Jak Barley, Private Inquisitor
and the Case of the Very Annoyed Viper Mages

Dan Ehl

Published by Rogue Phoenix Press, LLP

Copyright © 2022

ISBN: 978-1-62420-688-7

Cover Artist: Designs by Ms G
Editor: Sherry Derr-Wille

Dedication

To Kristin Watson, who once again dotted my Ts and crossed my crossed Is. And to old (in more ways than one) buddies: Russell Gabriel, Barry Walton, Ricky Stewart, Allen Shively, Ron Nichols, Doug Thomas, Dom Franco, Steve Miller, Scott Rohwedder, Roger Parker, Nikita Seliverstov, Neal Sheeley and Mike Neis; as well as to my muse, Barb Ehl.

Forward
G. Lloyd Helm

This is my eighth Dan Ehl book, seven Jak Barley and one called "Nicotine Dreams." They are all well written adventures in a world just as magically twisted and amusing as Dan's mind. The reader recognizes the parallels with this world and understands all the references made by Lorenzo Spasm, a visitor from this world to Barley's, though Jak is often confused by Lorenzo's references. And the magic! I love the magic, as will you.

Chapter One

"You are jesting, right?" I asked my friend Lorenzo Spasm. "How many times do I have to tell you I am taking a long goneaway? What other private inquisitor gets kidnapped by piss dragons, attacked by Ghennison Viper Mages or pursued by assassins while on a case involving a giant rampaging automaton resembling a rabid golden muskrat?"

"Are those rhetorical questions?" Lorenzo asked before taking another sip of ale in the King's Wart Inn.

"Whether rhetorical or not, my answer to yours is no."

"Don't you even want to know what it is?"

"No."

"Sure?"

"You are not going to wear me down. Keep your mouth closed unless it be for drinking."

I tried distracting myself from my friend's pesterings by glancing about the dim interior of the ale joint. A thick fog of incense hung in the air, burned to cover the body odor of the great unwashed masses. Many of the inn's clientele are not that fastidious about bathing on a regular basis. In a good mood, I lovingly describe my fellow patrons as loathsome scoundrels, gutter dregs, scofflaws, ne'er-do-wells, debaucherous rogues and blackguards.

I noticed several of the ever-present bar flies at the tavern had met their ale consumption limits. They were lying on their backs with tiny feet straight up in the air. I swept them off the table and then wiped my hand against my tunic. At least they were not buzzing so when passed out. During an exceptionally warm day a low drone of the inebriated insects can fill the King's Wart Inn.

"No," I repeated as I rose from my usual table situated in a dark back corner of the tavern. "I have to go to the water closet."

"You can't buy beer, you can only rent it," he replied, then added "Archie Bunker."

Lorenzo is always quoting strange sayings and sources, claiming he is from what he calls an alternate universe where magic does not exist.

"Parallel firmaments," my half-bother, Olmsted Aunderthorn exclaimed when being told of Lorenzo's claim. "Fjsten, a great metaphysicist, has hypothesized such manifestations."

I believe Lorenzo's tale, since he has proven impervious to spells and ones thrown against him rebound upon those who cast them.

The water closets are at the end of a long, narrow hallway, barely lit by two sourly smoking yimp fat lamps. The "Sirs" facility was almost as poorly lit, which is fortunate because it is best one does not see too clearly in such a malodorous chamber.

I hesitated at the door, recalling a rather unpleasant experience one other night at the King's Wart Inn. Upon opening the water closet door, a herd of small insects had scuttled for cover. I interrupted the slaughter of a number of army roaches. Whatever could bring down the armored cockroaches was an insect I would rather not meet. Then again, how many times had I been kept awake at night to the peeping bellowings of bull cockroaches as they fought in my walls and under the floor during mating season? I especially hated the tiny clicking sounds as they butted antlers, which were extensions of their exoskeleton. What if these other bugs could be bred as exterminators and released in pest-ridden homes? I pondered at the time.

Writings on the water closet walls are visible, if not always legible. Some are in cryptic runes, others in the unintelligible lettering of those from beyond the Misty Mountains. In the script of Glavendale are a number of witless musings, crude drawings of what appeared to be fertility goddesses and the addresses of maidens said to be exceptionally friendly.

"This wall soon to be made into a major theatrical production," read the only graffiti not dealing with body functions.

After relieving myself, I again contemplated that encounter from last year. I had crouched down, my nose wrinkling from the odor rising from the floor, and pushed a half-eaten army roach to a crack in the wall. The iron-grey cadaver, as big as my thumb, was sheathed in shattered scaly plates.

A furry green insect leg reached out and began pulling the carcass into the crack. I had placed a finger on the dead roach and began sliding it away from the wall so I could observe what manner of miniature monster I was dealing with.

This obviously was not what the mystery bug had in mind, for suddenly a pair of wicked pinchers shot out of the crack and latched painfully onto my finger. I jerked back in surprise and stumbled to my feet before slamming through the door. I floundered into the hall while wildly waving my hand above my head. Attached to my finger was what appeared to be a tiny lobster with long spider legs.

My hasty exit had taken three very unattractive giants by surprise. Wearing the bizarre facial tattoos and black hooded cloaks of Reverian Assassins, they were outside the door with knives drawn – which does not augur well for making new friendships. The odious insect finally let loose, only to fly into the face of one of the rogues. The thing gripped the scofflaw's nose with its pinchers. The would-be killer howled in both pain and surprise.

Gathering some of my wits, I kicked the second of the trio in the shins and dodged a dirk thrust my way by the third hooligan whose aim was hampered by his shrieking confederates. I took advantage of the confusion to hasten down the hallway and back to my friends. That had begun the Case of the Seven Dwarves, as entitled by my friend Sergey at the Weekly Tattler.

A vermin control crew was soon called and though the disturbing invaders were purged with several eradication wards, the familiar army roaches remain on hand to greet the ale joint's patrons.

~ * ~

"No, I really think you are going to be interested in this case," Lorenzo said on my return from the loo before I could even regain my seat.

"I would find a throng of juggling zombies riding giant chickens interesting, but that does not mean I would want to join in," I replied.

"Funny you should mention that."

I paused with my mug halfway raised. "I know you are not going to tell me the case involves juggling zombies or giant chickens."

"No, although outlandish and exotic creatures are involved."

I cocked my head. "Lorenzo, I am finally going to meet your family?"

"It involves the Duburoake Royal Exposition of Extraordinary Artifacts, Menagerie of Astounding Beasts and Unearthly Botanical Gardens," he continued, ignoring my quips as usual.

"Our city zoo, gardens and museum," I sighed. "What? Did a virgin sneak in and steal a unicorn? Maybe an iron-toothed mountain centipede ran off with a Third Dynasty chamber pot? Has someone been plucking purple blood pansies?"

"Scoff if you may, but this case has national ramifications."

"It sounds like a case right up your back alley."

Lorenzo shook his head and gave his usual excuse for pushing such matters onto me. "Can't. I'm not certified as a private inquisitor by the Duburoake Public Safety Council."

"Then go look for some out-of-work private inquisitor, one who likes pets and flowers."

Lorenzo shook his head. "The king wants you."

"No," I groaned. "He be personally involved in this?"

I first met the king when he was still Baron Garsten Stee Hragen. It was during a visit to Stagsford, the capital of Glavendale, that he assumed the throne thanks to help from me and Lorenzo. King Kenton was the former ruler, most noted for a number of sordid habits and vile

4

entertainments best left for the thoughts of those with baser imaginations. I have one more connection to the current king – he is my father.

I grew up never knowing who my real sire was. Father might not have been a very good parental figure for his numerous offspring – a downright miserable one since he did not remain to see even one of his many scions actually birthed – but he did leave behind an expansive network of kinship for his whelps. One that transcends the usual social and economic barriers of a provincial capital like Duburoake.

I have half-brothers and sisters throughout the city. Garsten was impartial when it came to pretty women, be they scullery maid or a duke's daughter. His whereabouts and state of health remained a mystery during my childhood, since many good fathers and husbands of the berg nourished ill feelings. Most believed he fled to a far realm to ply his talent among a less suspecting populace. It was during my time in Stagsford, the capital of Glavendale, that I learned the truth.

In other principalities such birthing's as this might be of some import but given the formidable proclivity of our father's youthful indulgences, it mattered little. So, we who knew of our parentage kept silent on the riddle of our siring. I like to believe that my fleeting time with Garsten, through a rather perilous ordeal, did endear me to him. It was long enough for him to seek my help when some matters were not suited to the normal channels of royal investigations. Though gradually changing under the new king's oversight, the CIA (Clandestine Information Authority) be still plagued with grifters, sociopaths, sloths and ne'er-do-wells.

"Stop right there," I ordered. "What in Hades could anything to do with that rundown park be of interest to the king? It be not as if Baron Ruble has kept the place up. The last time I was in the museum its roof leaked, weeds had taken over the gardens and the zoo animals were toothless and moth-eaten."

"It seems the baroness has taken it upon herself to promote the cultural side of Duburoake," Lorenzo answered. "Since pilgrim numbers have fallen with reports that Saint Riffus died in a still explosion and not in a fiery soul passage to the gods, the baron has decided the park could become a replacement tourist attraction."

"And...?"

"And?"

"Yes. Why would this interest Garsten?" I asked in exasperation. Lorenzo should have chosen the stage. He likes his pronouncements and adventures to be high drama.

"As part of the park revitalization project, the baroness imported a number of exotic animals for the zoo. Some of them were procured through reputable traders who observe ethical and sustainable practices. Others, maybe because the baron wanted to keep costs down, were obtained through murkier channels."

"You mean smuggling?" I asked.

He shrugged.

Before I could ask what this had to do with the price of pig jowls, he continued, "Certain intelligence sources have gathered vague hints that an assassin hides among the new additions at the zoo."

Now I was confused. "How can that be?"

"Many of the new exhibits are from such faraway and mysterious lands that little or nothing is known about them. The director of the zoo was hired more for his family connections than expertise."

"In other words, he would not know a kongamato from a skunk ape," I filled in. "This sounds more like a job for a bestiary scholar than a private inquisitor."

"As I said," he continued, "the newly acquired creatures are from unknown parts and so far, unidentified."

I still did not get it. Why and who would go to the trouble of planting an assassin in a backwater zoo like that of Duburoake's? If such a beast was smart enough to be a hired assassin, that meant it fell under the Human, Werefolk Accords. The treaty was originally established to keep intelligent beings off each other's menus, but was later to institute The Equal Beings Rights Amendment.

"So why is the king involved? This be of a bizarre nature, but if the king concerned himself in every odd occurrence, he would not have time to issue royal decrees, oversee revelries, attend ribbon cuttings or whatever else a monarch does."

"The baron has invited him to the grand opening of the new exhibits."

"What?" I yelped. "The king is coming here?"

Like any good Duburoakian, I felt a certain amount of pride in our relative independence. We are on a sliver of coastal land cut off from the rest of Glavendale by the Megaoulas Mountains. There are few royal troops this side and no royal navy to speak of – the court being more inward looking to the east where like locusts, hordes of pony men come swarming in every generation or so.

The lack of a large royal fleet is evidence of this disregard. Only two carracks, several brigs, a frigate and four corvettes comprise his majesty's fleet. The majority of ships docked in Duburoake are traders, with the exception of a few stealthy smugglers flying false flags. So, for the most part we appreciate our benign neglect.

"The king is coming here?" I again stammered. "Why?"

"Maybe Garsten is bored. Besides, with the new commercial dragon flights it no longer takes weeks to get here by caravan."

"This grand opening be when?"

"In six days."

"So, let me get this straight," I moaned. "I have less than a week to uncover a member of an unknown species of sentient beings hidden among a throng of other equally unknown creatures? If I do not, my father who also happens to be the king of Glavendale, will be murdered?"

I forced myself not to slap my forehead and said, "It be time to see Olmsted."

~ * ~

Olmsted Aunderthorn is a man for all five seasons, a brilliant alchemist whose clever mind far outpaces the impediments of his body. The hunchback is a seeker of all arcane knowledge as well as being my well-loved half-brother. Though Olmsted has a successful career as a metaphysicist and alchemist, he still maintains his laboratory and extensive library in a ruder part of Duburoake. Hanging in the air is the stench of wet sawdust, rotting animal hides awaiting tanning, coal-burning forges and workmen's sweat concentrated like the collected essences for some noxious perfume.

The cobblestone alleys are wide enough for freight wagons to pass in opposite directions, but the sidewalks are little more than narrow ledges. They are raised just enough to be above the street rivulets of slop thrown unceremoniously from the second-story windows of cramped and squalid apartments. One always keeps a wary eye cocked upward when walking these streets. At each corner are stepping-stones, spaced to allow wagon wheels to pass between them, while offering pedestrians safe fording above the effluent. It be not my favorite neighborhood.

I gingerly made my way through the district until coming to Olmsted's place of business.

"Olmsted," I cried as I passed through his open door and entered the dark interior.

Dust motes flittered like gnats in the shaft of light pouring from a stained-glass window in the shape of a two-headed carp. Passing through the colored glass, the rays went nova and exploded into shards of primary colors that danced across the pitted walls, ratty furniture and shelves of dusty jars containing aborted creatures, pickled eyeballs, shrunken organs and scaled parasites looking like grotesque, armored dew worms.

I found my brother peering into a lens tube at his workbench. He had crafted the mechanism based on instructions from Lorenzo and recently had been consumed with examining everything from pond water to fairy tears.

"Take a look at this," he ordered before I could even greet him.

"Olmsted, I have a..."

"Come, take a look," he cut me off.

My brother was excitedly swaying from foot to foot while pointing at the lens tube.

Sighing, I did as he bade and leaned over to place an eye to the device.

"What the...?" I gasped. "Be this a trick, some illusion spell?"

"There be an entire world invisible to the naked eye," Olmsted answered. "So tiny but yet as real as our own."

"What are they?"

"I named them sea monkeys," Olmsted answered.

Swimming about were two juveniles and two adult creatures. The adults appeared to be a male and female by their faces and all of them had three antennas ending in tiny spheres. Long legged, they also boasted tails. They were circling what appeared to be a floating castle complete with a turret.

I pulled away while shaking my head, forcing myself to file that scene away to when I had time to consider the moral implications of using the local reservoir as a source of drinking water.

I held my hand out to halt Olmsted's expected outburst. "I have something just as worthy of note. Listen."

His attention was completely captured within a minute and I went on to repeat the rest of my conversation with Lorenzo.

Stroking his chin, he hurried into the next room with me at his heels. It was his library. The shelves that reached to the high ceiling were crammed with the newest metaphysical journals to dusty and crumbling tomes, some written in ancient scripts now known only to a few scholars of the extreme arcane.

"This be my bestiary section," he said while waving a hand at a section of scrolls and tomes adorned with cobwebs and a thick layer of dust. "I have seldom need of them since I am well versed on local creatures. If your beasts be known, they will be among these manuscripts. We must visit the menagerie as soon as possible that I may take note of each specimen's appearance, diet, and hopefully any significant behaviors."

~ * ~

We entered the park on foot and followed a winding cobblestone walk through gardens that were yet to be fully pruned and weeded. I must say that I found the neglect romantic with old oaks draped in thick vines, crumbling marble fountains and toppled statues. We passed a hollow bulwark tree buzzing with bees and soon afterward a weasel crossed our path with a grouse securely clenched in its jaws. If a botanical garden is

9

to be a pantheon for nature, what better temple than to be one where the plants and animals have reclaimed their heritage?

Our path led to a wrought iron gate set within the fifteen-foot-high limestone walls that surround the zoo, which made it appear more a fortification than a menagerie. Of course, it served the same purpose, but to keep residents in rather than others out.

Two guards in new, if ill-fitting, uniforms lounged against the bars of the gate. They purposely ignored our approach with a slothfulness gained from years of disregard for the few curious enough to visit the almost forgotten menagerie.

I flashed my brass badge announcing my licensing as a private inquisitor.

"Well, lookee here, we got a ferret."

"That be private inquisitor," I replied by habit to the rude slang for my trade.

"... and a human camel," the knave continued. "Hey, how much water does that hold?"

His shorter and heavyset partner sniggered and added, "Bet at least a gallon or two. Maybe we should prick the hump, and see?"

Since childhood, I have been thin-skinned when perceiving slights to my brother's infirmity, though Olmsted seems to easily shrug off such insults. Subtle smirks or patronizing tones are one thing, but outright rude greetings are another.

Moments later, an apprehensive Olmsted commented, "I hope this does not mean we will not be able to view the beasts."

"Not to worry," I replied while unfastening a set of keys from one of the prone guards' belt. "They will be coming around in ten or fifteen minutes."

I downed the pair with my mastery of Kimchee, the ancient martial art of thumb fighting. My two digits are registered by law as deadly weapons.

"They are lucky I did not use the Flying Thumbs of Blindness," I added. Their insults did not meet the level of such a deadly attack and besides, I hate the unpleasantness of thrusting one's thumbs through bursting eyeballs and into a soggy brain.

We stepped over their bodies and unlocked the gate. From there we were guided by faded wooden signs directing visitors to various areas of the zoo. We followed the ones leading to the administration quarters that took us past an assortment of enclosures. They ranged from large wire aviaries and iron-barred cages to fenced-in pits complete with stunted trees and small pools of water.

The smell of new paint hung in the air and the sounds of hammerings told of on-going renovations. Olmsted was eager to observe the new arrivals, but first we had to introduce ourselves to the menagerie director. I was curious to see the invoices that accompanied each of the creatures. They should at least reveal points of origin and maybe even the creatures' correct names. That proved to be a disappointment.

"No, they all came from one exporter in the Amnesian Isles," Rahn Badtah nervously addressed my questions.

He was obviously disquieted by the sudden notoriety brought on by the baron's new interest and the scheduled visit by the king. "She, ah, well, did not seem to like paperwork."

We were sitting in his cramped office surrounded by stuffed specimens of past inhabitants. That they died of natural deaths brought on by old age was consolation, but it also meant they were not prime trophy mounts. The array of heads from both carnivores and herbivores looking down upon us through dusty glass eyes held several attributes in common – that of blunted or missing teeth and scraggly coats of fur. On every available shelf space were smaller creatures in a range of supposed life-like poses. A furry Mahngoalie death worm was most disturbing as it glared at me from the edge of Batah's desk.

The director had much in common with his deceased compatriots – he too would look much better mounted if the process occurred several decades earlier. He resembled that children's rhyme dealing with a spindly-limbed and foolish egg that in an intoxicated state, fell from a castle wall to be trampled and eaten by a herd of swine.

"You have no bill of sales?" I purposely asked with astonishment in my voice. "How can that be?"

"You see, the, ah, trader said she had other interested buyers and, well you know, sometimes you have to act fast for a bargain. These beasts, as unknown as they are, will also be a great attraction," the director spoke while his eyes anxiously darted from creature to creature about the room, never once looking Olmsted or me in the eye.

"Though she did supply me with each creature's wants," he added as an afterthought.

"Of course, you followed guidelines set by the Zoological Accord For Sustainable and Ethical Menagerie Exhibits?" broke in Olmsted.

Leave it to my brother, pardon the expression, to be a Jak of all trades. The already nervous director became even more fretful. He turned to stare at the stuffed remains of an eight-foot swine bear as if silently beseeching it to rid him of these unwanted guests.

I could further press Rahn Badtah on the subject. I suspected his pursuit of cut-rate specimens had more to do with him pocketing the spare change than cost savings for the baron. I reminded myself that I was not here as a fiscal scrutineer.

"All right," I sighed, "take us to these bargain beasts."

He led us out onto the grounds and stopped before a wire cage with a flagstone floor. A number of rope swings dangled from the enclosure's overhead mesh of thick wires. A giant snow-white bird glared at us with cold yellow eyes. It had paused in its preening at our approach.

Olmsted began immediately taking notes while quizzing the director. I listened as I studied the creature. It came as no surprise that its diet consisted exclusively of meat. The creature's sharp curved beak and nasty talons spoke of the violent rendering of flesh. Little else was to be gained from the zookeeper and Olmsted focused on the bird's physical attributes.

The next cage was larger and constructed of heavy iron bars. Its resident had an almost human appearance but that it had a grapefruit-size head and eyes in its feet.

"Now that be something you do not see every day," I observed.

Badtah related that the creature was a grain eater with massive jaws and broad flat teeth to grind its meals. The creature presented a problem. I was used to peering into the eyes of persons of interest as a tool in resolving both their nature and truth telling. It be very disconcerting to look eye-to-eye when such orbs are just above the toes. Its pear-shaped head – was there enough room in that odd shaped skull to house the functioning intellect of an assassin?

"Here we have a most unusual specimen," Badtah spoke with pride as we stopped at a fence ringing a large pit. "It should prove to be a big draw with the youth."

We looked down upon a hairless bear-like creature with spikes running down its back. It glared up at its captors with a palpable hatred that made me take a step back. Several scars running across its back spoke of unpleasant interactions with past owners. The beast hissed rather than roared when it opened its mouth to reveal dagger-like fangs. We were informed that its meals were best served while still breathing.

I shook my head. I remembered as a child when a knee-high ant deer with large green eyes was a favorite attraction. What be the matter with kinder nowadays?

We went on to eight more enclosures ranging from large wicker domes to more iron cages and a water-filled pit. There was a snake with a head at both ends. It arrived complete with its preferred diet of small rodents, though the snake only fed every two months. Next, there were a giant vampire bat, an apish creature with backward-feet, a snake bedecked in blue feathers, a ten-foot-long centipede, a blue metallic spider, a crocodile with human hands and what first appeared to be a normal horse until it revealed its curved fangs and retractable claws.

I had seen enough for the day, though I would need to return more than once to more closely study the creatures. Olmsted was anxious to return and compare his notes to his tomes.

~ * ~

The cellar-chilled ale at the King's Wart Inn was just what I needed. Lorenzo had been quizzing me upon my return.

"I am hesitant, for now, to rule out any of the creatures," I said while shaking my head. "First thought had the simian creatures more likely to be cunning, but be that a prejudice in body shapes? Still, I have never encountered a witty spider or clever snake."

"Why not plant some bugs?" asked Lorenzo. "The culprit might show itself when it believes no one be watching."

I had already thought of that. I did a lot of debugging when I first opened my office so I was familiar with a wide range of bugs that can send images back to a witch's crystal ball. Some pest removal services use toxic spells to rid such spies, but I preferred to release volleys of mantis, wasps, spiders and maiden beetles. That pretty well takes care of civilian bugs and does not leave nasty magical residues.

Now, military or CIA bugs are different stories. They favor purple-banded borer beetles that drill into woodwork. It can take an antlion to remove them. The military also loves dragon weevils because they are so heavily armored. There are no predators in the insect world that can handle those bugs. Lizards or tiger shrews are the only effective debugger.

I took another sip of ale before answering. "I mentioned that to the keeper, but he said the fortification wards cast to reinforce the compounds interfere with the surveillance. I will just have to spend the next few days at the menagerie seeking clues."

~ * ~

It was my fifth day at the menagerie and I was no closer to solving the case. I was getting desperate. Tomorrow was the grand opening and I, as yet, had no inkling to the assassin's identity.

Was it my imagination or was there a hint of intelligence behind the glaring red eyes of the bear-like creature? I stared as intently into its eyes as it into mine. Up to now I could only detect a fierce rage, something I could empathize with having suffered unjust imprisonment several times during my career.

I broke away to nod a greeting at one of the keepers, an elderly man who told me he had worked at the zoo for almost twenty years. I had gotten to know him and the four other staff members as I wandered between the enclosures. Every day I quizzed them, asking if they noticed any odd behaviors by the creatures. So far that proved to be fruitless, unless one counts the ape-like creatures self-stimulating, which Olmsted later related was not a rare behavior.

"Jak, I have news."

I turned to see my brother approaching with a sheet of folded parchment in his hand.

I stood and excitedly asked, "Have you identified the creatures? Do you know which one be the assassin?"

"Yes and no."

"Don't taunt me. What have you learned?

Olmsted unfolded the parchment and flattened it against his chest. "I have identified all the new exhibits, though it was not easy. I had to take a dragon flight to the Rooloo monastery to wrap up my search. That be a frigid flight through the mountains."

"Please, spare me the details for now. What about the beasts?"

My brother sighed as he looked down at the parchment. "It seems none of them have ever been reported as anything but dumb beasts."

I snapped the parchment from his hand and quickly scanned his notes.

The two-headed snake was identified as an Amphisbaena from desert climes and no, it exhibited no behavior different from other snakes. The vampire bat be called a Camazotz, which means death in a native tongue. According to Olmsted's notes the giant white bird be a Caladruis and the hairless bear-like creature was identified as a Chupacabra. The feathered ape was a Huitzilopochtli and the other, with eyes in its feet, was known as an Aigamuxa.

The large centipede was just a large centipede and the spider just a giant, if but a fancy, spider. The crocodile with human hands turned out to be a poor reptile that some wizard with a twisted sense of humor created. The scary horse was known by an unpronounceable name and as with the others, exhibited no higher level of wit.

I slapped my forehead and groaned. "It can only be that the tales of an assassin are false. That be the only explanation."

Olmsted's wince warned me of further bad news. "I spoke with Lorenzo before I left. He said a trusted source affirms the plot be real. The trader, it turns out, has connections to a foreign power – a nation that would gladly see Glavendale thrown into disarray."

"Yet you say that be impossible." I replied despairingly, before pausing with a new thought. "Could any of the beasts be in disguise?"

"Like you, Zak, I have carefully been studying the creatures. It be impossible, especially as the security wards would nullify any magical deceptions."

We were walking as we spoke, and I abruptly stopped in front of an enclosure to stare at its occupant. "Of course. How could I not have seen it? That be the only answer."

~ * ~

"You did good, little buddy," Lorenzo noted, as we watched the king addressing the crowd from a raised platform.

Inflated fish bladders of every color were anchored to the stage and swayed in the wind along with the snapping of hundreds of pennants. The crowd would soon be dispersing to view the new exhibits and visit the numerous food carts. It was the perfect day for the celebration, with its mild temperature and cloudless sky.

I had secretly met with King Garsten Stee Hragen before his public appearance. We reminisced of our first encounter and the chaotic adventure leading to his assuming the throne.

"Once again my trust in you has proven out," he said at the end of our visit. "The royal security apparatus is still riddled with dullards and villains left over from the last king. That is why I would like you to come to Stagsford and help with a CIA house cleaning."

I am sure the king could tell my answer by the look of horror sweeping across my face. The thought of being in the midst of the numerous petty court intrigues and the popinjays behind them made my stomach churn. Besides, I have already been on the scornful receiving end from CIA agents. To them, I was a ne'er-do-well ferret from a backwater berg. I gracefully declined the offer.

"I am impressed how you solved the case. Once revealed, it does seem obvious, but I am afraid even I would have overlooked it," he observed.

~ * ~

"That be it," I exclaimed to Olmsted the day before as we stood outside the two-headed snake enclosure.

"What be it? The bestiary at the Rooloo monastery gave a detailed account of the Amphisbaena, including its nature and habits. It would have noted any elevated display of cleverness by the snakes," Olmsted replied.

Ignoring my brother's skepticism, I quickly hopped the waist-high chain circling the snake pit and dropped into the enclosure. The snake was sunning itself on a flat rock and only one head turned to lazily gaze at me in disinterest. I returned the lack of interest and made my way to a large shipping crate in the corner of the pit.

"All right, the caper is up," I spoke firmly as I kicked the wooden container. "Do not even think about giving me trouble if you ever want to get home again. I am offering you amnesty if you surrender peacefully."

With that I threw back the hinged lid to view the supposed food for the snake – a pack of very startled rats.

~ * ~

"Well, once it was established that none of the exhibits could be the assassin, it left only one possible answer," I explained to the king. "As the two-headed snake eats only every couple months, why the need for the several dozen small rodents accompanying the reptile?

"Olmsted was able to identify the food stock as Pyrithian Desert Wolf Rats, rodents capable of speech and reasoning, as are the Old Town Rats inhabiting the abandoned tunnels beneath Duburoake, or the Djork Ship Rats that keep sea vessels free of vermin.

"The wolf rats were signed on as mercenaries as recent droughts made living difficult for them and their families. They were to swarm from their holding crate upon your arrival. With small blades hidden in the shipping container, they would have carried out the assassination with the proverbial thousand cuts.

"Once exposed, the rats quickly accepted equal pay and transportation home. They also revealed the name of several spies within the court aiding the plot."

A royal retainer handed me a purse as I left. It jingled pleasantly. I was now left to enjoy the rest of the day at the ale tent. The only thought to still plague me dealt with those damned sea monkeys. Looking down into my mug I could only wonder – was my ale brewed with well water or that of reservoir ponds?

Chapter Two

The pounding on the door was hellishly synchronized with the throbbing of my head. What kind of fiend would even consider inflicting such torment on another living being?

"Get up, Jak, it's late in the mornin', the rain is pourin' and we got work to do," sang the familiar and equally off-key voice of my supposed friend, Lorenzo Spasm.

His early morning habit of singing verses from his world is never appreciated after closing the King's Wart Inn but hours ago.

"Go away," I moaned.

"Come on. You've had four hours of sleep. That should be plenty of time for a real man to sober up. Anyway, I have a case for you."

It would be hopeless to believe that burrowing under my pillow and refusing to answer would lead to Spasm leaving. My lack of optimism proved correct.

"Come on. You have a client waiting in your office," he called, while resuming the pounding.

My attic quarters are above my second-floor office – handy for slipping out of the office by back-alley windows and climbing to my loft without being seen.

The neighborhood was once comfortably middle class, made up of prosperous burghers or elder yeomen who retired to town to let their sons and daughters take over the farmsteads. Not so anymore. The Dwarf Wars forced thousands of Frajan refugees to flee their dank mountains and many made their way to Duburoake. They now cram a ten-block area. Once comfortable townhouses were roughly divided into warrens of cramped lodgings sheltering families of old and young Frajans.

19

The city of Duburoake, like the rest of the nation of Glavendale, is composed of various peoples who arrived in waves through the centuries, blending until an array of looks can be seen in the marketplaces – from black to yellow hair, blue to yellow eyes and black to pale skin. Still, none are as ashen as the Frajans, with their white hair, faded blue eyes and bleached skins. They are often called spooks in jest, if not open derision.

I get along with the Frajans, normally a stiff-necked and cliquish tribe. That be mostly due to the bond with my half-sister Jennair. That our father had been able to seduce a Frajan maiden spoke more of his prowess than any other conquest.

"Have them come back later – how about a week from now?" I groaned. "Anyway, I already have a new case and it will certainly be less lethal than any you would bring."

"You don't want to keep her waiting, believe me."

I took a deep breath and sat up in defeat. "What? Who?"

The hint of gloating in his voice should have been enough of a warning. "It's Head Mistress Kahlan of the Kuu Academy of Mystical Arts and Witchcraft."

I had not taken a deep enough breath, barely able to stupidly croak out another, "What?"

That Lorenzo stopped his battering at the door offered only a minimal relief. What could bring the head witch of Morgana's academy away from that remote campus? Especially when graduation was but two weeks away.

Morgana is my intended and the daughter of Glavendale's most powerful and feared witch, Morganna (spelled with two Ns). My future mother-in-law makes no secret that I am not one of her favorite beings. She tolerates me only because of her daughter's love for me.

The mother witch displays no hesitancy in letting me know that her daughter could do better, even though I saved Morgana from certain death several times. It was also with me that her slumbering powers awoke while in the clutches of Dorga, the Fish Headed God of Death. Since then, for the past two years, Morgana has been away learning whatever arcane studies are taught to apprentice magic doers and has returned home only on weekends, spring breaks or pagan holidays. The academy is a day's ride by horse to the south of Duburoake.

"Ah, tell her I will be down very shortly," I surrendered.

"That's okay. I told her you were hungover from a night of ugly inebriation and wretched overindulgences in vices frowned upon by the dour, dwarfish priests of your troubled childhood."

"You did not."

"Just kidding. I'll keep her company until you make yourself presentable, or as close as possible."

I scrambled to the closet and sorted through a disarray of wear. I tended not to take the time to hang freshly laundered clothing, which meant my garb was often more wrinkled than the face of a two-hundred-year-old necromancer. I had a strong feeling that my slothful habits would end the same time as my bachelorhood.

My last stop was the mirror and water basin where I doused my face and attempted to rein in my tousled hair. I made my way down the stairs to my office door and paused to straighten my shoulders. This was the head mistress of Morgana's academy and as Morgana's intended, I did not want to make a bad impression. There really was no reason for me to worry. I last departed the academy on excellent terms with Mistress Kahlan after solving a dramatic endeavor Sergey entitled in the Weekly Tattler as "The Case of One Damned Thing After Another." Still, I knew many in Morgana's mother's circle were derisive of a witch wedding a magically-toothless commoner.

I ran my fingers through my hair and brushed hands down the front of my dark green tunic one last time, only to feel a small crusty patch. I peered down to see a blotch of brown. I sighed. I had last worn the tunic several days ago and somehow it mixed with my fresh laundry. I scraped away the reminder of an ox tail soup supper with my thumbnail until it mostly disappeared.

I greeted my secretary Osyani as I entered the outer office. Her appearance be that of a lithesome maid of late teen years with skin the color of honey. One would never guess Osyani was hatched a harpy who bonded to me soon after breaking through her shell. As a harpy, she had

21

matured magically fast. It be a long story involving an arduous trek through the Megaoulas Mountains. After being severely injured, she became fully human following a blood transfusion from the anti-magical Spasm. Osyani looks upon me as her father – and Lorenzo an uncle.

I pushed through the second door and into my office where both the witch and Lorenzo sat chatting over kaffee like old friends at a neighborhood eatery.

Mistress Kahlan be of slight build. Without the pointed hat marking her as a member of witchcraft academia, she barely topped my shoulder. She also had a suggestion of elfin blood with her slightly angled cheekbones and almost lavender eyes. It was hard to guess her age, though I believed it be at the end of middle years.

I took the chair behind my desk.

"Ah, I am honored by your visit," I greeted her, not sure how much polite small talk to make.

I could not imagine this as just a social call, which meant something of import brought her to the office of a rather disreputable private inquirer. I decided to let her broach the reason behind her unusual call. "I am looking forward to attending the graduation ceremony. It looks like we will have good weather for the occasion."

Mistress Kahlan threw her head back and laughed. "You do not have to worry about proper manners with me, Jak. I know you are dying to know why I make this visit when I should be busy with commencement preparations. So, I will get right to the point. We are under attack."

I bolted upright from my chair. "What? Under attack? I have heard nothing of this. Has anyone one been hurt? How is Morgana?"

She waved me back into my seat. "It be not a physical attack."

I looked at Lorenzo in confusion.

"It's a virus attack," he responded.

"What, a malady?" Olmsted has shown me through lens tubes the invisible world of malevolent miniscule beasts.

"No, it be a magical leech," the witch answered. "As you know, we witches have expanded the applications of our crystal balls. We long used them as a means of communication limited to among our sisters, but for the past couple years we have rapidly expanded their use on a commercial basis. It be now proving an important source of revenue for our guild."

This was common knowledge. Enterprising witches have opened offices where one can send instant messages to other offices throughout Glavendale. Many financial and governmental dealings now transpire over the magical ether. Ships at sea are even hiring witches specializing in messaging as well as an aid in navigation. Some are calling it a communication upheaval that threatens to make many trades such as couriers obsolete.

I was still mystified.

"Someone has devised a malspell that after hacking into one crystal, spreads among others in the communication chain," Lorenzo offered. "The virus than copies and transfers the messages to third-party crystals."

"We have promoted our service as a confidential means of communication," Mistress Kahlan continued, "and these breaches threaten to bring our endeavor to an abrupt halt. Who knows how much damage will occur to our clients? Our brightest students are working on counter wards, but Lorenzo says we can expect continuing attacks from newer spells. That maybe so, but I want the culprits behind this current assault found and punished as a warning to other would-be perpetrators."

I shied from considering what kind of example would befall the wrongdoers. Some witches have a morbid sense of humor when it comes to reckonings.

"What makes you such an expert on magical assaults?" I asked Lorenzo, "How can you know so much? What did you call it, 'hacking', when you say your world has no magic?"

He shrugged. "We have similar problems with what Olmsted calls metaphysics."

I shook my head and turned back to the witch. "Do you suspect anyone?"

"Wizards." She replied hotly. "They belittle women practicing magic, though it really be resentment over not having a monopoly on the craft. They also fear the idea that we prove just as adept. The wizards are now even more incensed with our messaging venture proving so lucrative and they have not the ability to master the crystals."

"If males cannot work crystal balls," I replied in puzzlement, "how can they be behind the attacks?"

"That be the maggot in the wound," Mistress Kahlan said after taking a deep breath. "A witch or witches must be abetting the wizards, though it be a foul thought to consider."

She straightened her shoulders and looked me straight in the eyes. "Coven representatives have decided our investigation would be best guided by one versed in inquiries as well as magical arts. We know of no individual who fits our needs, but we are well aware of such a pair."

Mistress Kahlan slightly smiled and continued, "Plans to become a private inquisitor by the daughter of one of Glavendale's most powerful witches has long been a topic of gossip, and even more scandalous since she planned a union with a rogue of questionable origins, shady acquaintances and dubious habits."

"Don't forget ugly inebriations and wretched overindulgences in vices frowned upon by the dour, dwarfish priests of his troubled childhood," Lorenzo chimed in.

I ignored my friend and asked, "Have you spoken to Morgana about this?"

"We have."

"And...?"

"Morgana says it be up to you. She spoke of your lack of enthusiasm when it comes to sorcery."

That be an understatement. Curses, dark arts, bewitchments and the like make my blood run cold. As abhorrent the thought of being knifed or bludgeoned, the image of being turned inside-out or erupting into a pulsating mass of maggot-filled pustules be many times worse.

"Be Morgana's mother aware of all of this?" I asked. "I have found wizards to be a testy lot. Such an inquiry could prove dangerous for her daughter."

"Of course. These are assaults upon all witches and as such, all are obligated to defend the covens."

What to do? I had been torn by the idea from the start when the young witch first spoke of becoming a private inquisitor. With her sharp mind, Morgana has proved more capable than most now holding private inquisitor licenses. Add to that her magical abilities and she presents a formidable force. With that said, I still struggle with the thought of her being in any kind of danger.

I shrugged, trying to console myself with the thought that as only a witch, she would face grave dangers, even without becoming a private inquisitor.

"When will Morgana be free for the case?" I asked the witch. "She told me she has been busy organizing events for the graduation activities."

"Morgana is available as of today. Resolving this threat be more important than arranging flowers and seating."

"I am catching an early dragon flight to Kaiserhelm tomorrow," I said. "I have another case dealing with the hijacking of a shipment of pixie gold in the Megaoulas Mountains. Have her meet me in Kaiserhelm and we can begin planning the investigation from there."

The meeting concluded with Mistress Kahlan listing a number of resources I could call upon. That included an elite cabal of young witches skilled in the new crystal spellings.

Chapter Three

I sighed. What now? I was in the reception area outside my office. It was still dark and Osyani had come in early so I could make last minute arrangements before leaving. By habit I gazed out the window to the gas-lamp-lit street below. Hanging outside the millinery shop was a sign in red lettering declaring 'HATS 20 PERCENT OFF.' I had an agreement with a number of neighborhood hang-abouts; if they were to spot any suspicious characters within sight of my building, they were to flip the millinery sign from 'HAT SALE TODAY' in blue letters to 'HATS 20 PERCENT OFF' in red lettering.

"Something appears to be amiss," I spoke while quickly scanning the rooftops and street below before moving safely from view. "I am not sure what, but I will be taking the back way out."

Osyani had been filled in on my two current cases and we were going over a code to be used when communicating by crystal balls. Lorenzo suggested the ploy, now that such correspondences could be compromised.

"I would tell you to be careful," said Osyani with a sigh, "but you have never listened in the past. I love Uncle Lorenzo dearly, but he does little to avoid danger. This time, though, you should at least be safer in the hands of Morgana. At least one of you will have common sense."

"I believe my quick wit and well-honed skills as a private inquisitor have always proven me a match for villains," I replied in mock defense. I smiled and shook my head. "You are right, though. Lorenzo be never content unless in the center of some maelstrom."

"I will tell you anyway, be careful," she laughed and gave me a parting hug.

Picking up my pack, I entered my inner office and paused at the narrow back window. It overlooked a trash and weed-filled abandoned courtyard, though at the moment it was shrouded in darkness. The wall encircling the courtyard was eight feet high and topped with broken glass.

With the removal of a few pins, the iron bars covering the window swung out as if made for the task, which they were. You never know when a hooligan, bill collector or irate lout might be waiting at the front door.

Sliding down a drainpipe and making my way to the wall, I pressed a section of stones that easily slid way to reveal an exit big enough to squirm through.

The alley be a lookalike of most back passageways in this old part of Duburoake. The perpetual dampness of the narrow alley has moss, tiny ferns and blossoming vines coating the old buildings to where little of the brick and stone can be seen. Darting about the foliage are glittering hummingbirds supping on both the nectar and insects. A jumble of rubbish be strewn along the alleyway – including a wheelless, decaying carriage body surrounded by pigweed growing up through the cobblestone.

The promise of coming dawn light was now revealing itself. Maybe it be not the most prudent action to take when attempting to flee unobserved, but curiosity drove me first to creep toward the front street with the aim of discovering what or who caused the shop warning. I was nearing the end of the alley when I spied three figures standing silently outside the back doorway of a rather disreputable hockshop. I quickly dropped behind a pile of broken crates.

Before they moved back into to the shadowed recess of the doorway, I identified the one wearing a purple peaked hat as a Ghennison Viper Mage. The other two were hooded ruffians grimly clutching bludgeons.

Damn those wizards. Ghennison Viper Mages are known for their arrogance, evil tempers and as loathsome students of the black arts. This be an unfortunate combination of personality traits and talents for those coming under the scrutiny of the notorious necromancers. Of all the necromancers, they prove to be the most spiteful. They harbor no love for me and seem unable to let go a grudge. That could be attributed to a number of mage casualties resulting from their attempts to violently interfere with past cases.

I was about to cautiously retreat when an unfamiliar beggar came limping around the corner. Such unfortunates come and go, either leaving for more generous quarters or succumbing to pestilences or infirmities. Greasy, knotted hair covered most of his grimy face. Leaning heavily upon a staff and clutching a gin flagon, the ragged figure weaved unsteadily on a course that would take him past the treacherous trio.

I grimaced and held my breath. Such thugs as those with the wizard boasted a repute of gleeful sadism, only exceeded by their monstrous masters. Please, I silently prayed to Saint Pysur, the patron saint of degenerate wastrels, let the poor sot pass safely. This was not to be. The beggar paused in front of the recess and cocked his head upon spying the ambushers.

"Hey, what be here? What nonsense be this?" croaked the derelict.

"Be gone," hissed one of the thugs.

The beggar was oblivious to the peril he faced. "Yah got a copper for a poor soul who has fallen upon hard times?"

"Fool, move on, or I will shove that staff up your arse."

"What? Because yah be some wizard's witless lackey, yah think yah can threaten me as if I be the putrid black bile oozing from beneath your hoof-like toenails, or the fetid green and yellow scum coating your cracked cow teeth?"

There was a moment of shocked silence before the oaf responded with a simple, "Well, ah, yes."

I was torn between somehow aiding the dimwitted beggar or creeping away from the about-to-be sheise storm. I fingered one of the slender dirk handles in my right boot. A best played-out scenario had one of the two louts falling quickly to a well-thrown dagger and then... That was it. It was unlikely the second hired blade would be so easily taken – and that was even if the mage were not present. Any scenario including a Ghennison Viper Mage could only end badly. By badly, I mean being reduced to an oily smoking bit of charred rag and bone. A wizard worth his damned soul would never not be sheathed in blade repelling charms.

Still, I knew a cowardly avoidance of this dark alley performance would haunt my slumber. Why me? I slid the knife from my boot and stood just as one of the two mage's mountainous minions stepped into the alley and roughly grabbed for the beggar's staff. Before I could blink, the beggar dodged and, twirling his staff until it was but a blur, dropped the miscreant in mid-step. The spinning walking stick led the beggar into the shadowed recess and the second oaf with a startled grunt toppled into the alley.

What a showoff, I thought as I slid the blade back into my boot.

An infuriated wizard's curse is painful to hear. It was followed by a searing bolt of purple lightening that burst against the shabby figure, only to rebound to the wizard who stood illuminated with hands outstretched but for a moment before disappearing.

"Yuck," the supposed beggar exclaimed as I approached.

He was gazing down upon a thrashing muck maggot. "It takes a real twisted bastard to want to turn a fellow human being into such a slimy and disgusting creature."

"Do not be so hard on your mother. I am sure she had no way of knowing," I replied. "Speaking of slimy and disgusting creatures, I like your new look. It be quite the improvement. May I inquire why you be so garbed and wandering down my back alley?"

"I often go incognito to avoid the mobs of adoring fans," Lorenzo replied.

"I was not aware there were that many ghouls in town," I spoke while nearing the end of the alley.

"You don't want to go that way," Lorenzo warned.

"A mob of adoring fans?"

"Only if you list Ghennison Viper Mages as admirers. Stakeouts were posted on both ends of the alley, as well as one down the street from your building's entrance."

"I guess that leaves only one other way," I sighed.

Minutes later we were making our way through the ancient storm sewers underlying the older sections of Duburoake. The dank, brick-arched waterways were once open flowing streams and are the only

29

monumental works left by the alien race that eons ago inhabited the coast. Much of Duburoake's older quarters were built with stones from the ruins of the ancient metropolis.

Duburoake's residents speak uneasily of these subterranean waterways, with tales of gibbering creatures crawling from the sewers at night to snatch unleashed pets or even errant children. As an errant child once myself, I had found the underground labyrinths convenient ways to escape annoyed guardsmen.

Lorenzo produced from his seemingly bottomless pouch two of his "not magical" torches he calls flashlights.

"Just how do you always seem to have an item to fit every occasion in such a small belt pouch?" I asked. "Be it a magical gift from Morganna?"

"Actually, I got it from another world line – one where the laws of its quantum physics allow this pouch to be a portal into a sixth dimensional wall locker. The String Theory is somehow also involved, though I'm not scheduled to take those studies until next fall."

I looked blankly at my friend. "You mean magic."

He sighed. "You might say that. As Arthur C. Clarke once said, 'Any sufficiently advanced technology is indistinguishable from magic.'"

We made our way along a narrow ledge running only inches above the flowing water. As a child, I had often followed the buried waterways to the bay.

Lorenzo did not comment on our bearing – in that it was not taking us directly toward the dragonport. If the mage ensnarements were related to the case given me by Mistress Kahlan, it meant the wizards were aware of my involvement. Knowing that much, they might also know of my flight reservation for Kaiserhelm, so I was taking an indirect route to the dragonport. The two stunned oafs in the alley would soon tell of the attack. From then it was only a matter of time for the wizards to deduce our escape route.

"I take it you are also going to Kaiserhelm?" I said as we reached the halfway point to where we would exit the sewers.

"Yes, I was getting a bit of cabin fever."

I did not bother to turn the torch on Lorenzo to check for ague or yellowed eyes and trembling limbs. I was used by now to his odd phrases.

"If you're wondering," he continued, "I have a change of clothing in a locker at the dragonport."

When Lorenzo was not in disguise, he stood out even in a city bustling with many races and hominoids. It was not just his preferred garb of faded blue breeches and colorful tunics sporting palm trees, long-legged pink birds and nubile females in grass kilts. There be nothing exceptional in his visage, but there be a shrewdness behind his brown eyes that belies his casual demeanor. He stands a lanky six-foot and his black hair, with traces of gray, reaches his shoulders.

Before finding that my friend was from a different world, I had tried guessing his origins through his facial features. His narrow nose could be Gevonish, but the brow and cleft chin were more that of the Brisbon sea folk. His cheekbones suggested Elfin blood. I hadn't even tried to place such barbaric names as Lorenzo or Spasm.

Many a time I puzzled about my friend, but usually when we were together there was little time for idle conversation. I took the current opportunity to satisfy my curiosity.

"Lorenzo."

"Yes."

"Just what do you do? I mean, besides involving yourself in such matters as we now face. You know – like how do you afford the number of what you call safe houses scattered about the kingdom, your informants, your many disguises and array of forged identity papers – or even simple things like meals and dragon flights? You seem never to lack for coin."

"Magic mushrooms."

"What?"

"Magic mushrooms."

I wracked my brain. "What? That sacrament used by the Second Unreformed Temple of the Devine Cosmic Wisdom of Inner Consciousness?"

"Yup. That's it. I have a monopoly since shrooms only grow in my world."

"Wait," I protested. "I thought there was no magic in your world. That be why spells have no effect upon you."

"There're exceptions to everything," he lightly replied.

"So, if they only grow in your world," I asked with some suspicion, "how did they come to be part of the temple's worship services?"

"Marketing."

I switched topics when he did not elaborate further. "So why do you spend so much time in my world? Have you no family at home?"

He stopped and sighed. "You said it. There's no magic in my world. And its natural wonders are quickly being destroyed by greed and shortsightedness. While I'm not saying more laws and rules aren't needed to prevent further damage, your world offers a kind of freedom long disappeared from my own. Too often, freedom where I'm from only means being able to continue poisoning or harming each other and nature."

I contemplated that for a while as we followed the meandering tunnels. Our echoing footsteps added to the faint dripping from the low arched ceiling.

"What about family? Have you none?"

"Oh, I connect with cousins and such during my return visits, though I do have a brother who actually resides in Glavendale."

That admission, causally given, stopped me in my tracks. "What? You have a brother here? You never told me – and do not say because I never asked."

Lorenzo shrugged his shoulders. "Guess it never came up."

"Do not tell me. Your brother be an evil twin, so you no longer claim him as kin?"

"No. He's somewhat of a hermit and prefers a quiet life."

"Why here if not for the excitement?"

"Cost of living. It's cheaper to live here. For just a few gold coins a month, you can have a servant or two and a modest mansion. The healthcare system sucks, but we can zip back to our world if the need arises."

"Be it that easy to cross worlds?"

"There are weak spots in the space/time continuum's fabric. If you know how to visualize such foci, it's possible to edge your way through."

"I would like to meet him," I announced.

"Who?"

"Who do you think? Your brother."

"As I said, he lives a quiet life. He worries notoriety might follow my visits."

I shined my light up and down his tattered garb. "I would assume you could visit him in disguise."

"There is always that. I have visited under the guise of a traveling broom salesperson. You and I both visiting might draw attention, thanks to the publicity Sergey has accorded us in The Weekly Tattler. Still, we could go as an itinerate musician with his trained dancing monkey."

"You are too tall to be a monkey," I observed. "How about a great ape? Hmm. That might not work as some apes are pretty intelligent."

"Actually, I pictured you as the monkey since less makeup would be needed."

"What brings the likes of you bigguns to the sewers?" a squeaky voice emerged from a dark side tunnel.

Stepping into the light was a large rat walking upright and wearing a leather harness from which hung a sharp sliver of steel. Past cases brought me into contact with several tribes of sentient rodents. Being here, the creature before us had to be a Downtown Tunnel Rat.

"Sewers? We must have taken a wrong turn. I thought we were in the baron's wine cellar," I answered.

"Very droll, yah are. Hee-hee. What are yah doing here?"

"We are..."

"I know who yah are. Spasm and his sidekick ferret."

"That be private inquisitor and Lorenzo be the sidekick." I turned to catch my friend winking conspiratorially at the rat from over my shoulder.

"We are taking a scenic route..."

"Bullturds," the rat again interrupted. "So, yah like to dally about while there be hordes of bigguns swarmin' the tunnels lookin' for yah?

Humph."

"What?"

"Yah deaf as well as dumb? Yah stirred up a hornet's nest and they be buzzin' about with plenty of stingers. The pointy-hats are blastin' anything movin'. They been heard speaking your names so me chief sent packs out to find yah. Seems your aidin' us in the past has placed a charge upon us. Any who find yah are to see yah to safety."

Damn. I had hoped to slip out of Duburoake unnoticed.

"Too bad I didn't bring along the monkey suit," Lorenzo said.

"What?" the rat asked in puzzlement.

"Ignore him," I answered. "He prattles nonsense. And thanks, but how will you know which tunnels are safe?"

"Scouts. They be trained to sniff out food upside amongst you bigguns. They now skittin' about, makin' a ruckus just out of sight of the bigguns, leadin' them off to the Abyss."

"Abyss?"

"A lightless hole. Our Speakers of the Past say it be bottomless and dug by the Ancient Ones. Some stories say it be a gateway to Hades. You bigguns boarded it over centuries ago, but now forgotten, the timbers rot. For a heavy biggun to cross the planks invites an unforeseen answering of just how deep be the Abyss."

That would be a brief journey of discovery for the thugs accompanying the mages. As for the wizards, they might be able to call upon a levitation spell in time.

"Lay on McDuff," Lorenzo spoke.

"Huh?"

"Just ignore his prattle," I again advised the rat. "Please show us the way. I do not want to miss my flight."

The Downtown Tunnel Rat, who had yet to offer his name, returned to the side tunnel with us following closely on his tiny heels. We had gone but ten or fifteen minutes when a second rat appeared before us.

"Turn about," she squeaked to our guide. "Bigguns ahead."

The rat ran past us and we quickly turned to follow. Other scouts came and went as they guided us through the watery labyrinth now swarming with Ghennison Viper Mages and their hired blades.

We were stopped for a breather when our guide informed us, "There be no way to continue that does not takes us past the Abyss. We must skirt close to it for you to find your way to the dragonport."

It took a moment for his statement to sink in. "What, you plan to lead us past some well to hell, the same one the mages are being lured to?"

"There be no other way. Never have our darkways seen such a horde of bigguns. They are as fleas and causing panic among our nests."

"We will make it up to you," Lorenzo tried mollifying the rat, "and this will be over soon. The mages and their minions could not care less about this underground realm. Things will be back to normal as soon as Jak and I reach the surface."

"That be the meat of the nut. All this havoc be laid at your feet," the rat replied. "It will take much of what you call making it up."

Lorenzo continued, "I know of a bakery that often has stale, unsold bread. I can see to it that it's dumped down whatever grate your tribe prefers."

"This be all well and wonderful," I interrupted, "but while you two discuss unloading moldy bread, the mages are likely tightening the noose."

The rat shrugged and again turned silently to continue our trek.

"I'll hazard a guess that this elder race was a quirky bunch," Lorenzo offered several minutes later, while slowing to observe one of the many reliefs carved into the brick walls.

"Why do you think they could be quirky?" I asked as I played my own light over the relief. "Just because most of the carvings depict a variety of unknown creatures torturing or having cross-species sex with each other? Hmmm. I wonder which are the Ancient Ones?"

"I vote for the skinny insectoids. They appear to be the more fun loving of the bunch," Lorenzo offered.

I slowed to observe the mantis-like creature snipping the head off what resembled a minotaur. "That makes me worry what you do for fun when I am not around. No, I believe them to be the ones that look like satyrs. They..."

"Are you wanting to keep unpunctured skins or to be art historians?" our guide huffed. "Keep watchful. We near the Abyss."

It was no hardship to turn my torch from those unsettling images and I hurried to catch up with the rat. We had long since been traversing passages never explored in my youth. We ultimately ascended a small flight of steps to emerge into a dome-roofed hall.

Lorenzo's non-magical torch revealed the chamber to be about eighty-feet wide. A number of tunnel entrances circled the hall like the spoke holes of a wheel. I stomped my foot and was relieved to find it solid stone. Eons of dust and grime hid what was solid footing and that of moldering planks. A fetid odor hung in the air and made me catch my breath.

"Which way now?" I asked. "This place gives me..."

"Quiet," hissed our guide.

He took the frozen pose of a startled hare, only one that also gripped the hilt of a sharpened sliver of steel.

The only sound besides my own breathing was the echoing plunk-plunk of water dripping from the slime-covered ceiling. I caught my breath and cocked my head. Yes. It was not some ear ringing but the faint sound of human voices. The rat's sharper hearing allowed him to identify the source of the interlopers. He pointed to an entryway that would be eleven o'clock if we were the six on one of Olmsted's newly acquired timepieces.

"This way," the rat ordered and we followed – to then halt at what would be five o'clock on the imaginary chronometer.

We stood at the exact opposite side of the chamber with the supposed well to hell between us and what most likely were mages and minions. I took several cautious backsteps to slip behind my friend.

"What? You're afraid of a couple spells?" he laughed.

"There be that, but I had been thinking more of thrown knives."

We did not have to wait long. A Ghennison Viper Mage and a pair of ruffians emerged in the wake of a luminary floating above their heads. The bluish light gave the necromancer's flesh an even more corpse-like hue. They paused to gaze about the chamber and their heads almost

36

comically snapped back in unison when spying us.

"There they be," shouted one of the oafs. His partner quickly followed in drawing his sword.

The mage spat a non-magical curse and shoved past the two. He grimaced and threw up a hand to shade his eyes as Lorenzo and I aimed our torch beams upon him. He uttered a curse, this time magical, along with a fling of the hand. It seems even objects from Lorenzo's world are immune to spells as our torches sputtered not, while the rebounding spell extinguished the wizard's light.

A new glowing sphere soon hovered above the opposing trio. The mage paused to consider the occurrence and inspect his adversaries before muttering to his minions. That he followed up with no further spells meant he had guessed facing him was the rumored outworlder – the one said to be impervious to wards and spells. He mumbled again to his lackeys. They responded by throwing back their shoulders and advancing across the chamber. Lorenzo and I responded by drawing our own blades.

The thugs confidently strode forward. Halfway across the chamber floor they grimaced upon hearing the sound of rotting wood crumbling beneath their feet, and to quickly plunge from sight. Frantic screams faded until once again only the echoes of dripping of water broke the chamber's stillness.

Though expected, I was still startled by the abruptness of their departure. The mage also appeared shaken. It seemed a standoff. The wizard could circle the chamber and get close enough to circumvent Lorenzo's blocking any magical attacks on me or the rat. If the strange torches were impervious to spells, the mage must be wondering if the same applied to Lorenzo's steel blade. Was the stranger's weapon also immune to protective wards? I knew the answer. It was not. He had gotten this particular sword at a Rum Island bazaar in the Amnesian Isles – not his home world.

There was also the fact that even if my friend was immune to magical forces, the domed ceiling was not. He could die just as easily as me from a ton of falling bricks. I forced myself not to look upwards. The Ancient Ones were masterful builders as demonstrated by the flowing arches of bricks meeting at the center of the dome. Blasting a hole above our heads might destabilize the entire inverted bowl of masonry. I said as much to Lorenzo.

"That's a thought," he replied, as if such an occurrence would be welcomed.

"Where to now?" I spoke softly to our guide. "We need to get out of here before the mage figures out a new line of attack."

"We go there," the rat asserted while motioning to a tunnel at three o'clock.

"What? That close to the mage?" I yelped,

My question was made mute by the arrival of two other mages and their minions exiting from tunnels at one and seven o'clock. Our guide did not wait for further discussion and burst off to the proposed escape tunnel. The mage and his two thugs at the one o'clock opening stopped to get their bearings. Upon seeing the three of us appearing to be charging at them, the hired blades raised their swords and the mage lifted his gnarled, clawish hands in a curse-hurling stance. A shout from the initial mage warned his cohort of the danger Lorenzo posed. This allowed us time to safely enter the new tunnel.

I ran past Lorenzo, who stopped and was rummaging through his pouch. I spun and while backpedaling, shouted at my friend, "What are you doing? There will soon be three mages on our heels."

"Just a sec," he replied and pulled out a grayish lump, another of his "non-magical" items I have seen him use in the past. He called it C-4.

I slowed to watch Lorenzo exit the tunnel. He paused long enough to stand upon his toes and stretch his arms out of sight above his head. This done, he sprinted back into the tunnel.

"Run. It's a short timer," he shouted, though by this time I was already frantically trying to distance myself from his latest unnerving gambit. I had experienced his use of the seemingly innocuous bits of clay on several occasions and was pressing the heels of my hands to my ears as I ran.

Lorenzo unceremoniously swept up the rat as we flew past him. There are times I do not know whether to curse or thank the otherworlder. Yes, I am grateful for the times he has almost miraculously extricated us from perilous plights. Still, do they have to be so dramatic and painful? Even with my ears covered and a good thirty yards from the thunder putty, I was slammed off my feet with ears ringing. I threw out my hands and tumbled heels-over-head.

I was forced to squeeze close my eyes and press nose and mouth into the crook of my arm as a shower of debris and billowing dust followed the earsplitting roar of the angry outburst.

"Was that entirely necessary?" I mumbled between coughs. "Have you nothing more docile in your bag of tricks?"

"Hmm," he answered hoarsely as he picked himself up. "I guess I could have used a lighter charge."

"It appears our guide has had enough," I observed as the patter of the rat's feet over the ringing in my ears dwindled down the dark tunnel.

After standing and dusting myself off, I turned to follow the rat's departure. I was eager to escape the choking cloud of dust. Lorenzo played his torchlight through eye-watering haze to regard the rubble blocking the tunnel's entrance to the chamber.

"Hmm. That should take care of them for a while, even if they managed to pop back in their tunnels in time," Lorenzo commented, obviously pleased with himself.

"Let us hope that rain of brick does not stir up what be down the pit," I said. "Old legends and tales always have a demonic beast lying in wait at the bottom of such pits, just waiting to stuff some wayward explorer into their slavering maw."

"There's always that possibility, but it would have to dig through a hell of a lot of dirt and brick. If I'm not mistaken, with the support of the ceiling gone, there could be one hell of a sinkhole somewhere above."

"Great," I replied. "Remind me to leave town when this is done. I do not want to be around to explain why a giant hole ate half a block of shops, only to be followed by an irate fiend from the deepest pit of hell erupting from the crater."

"Hey, no problemo. We're catching the last leg of a redeye to Kaiserhelm."

"True, but we have to return sometime. Speaking of which, we need to make haste if we are to make the flight on time."

Lorenzo retrieved a small circular object from a pocket that I first took for a snuff case, but then saw the top was glass with a small needle wobbling about. I had seen a similar device, though larger, in Olmsted's study. My brother called it a compass.

"This way. The game is afoot," Lorenzo cried and set off down passageway.

It was either dumb luck or the cave-in that was responsible for no further interactions with the mages. Either way, we safely made it to stone steps leading up to a rusty grate, that in turn overlooked a canal. Once on a cobblestone lane, I dropped and sat upon my canvas pack.

"Don't poop out on me now," Lorenzo said as he surveyed our surroundings.

"I am not 'pooping out.' After this morning's trials and tribulations, I believe I merit a short rest. We are but a mile from the dragonport and by the rising sun, we have at least two hours before departure. We can make it on time."

"Sure, if we aren't further delayed."

I looked closely at Lorenzo. "Do you know something I do not?"

"Sure, but we don't have time to go down the list."

"Lorenzo..." I firmly spoke.

"Okay, a source told me yesterday that a wackyweed cartel has been hired by some anonymous group to see that your investigation into the stolen pixie gold comes to an abrupt end."

"You be jesting, right"

When Lorenzo did not answer, I continued, "Wackyweed cartel? Is there still one? The king legalized the herb last year. I do not understand."

"You said it. The smoke is now legal, meaning that cartel members no longer have a steady income. It's forced them to look about for other endeavors and their flair for bloody mayhem does not lend itself well to organic farming or designer dog breeding. They aspire to fill the vacated niche following the annihilation of the Glavendale Assassins Guild."

I groaned in resignation and rose to my feet. "There are several wackyweed smugglers I know who patronize the King's Wart's Inn. Maybe I can buy off the cartel. That would not have worked with guild assassins, but these would be non-professionals."

We walked in wary silence until coming to the edge of town and the Duburoake International Dragonport. With dragon flights fairly new, the dragonport be but several years old. Many of the flights cross the Megaoulas Mountains to Stagsford, the capital of Glavendale. Their passengers are mostly wealthy merchants and royal officials. The flights are still too expensive for common pilgrims and holidayers. Those on more limited budgets still take the week-long trek through the mountains by caravans, which gather in Kaiserhelm.

The dragonport's painted dome ceiling was decorated with fluffy clouds against a dark blue sky, as well as several dragons depicted as circling for landings. Pink quartz pillars as large as ancient oaks supported the center dome. The floor's green quartz glimmered in the glow of the witchlights set in pink seashells dotting the walls.

People were coming and going in a rush, much like Duburoake's sea harbor. Only this gleaming port did not reek of fish and unwashed sailors. If there was more time, I would have steeled myself for the flight by visiting the dragonport's bar, even though the drinks were five times the coin as those of the Kings Wart Inn.

Lorenzo returned in his usual garb after disappearing for ten or fifteen minutes – just in time to arrive at a heavy iron gate and begin the boarding process of presenting flight vouchers and identification papers to guards of the Royal Glavendale Motherland Security Service.

"Ah, Jak Barley and Lorenzo Spasm. Yah're almost missing the flight. Yah be the last ones. Wait until I tell the missus who I seen today," the plump security guard exclaimed with a large grin. "Goin' off on some dangerous state of affairs, are yah? I often think I shouldah gotten meself into another branch, somethin' more excitin' than looking at tickets all day."

"Of course, that fella Sergey with the Tattler embroiders them stories a bit, I expect," he continued. "I mean, all that kidnapping by dragons, battling demons and fighting off hordes of evil wizards – that be a lot of storytelling, right?"

I was more surprised by the guard's friendly prattle then if he had ordered a strip search. My experiences with dragonport security have usually proven not this congenial.

"Well, as a matter of fact we are being chased by a horde of enraged mages and their thuggish minions – and maybe even a mob of assassins," I whispered to him in a conspiratorial voice. "So, you might want to call in backup or else make yourself scarce after you pass us through."

That brought a hearty laugh from the guard and, after handing back our parchment work, he thrust a heavy iron key into the lock and pushed open the gate.

"Have a good flight," he wished us through the closing bars.

"Ah, you best run for it. Here come the mages," I warned while looking over his shoulder. Coming in the dragonport entrance were several disheveled looking Ghennison Viper Mages, minus the hired blades.

Lorenzo grabbed my sleeve and yanked me into motion. I looked back as we ran and observed the unaware guard still laughing as the wizards came rushing to the gate.

After several messy incidences with rogue necromancers, royal government facilities were pushed to install safeguards against magical assaults. The dragonport gate would be warded, but the spell designers could hardly have foreseen the need for magical fortifications that could survive an onslaught from three powerful and very rankled wizards. I only hoped the wards held them back long enough for our departure.

We exited the dragonport into bright morning sunlight. Our fellow passengers were already safely harnessed – facing outward on cushions. I did not recognize our dragon's breed. Medium size, it sported highly polished, deep green scales edged in bright crimson. Larger dragons are used for more distant flights and feature a section of legless chairs for the more moneyed passengers, as well as a flight assistant who serves free ale and wine.

As anxious as I was, I still noticed the dragon's impatient glare at our tardy arrival. The large reptilian head may have suggested a wild beast, but its piercing golden eyes revealed a fiercely intelligent mind. We scrambled up the mobile stairway and upon a ground attendant's instruction, secured ourselves and belongings.

So far there was no sign of the mages. I expected any second to see them burst onto the dragon pad. I fought to keep from screaming at the ground crew as they took their time with last minute inspections of the webbing and harnesses.

"First time?"

"What?" I twisted around to view a grandmotherly-appearing woman looking at me in bemused concern. Her white hair glowed like a halo in the morning sun.

"This be your first time, right? I can tell. Once we be up, you will be fine. It be so beautiful. All the farmstead fields appear as quilt patches and the buildings like children's toys."

"Ah, sure. Thanks."

"Maybe a sip of this would help." She was holding out a silver flask. "I find it soothes the jitters."

"Then you better take another sip." I groaned my warning.

She was going to need it. Emerging from the dragonport were three very unhappy Ghennison Viper Mages. The ground crew scattered at the unnerving sight.

"They sure are annoying," Lorenzo sagely observed.

The wizards came to a stop not more than fifty feet away and raised their hands in unison. I struggled with my harness even though I did not know what I would do once free of the leather straps. I caught my breath and reflexively hunched down when they began a soul-wrenching incantation that in itself caused one's blood to run cold.

Their rising voices signaled the mages were at the finale of their curse when the dragon calmly turned its head and exhaled a searing blast of flame that engulfed the startled mages.

I was part of the chorus of startled gasps erupting from the passengers. That was followed by a shocked silence as all eyes were now upon the still standing flaming husks. I recoiled from the repulsive, yet paradoxically welcomed stench of burning Ghennison Viper Mages. After all, my being able to smell the odious conflagration meant that it was the mages rather than me burning.

I thought to turn to the kindly woman besides me, worried that she would be stricken with terror. Our eyes met.

"Now that be not something you see every day," she replied, as if having just sighted a rare songbird. "Maybe you should have a sip. You look tense."

She was again extending her flask and this time I accepted.

"Good morning," the deep voice of the dragon began. "I be Vaxen, your dragon for this Glavendale International Dragonways flight. Sorry for the minor disruption. We will now be departing for Kaiserhelm and should make landing at approximately noon. Forecasts call for a slight overcast with a heavier cloud cover upon reaching Kaiserhelm. We have a tailwind so we should be arriving early. Please make sure your safety harnesses are correctly buckled and remain so during the entire flight."

"Minor disruption?" I said to Lorenzo. "What would be a major disruption?"

Our conversation was temporarily halted by the loud whoosh from the dragon's vigorous downward thrust of its wings. According to Olmsted, a dragon's wings are too small to alone provide the lift needed for flight. It be magic that allows their massive bodies to defy gravity. Those sensitive enough can actually see this magic as it flows about the wings in waves that shimmer like the northern lights.

"Maybe your friend would like a pull," were the first words I heard once we reached level flight.

"Sure," Lorenzo said as he leaned across to accept the flask.

I leaned back during the transfer and then turned a wary eye to my fellow passenger. "Alright, just who are you?"

"Me?" she innocently answered.

"Yes, you. There are obvious indications that you travel in disguise. Who are you?"

"My dear lad, why would you think that?"

I sighed in resignation in having to point out the obvious. "Your homespun garb be at odds with such things as the number of white lines on your fingers. They point to the wearing of multiple rings – an extravagance unlikely for the commonplace facade you attempt to portray. Your teeth are brilliantly white and perfectly aligned, a rarity for someone your age not of the nobility or wealthy merchant class. Your accent, though well done, fails to mask an affluent and educated background. I could go on, but that be hardly necessary."

Her response to the unmasking was unexpected. She leaned over to pat my hand and said, "There, there. Nicely done, nephew."

Nephew? I realized my mouth had dropped open and quickly shut it. Nephew? I knew all my mother and stepfather's siblings. Nephew? My eyes widened in disbelief.

"Yes, I am Vilhema, the older sister to your father. Though I never would have believed that imp would become anything but a roguish layabout. Of all his vast brood, I have been wanting to meet you for some time."

I could now see a resemblance in the eyes and nose to my father, though the woman in front of me had not gained the later-age girth of her amply padded brother. If I had not been so distracted by the mages, I would have earlier noticed the disparity between her easy self-confidence and the outward appearance of a shopkeeper or seamstress.

"Why, ah, what are you doing here?" I stammered.

"I have discussed with your friend that you could be facing some danger on the way to Kaiserhelm where I have business interests. So Vaxen and I decided on a lark to accompany you there."

I turned and scowled at my friend, who held up his hands and said, "Don't look at me. I only found out yesterday. She asked me not to tell."

Looking back to my newly found aunt, I almost had to shout to be heard over the wind and rhythmic beat of the wings. "Do not tell me. Your business interests just happen to involve the stolen shipment of pixie gold. You are the one who hired me."

She answered with a smile. "How fortunate for me that my own nephew be a famous private inquisitor."

I thought back to an earlier comment. "Vaxen? The dragon we are riding?"

"Yes, we are old friends. He thought it would be great fun to be a passenger dragon for a day. He has been practicing that introduction all morning."

"How did he manage ..." I began. "No, do not tell me, you own Glavendale International Dragonways."

"I, along with my silent partner, Vaxen. He was the one who foresaw the potential of dragon carriers. I am still working with the archaic ownership laws, but under Garsten's new Human-Werefolk Accords, we hope to see dragons allowed ownerships in both dragonports and dragonlines."

Thinking back to the nonchalant way the dragon disposed of the mages, I continued my questioning, "I am guessing Vaxen's career has included more than being a private chauffeur."

"Oh, yes. Vaxen was a member of the elite palace guard until Garsten assigned him to me, over my protests, as part of a security team. I do so hate all royal trappings. I am perfectly capable of providing for my own protection. I quickly rid myself of the team – except for Vaxen. He immediately became indispensable and I lured him away from royal service.

"I informed Lorenzo yesterday about the cartel members hired as assassins. I have my own security people who I believe to be more resourceful than those bungling CIA agents. They are now seeking those behind the plot. Since I felt responsible for putting you in danger, I decided to personally escort you to Kaiserhelm. I must admit I was caught off guard by those mages. You will have to tell me about them. For now, I find this shouting very tiring."

I took the hint and spent the rest of the flight enjoying the view and looking forward to seeing Morgana.

Chapter Four

I am not a fan of Kaiserhelm. It squats at the feet of the Megaoulas Mountains like a skinless, bleeding toad and grows fat on the caravans that come and go through the only entrance through the mountains for one hundred and twenty miles. The whole village, from the cobbled streets to the squalid houses, temples and warehouses, is made of bricks from the surrounding red clays of the foothills. Constant rains keep Kaiserhelm glistening like the raw skin under a broken blister and wash down streams of odorous, scarlet water that oozes across the streets like the spilled blood of some murdered giant.

The innkeepers and peddlers are well versed in fleecing the provincials who excitedly anticipate crossing the mountains for their first views of the fabled wonders of East Glavendale and to gawk at the royal city of Stagsford with its many temples. Pilgrims excitedly jabber like children as they wait for the latest caravan to begin the trek over and through the perilous crags and gorges.

I took that torturous route several years ago and it was then that I first unknowingly met my blood father, Baron Garsten Stee Hragen. At that time, he was following his proud line of robber barons – taxing caravans for the privilege to pass through his lofty narrow valley. He joined Lorenzo and me on our trip to Stagsford. Not long after, he assumed the throne following the death of his cousin, a pig of a king noted for sordid habits and vile entertainments best left for those with baser imaginations.

A Weekly Tattler account of the events leading to Garsten assuming the crown, and my first run-in with a once powerful death sect was headlined "Jak Barley, Private Inquisitor, and The Temple of Dorga,

47

the Fish-headed God of Death."

We arrived at the small Kaiserhelm dragonport to be met by three carriages and a small security team. Vilhema spoke softly to the dragon before rejoining Lorenzo and me in the center carriage.

"I have a room reserved at an inn called the Decker House," I informed her.

"Do not be silly," she replied. "You and Lorenzo are staying with me. I will not have my nephew residing at an inn when staying in Kaiserhelm."

During the ride to her residence, Vilhema suggested I call her Auntie when we were alone. I observed that Auntie was usually reserved for use by small children. I also noted such a greeting might accidentally be overheard and reveal our tie, so we agreed I would call her Vilhema in private and Baroness in more official settings. As a supposed commoner, it would be considered gauche for me to publicly refer to Vilhema by her given name. To some imperial members, it would even call for harsh punishment.

She related her official title was Baroness Vilhema Stee Hragen, Defender of the Eastern Reaches, Noble Member of the Order of Merit, Companion of the King's Service Posse, Consul for the Dignified Order of the Nettle, Duchess of Windberry and Recipient of the Majestic Black Check Mark. I reaffirmed that just Baroness would work for me.

My aunt asked why I was against being identified as her brother's offspring. Already a moving target as a result of my investigations, why add anti-royalists to the mix? My father appears to be a wise and benevolent ruler, but who is to say following generations will not be witless monsters? I do not want my future children to become spoiled members of nobility as those ruling or in line to rule in my home city.

Vilhema's laughing approval of my reasoning was a relief and increased my growing fondness for the woman. She in turn spoke of similar feelings that included her rationale for not marrying. As a fiercely independent spirit, she had failed to find a suitor who did not expect a traditional male-dominated union. With that she looked at me sternly. I hastily replied that I agreed and my relationship with Morgana was one of equal footing.

The dragonport was located on the outskirts of the city and our route took us even further from the center of Kaiserhelm. A massive iron and wood plank gate swung open at our arrival. My aunt's villa was set flush against a natural flat face of the mountain. I was informed that it was an ancestral summer home she assumed upon the crowning of her brother. It resembled more a small fortress with its semi-circular stone wall encompassing a courtyard of gardens and a spring-fed pond.

Not all government personnel were gone. Garsten was adamant that a company of royal guard remain stationed at the gate and wall. Being sister to the king, he argued, now placed her in greater danger.

The manor was of the ubiquitous red stone and featured lofty turrets at both ends. The quarrying for the wall and grand hall resulted in vaults carved deep into the foot of the mountain.

"I believe you can feel safe here," Vilhema said after describing her residence's layout.

A circular drive boasted a large fountain. I sighted several garden gnomes. They had taken topiary to an extreme, with there being an assortment of bushes whimsically sculptured to resemble dragons, centaurs, dwarves, two-headed rocs, wolves, sharks and nymphs.

"Just think, something like this could be yours if you wanted," Lorenzo said as servants rushed to take our meager baggage.

"I would not mind once married, a less crowded neighborhood and a bit more flora, but in quarters more similar to that," I answered while pointing to a carriage house off the main residence. "Besides, there would not be much to go around if all my siblings were also recognized."

We paused after entering a blindingly white rotunda with its domed ceiling circled with gold foil leaves, jade vines and precious stone blossoms. Five stained-glass skylights let in a rainbow of sunrays. Statues of legendary statesmen and mythical heroes guarded three entrances to the main hall.

A jungle of vine-covered potted tropical trees crowded the center of the rotunda. In their branches were chattering parrots – their vivid plumage as eye-catching as the colorful blossoms. I expected a tiger any second to emerge from the foliage.

"I do so love house plants," Vilhema said from over my shoulder, "but they can get out of hand."

Several years ago, I would have been awed into silence by the opulence on display. Since then, my cases have taken me to even more sumptuous palaces and temples. Still, I had to admit that I was impressed.

Vilhema said there would be a mid-afternoon repast before ordering a servant to see us to our rooms. Lorenzo and I followed him up a gently curving marble stairway to a circular balcony overlooking the main floor, and from there into the right-wing corridor. Witchlights illuminated the hallway. The wall on our left was festooned with portraits of dour men and women clad in sumptuous furs, silks and gems.

"I see a family resemblance," Lorenzo whispered as he stopped in front a scowling, balding and toadish figure of a man posing beside a seated and equally severe woman who appeared walleyed.

"Not likely, you being from another world," I replied in an equally hushed voice. "Though maybe one of your distant sires also slipped through the veil."

We continued behind our guide until halting at two open doorways. He entered the first room and deposited my pack on one of several comfortably cushioned chairs. The room was also furnished with a fireplace, settee, table with four straight-backed chairs, small writing desk and a half-filled bookcase. Six extremely narrow windows overlooked the gardens we had but minutes before crossed.

"There be the water closet," the servant informed me while pointing to a door to our right. He then turned to a doorway on the opposite side of the room. "There be your bedroom."

He nodded when I thanked him, then turned to lead to Lorenzo to his quarters.

The apartment featured witchlights and one flared to life with a tap. A second tap extinguished it. There was no need for the wall lights while daylight streamed through the windows. At closer inspection, it appeared the window frames were purposely made for easy removal. The result would be arrow loops – slits that are common features of a fortress.

Further exploration revealed a large, canopied bed and a chest of drawers. The water closet was likely once a large closet. There was no chamber pot. Its plumbing was an appreciated recent installation. Not all manors are so modernized. My attention was immediately drawn to an ale chiller. A magic-spelled cooler is costly and nothing would signify my aunt's wealth more than if there be one in each guest quarters. With a red oak exterior, the lining be of a rare type of blood stone perfectly suited for maintaining long-term frigid spells.

With a bottle of Duburoake Star Ale in hand, I returned to the bedroom to inspect a suit of formal clothing laid across the bed. It consisted of a blue linen tunic, a velvet vest of a deeper blue and grey trousers. At the foot of the bed was a pair of expensive appearing boots that reached mid-calf. I sighed in relief. The latest garish styles called for one looking like a popinjay. Still, I loathe occasions calling for such elegant wear.

"Don't worry. That's not for lunch," Lorenzo said as he entered the room. "It's for the garden party tomorrow that she throws every year."

I groaned. "We are not nobles or rich merchants. How will she explain our presence?"

"Haven't you been following the Weekly Tattler society pages? It's in vogue to have at least one or two infamous rogues present at a gala – the more scandalous the better, whether it be an artist, actor or even a notorious ferret. I'm surprised you haven't been flooded with such requests."

I frowned. "That sounds like one I supposedly received from the Baroness of Duburoake. I thought it a jest by the fools at the Kings Wart Inn. I told Osyani to ignore it."

My friend laughed and shook his head. "Think of all the good food you missed."

I more closely examined the clothing. "It looks to be of proper fit. What about yours?"

"Perfect. The Baroness was right to brag about her spies," Lorenzo replied.

Even if she was my aunt, I felt uncomfortable being under such surveillance that even my inseam was known.

Lorenzo reached into his bottomless pouch and withdrew a brown glass bottle displaying an outlandish script within a heraldry. He casually popped the cap off with a small red device, which was followed by the fizzing of ale.

"Oh, sorry. Here's one for you," he offered, after pulling out a bottle of Duburoake Star ale.

"What be that" I asked. "From your world?"

"Yes, a type of ale called Falstaff."

"From your world and you are not going to share?"

"Can't. Being from my anti-magic world, I'm not sure the beer would be safe for any inhabitant of this one. Here, as a token of my affliction, is the bottle opener. It's called a Swiss army knife and comes with all these doodads."

"Clever," I admitted after playing with it for a minute.

We finished the drinks while gazing out a window onto the courtyard.

Lorenzo returned to his quarters and I continued to gaze out the window. The half dozen guards were pacing back and forth atop the wall and stopped regularly to peer over the parapet. Vilhema was right when she said I should feel safe here. Her villa was a stronghold in everything but name.

With a start, I pressed my face to the window to peer at a figure strolling across the courtyard. It was a wizard. My momentary panic was soon abated upon observing he was not a Ghennison Viper Mage. This wizard's robe and cowl were grey and he wore no hat to cover his tightly curled black hair. His complexion was that of a walnut stain. I was at a loss to identify his branch of wizards.

Though it made sense for my aunt's defenses to include a magical component, I found the presence of a wizard unsettling. Head Mistress Kahlan was convinced male spell casters were behind the attacks on their crystals. I needed to discover if the conspiracy was made up of Ghennison Viper Mages or was the hostility toward the witches' new enterprise universal among sorcerers?

Vilhema had expressed surprise at the dragonport mage assault. Was it genuine? It seemed unlikely if her intelligence gatherers were as capable as she claimed. I took a chair as other considerations buzzed through my head. One by one I attempted to organize all the details from both cases into an orderly arrangement.

Sometime later I bolted from my chair and found myself muttering an exclamation used by Lorenzo, "Crapola!" Morgana – I was to meet her at the inn.

I entered the hallway just as Lorenzo was leaving his room.

"Don't fret it. Vilhema can send a carriage to pick her up," Lorenzo tried calming me.

"I need go myself. She be too cautious to accept the word of a strange coachman."

I hurried to the ground floor and into the hallway my aunt said led to the formal dining hall. It was in the wing opposite our quarters. Grabbing a passing servant's sleeve, I demanded, "Where be the Baroness?"

He let me know of the rudeness with a singular glare and snapped, "Do you refer to the Baroness Vilhema Stee Hragen, Defender of the Eastern Reaches, Noble Member of the Order of Merit, Companion of the King's Service Posse, Consul for the Dignified Order of the Nettle, Duchess of Windberry and Recipient of the Majestic Black Check Mark?"

"Just how many baronesses do you have around here?" I snapped.

"We only have the Baroness Vilhema Stee Hragen, Defender of the Eastern Reaches, Noble Member of the Order of Merit, Companion ..."

Lorenzo cut short the litany with a rap to the oaf's noggin. "Give it up. Where's the baroness?"

Puffing up indignantly, he grudgingly replied, "In the library."

"Which be where?" I asked.

He pointed down the hallway and yanked his sleeve free to go scurrying away.

The two wings of the manor flanked the mountainside. The wing we were quartered in was mainly apartments, with commoners like Lorenzo and me on the second floor. Also quartered there would be foreign dignitaries and representatives involved in business dealings with my aunt. The first floor was reserved for Vilhema and visiting members of the royal court.

The vault corridor, of course, plunged straight back from the rotunda into the base of the mountain.

The left wing housed such things as the library, dining hall, kitchen and servants' quarters. Its interior wall was adorned with paintings of famous occurrences – warriors battling dragons, goblins, trolls and other human warriors.

"Ah, here is at least one scene commemorating a peaceful event," observed Lorenzo. He was stopped in front of a painting depicting a group of humans offering bolts of cloth, necklaces and iron utensils to a band of scantily dressed dryads.

I grimaced and replied, "That's Prince Drump's first meeting with a mountain forest folk. Not long afterward the area was timbered and the tribe went extinct."

I was saved from further contemplating the genocide when nearby double doors opened to reveal Vilhema. "I thought I heard voices. Come in."

The walls were covered with tome-laden shelves reaching from floor to ceiling. A table sat in the middle of the long room. On it were several inkwells and quills, blank sheets of parchment, scattered stacks of manuscripts, a very large map and of course, a large crystal ball. Potted plants muted the sunlight streaming in from the narrow openings.

I took in none of this. My attention was wrenched away from the room's décor and to a person sitting in one of the large, padded chairs – Morgana.

"The Baroness was kind enough to see I was met at the dragonport. She was about to see me to my quarters before finding you."

She stood as I quickly strode across the room and we embraced.

"I worried that you would be hesitant in accepting such an unexpected ride," I said after stepping back to hold her at arm's length.

"I would have been, but the Baroness contacted my mother. With your trouble at the dragonport, they thought I should take an earlier flight. It took some scrambling, but here I am."

"I, also," an all too familiar voice spoke from the hallway.

I turned to see Morganna in the doorway.

"Please temper your joy at seeing me," the mother witch dryly said.

I took a deep breath and cleared the surprised consternation from my face. I need brace myself before any meeting with Morganna. Intimidating be an understated description of my intended's mother.

The witch be an older version of her daughter, but Morganna's face holds hints of strength yet to be part of her offspring's features. Whereas Morgana has copper red hair and a darker complexion, the mother possesses coal black hair and extremely pale skin. They do have green eyes in common.

"Ah, so you and the Baroness are acquainted?" I asked to change the subject.

"Since childhood," interjected Vilhema. "So, I found it pleasing to hear a nephew was courting my friend's daughter."

"One of the reasons I let you live when you first began seeing Morgana," the witch added.

I recovered with, "As well as my wit and charm?"

Morganna ignored my quip and turned to my friend. Her smile warmed by a number of degrees. "Ah, Lorenzo. It be so good to see you again."

"You as well. I must say you are as beautiful as ever."

Such a compliment coming from anyone else would result in a withering stare at best and a painful curse at worst. Yet the most feared witch in Glavendale bordered on coy when around Lorenzo. I often wondered if the two socialized on the sly – not enough to inquire of my friend – and certainly not to the witch.

"We will have a light repast off the kitchen," Vilhema informed us as she gathered the arms of mother and daughter to lead us from the library. "This evening's meal will be in the great hall."

"Why does that make me nervous," I whispered to Lorenzo as we followed the trio. "I am feeling outnumbered already."

"It's not that bad," my friend offered. "Just think of it. After you're married, the four of you can go bar hopping – become regulars at the Kings Wart Inn."

"I cannot see that happening."

"Exactly."

We turned and entered a room before I could cuff him. A table was already set for us. Vilhema's ideal of a light repast included stuffed auks, smoked auroch ribs, spiced roc eggs, a variety of cheeses, breads of different grains and flasks of white and purple wines. The desserts were honey cakes and toadberry pies.

"Now then, why not get down to business?" the Baroness exclaimed as the remainder of our plates were cleared and the last servant left the room. "I just now am learning what laid behind the attack at the dragonport. Nasty bunch, those Ghennison Viper Mages. But with Morganna and her daughter, as well as my own wizard and a number of wards already in place, my residence will be secure."

"This trouble with the crystals does worry me. I have great trust in Arkhjin, previously a court wizard for my brother. I will question him in regard to that, though I hope Jak and Lorenzo can ascertain the extent wizards are involved."

"You can feel free to interview him yourself, Jak," she added.

"I, also, will enjoy visiting him," purred Morganna, like a cat contemplating an unwary songbird.

Egad. I know well Morganna's loathing of wizards. Visiting would not be my word for the witch's time with the man.

"Good," the Baroness continued, "but now for my problem. A shipment of pixie gold was to have arrived one week ago. It did not. Arkhjin informs me the caravan master and those with the wagon are telling the truth when swearing they know nothing of how the casks became filled only with rocks. Arkhjin also says a scan of the wagon and casks show no trace of switch spells. Another wizard I called in spoke the same.

"Those involved return to Stagsford in two days, so any further questioning must occur before then. I have in the library all the parchmentwork involved in the purchase and transportation of the pixie gold."

Pixie gold. I was vaguely aware that jewelry made from it was in high demand. Times like this had me wishing my walking encyclopedia of a brother, Olmsted, was near. He was not and I had to ask, "Just what be the difference between pixie gold and regular gold?"

"It be simple," Morgana was the one to answer. "It be regular gold charmed by pixies so that it takes on an almost spellbinding glow. Jewelry made of it dazzles both the eye and mind. The magic for the enhancement be held secret. That monopoly allows them to limit supply and keep demand high."

I thought a minute before asking, "Are all pixies able to do this? There are so many kinds of pixies, I find it difficult to believe keeping such a secret possible."

"No, they could not. An isolated mountain clan be the only pixies with the knowledge. Fairies and even other pixies have attempted to discover the magical workings, but to no avail. Helping guard the secret are the neighboring dwarves who mine the gold."

"How do you know all this?" I asked the young witch.

"It be common knowledge for anyone who does not spend all one's idle time in squalid taverns and associating with the dregs of Duburoake," Morganna answered for her daughter.

"Yes, it be a hardship," I sighed, "but somebody has to do it."

By now I am used to the witch's hyperbolic comments and I believe, though I am not about to test it, that she finds the game amusing.

I turned to my aunt and explained in a less glib voice, "Many of my investigations have been solved by information garnered in those murky confines. Not much goes on in Duburoake that does not sooner or later find its way to the lawless quarters. A maid may mention a master's mishap to her boyfriend, who speaks of it to a bar mate, and so on and so on. A thief's bragging of a jewelry theft, a murderer of their victim – this all drifts among the currents of Duburoake's hidden world, with bottom feeders filtering and ready to sell such tidbits. But one must be cautious. They are also shark-filled waters."

There was a brief silence before Vilhema announced a mid-afternoon meeting in the library to review all that was known regarding the heist. The wizard would be on hand. At that we dispersed.

"We also have a Whiz meeting in fifteen minutes," Morgana

informed me as we climbed the stairway.

"Whiz meeting? What?"

"We have witches specializing in communications. They wrote a spell that allows a number of crystals to link so many can attend meetings from around Glavendale."

I groaned, "That be a horrific fabrication. I hate meetings. Now there will be no getting free of them."

Morgana's rooms were just past Lorenzo's quarters. Lorenzo retrieved ales from her chiller as I collapsed in a chair and then straightened in surprise. "You have a flat crystal."

Just as its name, the opaque crystal was about two inches thick, two feet in width and a foot and a half in height. I had seen such crystals only once before as part of a casino security set up.

"It took some convincing with my mother and Mistress Kahlan. Older witches can get set in their ways," Morgana replied. "But with the discovery of ways to grow the crystals in mass and with sharper focus, flat crystals make so much more sense. "

"I wouldn't doubt that someday small handheld crystals will be in common use for everyone," Lorenzo offered.

I rolled my eyes. "Who would want something like that always nagging at you?"

Morgana moved the crystal to the table and aligned three chairs to face it. "We are about to start."

On cue, Lorenzo and I took a seat to each side of her. The crystal flared into brightness following Morgana uttering a string of numbers. I looked at her in puzzlement. "Key code for security," she answered.

I blinked in amazement when the top left corner coalesced into an image of the three of us. Before I could voice my surprise, one-by-one the four remaining squares came to life containing the likenesses of three witches. Their tiny mouths opened in greetings and accompanying voices emanated from the crystal. Morgana introduced Lorenzo and me and followed by naming those appearing before us.

Two of the squares unsurprisingly featured Mistress Kahlan and Morganna. The two remaining witches, appearing younger than Morgana, were introduced as Hexicona and Kodia.

"What do you have for us?" Morgana asked.

"We have tried tracking the initial malspell, but it skipped so many times from crystal to crystal and back again that it proved impossible," said Hexicona, who by appearance of her almond-shaped eyes and olive complexion was from the far northern border regions. "We have counter spells in place and are on alert for new variations that could slip by the wards."

"We believe the witch or witches responsible are from Stagsford," spoke up Kodia.

She had the high cheekbones and bluish black skin of one from the inhospitable salt wastes of the Frainian Desert. To survive such a harsh landscape called for an indomitable strength of will and fortitude. Her self-assured pose and commanding voice spoke of both.

"Why do you say that?" I asked.

"Sorcery was hit and miss when first harnessing the unseen energies we call magic," Kodia began, in a voice reminiscent of an academy lecturer. "Early advancements in incantations, conjurations, rituals, transmutations, charms and hexes were the results of random fumblings – adding something here, subtracting something there, or just rearranging. Modern thelemic research combines different schools of knowledge such as numerology, alchemy, psionics, astrology, eldritch casting and spiritualism; to name a few. Now within this academic research be a specialization for crystals.

"The methodical delving into these magical branches be ongoing in three of Glavendale's witch academies, each following different approaches to systems of magic – some which can be quite arcane. After breaking down the malspell attacking our crystals, an analysis revealed characteristics common to the line of work at the Stagsford Enchantress Preparatory Academy of the Occult Arts."

Kodia looked at me for further questions.

"Ah, oh, yes," I stumbled after her dissertation.

"How many have graduated in the crystal-linked studies?" Morgana asked. "Are we looking at a handful or dozens of possible suspects scattered about the country?"

"It being a fairly new study, the number is not that great, though it will be growing each semester," Kodia answered. "I believe those responsible are very recent graduates or still enrolled, since some elements of the malspell are of recent development."

"We are looking at how many?" I asked.

"There are eight currently in the crystal program and twelve graduates," she replied. "Of the twelve, four remained to join the academy's teaching and research staff, one is now a witch to the royal court, three have started up their own spellware companies and the whereabouts of three are unaccounted. The twelfth witch be me. I was freelancing as a consultant until the appearance of the malspell. I have returned to the academy to aid in the response."

"If you wish," she continued, "I will remove myself from this inquiry for possible conflicts."

"I do not believe that will be necessary," Morganna spoke for the first time. "I am sure we will be able to account for your veracity after I have met with you."

I did not envy Kodia. Even if this were to be a comparatively friendly inquisition, being scrutinized by the witch would be no picnic.

It was agreed that Morgana, Lorenzo and I would travel to the Stagsford academy after making a stop at the pixie colony.

"That be the state of things so far," Mistress Kahlan concluded the meeting.

Chapter Five

"You freshen up nicely," Morgana noted as she brushed a stray lock of hair from my face. "You should dress up more often. And quit fidgeting. This will be fun."

Morgana stopped by my room on the way down to Vilhema's garden party. I was fidgeting. Instead of rubbing elbows with snobbish aristocrats and moneyed merchants, I would much rather be on the first leg of our inquiry at the pixie settlement. Vilhema was insisting we spend another night with her before leaving, which included this afternoon's garden gathering.

The day was not a complete waste. The morning had been spent interviewing three guards, two teamsters and the caravan master. Why, I asked, did the pixies ship the gold overland rather than by dragon? After all, there are dragons large enough to haul the heavy load and it would be speedier. The caravan master answered that there be bad blood between the pixies and dragons over some incident neither would speak of.

As was standard protocol, the waggoners related how they witnessed the oak cask containing the gold being sealed before it was loaded inside the enclosed wagon. A ward was then placed on the shipment to prevent magical interference and an unauthorized unsealing. The guards and teamsters adamantly insisted that at no time was the wagon left unattended. Yet upon arrival in Kaiserhelm with the seal broken before the Baroness, the keg contained only river pebbles.

They took me to the warehouse where the barrel was still stored. I studied the open keg for several minutes and ran the small stones between my fingers.

"Seal this back up. I want this continually under guard until I can

61

have it flown to my brother's laboratory in Duburoake," I ordered.

Not to leave any stone unturned, so to speak, I would have Olmsted examine the pebbles. Maybe he could pinpoint the sources of the stones and in turn offer a new lead. I would also ask my secretary Osyani, via the witch crystals, to contact a witch in Duburoake to do an independent scan of the keg and stones.

If the teamsters' and caravan master's consternation and puzzlement over the missing gold were feigned, then they were wasting their talents by not taking to the stage. I came away believing their denials of any wrong doings.

~ * ~

The manor greens were beautiful. Vilhema moved into the ancestral winter manor after Garston's ascension to the throne. It and the grounds had been falling into neglect under their cousin King Kenton's reign and my aunt immediately set about to remedy that.

A large pavilion had been erected in the spacious open area near the pond, which was surrounded by ancient, moss-covered shade trees and colorful flowering bushes. Scattered about were guests wandering the gardens.

"Ah, here be that private inquisitor, Jak Barley, and the witch Morgana who have set Duburoake abuzz," Vilhema exclaimed to a small knot of extravagantly dressed guests. Playing the part, she introduced us as if we were juggling monkeys brought as entertainment.

"Where be your cohort, Lorenzo Spasm?" asked a simpering dandy.

I rolled my eyes and responded, "I am afraid he has been forcibly quarantined by the authorities. Something to do with virulently contagious seeping lesions usually associated with unnatural acts with... Ouch!" Morgana kicked me in the shins.

"Jak be jesting. Lorenzo should be down shortly," she corrected me.

She took my arm and steered me away from the group. "I am

62

taking you to the banquet tent where you will cause less trouble because your mouth will be filled with food and ale."

"I will drink to that," I agreed.

Halfway to the pavilion we were intercepted by a wizard who upon seeing us broke away from a huddle of guards.

"Master Barley, witch Morgana. I am gratified to meet you. I am the Baroness's wizard, Arkhjin. We have not yet had a chance to speak. I am at your service in the quest to find the stolen pixie gold."

I smiled and shook his offered hand. Arkhjin turned to repeat the act with Morgana, who gracefully responded. Though her smile was faint, I could tell she appreciated the wizard's openness on two levels. Some mages still look upon women as inferiors and such salutations to be reserved only for other males. Many wizards would not offer the courtesy because they believe wielding magic should only be under male auspices.

It also did not hurt that he was good looking – not the corpse-like figures most people associate with wizards. Along with broad shoulders, cleft chin and a height several inches above my own, his deep, melodious voice flowed like thick honey.

Our conversation continued as we made our way to the pavilion.

"Have you any leads?" I asked.

"No. I inspected the shipping barrel and found no traces of enchantments other than the protective ward placed upon it after the keg was sealed and placed on the wagon," he replied. "As a matter of fact, I went to reexamine the cask only an hour ago and found that it had been moved. The warehouse guard knew nothing of its current whereabouts."

The wizard looked at me questioningly and I replied to his unspoken query, "It be in safe hands. I wanted to further study the barrel and stones."

"They were brought here?"

"No, but I can assure you they will not be misplaced."

I could tell he wished to press me further on the matter, but the conversation was interrupted by our reaching the tent and its refreshments.

"I will leave you to enjoy the afternoon," Arkhjin said as we entered the pavilion. "We will have plenty of time to discuss the theft tomorrow."

We watched him retreat back into the bright sunshine. "I hope that does not mean he will be traveling with us. I do not trust him."

Morgana's laugh is always like fairy bells – delightful even when aimed at me. "He seems like a very nice wizard, Jak. Could it be because he has the appearance of a handsome young god?"

"All right, I know you are jesting with me. No. Did you notice him trying to hide his interest in the location of the barrel and stones? Why? We need a second opinion. We have only his word that there are no signs of magical tampering."

I paused while filling my plate with an abundant offering of meats, breads, cheeses, fruits and cakes. "If the wizard be in on the theft, he would cover any evidence."

"That be possible, though your aunt seems certain of his loyalty. I will contact the Duburoake coven and have them send a witch to your brother's laboratory."

I spent the next couple hours downing mugs of ale and vainly attempting to avoid my aunt's guests, many readers of our past exploits in the Weekly Tattler.

"Sergey owes me," I said to Morgana after escaping one such mob. "Until we came along, his Tattler was a market stand rag with stories about infants raised by chickens or scandalous affairs. I would wager circulation has risen ten-fold since he began reporting our cases."

A thunderous sound and the following uproar among the guests drew us from beneath the tent just in time to see a smoking object tumbling out of the sky. It landed with a sickening plunk only a dozen yards away. Morgana grabbed my hand and pulled me along to the smoldering corpse of a piss dragon.

Piss dragons. I hate piss dragons. Only a quarter of the weight of their more common relatives, the piss dragon makes up for its lack in girth with an insane ferocity, razor-sharp talons and dagger-like fangs – all under control of a brain more suited to a clam. Their ferociousness be only bested by their stupidity. I still have dark dreams from past experiences with the vicious beasts.

"Someone be testing our defenses," spoke Arkhjin from behind us.

"A blaze barrier?" asked Morgana.

"Similar," the wizard replied. "We call the ward an inferno cordon. Different name, same thing. Now we must ponder who was the dragon's intended victim and those behind the attack."

His victim uncertainty had to be rhetorical. The only question was who sent the dragon – those behind the pixie gold hijack or attacks upon the crystals?

I scanned the air to see three small dots circling high above. "There, are those more dragons?"

Lorenzo had just joined us and upon my question, rummaged through his pouch to bring forth a spyglass.

"Yep. That's what they are. If they have any kind of eyesight and even the slightest intelligence, they'll figure out that further attacks are useless."

"I do not know about their eyesight, but when it comes to..." I didn't get to finish my thoughts on their wits or lack thereof. One by one the dots spun off to grow larger in size as they drove toward us.

"This should be interesting," Lorenzo commented.

I thought so too, having never seen a dragon attempt to breach such a ward.

The lead dragon was about two hundred feet above our heads when it slammed into the invisible shield that flickered purple to momentarily reveal its bowl shape. Smashed like a boot-stomped cockroach upon impact, the piss dragon began sliding down the invisible dome before bursting into flames. At that point, now dead, it passed through the barrier and plummeted to crash not far from the first dragon. We had barely enough time to pull our gaze from the smoking corpse to look up and see the next dragon meet a similar fate.

That left the remaining dragon not wavering from its dive. I grimaced and prepared to watch another suicidal collision, but stepped back in surprise when the ward again flickered to life, but this time the dragon plunged safely through. It circled above the gathering, its beady-eyed head darting about while searching for its quarry.

I turned to the wizard. "Do something."

He appeared stunned and his mouth moved, but emitted no sound. I looked back to the sky to see that the dragon had picked its prey. Not again? I was at the end of its glide path. I frantically clutched for a sword that was not there.

I bent at the knees and prepared to dodge its wicked claws. My last-second leap did not save me from being struck by the dragon – or at least part of the dragon. A hunk of flying meat walloped the air from my lungs. Lying stunned on the ground, I looked up to see Morgana with arms still outstretched and wand in hand.

"You waited long enough," I groaned as I climbed to my feet.

Scattered about were shreds of dragon scales, organs, muscle and bones. Both the grass and I were also coated in stinking piss dragon fluids.

"Where were you?" I snarled at Arkhjin. "Morgana is yet to see her diploma, while you are reputed court wizard."

Indignation crossed his face, only to be quickly replaced by bewilderment and then consternation. "I, ah… Excuse me," he said, while trying to regain self-control. "I am sorry, but that should not have happened. My ward should stand off dozens of the beasts. It be no excuse, but I scarcely believed it happening. You are truthful, I should have responded. I have failed twice."

"Maybe not twice," Morgana said as she nudged a hinged brass cylinder with the toe of her boot. "Would this have fitted upon a piss dragon's ankle?"

I watched as she lifted the artifact with her wand. It bore strange runes that, once observed, had both Morgana and Arkhjin making startled gasps.

"Cfxzyth." Morgana was the first to respond. Arkhjin nodded in agreement.

I was well aware of Cfxzyth relics. Twice, rings forged by the long-vanished creatures saved my life. From the few skulls unearthed beneath desert ruins, those ancient holders of dark powers had the facial features of rats. Little be known of their mythical magics, but what tales survive terrify even the most malevolent of mages.

"That would explain the dragon's breach of the ward," Morgana observed. "Whoever be behind this attack has access to rare and arcane weaponry."

I turned to Lorenzo and observed, "You have been unusually quiet. Where have you been?"

He only shrugged, which made me nervous. Such silence usually foretells some sort of mayhem.

The Baroness approached, accompanied by several guards. Most of the guests took shelter within the pavilion and only a few hardy souls were venturing out.

"How dreadful," began my aunt with an exaggerated sigh. "I believe nothing will remove that bile and phlegm from your garb. And you looked so nice in them."

Morgana tilted her head while scanning me up and down. "He be a mess," she agreed, "but I think this might work."

Whispering while she raised her wand, Morgana dramatically brought her hand down and a shimmering enveloped me. This was followed by a foul mist bursting off my skin and clothing and quickly settling to the ground.

"My, I wonder if you could teach that to my maids," mused the Baroness. Now serious, she turned to her wizard and snapped, "How did this happen?"

"I believe this can explain it," Morgana interceded.

She displayed the artifact and described its likely role in the ward's breach.

"I know of no spells taking such an ancient relic into account," Morgana continued. "It might take a gifted wizard or witch weeks, if not longer, to fathom the magic behind it. Cfxzyth artifacts like this are eagerly sought by those hoping to remaster that forgotten lore."

Morgana's mother joined us and agreed with her daughter's conclusions. Not one for such festivities, she had been investigating the many tomes in Vilhema's library. More guests were leaving the confines of the tent and congregating around us, though not moving in too closely because of the messy carnage – as well as the stink of the dragon entrails.

"Do not worry, nothing more shall disrupt your garden party,"

Morganna assured the Baroness, who had wondered if she should call an end to her yearly gathering. "I am sure my daughter and I, as well as the wizard, can prevent further intrusions."

Eager to rectify his earlier failing, Arkhjin quickly agreed. The expression on the mother witch's face was one of outrage that anyone would dare attack a residence where she was staying.

Despite the stomach-wrenching stench, I forced myself to slowly examine the remains of the dragons for further clues. I bent to examine a still smoking corpse. Though charred, I observed a hemp netting across the dragon's back. That was unusual since piss dragons are considered too temperamental for safely transporting people or freight.

I reached into my waist pouch to remove a small parchment envelope and into it inserted a few hemp strands. Olmsted might be able to discern clues from the sample.

It was while inspecting the third corpse that I discovered another unusual item, a copper medallion attached to a leather collar. As with most magical instruments, it bore the squiggles and lines of a language unknown by me. I often wondered why wizards and witches didn't standardize their written and spoken spells into one modern language. Lorenzo explained that the required education needed to interpret the various tongues, some long dead, enabled the mages and witches to maintain a tight monopoly on the arts.

"An amulet used to negate magical barriers – one I did incorporate a defense for in my ward," spoke the wizard as I held it up. "It be an old one. By old I do not mean as the Cfxzyth relic, but ten or fifteen years."

I passed it to Morganna after she held out her hand. "It be a spell I recognize, though the medallion be strangely crafted."

The three spell casters huddled to discuss the attack, so I drifted back to the pavilion – the ale keg to be more exact. I was fairly surprised that Morganna was acting so cooperatively with the wizard.

I was immediately swarmed by Vilhema's curious guests. So much so that I almost wished to be still drenched in dragon slime. It took fifteen minutes and two ales before I managed to break free – almost. Lorenzo remained unusually quiet.

"All right, what be the scoop?" a familiar voice made me jerk around.

"Sergey, what are you doing here?"

The Weekly Tattler publisher had a roc fledgling drumstick in one hand and a mug of ale in the other.

Sergey and I are both in our early thirties. Yet for his even more intemperate lifestyle, Sergey appears to be but mid-twenties – except mornings. After a night of roustabouting, he often looks to be nearing forty. Of middle height and slim build, and with brown hair to his shoulders, Sergey cuts an unassuming figure. He says this lends itself to gathering gossip.

"Well, you know, free food and drink," he answered. "We scribes cannot resist."

I returned his sham innocent gaze with one of skepticism. "I know you are a hopeless beggar, but even so I find it difficult to believe you traveled all the way to Kaiserhelm for a free meal. Just how did you worm your way in?"

"Your escapades at the Duburoake International Dragonport are not easily ignored. It be not often that three Ghennison Viper Mages are roasted by a dragon – one in the service of the king's sister – and with you and Lorenzo on board."

"And," he continued while looking about, "please do not tell anyone how I got in. I would not want to get the caterers in trouble."

I am never without amazement at Sergey's ability to insert himself into places no matter how the tight the security. Though he might not have the most sterling reputation among fellow chronicalist, he is a legend when it comes to his wily ways. He be near as skillful with disguises as Lorenzo.

"You know you owe me," he now said in a serious tone. "If not for the Tattler, you would be a drained husk after that bloodsucker business."

That was true. I took a deep breath and asked, "What are you getting at?"

"I want to be embedded with whatever investigation you are on."

"Embedded?" I asked confused.

69

"It be a word Lorenzo described for how I was part of the vampire case. That was some of my best writing. Even won first in news reporting from the Glavendale Press Association. I do not know what is going on now, but from that mage sheiss at the dragonport, it has to be hot."

"You will recall," I said, "you were almost dismembered and turned into an undead several times."

"Yeah, that was exciting."

I did like Sergey and he had proved surprisingly resourceful. "Both the witches and the Baroness must approve your accompanying us. There are matters the Baroness might not want to be common knowledge. That might prove difficult."

"Morgana told me she believed it would be all right as far as the witches are concerned."

"What?" I exclaimed. "When did this happen?"

"Just a half hour ago. She said it was about time the covens used social media to their advantage."

"Social media?"

I turned to Lorenzo. He again just shrugged.

"There still be the Baroness," I continued. "She might not like her problem becoming common knowledge. It might look bad."

"What would look bad?"

Damn. Vilhema was as bad about sneaking up on one as Lorenzo and Morganna.

"Ah..." I struggled for how to explain.

"Are you going to introduce me to your friend, Sergey, the infamous chronicler of The Weekly Tattler?" the Baroness asked, leaving me even more tongue-tied. "Come, come. You do not think my security would be so lax? They have been watching Sergey since he arrived."

It was Sergey's turn to be at loss for words.

"I have been telling guests that soon the notorious Sergey Varvervane will also be arriving. It be the social coup of the year to have the four of you at my garden party. Now, tell me, what might look bad?"

I let Sergey explain his wish to be part of the investigations into the malspell attacks and mage burnings at the dragonport. He had only just learned from Morgana that we were involved in two separate inquiries, leading him to question the Baroness's involvement. The chronicalist was still unaware of the missing pixie gold.

Sergey brightened at my aunt's first comment. "I assume nothing will be printed until, and only if, my case comes to a satisfactory conclusion?"

"I can assure that," Sergey eagerly agreed.

"If the culprits are apprehended, that might be a warning to other would-be villains," she spoke softly, as if to herself.

"Then again," she said in a louder voice, "such publicity might send the wrong message if the scofflaws escape capture."

"Ask Jak, I may be accused of being a drunken ne'er-do-well layabout, but never as an oath breaker," Sergey said.

"So, you are saying the inquisitor and you have a great deal in common."

It took a moment for Sergey to recognize the jest behind the Baroness's comment. He was clueless about our relationship. She continued, "I will accept your pledge under the condition Jak has the final say on your account."

Sergey stiffened. I knew why. He replied in a sober tone, "I can only promise that if the case be solved, I will report nothing that be not true. Jak can fact ensure it, but that be all. I am not anyone's public issues manager. I will not paint something that it be not, no matter how uncomfortable it may make some."

The Baroness considered his declaration for a minute. An air of silence hung over us while festival clatter filled the surrounding greens.

"I agree. That be all I want, just the truth," Vilhema finally spoke. "Jak, you may fill your friend in on my case. I will have a servant ready his quarters for him. The dragon leaves for the pixie settlement at dawn."

The Baroness paused before leaving. "All this on one condition."

"That be?" Sergey hesitantly asked.

"That you now mix with my quests and enjoin them of those wild tales printed in your journal."

"That will be a hardship," I laughed. "Just ask those forced to listen to him at the Kings Wart Inn."

~ * ~

That evening I sat with Morgana and spoke of several bothering's. "Do you believe Arkhjin is telling the truth? It could have been an act. I am still not sure we can trust him."

"He seemed genuinely shamefaced about the breach," she replied. "As I said, that Cfxzyth relic would have taken any witch or wizard by complete surprise. I do not know if you realize how rare such artifacts are. That you came in contact with two such rings be unheard of."

"Well, I guess he will have to be kept under close watch. I will feel better when we have a report on the shipping barrel."

Morgana looked at me closely. "Something else be bothering you. I can tell."

I nodded. "Have you noticed Lorenzo is acting strange? I left him plenty of openings and not one insult. It be unnatural for him to be so quiet."

"Yes, I noticed that too," she replied as I made to leave. "It be very unlike him. You should go to Lorenzo before we leave. Tomorrow may prove quite hectic."

Lorenzo answered the door on my second knock and I unceremoniously brushed past him to take a seat.

"Hello, won't you come in," he said dryly.

"Sit down," I ordered while pointing to a nearby chair.

He raised his eyebrows, but followed my command. "I take it that you have something on your mind."

"Yes, what be the problem?"

"There's a problem?"

"Yes, problem. And do not answer a question with a question that includes 'Do I?'"

"Why do you think there's a problem?"

"That be answering a question with a question," I kept to the point. "Again, what be the problem? I have known you long enough and under many circumstances to know something be amiss."

He let out a sigh – one I could tell this time was not theatrics. "You might've wondered why I suddenly mentioned a brother after all this time."

I nodded for him to continue after a long pause.

"It's because he's been on my mind. I received a note from him several days ago. We correspond regularly. Almost as an afterthought, he mentioned he had been receiving threatening death notes."

"What?" I said and stood from my chair. "Who sent it?"

"That I don't know. I have feelers out."

"You are now just telling me?" I almost shouted.

"We have our hands full enough. I didn't want to distract you."

I was now pacing back and forth. "It would not be the first time I have had to multi-chore. This be dreadful. Tell me all you know."

We went back and forth with questions and answers. He seemed to be taking the threats too lightly. Lorenzo's brother's name be Michael, an outlandish forename, but then again, the two are from a different world. Lorenzo said he was having his brother send one of the notes to Olmsted to trace the ink and parchment, as well as analyze the writing. Odd spellings and grammar can reveal much, as well as the style of handwriting.

"You told Morganna, correct?"

"Not yet."

"Why not? I am thinking that anyone outside our circle to discover your otherworldly origins must be a magic user. If so, Morganna can help."

I was now on a roll, as well as in an uncommon role – that of telling Lorenzo what to do. "Of course, we will not notify the Clandestine Information Authority. We do not want to reveal your origin to the bunglers in the CIA and they would only get in the way."

I stood silent for a moment, then added, "Until this be settled, I think it be best for you to disappear. I will let it be known that you abruptly departed, and we have no idea why or to where."

He listened to me with a maddeningly bemused look and said, "I don't think that'll be necessary."

"Nonsense. I would do the same for any of my brothers or

73

sisters...those I know of, anyway. This way you can aid your brother. I only wish I was free to join you."

"Hah," Lorenzo laughed.

I looked at him in surprise. He answered my startled look by saying, "Calm down. You don't know my brother. I would be more worried for the safety of those foolhardy enough to threaten Michael. I'm the timid one of the bunch."

I waited to see if Lorenzo revealed he was but jesting; maybe a way to deal with worry for his brother's safety. The relaxed smile did not leave his face. My gods! If my friend was the considered timid one, what must his brother be like?

~ * ~

A servant's loud door rapping caught me in the middle of packing. Minutes later I was in the hallway and following the fellow down to where the rest were partaking in a light breakfast.

We were leaving at daybreak by sandglass rather than the sun since it did not rise over the mountain peaks until late morning. I donned a wool outer garment in preparation for the frigid winds whipping through the mountain peaks.

"My gods," I exclaimed again after stopping dead in my tracks upon seeing the dragon that was to carry us to the pixies and then onto Stagsford.

"Ah, it be the buffoon monkey again," a deep voice roared back.

Dominating the greens was a copper-hued dragon at least forty feet in length from its nose to tail tip. While many such beasts have narrow snouts like crocodiles, this dragon had a shorter and squarer jaw that gave it a milder appearance. Its back and lengthy tail also lacked spike plates. It was no other than Adalbert, the dragon that first joined our group of questers for the Dark Lords Conspiracy and several following adventures.

"Ah, I see it be the giant freakish lizard with glandular problems," I shouted.

"That be hero dragon of the Cyan Isles clan," he roared back.

74

"That be human private inquisitor," I hollered in return.

It be an eerie feeling to look into the icy eyes of a dragon from but several feet away, not to mention the close proximity to its dagger-like fangs. As irritating as the dragon be, Adalbert has proven a stalwart traveling companion. We climbed up the netting and set to securing ourselves and baggage.

Adalbert launched into the air with a powerful downward thrust of his wings. The next ten minutes of flight was spent circling to gain altitude. The dragon was taking advantage of the updrafts created by warmer winds forced upward when hitting the mountainside.

I could not stop nervously scanning the sky for signs of an aerial attack. My neck muscles were thoroughly knotted by the time we set down. We came to rest in a long narrow glade surrounded by fir trees. A herd of shaggy aurochs grazed within a split-log fence and small gardens were situated alongside a row of thatched huts. Giant flightless moas guarded a flock of sheep grazing freely in the high mountain valley. One log building stood out because of its larger size. It was here, I guessed, that the magical alchemy takes place.

A contingent of three pixies and three dwarves solemnly paraded from the buildings to greet us. The Baroness warned us to be very tactful as the two bands of folklings were distrustful of outsiders, especially bigguns like us.

Morgana stepped forward and introduced our party.

"I be Amerate," one of the pixies declared. She, like her two pixie companions, was dressed in wool and leather. They stood about two-feet tall and appeared stouter than the pixies I am familiar with, though that could be explained by their bulky cold-weather garb. Amerate ignored naming her companions.

About four feet in height, which had him towering over the pixies, the lead dwarf identified himself as Smelt. He named his companions Shale and Breccia.

That was the entirety of the ceremony. Amerate abruptly spun about and waved us to follow – the pixies in front and the dwarves bringing up the rear. There were several doors along the length of the building and we entered one that opened into a meeting hall. A large fireplace held glowing coals. It would be refilled with logs as evening neared. The tables and chairs came in two sizes – pixie and dwarf. The four of us were motioned to take chairs scaled for the dwarves. That meant sitting with knees almost to our chins, much like parents visiting a classroom for kinders.

"What do you want?" asked the pixie in as stern of tone possible when given in a squeaky voice.

I was startled. "Has not the Baroness spoken with you?"

She shrugged. "This be not our business. We supplied the gold and are not responsible for biggun bungling when leaving our valley."

Vilhema warned me the pixies might take such a tack. "Of course not. Yet once the theft becomes common knowledge and unfounded rumors begin, it could impact your reputation, future sales and maybe even an investigation by the CIA. After all, the Baroness is the sister of the king."

"Be that some ill-framed threat?"

I held up my hands palms outward. "Certainly not. I am just mentioning the possible consequences of not solving the disappearance of the gold shipment."

With a deep sigh, Smelt spoke, "Do not get your dainties in a knot, Amerate. Tell them what we know. It be to our advantage."

Smelt shifted his gaze to me. "We dwarves know of you and Spasm. We hear no ill tidings. Even the coal dwarves speak well of you, if grudgingly."

That was a relief. The seven dwarves had been a bit testy when I investigated the magically induced slumber of Frost Ivory.

"Can you just relate the movement of the gold while in your charge and the last you saw of it?" I asked.

Smelt spoke first. "We store the gold deep within the mountain after it be refined from ore. It be impossible for outsiders to make their way through our labyrinth of shafts. When there be enough to fill a cask the size of an ale barrel, we divide the gold into packs and carry it here under guard."

He paused a moment and looked to me, "I expect this account to travel no further than amongst us. I would not want thieving bigguns to use such information against us. Can you pledge that your friend will also keep this trust?"

He was obviously speaking of Sergey. I looked to my friend and lifted my eyebrows. He vigorously nodded his head in affirmation and spoke, "On my word as a journalist."

I sighed. "You might want to ignore that last part, but I can attest to Sergey's word of honor. He may be a noted wastrel, but one who prides himself on keeping vows. I will stand for him."

The dwarf might have looked doubtful, but he continued, "We travel with a heavy guard and wind our way beneath the forest canopy so as not to be seen by prying eyes from the sky. The pixies weigh the gold after we arrive and that be the last we see of it."

He turned to Amerate. It was now her turn and she grudgingly continued. "We value-add the gold and sell it."

She returned my stare with a glare. "What? We pixies are not as trusting as the dwarves. You do not expect me to give away our closely guarded secrets."

"No, I do not. Start from after the transformation. Who oversees the packing? How be it transported to a caravan? What precautions do you take?"

"Go on, Amerate," Smelt urged as the pixie huffed up like an angry fighting cock. "We need to see this settled."

"I oversee the packing," she spoke, as if issuing a challenge. "The pixies involved in the transformation fill the casks. Guards from the caravan arrive and witness the meddle-proof cask being securely sealed. Ask the caravan master. They be bonded for any loss. We take no responsibility after it leaves our valley."

"So, you personally saw the sealing of the gold-filled cask and its transport onto a wagon?"

"You deaf? I said so," she snapped.

"I would like to follow the path taken from where the gold was transformed to the wagon, as well as speak with each of the pixies involved."

"What?" It was more of a squawk that a question. "Did not I just tell you I oversaw the transfer?"

"I have no reason to doubt you, but if I do not carry out a thorough investigation, I will have failed the Baroness."

It took some further persuasion before the pixie capitulated. She strongly protested allowing a witch to see where the magic was performed, fearful Morgana might pick up hints of the workings behind their spells. We finally agreed that the area could be first cleared of any numinous diagrams, gemstones, talismans, athames, besoms, cauldrons or any other magical tool used in the transformations.

The following interviews seemingly proved fruitless. All four of us took part in the questioning so there was no turtle left un-flipped. It turned out that Sergey's experience in interviewing news sources crossed over well for the interrogations. The pixies swore the transformed gold was never left unwatched until given over to Amerate.

"There be always at least one of us with the gold after its transformation," spoke a pixie named Nandie. She had been introduced as foreman of the laboratory. Her outer attire, like the rest of her crew, was a one-piece blue garb with a bibbed front held with shoulder straps. Beneath that was a simple white tunic.

I had chosen an informal setting for the interview, not wanting the pixies to feel intimidated, yet still unsettled enough that they might reveal more than intended. We sat in a circle in the now emptied laboratory – us four and the pixies directly involved in that particular shipment. We had to sign a logbook at the door that kept track of all entering and leaving the site.

"You say there be one pixie of your crew not present?" I asked.

"Yes," replied Nandie. "Airahka – we fear she wandered too far in search of certain ores and fell prey to one of the giant centipedes that infrequently wander into our valley."

I shuddered, having been attacked by one of the devilishly large beasts during that one overland trip to Stagsford.

"You say centipede intrusions are not uncommon?"

"Well, I would not say such occurrences are common, but they have been known to occur," she replied. "We rely on the dwarves to keep the valley free of dangerous beasts."

"Finding ores, you say?" I continued questioning about the suspicious disappearance of the pixie. "Would not that be a job for the dwarves?"

"Airahka liked to hike in the woods and she used the searches as an excuse," Nandie answered, and added, "If you believe she was involved in the disappearance of the gold, I can tell you that she went missing before the cask was inspected, sealed and warded at the caravan grounds in Stagsford. She was only involved with it leaving for Stagsford. Just ask your wizard."

I twisted in my seat to glare at Arkhjin and exclaimed, "You were here? What, you did not think that was something I should know?"

The wizard shrugged and replied, "It was of no import. I was already back in Kaiserhelm when the pixie gold arrived in Stagsford. I wanted not to distract from this investigation since I could not have been involved."

This did nothing to sooth my rising ire. "As far as I am concerned, your lack of candor automatically makes you suspect, no matter what be your excuse."

"It be inexcusable," Morgana joined in. "I am not comfortable continuing this investigation with you present. You need to excuse yourself and return to Kaiserhelm."

"You cannot make me," he heatedly replied. "The Baroness will hear of this."

"I am in charge of this investigation and I am ordering your removal," I firmly added.

Though Morgana's order took me by surprise, I echoed her declaration because not only was I in total agreement, but to affirm solidarity with my partner.

"I should have expected nothing else from a witch," the wizard shouted angrily as he leaped to his feet and brought his hands up, either in anger or to fling a magical assault.

I did not wait to find out. I reflexively leaped to my own feet and stepped forward to perform the Striking Snake, a basic Kimchee move that is taught to all novices of the ancient thumb martial art. It entails lunging with one foot thrust forward, an explosive straightening of the arms and leading with both thumbs to stab into nerves located beneath the shoulder blades. The victim's arms immediately fall numb to their sides.

That he failed to have a basic ward for such a simple assault showed an inattentiveness on his part.

"Start to say anything, anything at all, and it will be the last words you ever utter," I spoke while now holding a blade to his throat. "You have left me no choice. Even if your claim of innocence be true, your actions speak otherwise. You will not be going with us to Stagsford. I will notify the Baroness and if she wishes, send a dragon for you."

Arkhjin looked as if to protest, but the added pressure of my dirk quickly dampened any response.

By now all in the room were standing. The pixies were following the drama in shocked silence. Sergey appeared just as speechless.

Lorenzo reached into his belt pouch and produced a stubby grey tube. Unwinding a ribbon from the roll, he tore off a section and pressed it over the numbed wizard's mouth.

"It's amazing all the uses for duct tape," he said after pushing the wizard into a chair and tearing off several more strips to further bind him. "This should keep him quiet for a while."

"Let me extend Jak's restraint," Morgana volunteered. I stepped aside for her to whisper a spell that resulted in Arkhjin's eyes closing and his chin dropping to his chest. "That should last until a couple hours after we have left."

I next had the pixies show me the route from the laboratory to the loading area. It proved straightforward – out the laboratory's door and across the open yard to an empty green space. There were no buildings or shrubbery to impede a continuous observation that would allow for sleight of hand.

With no further reasons to remain, we returned the landing area and waited for Adalbert to finish whatever tedium-breaking explorations he was pursuing.

"I do have one question," I said as we waited. "Why should a duck need taped?"

A half hour later we were given a much more enthusiastic sendoff than the earlier welcoming. They were obviously glad to see us go. I watched the figures dwindle and wondered of the conversations that must now be occurring. Did they hide secrets we missed? I could see no reason for the pixies lying or being involved in the theft. The dwarf testified that the raw gold was delivered to the pixies, so there was no need on their part to conceal a shortfall with a sham theft.

I considered the actions to be taken in Stagsford. On the list were a questioning of the caravan mage who placed the protective ward on the pixie gold, finding the guards who accompanied the gold from the pixies to Stagsford and viewing where the caravan members gathered for the trip.

I would also visit the Stagsford Enchantress Preparatory Academy of the Occult Arts with Morgana and speak with the students and staff. The young witch Kodia would be one of the first contacts. Without Morgana's knowledge of the arts, I feared I would miserably fail the case. *Maybe,* I thought, *the case should be turned entirely over to Morgana and I focus on the gold theft?* Considering that, I remembered Morganna saying she also planned on meeting with Kodia. The best plan of action would probably be to have the two witches deal with the malspell.

~ * ~

"What? You do not want to work with me?" Morgana responded to my thoughts on dividing the cases. We had just finished settling with Adalbert when to meet again and were crossing a newly laid cobblestoned landing site at the Stagsford dragonport.

"Huh?" I answered in surprise. "No, of course not. I know little of magic. That be your specialty."

"So it be, but no one can be an accomplished witch immediately out of academy. That be why I am grateful my mother and the young witches here will be aiding me. Though I plan to become an incomparable private inquisitor, right now I know my limitations. Working with you will help me hone those skills."

"Sure, ah, after we register at the inn, we can..."

I was cut off by the sudden appearance of a dozen royal dragoons. They were easily identified by their black uniforms, unadorned leather harnesses, knee-high boots and narrow-brimmed caps that completed the black ensemble. They flowed around us like wolves circling a musk ox.

"Come with us," ordered the leader, easily identified as such by her excess of ribbons and medals.

"What? Why?" I stammered.

"I have orders to escort you to the palace. Come, the King awaits."

I was afraid of that. I hoped Sergey would not think it strange that we were being accorded this special attention. I would think not. After all, we were on a mission for the King's sister, the Baroness Vilhema Stee Hragen, Defender of the Eastern Reaches, Noble Member of the Order of Merit, Companion of the King's Service Posse, Consul for the Dignified Order of the Nettle, Duchess of Windberry and Recipient of the Majestic Red Check Mark.

Awaiting us were three ominous black extended carriages. The guards hustled us into the middle one. We were joined inside by one of the dragoons as another climbed to sit with the driver. The rest split up to board the other two coaches.

I was curious to see if the inside of the new Stagsford dragonport terminal was more opulent that Duburoake's, but we skirted around it.

"Do you think we will actually meet with King Stee Hragen?" Sergey excitedly asked.

It would be quite the scoop for his weekly publication.

"The Royal Dragoons are only involved in matters directly relating to the King of Glavendale," I answered. "This escort certainly means we will be honored with the presence of His Majesty, King Stee Hragen."

Morgana and I locked eyes and she returned my smile. This would be her first time meeting the father of her intended, though it certainly would not follow the common routine of family introductions. Our public meeting would follow the stilted royal protocols of the court, but I had no doubt that later there would be a much warmer and informal introduction between Garsten and Morgana. After all, it was because of my blunderings that the former king wound up deceased, rolled in a carpet and hung from a castle window – all which resulted in the baron assuming the throne. That is one narrative that will never find its way into The Weekly Tattler.

King Garsten was undertaking a modernization spree for Stagsford's roadways. Not only had the king commissioned the new dragonport and was replacing many of the ancient and crumbling bridges, he was constructing a byway from the dragonport to his castle, the center of Glavendale's government. The new four-lane pathway swung around the outskirts of Stagsford to avoid the clogged and narrow city streets.

"Damn," I heard our carriage driver curse loudly. "Cannot they do this work at night?"

We had come to a dead stop and I opened the door to peer out. This new throughfare was much wider than customary roads. A flagman was halting those bound for the castle as construction signs herded passage to only one lane. A steady stream of everything from heavy freight wagons to passenger cabs flowed past us from the opposite direction.

"Damn," the driver again swore loudly. "Me thought all this section was done months ago."

Lorenzo and I locked eyes. Turning to the dragoon, I asked, "Do you often travel this way?"

He hesitated as if unsure he should be speaking with his charges. "Yes," he finally replied to the simple question.

"Has this section of the road been finished for months?"

"Ah, yes."

Lorenzo and I nodded in silent agreement. Morgana sensed our apprehension and straightened in her seat.

"This could be a trap," I snapped to the dragoon as both Lorenzo and I drew our blades.

Both our escort and Sergey looked startled at my exclamation. After all that occurred, I would rather look foolish than be caught with my breeches down.

I yelled up to the driver and other dragoon, "Heads up. This could be an ambush."

I dropped to the center of the highway as Lorenzo exited from the opposite side. The sky was clear except for a few scattered clouds. Several new inns were under construction in what only a year ago had been filled with crops and pastures.

"All clear," Lorenzo cried.

Both Morgana and the dragoon were now at my side.

"What be going on?" the soldier riding with the driver yelled to his cohort.

"He thinks this be a trap."

"What? Here? This close to Castle Raven?" the other scoffed.

I strode past the first carriage to confront the flagman. "What be the holdup?"

I could not blame the fellow for his startled appearance after being approached by a sword-wielding stranger. I tried allaying his fear by saying, "Our party be on royal business and we have an appointment with the King. Speak up, why the delay?"

"Ah, I, ah, just work here. Yah have to ask me bosses."

I placed my sword against his throat, a move I would normally be fain to do in such a situation, but this knave was definitely not a road hand.

"One quick whisk of my wrist and your last few moments will be spent wishing you had been more forthcoming."

"But I be..."

He gasped as I pressed the sword harder against his throat. "It be curious how a lane worker spending all day in the sun can be so pale. I am also surprised how polished are your boots and new be your tunic. There be also the..."

"Are you mad?" demanded a dragoon from the lead carriage as he approached us. "Leave that fellow alone."

"Speak," I again demanded of the supposed road laborer.

"I said..." again began the dragoon.

"Quiet," I heard Lorenzo's voice from behind, which followed with the sound of a head being clouted.

"Seven, six, five, three, two..." I counted down.

"Ah, you forgot 'four,'" he gulped.

"I grow impatient."

"Alright, alright," the rogue grudgingly gasped. "A mate of mine said a wizard would pay in gold for a number of us to ambush your party."

"What?" exclaimed the dragoon, whom I continued to ignore.

"It be difficult to imagine you and your friends being fool-hardy enough to attack a contingent of royal dragoons," I pressed the knave.

"With the new king, there be many soldiers discharged for breaches of his dim-witted decrees," he began babbling freely as I pressed the blade almost to the point of drawing blood. "Me, I served eleven years, only to be booted for something of no matter. There are plenty of us now almost beggars."

Under King Kenton, the army had become filled with thuggish miscreants and I did not want to know what his definition of 'no matter' was.

"How many?" I demanded while keeping an eye on the oncoming traffic.

"Huh?"

"How many malcontents are in on this?"

He suddenly straightened and snapped, "Ask them."

I turned to where he motioned with his chin. The flow of opposing traffic was halted by two large freight wagons, each drawn by four-horse teams. Canvas covers flew to the ground and spilling from the wagons was as motley a crew as can be imagined. Most were ill kempt in appearance and another commonality they boasted was an apparent aversion to washing, both for themselves and their garb. These were former soldiers who had fallen on very hard times. I would have almost felt sorry for them if not for an inkling of the transgressions they had to have incurred to be booted from the army.

I removed the supposed flagman from the upcoming mêlée with a cuff to the head. By now even the most skeptical of the dragoons were rushing to collect about the middle carriage.

"Come," the soldier at my side curtly ordered as he grabbed my shoulder.

He did not have to speak twice. This was just the kind of occasion that called for having a witch at one's side. The three of us quickly rejoined the others. The ambushers were also forming into a knot.

"This should be simple, right?" I asked Morgana. "You know, maybe a violent wind to blow them away. Oh, I know, do you have a spell to give them diarrhea?"

"It normally would be easy," she replied in a distracted voice. "Not so at the moment."

I followed her gaze back to the advancing attackers. Amidst the mob of a dozen or more was a figure I was becoming very weary of seeing – a Ghennison Viper Mage.

"Quick, Lorenzo, to the front," I yelped.

The ancient appearance of the necromancer spoke to scores, if not centuries, of being a magic wielder. Morgana might be top of her class, but before us was one of the Ghennison Viper Mages' eldest member. As a child, I would carve faces into peeled apples and let them dry. The resulting works of art mimicked the shrunken heads of the Outer Amnesian Islanders – desiccated and deeply wrinkled. Coming towards us was one of such countenance.

Lorenzo stepped to the front, which brought a sneer to the mage's lips. If not for the wizard's venomous reptilian-like eyes that blazed with a malignant intensity, his face could have been that of a millenniums-dead mummy. It was obvious that the wizard was aware of my friend's curse-repelling power. He waved the mercenaries out of his way and raised his claw-like hands. Morgana stepped past Lorenzo and flung a blinding purplish fireball at the mage, who contemptuously brushed it aside with a scornful flick of his fingers.

A multitude of possible attacks by the mage raced through my mind, all of which could bypass Lorenzo's anti-magic attributes. How to respond to the sundering of the earth beneath our feet? Bolts of lightning drawn down from the heavens? A mini-tempest? A...

My frantic musings were cut short. In the proverbial blink of an eye, I found myself open-mouthed. It was only after turning my eyes to the sky that I realized what the flashing streak of motion had been. The mage was now tumbling head over heels after being released from the talons of a dragon – that dragon being Adalbert.

A wizard's wards prevent most folks from physically assaulting them, but not from a dragon's sneak attack. The wizard making contact with the ground sounded like what would be expected from an over-ripe watermelon. The abrupt removal of the mage resulted in immediate chaos among the attackers. The promise of a wizard ally would have been a powerful inducement for the thugs to participate in such a dicey endeavor. The drivers of the two wagons began frenzied whippings of their horses and the panicking assailants turned to chase after them.

"Hmm, I would have never guessed he had that much liquid in him," Lorenzo observed as a black pool of blood sluggishly spread about the mage's body.

"We will never hear the end of this," I moaned, while watching the dragon recede into the scattered clouds. "His feigned humility by not returning to hear our thanks means Adalbert will be expecting even more gratitude later on."

"So cynical of you, but probably true," Lorenzo agreed.

"Quit it," Morgana laughed in obvious relief. "Adalbert deserves more than whatever praise be given. That mage was one of the almost mythical Elders of the Ghennison Viper Mages. There are no more than four or five of them and I cannot exaggerate how powerful they are. The last reported sighting of one was sixty years ago. It be hard to believe we actually witnessed the appearance of an Elder, let alone to have survived."

That took a few moments to sink in. "And is sabotaging your witches' messaging service be enough reason for one of those Elders to attack us? It be that important to them? Why?"

Morgana shook her head in puzzled agreement. "It makes little sense."

Our conversation was interrupted by the dragoons who were recovering their wits after the startling attack.

"Come, we must continue to the castle," ordered the soldier who had been riding inside with us. "The King is waiting."

We were herded back into the carriage and once again set off for our meeting with Garsten. Soon I spied the famous Stagsford skyline that included the crumbling towers of the former temple of Dorga, the Fish-

Headed God of Death. The dark Castle Raven loomed above it all, perched upon its forested hill like a monstrous bird on its nest.

The drawbridge began lowering as soon as the guards sighted our group. The horses thundered across the wooden timbers and we entered a large garden between the inner and outer walls. It boasted ancient elm trees and multitudes of flowering bushes. I was able only to get a glance at the rustic setting before passing through another gate.

Our carriages crossed a large courtyard, also agreeably planted with a variety of foliage, before halting in a circular drive. A flight of marble steps led up to massive doors fit for giants.

I know Lorenzo so well that I could tell he was dying to quip about arriving at my father's royal domicile. I leaned over and whispered so that only he could hear, "I know – living in my parent's basement and being ordered to my room would mean being sent under guard to the dungeon."

Lorenzo hides his thoughts well, but I could tell by the slight rise of his eyelids that he had been planning such a jest.

Our party was escorted up the steps and through doors opened by castle servants garbed in a colorful livery of greens, reds and gold trim and braids. High vaulted ceilings soared above our heads. The hall was a manmade cavern of finely fitted stone blocks, carved marble support arches and a brilliantly polished granite floor. The only concession to softer colors were the tapestries depicting royal hunts and historic battles, along with velvet curtains framing the narrow windows cut through the thick stone walls.

As befitting the royal seat of Glavendale, the main hall was no longer lit by oil lamps, but with costly glowing witch orbs. They floated in shallow dishes held aloft by brass figures depicting both real and mythical creatures.

Our arrival threatened to prove exhausting. We were handed off to different servants each time we entered a deeper section of the fortress. These progressively older additions were much like the layers of an onion. The labyrinth hallways grew more narrow and ruder in appearance as we continued farther into the bowels of the citadel. Each stride was a step further back into antiquity until we arrived at Castle Raven's heart, the original stronghold raised when only ferocious beasts inhabited the land.

Even though the small outpost did not present an imposing sight, I still felt a bit of awe to stand amidst these center stones. The roughly hewn rock walls are tightly woven into the country's folklore, even while many of the heroes of that mythical time have been forgotten. I glanced over to see Sergey running his fingers in wonder over the cold stones. Few among the past dozen generations of Glavendale citizens have trodden here.

The simple hall, not much larger than an inns common room, was lit by oil lamps. Facing us was a graceless stone throne bereft of carvings or inlays. And looking down from the ancient High Seat of Glavendale was King Garsten Stee Hragen. Our party immediately fell to one knee as the servants bowed and backed out of the room.

"Rise," Garsten spoke, echoing the command with an upward motion of his hand.

If Garsten had lost weight since we last met, it was not evident. Having unlimited access to all the culinary delights of the kingdom be not the best inducement for shedding pounds. Since receding hairlines can be hereditary, I was glad to see that while his hair was graying, it remained thick and reaching to his shoulders.

"Your Highness, we as loyal servants to the throne greet you and express our gratitude for the favor of your presence," I intoned a simple standard court salutation.

There are more flowerily greetings given to stoke a sitting monarch's pride. Such flatteries are unneeded with Garsten and even if he were not my father, I am no candy-mouthed bootlicker.

"Welcome, sirs and mistress," his deep baritone voice followed. "I will not forget your masterful sleuthing at the Duburoake Royal Exposition, Master Barley. Well done. My sister has spoken of your new quest dealing with the stolen pixie gold and begged that all doors in Stagsford be open to you. I cannot allow such slights against a member of the royal family. My court advisor will have notes of royal endorsement for you by early afternoon."

"Thank you, sire. You are most kind," I replied in the expected deferential voice.

"I have heard much of your companions," he continued, "Witch Morgana, I believe from my reports that you will prove to be as capable a sorceress as your renowned mother.

"Master Spasm, it be good to see you again. You must not make yourself such a stranger at court. I am still smarting after that last game of hnefatafl. I look forward to a rematch."

"I am at your beckoned call, Your Majesty," Lorenzo replied.

The King of Glavendale next turned his gaze to the publisher of The Weekly Tattler. "Sergey Varvervane, I hear much of your writings from my CIA director."

My friend visibly paled. Sergey has more than once ruffled the feathers of various powers that be, whether those of rich merchant guilds, influential families or local government officials.

"I have one question and I want an honest answer," Garsten dropped into a stern voice.

"Ah, of course, Your Majesty."

Poor Sergey. His mode of operation when confronting threatening adversaries be first consuming a large number of ales. He also be one of the few people I know who actually becomes wittier by the mug – to a point, of course. Here he now be within the sacred ancient hall of Glavendale standing before its king while stone-cold sober.

The King continued. "Be there really youths raised by savage chickens in the sewers of Duburoake, a hybrid child known as Bat Lad and swine mutilations perpetrated by denizens of the moon?"

Ah-hah. Sergey was going to have to come clean. The Weekly Tattler, sold at the counter of many food stands in the market, has been accused of printing outrageously wild stories to boost circulation. That be why many question the actual accounts he has printed of my past cases. I do know for a fact that there be a Bat Lad. I had met the creepy little bastard in what Sergey titled, "The Case of One Damned Thing After Another."

"Ah, there be a Bat Lad," Sergey hesitantly began. "You can ask Jak. Ah, as for savage sewer chickens raising foundlings, well, I believe that was a valid conjecture. Said poultry were never actually seen, but why else would those rescued gutter toddlers only cluck and sleep with their heads tucked in their armpits? As far as being described as savage, I have never met a cultured chicken. And as for the swine mutilations, we, ah, did print a retraction."

"Really?" I broke in. "I never saw it."

"Well, maybe it was kinda in small print."

"Must have been real small."

Sergey shrugged and continued, "It turns out to have been roving bands of poachers. I guess it was fad for pig tails to adorn the hats of lady trolls. We are now hearing farmers complaining of severed ox tails, but I am chalking that up to the recent popularity of nouvelle cuisine soups."

There was a moment of silence after Sergey's pronouncement.

"Yes, well, I guess that answers that," Garsten said. "Now I must speak in confidence with your companions. Do not take it as a personal slight. I will leave it up to Barley and Spasm as to what of our conversation can be shared."

Garsten reached to a gold cord hanging to his right and seconds later two servants responded. "See that this fellow be taken to the commons and fed, as well as provided with the best from the ale cellar. He looks to be parched."

Sergey deeply bowed and turned to follow his escorts. I know he would have liked to hear what followed, but the chance to savor the King's famous collection of brews be a once in a lifetime opportunity. Breweries across Glavendale compete every year to be judged a royal favorite. Sample kegs fill the caverns beneath the castle. No doubt Sergey was already relishing the thought of publishing an exclusive review of the ales.

Garsten rose to his feet as the door closed behind the servants and made his way across the room.

"It be good to see you, Jak, and you as well, Lorenzo. I have been very keen to meet you, Morgana. I have heard much about you," he declared after taking her two hands into his. "You must be very brave or exceptionally foolhardy to be betrothed to this layabout. No matter – I welcome you to the family."

His bantering tone turned serious when again addressing me.

"That be something we must someday speak of, Jak. I have no official heir. I would not see the kingdom torn apart by competing distant cousins fighting to claim the throne."

"Yes, I know..."

Garsten stopped my reply with a raised hand. "You find abhorrent the prospect of being confined by the shackles of court life. Even now there are intrigues about and I fear some would-be-assumers of the crown are not a patient lot. Such conspiracies would be stymied by the announcement of an heir apparent."

"Why me? It be not like you lack offspring to choose from," I protested.

"Your dissent in itself be a good recommendation. Those who seek power for power's sake make poor rulers. I also see my younger self in you."

He quickly added, when seeing Morgana about to protest, "Of course without some of my juvenile proclivities."

"Those proclivities created a number of problems, namely my many half siblings in Duburoake," I observed. "Duburoake be a small enough city that such prodigious penchants of a mysterious visitor could but only make for scandalous gossip. There was much hand wringing by innocent maidens, spinsters and wives after your departure, as well as outrage from fathers and cuckold husbands."

This was as close as I have come to chastising my father. I took his silence as contrition.

"Many of your Duburoake offspring are well aware of their kinship, yet only I, two brothers and a sister know you to be our father. To proclaim me as your son would be acknowledging parentage to many of your brood. You worry of the chaos created by cousins fighting for the throne? Think of the maelstrom that would follow in Duburoake. Even those with no political desires would be made pawns by court jackals."

The King sighed, "Yes, you are right. Still, it be a problem that must be resolved. We will speak again of this. Down the road you may feel differently. For now, we can put such quandaries aside."

Garsten strode to the door. Opening it revealed half a dozen servants in waiting. They smoothly brought in chairs, a table and food and drink – disappearing as quickly as they appeared.

"I do not often visit here, but it offers a privacy lacking in the official assembly quarters," Garsten explained.

Our conversation drifted from topic to topic. As well as details relating to the missing pixie gold and attacks upon the witch crystals, I spoke of local happenings in Duburoake. Historically, the country's remote coastal strip drew little attention from the Crown, for which city residents are thankful. It be commonly believed that the farther removed from court drama and its arrogant popinjays, the better.

I was not happy to learn from Garsten that with dragon flights now offering greater accessibility to Glavendale's only port, interest in Duburoake was growing among Stagsford business cartels. Such robber barons are always interested in new exploitations. Adding to the mix be the instantaneous communications initiated by the witches.

I like my home city just as it be and was glad to leave that depressing subject to hear from Morgana. The King was surprisingly knowledgeable of the young witch's life – not all of which could be gleaned from accounts in the Tattler. He asked about her academy and if she had a business plan for the new private inquisitor agency with me. I listened with interest, just now realizing how my recent cases and her finishing classes had given us little time for such conversations.

The same went for Lorenzo. Garsten turned his questioning to my friend. Our afternoon discussions at the Kings Wart Inn have lately been few and far in between. By now I should not be surprised by his other diversions, and yet... It seems Lorenzo spent his five-day absence last month teaching what he calls paragliding.

"Olmsted helped me with the construction," Lorenzo related. "Made them out of wolf spider silk. They're kinda like giant kites. We bought a high spot right outside Duburoake for a launching lodge. It will utilize the same updrafts that boost dragons and allow vultures to glide for hours. I can see the sport really taking off, no pun intended, in a couple years."

"What? We?" I asked in disbelief. "Are you saying my brother be partners in an inn that caters to people jumping off cliffs?"

93

"That about sums it up. Olmsted was adamant that we wouldn't promote it for covert military purposes, even though that's where most of my experience comes from."

It was then the King's turn. He related both the latest in foreign and court intrigues. If the purpose of the account was to pique my interest in royal affairs, it failed miserably. I shuddered to think of such a stifling life.

Garsten was startled to hear of our suspicions in regards to the former royal wizard, Arkhjin. The mage had been well thought of at court. He promised to look further into Arkhjin's background.

It was late afternoon when we left Castle Raven – the same carriage caravan now taking us to a modest inn in the heart of Stagsford. The King offered us rooms in the castle. I explained our need for coming and going freely while carrying out the investigations. I would also feel more at ease quietly sipping ale in the Hamberg Inn's tavern than surrounded by servants and other prying eyes.

Sergey's only half-hearted attempt at learning the details of our meeting with the King was due to his glassy-eyed state of inebriation. He had yet to learn that to taste test a wide array of ales does not involve swallowing the samples.

The arrival of three extended black carriages in front of our inn caused a mild stir. Those on the street paused in their errands to watch as we climbed from the coaches. No doubt all Stagsford citizens could easily identify the vehicles and accompanying dragoons as official arms of the royal court.

The Hamberg Inn was located in the older section of the city, with no building being over two-stories tall. As with the inn, the surrounding structures are of limestone, many with balconies running the lengths of their fronts.

I had asked Osyani to find an inn within close proximity to both the Stagsford Enchantress Preparatory Academy of the Occult Arts and the traditional gathering meadow for the caravans crossing the mountains to the coast. I was told the rising cost of real estate was fueling the demolition of older sections of the city to be replaced by towering buildings of three or four stories. It might be not that much longer until the inn suffers a similar fate. Even the centuries-old caravan field was soon to be relocated to the city's outskirts along the King's new roadway.

Servants from the inn scurried out to take our luggage. I scanned the street as the carriages pulled away. Several food carts were parked in a tree-shaded commons that also boasted a small fountain and a few benches. The carts most likely catered to those working in the shops, their customers and freight haulers.

My eyes were drawn to one singularly looking figure standing in front of a cobbler's shop – who boldly stared right back. What little I could see of his hood-shadowed features were greenish locks and a pallid cast. What stood out, seen even from across the street, were his blazing yellow eyes.

"I think that guy has a crush on you," Lorenzo spoke from over my shoulder. "He can't seem to take his lizard eyes off you."

"I am sure he looks your way. Must be that bestial magnetism you exude. I guess it works on more than just ghouls and dung toads."

"I think those yellow eyes color-coordinate very nicely with that green hair," Morgana joined the conversation. "To set the record straight, he be gazing in entrancement at me."

Coming under the scrutiny of all three of us was enough to turn the stranger about. We watched the odd figure until he disappeared around a corner.

"Your friend has already taken to his room," the desk clerk informed us of Sergey. "He seemed out of sorts. Your baggage has been taken to your rooms – the ones with balconies. Please let us know if we can be of further service."

I hefted the heavy ornate brass door key the clerk handed me and looked around at the faded drapes, worn carpet and peeling wallpaper. The richly embellished key added to the impression that the inn had once been a prosperous establishment.

"I am going to change in my room and then head to the bar," I declared. "That will be as good a place as any to discuss our plans."

The lock and deadbolt seemed sturdy enough and the door itself appeared as sound. Several past experiences have led to such inspections upon entering new quarters. I next checked the twin doors leading onto the balcony. They were a cause of concern with their numerous glass panes. That was compounded by the fact that even a slightly agile rogue could leap the gaps between balconies.

Lorenzo appeared on his terrace, carrying out a similar inspection. He turned and leaning back against the wrought iron railing, said, "Wouldn't take much to drop down from the roof, either."

"Osyani booked the rooms from a witch crystal cafe," I spoke of my secretary. "She will have to ask about layouts in the future."

"Really? Let's hope none of those hackers know of our location."

That thought was troubling. "Do you think we need different lodgings?"

"Do not be such worry warts," Morgana chided us from the balcony on the other side of my own. "It be a charming view from here."

"Charming until some hired blades visit," I replied.

She laughed. "You forget, Master Barley, who you are now partners with. It be a simple task to ward these terraces against common thugs. The charms will also trip an alarm if a witch or wizard attempts a breach."

I snapped my fingers. "Oh, I almost forgot. Morgana, will you please send a message in our code to Osyani and tell her we arrived safely in Stagsford. She was also going to have a few of my snoops see if there be any truth behind the rumor of wackyweed cartels being hired as assassins. Can you recommend to Osyani a witch you trust in Duburoake to examine the pixie gold cask at Olmsted's?"

Morgana smiled. "It be already done."

~ * ~

Sergey was somewhat recovered from his encounter with the royal ale cellar. All four of us were finishing our meals and relaxing around a

96

table while outlining the next day's tasks. A cab hired for the next day would first take us to the witches' academy and from there to where the caravans assemble. I could only hope the visits would provide additional leads. A notion was already forming in regard to the pixie gold theft, but it would require further inquiries. I was counting on Morgana for any progress with the crystal attacks.

Chapter Six

A soft rapping on the door brought me instantly awake. Unlike when between cases, I do limit my ale consumption when on the job. I slid into my breeches and drew my sword from the scabbard hanging on a wall hook.

"Who be it?" I asked.

A past sneak attack through a peephole kept me a cautious distance from the door.

"I need to talk with yah," an unfamiliar voice replied.

"Why?"

"About yah case."

"Which case?"

"Yah know, what brings yah here."

"What brings me here?"

There was a moment of silence. I was not about to open my door in the dead of night to a stranger after the recent attacks.

"Ah, I am to deliver a message."

"Go ahead."

"How am I to know you are to whom it be addressed?"

"How would you know if I opened the door?"

"Well, yah see, I was given your description."

"What was it?"

"Ah, this ferret Barley be middlin' height, slim in build, trimmed beard and hair past his ears."

"No problem, then. That be what I look like."

"For sure?"

"Yup."

"Alright, then. Yah is suppose to come alone to the loading dock behind the Kahlownah Brewery down the street."

"When?"

"In two hours' time."

"No."

"No?"

"Do I have a tongue impediment? No. Do you take me for a dullard? It would be a lunacy to do such. I am now going back to bed. Whoever they be, you can relay my reply that they may contact me here before breakfast. Good night."

"They say they can help solve your case."

"What case?"

"Come on; that all they are telling me."

I sighed. "All right. I will meet them in two hours."

"Sure? And alone? You must come alone."

"Yes, alone."

"Truth?"

I did not answer.

The floorboards outside the door creaked for a minute as if the messenger stepped from foot to foot in befuddlement as to what to do next. He finally gave up and retreated down the hall.

I quickly donned tunic and boots and belted my sword. Easing open the balcony doors and kneeling by the railing, I soon spied a retreating figure scurrying through the pools of light cast by the gas street lamps.

Morgana's ward was cast to keep unwanted intruders from our rooms, not to prevent me from leaving. I quietly climbed over the railing and hung for a moment before dropping to the ground. It was no great feat to remain in the shadows while following at a safe distance. I stopped as he continued past the brewery – a squat brick building set back a dozen yards from the street and enclosed behind a brick wall. Its iron gate lay rusting on the ground. By all signs, it had been abandoned for a number of years.

The messenger continuing past the rendezvous meant the sender or senders were not yet at the brewery. Fine with me. I stealthily made my way into the enclosure and circled back to the loading dock. A quick search of the area revealed several hiding spots. I considered the dilapidated wagons, piles of broken kegs and discarded packing crates. They provided adequate hiding under the cover of night, even with the full moon, but would be less concealing at daybreak. I continued my inspection to the other side of the building where a spindly tree managed to grow in the cramped space between the brewery and the wall.

I settled for a wait on the roof – the only way to accept such a dubious invite. I did not have to wait more than a half hour. A soft wind tussled my hair and carried the night chirps of dragon crickets.

Others had the same idea about arriving early. Six hooded figures appeared as the night sky had yet to reveal even a hint of morning. Five of the group spread out to inspect the surroundings. The sixth member remained in the center of the yard until the rest regrouped around him. He waved a hand and they scattered to hide behind the very concealments I had snubbed.

Damn, six of them. I had been hoping to ensnare whoever sent the messenger. That was not going to happen. There was no recourse but to wait until they lost patience and hopefully glean some clues by following them. I sprawled out and peered over the edge to watch the lone figure standing as stationary as a statue.

Time passed and I had almost fallen asleep when a new actor appeared on the stage. Entering the yard was another hooded figure obscured by the shadows.

"You came alone?" asked the leader of the five.

"Yes."

"You are a fool, Jak Barley." With a snap of his fingers the mysterious being signaled his minions to erupt from their hiding places. They rushed forward with knives drawn.

Even for Lorenzo, being this outnumbered was almost certain doom. It was just like him to secretly follow me. I leaped to my feet and sprinted to the tree peeking above the edge of the roof. One by one a chorus of screams grew as I dropped from limb to limb. I stumbled once and quickly regained my feet at the foot of the tree. An abrupt silence, more foreboding than battle cries, stopped me mid-step. I took a deep breath, tightened the grip on my sword and fearfully rounded the corner.

The cause of the sudden stillness was as surprising as it was obvious. They were all dead. Five of the sinister welcoming party laid crumpled on the ground around the smoking remains of their leader.

I shook my head and found it difficult to speak. "Whoa, Lorenzo, what happened? The wizard be no surprise, but five hired blades in a minute? I mean, well…"

My friend did not answer. The growing morning light revealed him garbed in an unusual outfit – a grey hooded robe draped to his ankles.

"What, griffin got your tongue?" My next comment caught in my throat as the figure turned and for a brief moment revealed a glimpse of startling yellow eyes.

~ * ~

"I tell you, he just vanished," I repeated at breakfast. "I rushed to follow him to the street and he had disappeared."

Sergey was busily scribbling on his pad. "Yellow eyes? What folk have yellow eyes?"

"I wasn't close enough to fully view his face, but there be a race of scaled beings inhabiting the Kearal Islands. They have yellow eyes. I only know of this because I once met a woman of mixed human and Felidian ancestry. She had the eyes of the islander folk, but not the scales."

"Still," said Morgana, "he must be a magic wielder to incinerate a wizard. Were there clues to be had?"

"The thugs wore cheap robes and boots commonly sold at the market. They carried neither identification parchments nor jewelry. Their bodies all bore sword wounds. As for the wizard, all that was left were sizzling bits of greasy flesh and charcoaled bones. I do know that he was tall and gaunt."

"Just what we need," I sighed and continued, "another mystery."

"It would be nice to know if he stumbled upon them after

following you or purposely crashed the party," Lorenzo said. "Besides being a wizard, he has to be an excellent swordsman. More than just excellent to have dispatched them in the time you say."

"Unless he stole their senses with a spell," countered Morgana. "I must visit the brewery to see if there remain traces of magic. I might detect what kind of sorcerer he was. After that we can visit the academy and interview the witches."

The four of us were at the scene an hour later. Morgana kneeled and closely examined the blackened remains of the mage. She grasped her wand with both hands and closed her eyes. Bits of cinder, shards of blackened bone and scattered teeth began vibrating and slowly coalesced to form the vague shape of a skull. Once completed, she murmured softly and a glowing haze formed over the grotesque visage. It solidified into a lucent image of a face.

Morgana dropped her hands and stood. We all watched entranced as the vision faded and the skull dissolved into a pile of ash and cinder.

"It be a Ghennison Viper Mage," she declared after a long sigh. The casting had proven strenuous.

"Good," I answered.

"Good?" asked Sergey.

"Good in that we already know the Viper Mages are involved. I do not need another circle of wizards entering the fray."

~ * ~

Our cab was proving not as comfortable as a royal carriage, being cramped in comparison and rattling noisily over the cobblestone.

"Have you considered moving to the castle?" asked Morgana.

"What?" Her question caught me by surprise. "Why would we?"

"Think about it."

I stared intently into her face and considered her words. I thought we agreed that the inn offered more flexibility. What did the castle offer over our current quarters? I began reviewing our cases and incidents from the past few days. Slowly, I had to admit, an overlooked concern took shape.

"The mages."

The young witch smiled. "Yes, the Viper Mage Council must be severely vexed over their recent losses."

"So, they will be reviewing their failed tactics," I continued. "They have two choices, either quit while behind or..."

"...up the ante," she finished my thought.

"Egad. That would be staging an all-out attack," I groaned. The image of a horde of irate wizards descending upon the inn was unsettling to say the least. Morgana's wards would instantly crumble under their combined assault.

"Just a thought," Lorenzo joined the conversation. "Are the court wizards up to defending against a concerted attack by an entire faction of mages – and would they want to?"

"Want to?" I echoed.

"Yes. It's one thing to manage the more mundane duties of a court wizard and another to face Armageddon from a horde of badass mages. I'm guessing that's not included in their contract's fine print."

Morgana straightened in her seat. "Who needs a bunch of wimpy wizards anyway?"

"Not us?" I asked.

"Not us. Not when our clients are the covens of Glavendale. I am sure my mother would agree. The Council could send out a call for all available witches to gather at the Stagsford Coven Hall. Many will be coming anyway for the graduation ceremony in three days – two weeks before mine at the Kuu Academy."

"So, if all the covens sent witches, the mages would be outnumbered, right?" I asked. "I mean, how many Viper Mages are there?"

"That be the question," replied Morgana. "Of all the wizard cabals, theirs be one of the most secretive. Their headquarter be in the Cythnian Desert and it be death for all, even other wizards, to venture near. It be an exaggeration to call some wizards necromancers, but not the Ghennison Viper Mages. They truly are death wizards.

"As to how many there are, we know their misadventures over the past couple years have reduced their numbers, but to what point be unknown. If they are in desperate straits, that will make them all the more dangerous."

I closed my eyes and shook my head. "Maybe, just maybe, we should consider a different line of work after we are wedded. Something less stressful. I hear there be a growing demand for neighborhood-grown vegetables. I could do the planting and selling at the market and you could perform charms against pests and spells to make the crops grow bigger and faster."

"Here we be," announced our driver.

We were stopped in front of an arresting structure – the most notable aspect being the dozen slender spires and a connecting web of delicate arching skywalks. Banners representing the various covens of Glavendale flew from the steeples. It could be a breezy fairy dwelling if not for the intimidating blackness of its stone and the skull motifs framing the windows and running along the rooflines. The ghastly gargoyles did not help.

Morgana read my bewilderment as I stood at the flight of steps leading to iron doors. "At the time the academy was being proposed, two of the more powerful covens demanded their own preferred designs and architects be used," she explained. "Members of Murky Forest Coven were noted for their white-hot tempers and rumored dalliances with the black arts, while the Highland Glade Coven was associated with the healing earth magics. The matter was brought before the Council and to prevent the quarrel from growing into an outright schism, it ruled the two must compromise in the designing process."

"This be the result," she concluded with a wave of her hand.

I contemplated the edifice looming above me. "Normally I would guess such an arrangement was doomed for failure, but it works in its own quirky, appalling way."

"It's kind of Cinderella Gothic," Lorenzo offered one of his usual enigmatic comments.

Our architectural critiques were cut short by the large iron doors swinging silently open to reveal three witches, two of whom were familiar

– Morganna and Head Mistress Kahlan of the Kuu Academy of Mystical Arts and Witchcraft.

"Greetings. Please enter," spoke the third witch. "We have been expecting you. I am Head Mistress Mirthia of the Stagsford Enchantress Preparatory Academy of the Occult Arts."

Mirthia was what could only be described as rotund and cheery – resembling more a seamstress or baker than head of the largest of witch academies in Glavendale.

I in turn introduced Lorenzo and Sergey. Morgana knew Mirthia because of the head mistress's friendship with her mother.

After viewing the outside, I should not have been surprised at the interior – yet I was. Maybe the Highland Glade Coven believed that an all-white ambiance would offset the Murky Forest Coven's contribution to the layout – it did not. Circling the rotunda were at least two-dozen alabaster statues made in the likenesses of demons, ghouls, malevolence spirits, horrendously tortured beings and others unidentifiable in their hideousness. It was hard not to shudder at the tormented faces gripped in madness, malformed bodies and almost human hands tipped with sickle – like talons. Having them carved in a stone representing purity made them all the lewder.

"We do not hold many social events here," Mirthia dryly commented as she led us into a side hallway.

"Ah, so, what about these Murky witches?" I asked Morgana. "Will they be here?"

"Such as my mother?" she answered, which brought a chuckle from Mirthia who obviously overhead my whisper.

"Just jesting," Morgana joined her in laughter.

"Over the centuries some covens prospered and others died out," Mirthia volunteered. "The last surviving member of the Murky Forest Coven passed away more than a century ago. Some say the coven's exacting initiations were the reason."

Minutes later, we entered a room bereft of adornment and, without my asking, the head mistress explained that through the years the academy removed the more malicious adornments. The main entryway was preserved as a cautionary tale.

"Some said it be an erasing of history," Mirthia offered of the renovations, "but that which glorifies evil should never have been created in the first place. At the time there was quite the controversy over the removals."

This was new to me and it piqued my curiosity. "Are there still those objecting to the change?"

The mother witch and two head mistresses might have thought their fleeting eye contact went unobserved. It did not. I could feel a subtle tense undercurrent. After a moment's silence, Mirthia cautiously spoke, "There be some who would have us seek power over the wizards with dubious magic."

I was getting nervous. "Just what do you mean by 'dubious?' Even more to the point, I know there have always been minor skirmishes between witches and wizards, but are you saying there are witches wanting outright war?"

Morgana appeared surprise as I by this line of discussion. "Mother, be there something you have not told me?"

When came no reply, Morgana continued, "So there are those who would use the black arts against wizards? What about the mages? Do they know this?"

Mirthia raised a hand and snapped her fingers. A young witch appeared from nowhere.

"Sergey, may I ask if you would be kind enough to follow Ahraygana to our reception lounge? We have a wide range of wines and ales. I am sure you will find something for your approval. I will leave it up to Morgana to decide what can be shared with you."

Once again, my scribe friend was being expelled from a conversation he would dearly love to hear. Yet, as with the King, there was no arguing with Mirthia. He turned to the young witch who was also comely and asked, "Will you be joining me?"

"Yes, Ahraygana, please keep our esteemed guest company until we can join him," Mirthia consented with a smile. "But please, do not try to keep pace with his imbibing."

"We are not preparing for war," Morganna firmly answered

Morgana's earlier question. "Yes, there have always been some dissidents and the more radical are outcasts. We keep an eye on them. The wizards also have their counterparts, but they too are few. "

I took a deep breath before saying, "If Morgana and I are to solve this attack on the crystals, there can be no secrets. I can tell you are holding back. The outcast witches you speak of make likely suspects for the attacks on the crystals. I am familiar with clients holding back sensitive or embarrassing information because they believe it has no bearing on a case, but that be for Morgana and me to decide. Would these rebel witches have even been mentioned if not for my curiosity about the academy's architecture?"

"It be something we are loath to discuss outside the family," Morganna answered, "or even among ourselves. They are an embarrassment. Since they seldom do little to attract attention, it makes it even easier to ignore them."

"How many are there?"

"We do not know," Kahlan spoke. "Some have been officially expelled from our covens and we believe others who dropped from sight may have joined them."

"In other words, you are describing a rogue coven of witches who have gone to the dark side."

"Yes," declared Morganna, who then turned to the two academy head mistresses. "We cannot afford to continue our inattentiveness to this problem. Even if no direct action be called for, the Council needs to begin more closely monitoring the activities of our wayward sisters. The danger of a number of witches uniting in the dark ways is too dire to ignore."

"Mother, if you mean to discuss this topic with other council members, I suggest it be not by crystal balls," Morgana warned. "Not while they are being infected with malspells."

"You are right. Many of them will be arriving soon for the graduation ceremony. We can discuss it then," the witch replied.

"While we are on this subject..." Morgana began, then went on to relate the possible peril of an all-out Viper Mage attack.

The three witches readily agreed a call should immediately go out for a Grand Gathering, a rare assemblage of Glavendale witches not invoked for more than a century. The keepers of several inns near the Glavendale Coven Hall were soon to be shocked that a mostly forgotten accord with the covens would have them clearing out their guests for a flood of witches.

A second young witch was called for and as with Sergey, we were politely directed to remove ourselves so the witches could further confer in private. I gladly submitted, knowing Morgana would fill me in on matters connected to our cases. The thought of a chilled ale also soothed any feeling of exclusion.

"Another fine mess you've gotten us into," Lorenzo gleefully observed as we were steered through a maze of hallways and stairways. "Did you like to stir up hornet nests as a child? We have a possible all-out assault by an entire circle of mages, a call to arms by a dozen witch covens and a potential cataclysmic war between the two."

I ignored his idea of a jest aimed to rankle me.

"Before anything else, we need to interview the wizard responsible for inspecting and warding the pixie gold cask," I steered instead to important matters. "I would like to get that out of the way before mages rally their forces. The prospect of being ambushed on the streets of Stagsford be not appealing."

Our journey through the academy ended in an airy room beneath a stained-glass dome whimsically depicting what I first took to be a swarm of blackbirds, but upon closer inspection saw that it was a flock of broom-riding witches soaring amidst cotton ball clouds.

"Lorenzo, Jak. How goes it?" Sergey hailed us from a semicircle of overstuffed chairs near an unlit fireplace. A large smile and a half empty mug signaled that his self-medication with hair of the dog was successful.

~ * ~

Other than small talk, not much was said during the evening dinner. It was odd to be sitting at a table that could seat twenty or more guests when there were but the six of us congregated about one end. Still,

Head Mistress Mirthia treated the meal as a formal affair with apprentice witches acting as servants waiting at our elbows.

It was decided we would stay the first couple nights at the academy. Until the arrival of the mobilized covens, there were more witches housed in the witches' school than at the Stagsford Coven Hall. Many of the witches here might be students and novices, but they are buttressed by a staff of spell-casting veterans.

Mirthia called an assembly to explain the situation and assign sentinel duties. Excited murmurs rippled through the younger witches and students. The older witches remained silent, but their grave expressions said they were more than aware of the gravity of such a threat.

The academy was breaking a longstanding tradition of females-only by allowing Lorenzo, Sergey and I to remain overnight. The outrageousness of the assaults by the mages were enough reason to break from custom.

We were guided to the central most secure quarters of the building where Lorenzo and I were to share a room and Morgana situated down the hall.

"Try sleeping with your head under a pillow," Lorenzo said as we prepared for the night. "We do not want to alarm the young sentries with the fear that some monstrous growling beast had invaded our room."

"Very amusing. I do not snore, no matter how many times you accuse me of that."

"Whatever."

Chapter Seven

The morning was off to a good start. I slept well, enjoyed a light breakfast and was now on my way with Lorenzo to visit the caravan staging area and speak with the wizard who warded the pixie gold shipment. Rather than wait for coachman and carriage, Lorenzo and I opted to drive ourselves in a two-wheeled chaise used for light errands by the academy staff. Lorenzo swore he could find our way with directions given by a witchling.

Morganna had cast a protective spell upon our horse and cart, which would also alert her to any magical attacks. Still, I was nervous traveling the crowded streets of Stagsford without Morgana along. She stayed behind to line up interviews with the witches involved in the Crystal Ball spellware attack.

I was less concerned about a physical assault. Lazily circling above us was Adalbert. We were not traveling by dragon because his appearance at the gathering field would cause a stampede of terrified draft horses and oxen. Instead, he guarded from above. That did not mean I could relax my vigilance. A gang of assassins might stand out amidst the chaotic swirling of street traffic. In turn, they would be quickly identified and dispatched by the dragon. But a lone hired blade could suddenly erupt from the crowd with drawn knife.

"There's also the possibility of hidden archers," Lorenzo volunteered after I mentioned my concern. "They could turn us into pin cushions before Adalbert even noticed, not to mention throw poisonous snakes or darts, or even..."

"All right, all right. I get the point," I interrupted his gleeful recital.

"Say, does that protective ward work against creatures called forth by magical means?"

"Why?" I replied.

"Just wondering."

Lorenzo just wondering always made me uneasy. He was looking over his shoulder. I shut my eyes and would have prayed to one of my childhood gods if I had not already offended every one of them. The sudden sound of excited voices quickly changing to ones of panic forced me to turn and look.

The street was quickly emptying as merchants and shoppers stampeded into shops and taverns. Horses were rearing in terror, sending carts and wagons careening toward us. Several enormous swirling clouds of brilliant speckles pulsated in the street like swarms of angry sun bees. The haze began coalescing into vague shapes. The terrified screams of the horses panicked our own mare into a full-on gallop. Arching backward with reins pulled tight, I was just able to slow the horse enough for those in front to throw themselves from our path.

Above the screams and shouts came bloodcurdling roars issuing from the throats of no beasts I knew of. I turned again to see the three swarms solidifying into a confusing mass of twisting shapes. The radiance subsided and disappeared to reveal very solid monsters – balauri. I had seen the seven-headed dragons only as illustrations in my brother's ancient tomes. They were depicted as either mythical creatures or long extinct – yet here was not one balaur, but three.

Rearing onto their back legs, the beasts towered nearly twenty feet when any of their weaving necks snaked upward. Dropping to all four legs, the top of their backs reached ten feet and tails added another dozen feet to their lengths. Wickedly sharp spines ran down their purple necks to join into one line to their tails. At least the heavily scaled dragons were wingless.

I quickly gave full rein to the mare. There was no doubt as to why the creatures magically materialized along our route to the caravan grounds. We were their target. The only question of the sending was by whom – the Viper Mages or rogue witches? For now, that was a mute query. I continued precariously gripping the side rail of the wildly weaving cart with one hand and the reins on the other.

"How close are they?" I yelled to Lorenzo above the clattering of the iron tires upon the cobblestones and the shrieking of the balauri.

"Two of them are a good twenty yards behind," he yelled back.

"What? Where be the third one?"

"Look up."

I tilted my head back and gasped in shock. Passing not twenty feet above us were the writhing heads of a maddened balaur viciously clashing its beaks like a clutch of angry snapping turtles. Adalbert gripped the beast by its tail and I could see he was struggling to gain altitude with the heavy load.

"That's something you don't see every day," Lorenzo remarked.

"You say that way too often," I replied.

"Come on. You love the rush."

"If you mean excitement," I struggled to say, while being severely tossed about by the unchecked flight, "the answer be no. Just tell me how far behind are the other two."

"They're not the most fleet of monsters, still they are slowly gaining on us."

"Yikes," he added.

"What?"

"One of them got the munchies."

I was barely able to keep from being jolted from my seat – still I had to twist about.

One of the balauri was falling behind its companion, slowed by several of its heads feverishly worrying on an unfortunate bystander. They were messy eaters and I quickly looked away. Adalbert was several blocks ahead and gained what he must have considered a sufficient altitude. He released the balaur and it tumbled heads over heels until grazing a shop front, only to burst like an egg melon. The outraged bellowing of two remaining balauri was pure torture to my ears.

The bloody balaur carcass blocking the street slowed our horse's mad rush. The mare skidded against the cart's momentum and managed to turn into a side street with our cart precariously tilting. Lorenzo grabbed my tunic as I almost tumbled overboard. The mare's breathing was becoming labored.

"We cannot remain in the cart." I warned Lorenzo. "The horse cannot keep this up."

I looked back to see both balauri continuing in pursuit. Adalbert circled back and was positioning for a second attack. The first assault caught the monsters by surprise, but now the two remaining beasts were defensively drawing closer together.

"There," Lorenzo shouted. He was motioning toward a quickly approaching alley. "It looks too narrow for them to enter. After me. Remember to roll."

He followed the command by grabbing my tunic and tugging me to his side of the chaise. There was no time for deliberation. I clenched my teeth and paused but for a second before following my friend's leap.

All right. I might not have been the most bookish of students while attending the Duburoake Academy of Private Inquisition and Methodical Deducements. Between a youthful preoccupation with the riotous late-night environs of squalid ale joints as a part-time lead zitherest in a thump band and the, often in-vain, pursuit of young maidens, I did acquire a number of eclectic skills.

All right, maybe my classes were not chosen with a calculated eye towards a career when leaving the barely-hallowed halls of the academy. And maybe many of the classes I signed for were the only ones left after arriving late with hangovers at registration. Still, it did result in me becoming a black suspender in the obscure martial arts school of Kimchee – a skill that has saved my life on a number of occasions.

I can credit my survival from the cart that resulted in only a few cobblestone rashes to Emergency Exits From Briskly Traveling Vehicles 101. It was another of those last available choices. I completed the course with a number of bodily grievances – some resulting from the practice wagon leaps and even more from Master Blenedar's rod when he concluded a student was not giving their full commitment.

Hanging from the side of the wildly careening chaise, I leaped to hit the ground running before tucking and rolling a number of times. I regained my feet and staggered after Lorenzo.

"This alley does not appear that narrow," I observed as calmly as possible once off the street.

"You're right. My mistake."

No further deliberations were needed to spur my flight deeper into the alley hoping to find a narrower one or any other avenue of escape. Lorenzo followed. We arrived at an intersection just as the balaur entered the alley. I looked over my shoulder when Adalbert's familiar roar was followed by numerous, albeit not as loud, bellows. The dragon once again seized the tail of a balaur, but the tight confinement of the alley was preventing him from fully spreading his wings for flight. I would have paused to see the outcome if not for the remaining monster's continued pursuit.

We would have been in trouble if the creature had the standard number of heads – that being one. Its physical unwieldiness alone made it not a swift creature, but how that many heads could coordinate any action was a puzzle I had no time to contemplate.

We crossed into the next alley. I briefly paused to test several locked doors. There were no sewer grates or fire escapes. A bend in the alley brought us abruptly to a dead end in the form of crumbling brick wall.

Lorenzo and I spun around and drew our swords. We could but wait for the balaur's arrival.

"Maybe we can catch it by surprise as it comes around the corner," I suggested half-heartedly.

"You take that side and I'll wait here," Lorenzo agreed. "Maybe we can confuse the heads from two sides."

It was not much of a plan but there were no other choices. We did not have to wait long before the lumbering beast rounded the bend. It stopped with several heads turning to me and the others examining Lorenzo.

"Hah, we gotcha," spoke the middle head. Now up close, I could see it was the slightly larger of the seven.

"Yah, gotcha," chortled the other six in a perfect unison that created a buzzing effect.

"Who's the boss here?" Lorenzo addressed the head closest to him.

"I speak for all," answered the center one.

"Really? When this head looks so much more intelligent?" I entered the discussion while pointing to the head nearest me."

"Sorry, Jak, but this head has to be the intellectual superior," Lorenzo disagreed.

All seven heads laughed in unison. "Try not to distract us," boomed the dominating head. "We see you attempt to divide us. All know that I am the cleverest because it has always been and always will be that the middle head be the leader. Right?"

"Right," echoed the others. "Has always been and always will be."

"Ah, what about the prettiest?" I wondered.

"What?" the heads responded in a puzzled tone.

"The prettiest. I see that each of you has a slightly different coloration and shape. I believe you are the prettiest," I decreed, while pointing to the head second from my end. "You have the prettiest red eyes and yellowest fangs."

"No, you are wrong," my friend chimed in. "I believe that honor goes to this one. One can but admire the rakish tilt to its unibrow. Do you all have names?"

"Hold it," I shouted after their muddle of words. "You cannot answer at the same time. How about you first?"

"No," I interrupted as all six began opening their mouths. "I said one at a time."

"Stop this nonsense," roared the middle head as the others appeared flummoxed at the possibility of speaking individually.

"Ah-hah," I crowed. "So, it has always been the middle head as the leader, but who says he gets to be the prettiest? You there – I believe that frill about your neck to be much dandier than his."

Its fellows twisted round to examine him.

"You," Lorenzo pointed to another. "I don't think I've ever seen a more majestic snout."

"What 'bout mine?" queried a different head, which then gasped in startlement, along with the others at its unexpected audacity.

"Or mine?" another broke form.

"DESIST." the leader bellowed angrily. "This be not allowed. Only I speak out of union."

"And your name be?" I asked the closest head.

All six of the minor heads opened their mouths, followed by five struggling to close theirs. They finally succeeded and the head I addressed answered, "One."

"Two," volunteered the next head, to be followed down the line with the expected proceeding numbers, except for the leader.

"You are?"

"Ahg-g-g-g," it shrieked.

"Hub," the others again spoke as one. "He be Hub."

"Quiet. Enough," it howled even louder.

"You could vote on it."

"What, what, what, what, what, what?" I was not imagining it. They were out of sync.

"Each head can have two votes as to who be the prettiest, since obviously you would all vote for yourselves with one vote, resulting in a tie."

The balaur's body trembled violently before taking one step forward. Hub was struggling to attack me. It appeared that while he directed the body's movement, Hub still depended upon a unified effort for seamless movements. It was made all the more difficult when its fellow heads were not in full agreement. In frustration, he drew back his head like a viper, but was not close enough to strike.

"I have to admit, you are all fine specimens of heads. It would certainly be difficult deciding who be the prettiest," I observed. "There also be who has the most melodic voice."

"Huh, huh, huh, huh, huh, huh? Melodic, melodic, melodic, melodic, melodic?"

"We must kill them. It be so ordered," Hub cried in frustration.

"Just who ordered this?" Lorenzo asked.

"Make no mind," Hub answered, his voice growing shriller.

"Notice that you seem to be alone," Lorenzo continued. "You've seen with your own fourteen eyes that your compadres have bit the dirt and that only you remain. Now tell me, did whoever employ you warn of the dangers you might face? Did they mention how you were to return home after killing my friend and me?"

Even Hub seemed stumped.

"Thought so. You've been suckered. Do you think you can survive here even if you succeed in your task?"

One through six all turned to look questioningly at Hub.

"We were promised plenty to eat," Hub grudgingly answered. "We near starve on our island."

"It be hard to dine when dead," I observed. "That dragon you saw will be coming for you. Your only hope is to throw in with us. We promise food and safety if you agree."

Hub's head weaved back and forth in agitated indecision.

"Do it, do it, do it, do it, do it, do it," he was urged.

The balaur's body drew in a deep breath and Hub looked to his left and right. "I consent, but this dissension must end."

"Agreed." Once again, the six answered as one.

With the danger ended, the release from what Lorenzo calls an adrenalin rush threatened my wobbly legs with collapse.

"Run," came a cry. "It be too narrow for me to land."

Nine heads turned upward and I answered," It be all right, Adalbert. We have come to an agreement. Meet us at the next street."

A disbelieving snort was his only reply.

"This way," I spoke to the balaur. "You are now under our protection."

With the creature again under united control, it docilely followed. I did, faintly though, hear one of the heads whisper, "But who be the prettiest?"

~ * ~

We emerged onto the next street to face a hastily mustered semicircle of Stagsford Municipal Royal Guards with pinched faces,

117

nervously clutching drawn swords. With duties normally confined to rousing drunks from doorways come morning, chasing down cutpurses or ticketing speeding wagons, being called to do battle with a raging monster was very much outside their job description.

"It be all right," I said after stepping forward. "We have everything under control."

Relief flashed across their faces, though the captain of the group appeared unappeased. "Be that your monster? Somebody must be held accountable for the mayhem incurred. There are two deaths and much property damage, as well as a cleanup bill for the bloody messes."

A low growl emerged from Hub. "Nobody's monster."

"You want see bloody mess? I will show you bloody mess," Adalbert irately added, who had landed on a nearby roof.

The guards went back to being nervous, though the captain stubbornly stood his ground. "What be that? An escaped menagerie beast? Do you have an exotic pet license for it? Why be the dragon perched on that building? I believe you better come with us to the station."

"I understand why you are concerned," I attempted placating him while pulling the parchment decree from a pocket, "but I am a private inquisitor under royal appointment. We are to be aided by all government officials and hindered in no way."

"What? A ferret? Tell me another one," he scoffed.

"That be private inquisitor," I rebuked him. Most constables and the like hold little esteem for my trade.

"Save your breath and whatever bogus documents you have," he continued in contempt. "Never met a ferret yet lived up to their puffed-up repute."

"That be private inquisitor," I repeated before half closing my eyes and beginning a slow examination of the captain from foot to crown. "You regularly force ladies of comfort, under threat of arrest, to serve you without compensation; take bribes; and resort to torture for guilty pleas."

He began sputtering, but was abruptly silenced by, "That will be enough, Captain. Remove yourself and your men now. We be on king's business."

Morganna had literally magically appeared before us. Her stern voice rang with an ominous tone that chilled to the bone. She wore a deathly cold aura like a cloak and even the balaur retreated a few steps. Her long black tresses framed a startling pale face that could have been molded from packed snow.

"Gotta love her," Lorenzo chuckled from behind.

Not even the pretentious captain could stand against that steely gaze nor ignore the powerful currents swirling about the witch. He hastily spun and ordered his cowering troops into a marching formation.

She turned her focus onto me. "Am I expecting too much to believe you capable of going even half a day without leaving a trail of mayhem in your wake?"

Adalbert sniggered as I contemplated her question.

"Well?" she snapped.

"Oh, I thought that was a rhetorical question," I replied. "As you well know, this mayhem was most likely the result of your witch crystal troubles. I might also ask what took you so long to arrive?"

After several years of dating her daughter, I was becoming better at not visibly cowering in front of the witch.

She chose to ignore my reply and continued, "Why is it you are always bonding with such an ill-assortment of creatures? I thought associating with Blackwatch Goblins was appalling enough, but now you have a balaur amidst your ranks?"

Before I could reply, the witch turned to the dragon and said, "A balaur. What are you doing off your island? The diktat of 2408 says your kind must remain there until deemed otherwise."

"We, ah, hungry. Food scarce," Hub replied in a timorous voice.

"Why did you come here? How? By whose hand?" she persisted.

"Person like you. She says she bring us where much food. Wave paws and speak tongue we not know. Now here."

"A witch?" Morganna asked in outrage. "A woman?"

The balaur took a few steps back. "Female, yes."

"What did she look like?"

Hub looked to his brethrens' heads in confusion before answering, "Not know. You skinbags look all same to us."

Adalbert chortled again. Skinbag be one of his favorite slurs when talking about humans.

"I must return to the academy with this news. Stay here until I can send Morgana to join you," she ordered. "I doubt the mare with the cart is in any mood to continue for the rest of the day. Especially with your new friend."

I blinked and she was gone.

"We new friends?" One through Six chimed.

"Yes," I sighed, "as long as you do not eat anything we have not approved."

"We hungry."

"Adalbert," Lorenzo called to the dragon. "How about flying out of town to pick up an antelope. That should hold them until we can get a take-and-go order from the local abattoir."

"Anything to get away from this barmy bunch," Adalbert agreed and took flight with a spring and powerful downward thrust of his wings.

"Okay, I've got to tell you," Lorenzo spoke, "that was some pretty quick deductions on your part with the captain. What were the clues?"

"I did not bother deducing."

"What?"

"He just looked the type," I answered with a shrug, which sent Lorenzo into a laughing fit.

I spent the time waiting for Morgana by questioning the balaur. From the description of the vegetation and weather, I guessed their island to be in the subtropics. Brother Olmsted would know where, as well as the story behind their exile. If not, I was sure he had some musty treatise on the subject.

My curiosity was driven by a hesitancy in trusting the balaur. Were the dragons exiled because of their treacherous nature? Was there not enough food on their island because of their voracious appetites? Hub's answers were vague, though I got the impression that they were more of a naive nature than evasion.

Morgana arrived by carriage as her mother's magical materialization was taxing for a novice witch. The driver was forced to climb down from her seat to calm the horse. It did not like the balaur.

"You appear hale and sound," Morgana concluded after examining me from head to toe from her coach window. "I was led to believe you were in dire straits. Where did you get that dragon? Here I thought you were off on our case, yet I find you picking up pets."

"I thought you needed a quirky pet to snuggle up to at night and yet scare away the rats," was my answer.

"Sweetheart, that be why I am wedding you," she replied with a smile.

"All right, you win. We need to be off for the caravan grounds." I paused to consider the dragon. "What do we do with you? Your presence would create an uproar among the draft animals."

"Tell you what," Lorenzo spoke up. "I'll stay with these guys and wait for Adalbert to return with lunch. They can eat in the alley away from the more timorous eyes. Afterwards, I'll take them along on an errand."

I eyed the dragon and then Lorenzo. "What kind of errand would you be on that could include a balaur?"

He just smiled, a look that had often preceded risky misadventures, some from which I still bore a small scar or two.

"Never mind. I do not want to know. Better the balaur than me."

I gave Morgana a hug after joining her in the carriage. The horse gave a quick start that had me grabbing for a looped strap hanging from the ceiling. No doubt it was all too happy to be away from the frightening beast.

"What could he be up to?" Morgana wondered as she watched Lorenzo and the seven-headed dragon recede from sight.

"Gods know," I exclaimed. "Stagsford citizens think of themselves as jaded cosmopolitans who have seen everything, but with Lorenzo roaming the streets with a seven-headed dragon, that may change."

It was but a thirty-minute ride to the gathering grounds. I nervously scanned the side stones. After the last few days, I half expected every knot of pedestrians to throw off their guise and erupt into sword-waving assassins.

~ * ~

The wizard suspiciously eyed the two of us. He was the next thing to a hedge wizard, Morgana whispered while watching him approach – meaning he had the barest of formal learning – just enough to join one of the lesser mage cabals. His threadbare robe spoke not of a very successful career in magic.

"I am Wizard Alon. You seek me?" he said in a slightly surly voice.

"Yes. Are you the wizard who placed the security ward upon Baroness Vilhema Stee Hragen's pixie gold shipment?" I asked.

"So, what if I am?" he heatedly answered.

I was slightly taken aback by his vehemence. "We just need to ask a few questions. I have been hired by the Baroness to discover at what point the gold was replaced with river pebbles."

Addressing his reply mainly to Morgana, he snarled, "So, everyone just assumes it be my fault 'cause I am not some well-heeled wizard. That be what the others think. I am tired of being hounded about that pixie gold. My ward be as good as any you can place."

"We are not saying that," Morgana said in pacifying voice. "We follow the gold's path from the pixies all the way to Kaiserhelm."

"Yeah? What be he doing here? He be no wizard. I can tell that."

"I am a private inquisitor. Morgana and I are working together," I answered for the witch.

"A ferret?" Alon sneered before abruptly stepping back and a look of panic replacing his churlish countenance. "Morganna, you say? Wait, you be too young."

"I am Morgana. You are thinking of my mother." Being the daughter of the infamous witch was enough to intimidate many.

"I, ah," he stammered. "I will, ah, be placing a similar ward on several crates of saffron for a spice trader. There have been recent cases of the shipments being diluted by disreputable shippers. You can see for yourself that my spells be as good as any."

"That would be most helpful," I agreed. "Lead the way."

The field was divided into a number of areas for the different caravan destinations and departure dates. We headed to the staging ground for Kaiserhelm and beyond, due to leave the next morning. We arrived at the tent of a wagoner, who along with his two teenage daughters was packing supplies for the arduous mountain passage. Their tent, cooking ware and sleeping gear would be loaded the next morning.

Three wagons were already packed with wooden crates and bales of colorful cloth soon to be covered with a canvas tarp. Another was filled with rugs. A fifth wagon was only partly filled, but on the ground near its tailgate were three large barrels.

The owner of the wagons warmly greeted Alon. He had broad shoulders and a face weathered by sun and wind. He wore the typical beige canvas tunic and knee breeches with the rugged knee boots of a teamster.

"Alon be a good wizard," the wagoner named Aarpstring offered, after we were introduced, and our presence explained. "Ne'r a bit of trouble with goods placed under Alon's wards. Until that pixie gold business, never heard a hint of anyone being unhappy with his spells."

Alon walked to the barrels and inspected their contents. Lolling nearby were two men who approached the wizard and displayed a certificate testifying that the containers came straight from a spice merchant and were of guaranteed purity. Aarpstring examined the parchment and rubbed his thumb across the seal before nodding his head in acceptance, after which Alon closed and sealed the solid oak casks. The wizard motioned for us to step back.

"You can remain," he said to Morgana, and began a whispered incantation while slowly moving his hands back and forth above the containers.

Those with even a hint of magical talents say they can see a shimmering when spells are cast. I saw nothing. Morgana nodded her approval and smiled when he was finished

"A very proven ward and masterfully cast," she exclaimed to the small gathering. "It be more than enough to cancel any switch spells and protect the barrels against all but the most powerful counter-spells. And as such, would also sound an alarm if a breach were attempted."

"Did the pixie accompanying the haulers to the caravan have a certificate as that presented by the spice merchant?" I asked, as the three of us left Aarpstring's encampment.

"Yes. I have secured many such shipments and all seemed in order. As I have told the others, I watched the kegs be sealed and the casting of the ward."

"What about this spell? What all does it do?" I addressed the two.

The wizard looked to Morgana to answer. "It be an all-around charm that will clear any malspells, fashion a strong ward against breaches and alert against attempted tampering."

"Malspells?"

"Yes. An earlier spell, let's say, that can hide beneath a later ward and burst open a chest upon a magical command."

"Hmmm. I see. Would Alon's spell remove such a malspell?"

"Yes, the ward he used would cancel any previous incantations.

"You appear pensive," she added, while gazing intently into my eyes. "I know such a look. Have you deciphered this puzzle?"

"Maybe," I replied, before realizing I was mimicking Lorenzo in not being more forthcoming. Still, I did not want to prematurely cast accusations.

"We best be back to the academy," I changed subjects. "There are witches to interview and the less we travel about, the safer we will be."

The return trip was unexciting, thank the gods. It gave Morgana and I time to go over the chaotic past few days.

"Do not forget the yellow-eyed stranger," Morgana reminded me. "He must be a wizard, and a powerful one at that to have defeated the viper mage. Maybe the academy archivist can enlighten us. The library be renowned for its expansive collection. There must be references to such wizards."

~ * ~

"After several misdirections, we narrowed the crystal intrusions to a general location in the Cythnian Desert," Kodia spoke. She and

124

Hexicona, the two young witches we had spoken with over Morgana's flat crystal in Kaiserhelm, sat across the table from Morgana and I in a musty library. It reeked of age and some ancient secrets best not dwelled upon.

"That pretty much counts out the students and staff here at the academy," I observed. "Has anyone tracked down the three witches – the ones whose whereabouts are unknown?"

'Two for sure," answered Hexicona. "One is setting up a crystal café in the Amnesian Islands. Her recent activity is well accounted for. The other witch recently joined the staff at Morgana's academy."

"So, there be one left unaccounted for," exclaimed Morgana.

"Yes. Her name be Yansey. She was in several of my classes," Kodia said. "The quiet kind who kept to herself, yet deft in spellware development. I was surprised when she left instead of joining the staff. Though we have traced the malspells to the Cythnian Desert, there be no evidence our missing witch is there or involved in the attacks."

Morgana turned to me as I groaned, "Not the same desert where Ghennison Viper Mages are? Why could whoever be behind the attacks not pick a seaside resort south of Duburoake or even Rum Island in the Amnesian Isles? I hate deserts. There are inferno scorpions, needle burrs, pit spiders, sucking sands and sting flies."

"We need follow that trail. A large expedition of coven witches would prove too noticeable and dangerous," Morgana spoke as if wondering out loud. "And I can think of no sly way for us to avoid alerting the viper mages of our desert search."

I eyed Morgana suspiciously. Was she speaking truth or slyly goading me?

"Oh, there might be a way," I casually replied.

All right, I fell for it. I could not help myself.

"Really?" she asked innocently. "How?"

"Give me time. I will have to smooth off the rough edges."

I suspected I saw a hint of a smile on Morgana's lips when I left the witches in search of an ale. I rationalized that I needed a brew to bring out my more creative faculties – something drastically called for if I were to come up with a plan to cross a hostile desert littered with the fallen granite bones of lost cities and malevolent temple ruins, built eons ago by extinct races not human and said to have ensnared many an unwary adventurer. And then beyond the normal pitfalls of such a wasteland, escaping the notice of said viper mages. Another dismal thought occurred – what if the witch or witches joined forces with the viper mages and was in their lair?

Sergey was catching a late dragonflight back to Duburoake. He was to return after getting the Tattler printed with its first in a series recount of his recent experiences. He did not know what he would be missing.

~ * ~

I awoke groggy with a headache and confused, as if waking from an afternoon nap and bewildered to time and place. I had a right to be confused, with hands tied behind my back and bound tightly to a chair. I was in a poorly lit and near empty storehouse. Various sized crates stacked four and five high lined the wall to my left. To the right were boarded windows with thin streams of light flowing through the cracks. A table at my elbow was covered with a cringe-worthy assortment of pliers, hooks, slim blades and large screws. The buzzing drone of flies filled the air.

As my eyes focused, I became aware that another figure was seated a dozen feet away and also bound, with a hood drawn over his head.

Front and center were a line of four chairs seating a rogue's gallery of thugs – their countenances displaying a wide array of features that included pinched shrew-like faces, swinish jowls, beady piggish eyes, broken noses and jagged scars. A common thread running through them all was a disturbingly cruel air.

Another shadowy figure lumbered out from behind the four and stopped beside me. Several minutes passed in silence before one of the sitting kidnappers asked, "Have you no questions, ferret? Why you are here?"

"That be private inquisitor and sure I have a question. What does a guy have to do to get an ale around here?"

The ruffian at my side smacked me alongside the head as my interrogator replied, "Wrong question."

"Hey, stop that," I snapped in an indignant tone. "That hurt. How would you like someone doing that to you?"

"Again, wrong question," the toneless voice spoke as I received another whack. "Grunt, how many times do I have to tell you? Put some weight behind it. You hit like a dryad."

I was now decidedly irked and decided not to play their dim-witted game. My silence was not appreciated.

"Listen, Barley," continued the speaker. "There be no time for fun and games. We have a schedule to follow. You and the other were squeezed in at the last moment. So, what be your progress on the crystal curses?"

"Schedule? Fit me in? What are you talking about?"

"Hah, so yah do have questions?" he chortled. "We get them out of the way, then it be you answering. My coworkers and I take clients who lack the skills and maybe, should we say, the needed fortitude for enhanced interrogations. They give us a list of questions and we provide the answers.

"We are pressed for time, as in an hour the courtesan of a rich merchant is to be delivered. Young maidens do add a dash of fun to an otherwise dreary day."

"It must be an interesting business model you have. Ever think of franchising it? Maybe as 'Pain Be Us' or "World of Whips'?"

"Funny you should mention that. We have been putting out feelers about supplying consultants for those who want to keep their curiosity in-house."

"Hmm. I do not suppose I could outbid these clients of yours?"

"Now how could we do that? Our business is built upon trust. We have a reputation to maintain."

I was feeling a little unnerved as I identified the mixture of odors wafting about that included the sickeningly sweet smell of blood, acidic stench of vomit and the reek of burned flesh.

127

"Oh, sorry about the mess," he continued. "We had no time for freshening up after our last subject. He was one of those stubborn cases, as exemplified by those fingers scattered about the floor. Not to complain, though. Such exertions keep us from becoming complacent and sharpen our expertise. Grow or die, as I say."

"In my case, who are your clients?"

"Sorry. No more questions. We just wanted to impress upon you the futility of resistance."

"At least tell me how I came to be here."

The rogue sighed. "Obviously there be a traitor among those you mingle with. You arrived here drugged and unconscious. Now, tell me of your investigation into the crystal ball attacks. Have you determined those behind it?"

"Who's that beside me?"

I received my third thump alongside the head. It did not help my headache.

"He be our next subject, still unconscious. Now, I must inform you that each of us be an expert in our own field of enhanced interrogations. We use Grunt, who you now have met, for the cruder warm-ups. Livoo be a master of the saws and snipers. Flum has the hot irons down to an art. Some of his patterns be quite exquisite. Quop be a master of the clamps, pliers and screws. I, Hvsun, am the concert master who orchestrates the music of your screams.

"I am giving you the chance to cooperate and avert a prolonged interval of intense physical pain, not to mention the mental anguish that accompanies extreme mutilation."

During this time, I slowly drew a slim blade from my left sleeve. Unless the arm of my tunic be pulled back, the long sliver of metal be undetectable beneath a regular pat-down. I tried not to show my startlement after a side glance at my fellow prisoner revealed slight motions of his hands that were also tied behind his back.

"You make it sound so appealing," I replied, as the severed cord unwound and fell from my wrists. "I am assuming no amount of cooperation will result in me being released."

"Sadly, no, but you will escape the torment of a badly abused body. Quop, would you like to be the first to work your artistic endeavors?"

"All right. I have been showing great restraint up until now, considering Grunt's boorish behavior," I spoke as Quop rose from his chair. "Release me now or face the consequences."

Hvsun sighed again. "Try not to be so droll. Quop, carry on."

I steeled myself for action. When Quop reached my side, I would spring from the chair to thrust the blade beneath Grump's jaw and into his obviously tiny brain. Quickly withdrawing the knife, I would then hurl it at Quop and rush the other three. Rubbing my feet together earlier had revealed my boot blades were missing, so I would fall back on the ancient martial thumb art of Kimchee.

The big question was would the other prisoner be able to join the fight? That query was answered as he calmly shook the cords from his wrists and removed his hood.

"It be about time," I spoke as Quop approached. "Thought you were going to nap through the whole thing and I would have to save your ass along with mine."

"I wanted my brave compatriot to have the time to display his amazing courage in the face of overwhelming danger," he replied.

The torturers leaped from their chairs with startled grunts. I crouched, with blade tightly gripped in preparation for the attack.

"I could use some help over here," I snapped at Lorenzo.

He responded by placing his two small fingers to his mouth and releasing a loud, shrill whistle. The bizarre action caused me and the others to pause in surprise. Before I could ask what in the Hades he was doing, a set of double doors exploded into splinters. Silhouetted against the evening sky were seven bobbing heads.

"Who we fight?" bellowed Hub.

"Hold on…" Lorenzo began.

Too late – the impetuous balaur stormed across the storeroom and immediately pounced upon Hvsun, Flum and Livoo.

I grimaced as the severed fingers on the floor were quickly joined by chunks of the dismembered villains. I hate the fetid smell of entrails.

Quop and Grunt stood frozen with mouths gaping.

"Stop!" I shouted as loud as I could, while jumping between the two and the dragon. "We need to question them."

I was surprised by how quickly the dragon responded. The balaur halted and all heads looked down upon the remaining torturers and me.

"No?" Hub and One through Six asked in unison.

"They must be questioned," I repeated, before I turned to the two and observed, "It seems the screw be on the other foot."

Grunt and Quop stared slack-jawed at the gore. For hardened torturers experienced in the myriad ways of mutilation, they seemed overly disconcerted by the bloody fate of their accomplices.

To add to their dread, I spoke loudly to the dragon, "Remember what I said, there be no eating unless I say so."

"Sit down," I harshly ordered the pair while pointing to the chairs recently vacated by me and Lorenzo. "You are going to tell me everything I want to know or…"

I let the unfinished sentence fire their imagination that must already be overtaxed by the evisceration of their cohorts and the deranged vision of the towering balaur.

"Ah, what? Me just do the cuffing," Grunt blurted in panic.

"Shut yah mouth," snarled Quop, who had composed himself. "Tell them nothing."

"Grunt, stand up," Lorenzo ordered. "Now tie Quop's hands behind his back."

Grunt looked conflicted as he bound his cohort.

"A man of your wit and intelligence must feel frustrated by the servile role given you," Lorenzo continued. "The others get to express their creative impulses while you are given only the more mundane of jobs."

"Huh?"

"Haven't you ever wanted to do more than just the whacking? Did they ever let you try out the brand or blade?"

"Ah, no."

"How would you like to try it now?"

"Ah," Grunt said in a confused voice as he eyed his fellow partner in crime.

"You arse, you dimwitted lout," growled Quop. "Keep your stupid mouth shut and sit down."

Grunt eyed Quop for a moment and then said, "Maybe."

"Good. What takes your fancy?" Lorenzo asked. "Pinchers, screws, hot irons, scalpels, a vice, saws? I see there is a wide assortment to choose from."

"You crooked-nose milksop. What do you think you are doing? Hit them and cut this cord. Quit acting the churl you are."

"Ah, gee," Grunt replied, while studying his former partner in slime. "I do like fire."

"Alright, alright. Grunt, please, old comrade. We go back a long way. Remember when we found you? We picked you out of that asylum when you were but a lad," Quop pleaded, after realizing his insults were not having the desired effect.

"Ah, look how these coals glow." Lorenzo said to regain Grunt's attention. He was wheeling over a small charcoal brazier. "Looks about ready."

Quop began to sweat before an iron was even put to the coals. "Ah, what be it you want to know? I, ah, guess I could tell you some things without violating my torturer's code of conduct."

"Who hired you?" I rejoined the conversation.

"Cannot tell you," Quop replied.

"How do you like this one?" Lorenzo asked Grunt while holding out branding iron, the end in the shape of a spiral. "One press covers a lot of skin."

"No, I mean it," Quop squealed. "Hvsun handled the business end. He never shared those behind our jobs."

"Grunt," I said. "This be true?"

He frowned as if it took a great effort to consider such things. "Hvsun never speak but of who and when to torture."

I scrutinized Quop. "Hmm, not even a hint? He said nothing?"

"No, I swear," he pleaded. "We just show up here every day. Yah know. It be just a nine to five job."

"I bet the traffic home must be terrible at that time," Lorenzo responded.

"You bet. Especially when there be cobblestone repairs."

"Yeah, too bad you cannot work from home," I added.

I looked to Lorenzo. He nodded in agreement. The cowering torturer was telling the truth. He did not know who was behind my abduction.

"Grunt, the city constables will soon be arriving. They should be getting a note on this place right about now," Lorenzo spoke. "If you give me your word that you will never torture again, you can leave with us. Quop, of course, will remain here."

It took a minute for Lorenzo's words to sink in.

"Constables? No like," Grunt mumbled.

"I can get you a job at the caravan field loading cargo," Lorenzo continued and pointed to the dragon. "I mean it. Russell here will come looking for you if you become involved in criminal ventures."

"Criminal ventures?" Grunt asked while eyeing the dragon.

"Things that hurt other people. Robbery, fighting, torture. That kind of thing."

"I get paid?"

"Yes, as long as you don't get into trouble."

"Good," he said and grinned.

"No, you cannot leave me here. I answered your questions," Quop protested as he strained at his bonds.

"Can and will. Well, we're giving Grunt the benefit of the doubt because of his…" I paused and then continued, "because of his being Grunt. You have no excuse."

We ignored his further protests. I took a deep breath of welcomed fresh air as we escaped the vile vapors of the storehouse.

Lorenzo gave Grunt instructions for whom to meet at the caravan field the next morning. "Tell the man with the camels that Steve Jobs sent you."

"Steve Jobs?" I asked as we watched Grunt walk away.

He just smiled. I shrugged. I was only too aware of the many

132

assumed identities Lorenzo used in the past. I turned my attention to the balaur. All seven heads appeared content to just tag along behind us.

"All right, Lorenzo. Would you like to explain how I wound up in the hands of those demented scoundrels? The last thing I remember was…"

"And?" Lorenzo urged me to continue.

What was the last thing I remembered? "I was at the caravan field. Oh, yes, Morgana and I interviewed Hexicona and Kodia. It be hazy after that. I went for an ale and… I am not sure. I know I did want an ale."

"That could be any time of the day or night for your entire adult life – and maybe even puberty."

I rubbed my brow in frustration. "How did you and the balaur so conveniently show up at my torture session?"

Lorenzo began to relate his excursion into what he called the sordid underbelly of Stagsford.

"You did this while being followed by a balaur?" I interrupted.

"I left him in the care of an acquaintance who owns an abattoir. It seems balauri are the goats of the dragon world."

"How so?" I asked.

"Goats will eat scrub brush that other herbivores won't touch. Balauri are the same in the world of carnivores. Our friend here will chow down on the bones and offal slaughterhouses pay to haul away. I think Russell has found a permanent home."

"What be that all about? Calling the dragon Russell?"

"Well, we can't just keep calling him the dragon or the balaur. We needed a name for their collective heads. Russell seems as good of a name as any."

"It sounds foreign, but it be a good ideal. What do you think of it, Russell?" I asked the balaur.

"It be strange for us to have one name, but we like it," answered Hub, and the other heads nodded in agreement.

"I got sidetracked," I said to Lorenzo. "How did you so handily become another prisoner?"

"It's been a while since I've hung out in Stagsford, but I found some old acquaintances."

"Like the one who owns a slaughterhouse? How do you meet these people?"

"It's my bubbling and outgoing personality. It wouldn't hurt if you were a bit more…"

"Never mind. Sorry to again interrupt. Please go on."

Lorenzo shrugged. "There are parts of the city that so far have escaped the king's gentrification efforts."

"Gentrification? Oops, sorry."

My friend sighed and continued, "There are still old quarters of Stagsford retaining the ambiance of, shall we say, its ancient disreputable days. One connection led to another. I finally got word of whispered queries dealing with recent visitors from Duburoake. Hearsay was that a mysterious group was offering a small fortune to make them disappear. There weren't many takers once it became known that an important witch was among the group.

"My wit and charm finally gained me a tip that our most recent friends here were getting a rush job for a ferret. It didn't take much for an old acquaintance to reserve another last-minute scheduling for me."

"You make it sound so simple," I said. "Did you happen to find out how and by whom I was drugged and kidnapped?"

"Sorry. Russell was just a tad too impetuous. Still, it had to be with the aid of someone in the academy."

"What are we going to do with Russell for now?" I asked.

"Russell can spend the night in the academy courtyard. He's eaten enough to keep him happy for at least a week. Dragons that don't fly need fewer meals. I will see that he is later taken to the slaughterhouse as a permanent garbage disposal."

Chapter Eight

"That was the last I saw of you," Morgana concluded. "You said you were going to find an ale. I looked for you later, but you were not to be found. Unless you left the academy grounds, I can only surmise one of the staff or students was involved. My mother said she would look into it."

"Hvsun said there was a traitor among those I mingle with and that I arrived drugged and unconscious," I pondered. "That can only mean someone slipped a sleep potion into my drink. It be maddening, but I cannot recall anything after leaving you."

"Of course, you won't be saying that in public," Lorenzo spoke.

"What? Why not?"

"Ah, yes," Morgana agreed and nodded her head.

I hate it when I seem to be the last to catch a joke, but was not going to ask what they meant. I instead considered his statement.

"Oh, yes," I finally comprehended. "I now remember the culprit behind my abduction. What say we announce I will reveal the traitor tomorrow during a meeting with Head Mistress Mirthia, but for now I am keeping the matter to myself?"

"Perfect," replied Lorenzo.

"I will need guard tonight." I said to Morgana. "If all here are suspect, even Mirthia, you must ask your mother for help."

"Do not give me that look," I quickly responded to her frown. "What if several senior witches are involved?"

"You are right," Morgana grudgingly agreed. "I will call for her. Still, there will come a day when such aid will not be required."

"So, this means we do not reveal our plot to anyone but

Morganna? Right?" I asked the two.

"I think it best," Lorenzo replied.

"Hmm. Be our trap too obvious?" I wondered out loud. "Why would I wait until morning?"

"Because," Morgana sat up straighter and continued, "more witches will be arriving tomorrow. It will be safer with them present when unmasking the traitor or traitors."

"That really makes no sense, but I guess we can only wait and see," I sighed. "Thanks for the ideal, Lorenzo. Next time, though, I hope I can come up with a plot involving you being the goat staked out for the cave lions."

~ * ~

"I placed a ward on your quarters," Morgana explained in late evening, before returning to her own room. "It can only be breached if attacked by a high-level wielder of magic or a number of witches of lesser abilities. If an attempt is made, the ward will sound an alert. My mother has already slipped into my room and together we will respond to any attack."

"And I, little buddy, will be there as backup," added Lorenzo after Morgana left.

I was about to give a pithy reply when we were violently thrown to the floor by a thunderous quake. The dark sky outside the window blazed brighter than midday.

"What in the …?"

A second blast drowned out my curse.

"This be not the work of a witch or two," I exclaimed. "It be an all-out assault on the academy."

The floor beneath us rolled like that of a storm-tossed ship and plaster exploded as cracks snaked across the walls and ceilings. Outside, lightning flashes of purple and scarlet battered against an invisible barrier.

~ * ~

Not again. For the second time in two days, I awoke with a headache and this time chained to a chair. An overall smarting spoke of rough handling. I did not lift my head nor open my eyes. The air felt clammy. I was surrounded by a deathly silence and a fungal odor. Obviously, no one at the academy expected such a fanatical assault, having been preparing for an attack but by one or two rogue witches. As they say, the finest tactics of rats and hominids often go astray.

"We know you be awake, ferret," spoke a voice as chilling as one emanating from the lipless mouth of a skeletal corpse.

I opened my eyes to find myself seated in a large cavern – its gleaming black walls studded with glowing blood-red wizard orbs that did little for a welcoming ambiance. An exceptionally brilliant sphere floated just above my head. Three Ghennison Viper Mages wearing their signature pointed hats hovered several feet above the rock floor with arms and legs crossed. I looked about. No one else was present.

I gazed about the cavern. Corpses in varying states of decay were shackled along one wall. Carrion beetles scurried about their feet as bits of rotting flesh dropped to the floor.

"That be private inquisitor. I like what you have done to the place. Did you get a decorator or do it yourself?"

"We will see how humorous you act by day's end," spoke the middle mage. Like his cohorts and Ghennison Viper Mages as a whole, he wore the purple peaked hat that sets them apart from other wizards. They also had the sallow complexion of a fading bruise and deep sunken eyes. The three had the mummified appearances common to the Ancient Ones of their cabal.

"I like how you color coordinate between your teeth and complexion. Yellow be a good look for you."

"You have plagued us for the last time," he ignored me and continued. "On too many occasions your blunderings interfered with our works, as well as costing lives of our members. The last straw was preventing us from gaining the controlling faraway wand to the automaton idol that you so inanely called the Golden Muskrat."

My head was finally clearing. I wanted to believe I would be saved by avenging witches, though the odds of them breeching the Viper Mage stronghold did not look good.

"You must be pretty upset to stage such an attack," I spoke. "Was I getting too close? Who of the covens has been aiding you in the recent attacks on the crystals and myself?"

"Hah, so your meddlings have made you other enemies?" he cackled. "Why should we care what those lesser females do? We seek only vengeance and to make a lesson of you. We cannot allow your insults to stand. There be our reputation to protect."

What? The mages were not involved in the malspells? I was confused. What gain for the mage by such a lie?

"What of my friends?"

"That be of no concern to you."

I took that to mean they were safe otherwise he would be gloating. Morgana and her mother would have responded swift enough to raise a magical shield, though obviously not in time to reach my room. Lorenzo, well, he be Lorenzo.

"We leave for other duties, but fear not, we will return soon with our brothers. A call was sent and all are gathered to enjoy your painful and timely demise."

"It be so nice that you can get the family together," I observed. "Often times it be just for funerals. Will this be a catered affair?"

"Oh, it will be for a funeral," he chortled.

The three floated from the room like leaves drifting in a river current.

I strained and wiggled as best I could, which told me the mages had been more thorough than the assassins. All things metal had been removed but they had missed my ivory picks hidden in the heel of my left boot. I slid my feet beneath the chair and after a bit of contortion managed to retrieve them. The lock was simple and the chain clattered to the floor. It seemed too easy and I feared to be interrupted at any moment.

It appeared the mages were too smug and complacent when it came to prisoners in their impregnable stronghold. They learned nothing from their past brushes with me. None be quicker at picking locks, except perhaps veteran members of the thief's guild, than a competent private inquisitor.

Still, I was wary of such an easy getaway. Circling the cavern were ten recesses. I cautiously made my way to the one directly opposite the exit taken by the mages. It was dimly lit by wizard orbs. Why worry of getting lost when I had no idea where I was or where to go? Even so, past experiences had verified the wisdom of marking trails. I wanted no sign that could be detected by the mages and decided to alternate between right and left choices when coming to forks in the passageway.

The tunnel I chose had few branching's, though it did wind forth and back as if following softer veins of rock for excavating. It was an effort to maintain hopeful spirits as time progressed. There was no way of knowing if I was plunging deeper into this viper nest or nearing the surface.

I stopped when observing a hole in the wall, two feet above my head. Gripping its edge and hauling myself up, I was greeted with a slight breeze that lacked the staleness of the caverns. It could only be an air vent. Even lightless, it offered more allure than the endless passages I traveled.

Minutes later a pinpoint of light appeared. Not the nauseating crimson of the wizard orbs, but a clean glow that promised white clouds and blue sky. I found myself reenergized and hungrily crawled toward it as a moth to the flame.

I blinked and grimaced beneath the blinding glare of a noonday sun as I crawled from the tunnel. A wall of heat struck me as the opening of an oven door. The shaft exited onto a ledge running twenty to thirty feet on both sides and a dizzying two to three thousand feet above a desert floor.

Dozens of vibrant green pinnacles towered like giant sentinels and gleamed as polished gemstones. The red lights of the wizard orbs had hidden the true color of the cavern and tunnel walls of the mage stronghold.

I knew it had been too easy. What would I do even if I found a way down to the harsh beauty of the Cythnian Desert, its floor littered with wickedly sharp splinters of crystals?

"New in purgatory. Come here often?"

I barely controlled a start that would have sent me tumbling over the crag. "Just scouting out the real estate for Lorenzo. This would make a great jump-off lodge for his air sailings."

"I just cannot keep track of you. Every time I turn around…"

I silenced the rest of Morgana's quip by spinning about and crushing the witch in my arms.

"Hmm. You seem glad to see me."

"No, just saving you from tumbling off the ledge."

"Then you can let go now," she laughed, which I reluctantly did.

"How did you find me and how did you pass their wards? I thought they were almost impregnable."

"After losing you to those torturers yesterday, mother and I worked a connection spell on you last night before the attack. You do have such a habit of wandering off to the strangest places. As both a beacon and anchor, you enable me to be drawn like a magnet to iron. An unexpected benefit is that it also exploits a chink in the mages' magical protections that are weaker outside their warrens, though it did take time to prepare for my jump."

"Great. Let us get out of here before the mages come looking for me," I urged. "They are not the most welcoming of hosts."

"First things first. You are not the only one who now acts as an anchor," she replied, and turned to face the sky. In an eerily echoing voice that set my teeth a buzz she cried, "Let it begin."

I stared at her in bewilderment until her call was answered by the one-by-one emergence from thin air of two-dozen witches. They hovered above us until the last of their number appeared and then glided onto the ledge. Satchels hung from their shoulders and each grasped a staff I knew to be magical flame hurlers.

Morganna made her way to our side and sniffed, "So, you survive?"

"You sound so joyful," I sarcastically replied.

"I am. We were not sure if the spell would work with a corpse."

"I am guessing you are not just here to safely chaperone me home," I said, while observing the stern expressions about me.

"We cannot let their attack upon a witch academy stand," the mother witch replied. "Their evil machinations have plagued all hominids for too long. Finding you outside and free does make this simpler. My daughter insisted we rescue you, which would have called for an inner assault upon their citadel."

"I am so glad not to have inconvenienced you, but how are you to assail them from here?"

"Does this opening lead to their warrens?"

"It does."

"We begin our attack like this." Morganna motioned to the other witches and they began slipping off their shoulder pouches.

"This borders dangerously close to the black arts, but it be our only option," the witch spoke in an ominous tone.

I watched the witches line up before the shaft and one by one begin emptying the contents of their satchels – marble-sized orbs so colorless they seemed as light-sucking holes into a hellish abyss. They flowed like beads of black mercury into the opening.

"They will spread throughout the stronghold," Morgana whispered to me. "Minutes from now they will activate and latch onto the wielders of magic."

"And?" I asked

"Suck the souls from their bodies, leaving only dried husks."

"Yes, I have to admit, that sounds like bordering on the black arts," I observed with a shudder as the last of the shoulder bags were emptied.

I would have been appalled by the slaughter if not for the insane evilness of the cabal. "Can we go now?"

"All right, what have not you told me?" I asked, after Morgana gave me a quick hug and gazed worriedly into my face.

"The travel spell, as with the black orbs, works only upon those with magical powers. You cannot leave with us, but Adalbert be on his way and will find you here once the mages are dead and the wards fallen."

"Hmm. I am guessing if Adalbert waits for your return, he will not arrive here until next morn. Am I right?"

"Yes, but you will be safe with the mages purged from their

141

warrens. Just be here at sunrise."

"You did not happen to bring any food or drink with you?"

Morgana winced. "No, but their pantries should be well stocked. You will be safe. The death beads only are drawn to those who wield magic."

"Fine. I will be safe until then, but you better leave now before the soul sucking starts."

She gave me a deep kiss and stepped away as the witches began disappearing, leaving only popping sounds in their wake.

I sighed at once more standing alone on the ledge. I was hesitant to imagine the offerings of a viper mage's larder. Pickled dwarves, candied eyeballs, infant jerky? Most important of all, did viper mages drink ale?

The passage back was uneventful, though once I thought to hear faint shrieks of terror and pain. At first glance, the cavern where I had awoken was empty. It was while circling the chamber that I realized the scattered robes contained the ash and brittle bits of bone belonging to former mages. I counted eight of the heaps. It was a relief to find the orbs worked as claimed. Now I could only hope they continued their incinerations throughout the entire maze of warrens.

I will not describe all that my search revealed. It did reinforce the horrid tales whispered of Ghennison Viper Mages. Those twisted, unspeakable sights killed any appetite for food. Thankfully, the wretched victims were dead, because I did not want to imagine them still living with such mutilations. Other quarters were left unexplored because of foul stenches emanating from their doorways.

Walking the silent halls was almost dreamlike, or nightmarish – the chambers and hallways occupied only by the grit and robes of dead mages. I occasionally froze in dread upon hearing some far-off echoing, but nothing came of it. Maybe it was the angry protests of the newly born ghosts. It made me hope they died quickly – not because of any feelings of mercy, but so they had not the time to curse those still living.

I stumbled onto the mages' treasure vault. Chests and casks overflowed with jewelry, precious stones and coins, as well as silver and gold plates and chalices.

I scooped up a fortune in gems and mused that I could spawn a small industry in fake treasure maps and trek outfitters if I related only the vaguest hints of the hoard's whereabouts. It be so with Pirate Rik's buried treasure. Dozens of gullible visitors to the Amnesian Islands scour the beaches each year in search of the mythical loot. There are regular deaths, either from those who prey on the moneyed fools or from the sudden and violent ocean storms. No doubt many crossing the Cythnian Desert in search of a rumored mage treasure would also suffer lethal fates.

I would instead confer with Morgana and Lorenzo on how best to deal with the hoard. Fortunes of but a fraction of this wealth have driven men to horrific deeds. I emptied my two handfuls of gems into my pouch and continued the search for something to ease my thirst. By now I did not even care if it was water.

The shriveled remains of wizards filled the passageways and chambers. I gave up counting after one hundred. Occasionally, a black orb would emerge from a doorway or around a corner or hall. I would stop and hold my breath as they rolled by, but I proved of no interest to them.

I was continually astonished by the rich tapestries, graceful statuary and the stunning paintings revealed during my explorations. I could but believe the vile mages valued the artworks only as plunder and not for their beauty.

The wanderings finally brought me to a large dining hall. Crumpled robes filled some of the chairs set before half-finished meals. The smoke-filled kitchen reeked of charred meats atop still glowing coals. My stomach remained unsettled, but I was relieved to find a cask of apple cider. I quickly downed three cups and filled a jug.

Several blankets joined the cider jug while retracing my steps. I had no intentions of spending the night in this ghost-filled lair. I would move back into the ventilation shaft if the desert night proved too chilly.

Once again, I was moved by the exotic beauty of the crystal summits as they were transformed by the setting red sun from rich emeralds to black gleaming crystals. Volcanoes can leave empty lava tubes. Could these towering shafts be the opposite – flows of obsidian left after the outer rock eroded away?

A lone ghoul vulture circled a distant pinnacle and I took that as a sign the last of the mages were dead and the wards fallen.

~ * ~

"How am I to land on such a sliver of rock?" a booming voice jerked me from a fitful sleep.

"You might be able to if you would lose some weight. Soon you will be like a fattened farm chicken, too heavy to fly and fit only for pulling manure carts," I replied, not feeling overly jolly.

The abuse pangs from the mages had been magnified by sleeping on the rock floor.

Adalbert was right. The ledge was not wide enough for him to land sideways with outstretched wings. The dragon could land straight on, but his head would be pressed against the mountainside. Turning around would be tricky.

"You need to jump, and I will catch you."

"What? Are you mad?" I blurted.

"You do not trust me? I am hurt," Adalbert responded in mock grief. "We must hurry. This hovering tires me."

I eyed the dragon and tried estimating how far I needed to jump. He had slowly descended and was now ten feet below me.

"There be not the room for a running start," I firmly stated.

"There be. Do it."

"You will be forever haunted by remorse and guilt if this does not work."

"Do it."

"It would be hard explaining to Morgana."

"I will get a bonus from her mother. Just do it."

I took a deep breath and, pushing myself away from the rock wall, sprinted to the edge and leaped into the void.

Adalbert had rolled back and snatched me as I dropped past him. "Oof. It be you who needs fasting."

Several minutes later we were on the desert floor. Adalbert picked a clearing fairly free of the splinters from the towering crystal summits. The gems ranged in size from my little toe to the trunks of fallen firs.

"If not for the viper mages, this region would long ago have been plundered by crafters of cheap jewelry," I observed while holding up a gleaming shard for examination. "If not for the crystal being in such vast quantity, no doubt it would be highly prized."

"Quit your babbling and climb on," Adalbert said impatiently. "It be a long trip back. First, though, fill the webbing rucksacks with the stones."

"Sure, but they will be of little value."

"Maybe so, but not until the site be found," he chortled.

~ * ~

"That be how I bravely led your troop of witches to the viper mage stronghold, and risking a venomous vengeance, scouted their evil warrens to verify all were dead," I concluded before a group of young academy students.

"It is interesting how you manage to lead people when you were unconscious," Lorenzo interjected.

"It does take a unique skill to lull foes while comatose," I replied, while waving for another ale.

We were gathered in the academy canteen and I was sorely in need of rehydration after the grueling time in the desert and the long flight back. It had been a nerve-racking last couple of days even when compared to the time I was a temple prisoner of Dorga the Fish-Headed God of Death, kidnapped by a piss dragon, held captive by vampires or pursued along narrow crag paths by an ancient leviathan deity. If anyone deserved an ale, it was me.

Earlier, I spent time with Lorenzo and Morgana, discussing the latest progress of our cases. We decided the most recent viper mage attack was solely vengeance driven. That meant the malspell attacks were from an independent group of viper mages with the aid of rogue witches. It was easy to see why wizards would be jealous, or even fearful, of the expanded influence that the crystals would bring their female competitors. That left the question of why would some witches be in league or acting on their own? What did these witches hope to gain, or fear losing, with the crystal message links?

"Maybe it be as simple as one or two disaffected witches out to sow discord," I hazarded a guess.

The puzzle was giving me a headache.

"We at the academy will continue attempts to track the source of the malspells," Morgana said. "Those behind the attacks showed themselves very adept at crystal magics. That was proven by the false lead to the viper mage stronghold."

I grimaced before speaking aloud a thought, "But was it false? The search was narrowed down to the Cythnian Desert. It be a big place. What if the attacks are from the desert, but not from the viper mage lair?"

"Could be," admitted the witch. "It should be safe to thoroughly investigate the desert with the Ghennison Viper Mages gone. I can leave tomorrow with a cadre of witches, some being the first answering the Grand Gathering. To travel to and back, along with the search, will take four to five days."

"Will the gathering still be called for with the viper mages no longer a threat?" I asked.

Morgana shrugged. "It may be needed even more."

"How so?"

"Because of the other wizards?" Lorenzo asked.

"Exactly," Morgana answered. "Envoys are being sent to all of Glavendale wizard cabals and schools. As with squabbling family members, the cabals might close ranks with the destruction of one of their own. It all depends upon the degree the wizards loathed their venomous brethren, as well as us witches."

"Are you talking war?" I blurted in shock.

A wizard-witch war occurred centuries ago and the horrific devastation still echoes down the ages in ballads and children's rhymes. Other reminders include buried deposits of ash, shattered ruins and great rifts in the earth.

"We think not, but there be that possibility." Morgana replied. "The Grand Gathering be a two-edged sword. We may need such a defense, but the calling could also provoke the wizards. The envoys hope to persuade them we are not preparing for a wider conflict and our attack was justified. A lesser response to the viper mages would have only spurred them to launch an even greater assault. The insidious nature of the Ghennison Viper Mages be common knowledge."

"It makes finding a lost pixie gold shipment seem frivolous," I said.

"Yet we must all continue with the investigations," she replied. "No doubt the wizards have their own feelers out. Our investigations into the malspells and theft of the gold be well known. It would appear suspicious for us not to continue as normal."

I could but reluctantly agree to Morgana's trip and detailed my plans for the next few days. I would focus on finding who ordered the hiring of the torturers.

I stopped and clasped Morgana's shoulders. "Are you sure it be safe for you tomorrow? Even without the viper mages, the Cythnian Desert be a treacherous scape. There are tales of giant poisonous scorpions, voracious jackal ants and ruins said to be still haunted by ancient curses."

Pecking me on the cheek, Morgana spoke to allay my fears, "Be not such a fretter. I will be in the company of seasoned witches. Those arriving for the Grand Gathering are veterans of battles with sinister creatures and forces that would cause you sleepless nights if known."

I gave another hug and observed with a smile, "It be a good thing I will have a wife to keep me safe at night."

"Among other things," she laughed.

Chapter Nine

Though still beset by minor aches reminding me of the recent days of rough handling, I felt recharged by the night's sleep. I went to bed knowing the viper mages were no longer a threat and I was being protected by Morganna's wards against rogue witches through the night.

Today I would venture into the shadowy underbelly of Stagsford where I might hear whisperings of who planned my kidnapping and subsequent rendezvous with the torturers. A good place to start would be the seedy taverns near the caravan assembly field. They, like the disreputable inns along ocean docks, are where both scoundrels and rumors congregate. For that I need go in disguise.

"No," I spoke to Lorenzo when he showed up after breakfast, "I do not need your idea of a fitting masquerade."

"I guessed you would be going undercover and I have just the outfit for you. I took the liberty of visiting several shops and brought this back," he said while depositing a bag at the foot of my bed.

I looked dubiously at his gift. It be not as if I am unable to pull off a successful disguise without such aids. I scored quite well in subterfuge during my apprenticeship under Phen the Razor. A credible guise does not always necessitate elaborate wigs or costumes, but a shift in gait, expression, manner and a sweep of the comb. I was also suspicious of Lorenzo's idea of a fitting cover.

"You can go as a milkmaid," he said, while laying out the garb with a flourish.

"This be just your twisted idea of humor. I am not going as a milkmaid. First, what milkmaid in her right mind would visit such sinister dens? You have tried foistering such upon me before. Quit looking at me like that. That skimpy gown does not even belong to a milkmaid. I have never known one to wear fishnet stockings and a push-up bra made from the eyelids of a mastodon."

"You must not hangout with the same milkmaids as I do," my friend said, before giving a dramatic sigh of disappointment and turning again to his bag. "I was afraid you'd act this way, so here is Plan B."

~ * ~

"What?" I snapped at the elf halfling sitting next to me at the bar.

She favored her human side and was casting uneasy side-glances at me as one afraid of attracting the attention of drunken weasels exiting a dark alley while ranting of pigeons in league with invaders from the second moon.

"What?' she nervously echoed.

"Do I have a tattoo on my forehead reading, 'I am a leper'?"

"What?"

"Never mind."

I would not have taken the woman for the timid kind. She was short, the top of her head just reaching my chin, but her well-worn black leather skirt, tunic and knee-high boots spoke of a seasoned mercenary, even without the no-nonsense sword hilt arising from a well-scuffed scabbard. She also had a faint scar crossing one of her high cheekbones. The woman appeared to be in her early thirties, though it be hard to tell with those of elf heritage; given away by her slightly pointed ears and pinkish porcelain complexion.

I would normally have let it end there, but her peculiar manner piqued my curiosity. I also needed to begin my search. "Buy you a drink?"

Her lavender eyes widened and she paused before answering, "I, ah, sure. A cider."

I motioned to the barmeister. "A cider and another ale."

He ambled over and placing both palms on the bar, leaned over and growled, "I serve yah, but me wants no trouble out of yah."

Damn that Lorenzo. Still, who could guess that this disguise would create such responses?

The mercenary, seeing my puzzlement, whispered, "What do yah expect coming in here as yah are?"

"Why? Are there killer inn ringhops terrorizing the town? I just got off work at a hostel and needed an ale."

"Sure. Dressed in that cutesy velvet red blazer and pillbox cap, and yah come to an ale joint like this? Look around. Yah be surrounded by those who would kill and eat their best friend for coin. Only a madman spoiling for a fight would be so garbed among the likes of them. Might as well come dressed as a milkmaid. I am just saying."

I was stumped for an answer and, while considering a suitable reply, a hulk of man pushed back his chair and stood. From the corner of my eye, I watched as he lumbered over and silently cursed Lorenzo for the fifth time that morning.

"Nice outfit. Yah must think yahself pretty tough comin' here like that? Itchin' fer a fight, are yah?" he growled, while towering above me. He had to be nearly twice my weight and eight inches taller.

Taking in the apeman, I observed a crooked nose that spoke of more than one contact with adversarial knuckles. The rest of his scarred face was also the beneficiary of such conflicts and most likely from fists graced with large rings worn for just that purpose. It did not help that the barmeister now loomed on the other side of the bar with eyes narrowed. The question was, even if I managed to down the miscreant with a series of Kimchee moves, could I make it out the door before being set upon by the other patrons.

"You gotta a lot of room to talk," I replied in a voice much more confident than I felt.

"Huh?"

I went for broke. "Come on, look at your tunic."

"Yeah?"

"That cut went out of style with your granny. And those pantaloons. The last time I saw a pair like that they were on a corpulent syphilitic eunuch. Do not get me started on those earrings. You must think they give you the swashbuckling air of a pirate, but they suit more a courtesan of some backwater court."

The hush falling across the tavern was as explosive as any outraged uproar. The giant looked down at me with startlement and took a step back to get a better notion of this clearly demented stranger. I tensed in anticipation of dodging a blow from his meaty fists.

The blow came, but by an open palm on my shoulder that nearly knocked me from my stool.

"Hah, yah crazy tiny bastard," he roared. "Yah be the pluckiest little fella I ever met. Men much bigga have trembled and wet themselves before me. Barmeister, bring him another round of whatever he be drinking."

That unusual blessing was followed by a palpable easing of tension about the tavern. The barmeister even smiled.

"Thanks, ah…"

"Rahjar be my name," he replied.

"It be a pleasure meeting you. I go by, ah, Keef the Knife."

"Be yah really a ringhop?"

"Ah, no. I killed and ate the real one," I answered, now getting into the spirit.

That brought a loud guffaw and another hearty cuff on the back. "Yah slay me."

"Did you really kill and eat a ringhop?" whispered the halfling after Rahjar returned to his table.

I took a long draw from my mug before turning to the mercenary and with faux sincerity asked, "Why? Would that come between us?"

"Yes, you are mad, Keef the Knife, if that be your real name, though I do detect a blade beneath a sleeve. What do you seek here?"

"Why, just an ale to wet a dry palate."

"Nay, I know better. You are a puzzle. I have made a study of many weapons and fighting styles. It be handy in my line of work. When Rahjar approached, your posture was not to draw your blade."

"No?" I causally replied, though completely focused on her speech.

"No, you kept your hands to your side, but with fingers curled and thumbs extended."

"Really?"

"Do not play the stooge. I am well aware of Kimchee. One would be very confident in the obscure martial art of thumb fighting to choose that over a blade."

"Kimchee? Why, I never… Oof." I exclaimed after being thumbed by the mercenary.

She had performed a classic Kimchee move called the Stinging Wasp. The strike upon a nerve cluster momentarily paralyses an opponent's arm. I was forced to hastily grab the falling ale mug with my other hand. The mercenary returned to clutching her own drink on the bar with both hands, a purposeful move to show she planned no further attacks.

"One can ask the same question of you," I spoke while massaging a spot below my right shoulder. "As you noted, Kimchee is an obscure fighting form and you clearly have more than passing knowledge of the art. More, at least, than one would expect from a common mercenary. While we are at it, what be your name?"

"Hiilda, if you need know."

"Hiilda, why are you here? Even as a seasoned mercenary, this crowd be dangerous for a woman who be also a halfling. Your adornments say you can afford a higher-class establishment and fellow patrons."

I referred to her jeweled gold rings, torc and bracelets. Mercenaries carry their wealth as jewelry rather than in land ownership or promissory notes. A hired blade flush from a successful conflict will invest pay and plunder in that which can be worn. A lack of jewelry reveals a mercenary down on their luck.

"I am to meet someone about a hire. I believe I have been stood up," Hiilda replied and, looking across the table to where Rahjar sat, asked, "Did you really plan for such to happen wearing that popinjay outfit?"

Rahjar, seeing our attention, smiled and raised a mug.

"Ah, sure I did."

"You sound not so certain."

"Well, ah, it was a friend's idea."

"A friend? Really? Does he mean for you to be killed?"

"Sometimes I wonder," I replied, thinking of perilous escapades Lorenzo had drawn me into. "I am in search of information and hope to gain it by drinking with such as Rahjar."

"Be careful, ringhop. Rahjar and his crowd see you now as an amusement, much like a dancing monkey. That may not last if you become an annoyance."

I studied the mercenary for a second and said, "I would like to speak with you later in the day. Will you be available?"

"Sorry, Keef the Knife, but you can keep your blade in your sheath. I have a companion and she would make quick work of a ringhop."

"As with me," I laughed. "No, I am thinking of employment. I may have need of an extra sword arm. Have you ever been a bodyguard?"

"I have." Her look spoke of half curiosity, half wariness. "It would depend upon what I be guarding against and if I need be seen with you in public."

I decided to be forthright. "I have been attacked several times by would-be assassins. I am now seeking information about those behind the assaults. And no, you would not have to be seen with me wearing this garb."

"I come as a pair," the mercenary firmly stated, "and she be as competent as I."

I nodded in agreement. "Can you be at the Stagsford Enchantress Preparatory Academy of the Occult Arts at near dusk?"

Her eyes widened. "Now you really do surprise me, Keef. Are they friend or foe? I may be foolhardy, but not enough to go against a coven."

I sighed and took the final leap. "They are my clients and my name be not Keef the Knife, but Jak Barley of Duburoake."

She sat up straighter with a jerk. "The ferret?"

"That be private inquisitor."

Her eyes opened even wider. "Then…" she began and paused, "that could only have been your Lorenzo Spasm who drew me here today."

~ * ~

"What?"

"Do not 'what' me, Lorenzo," I snapped. "First, you send me out in that monkey suit."

"Hey, don't blame me," he interrupted. "You turned down the milkmaid outfit."

"Then, without telling me, you sneakily maneuvered me into hiring two mercenaries."

"Nobody forced you, and you must admit, seasoned mercenaries as Hiilda and Hiidee are equal to a dozen royal guardsmen. They come with very good references."

"If you are so worried about my wellbeing, you have a strange way of showing it. I cannot believe you talked me into that costume. Do you know how close I came to being made a lad toy?"

"I knew you would be okay. As I have said before, I worry…"

"Stop right there," I ordered. "Yes, you worry I become too complacent and need such encounters to maintain my wits."

"Yes, and I was right. I knew you would overcome any difficulties. And you said you gained promising tips at the tavern."

I sighed. There be no arguing with Lorenzo. "I will follow those up tomorrow. Right now, we must meet with Hiidee and Hiilda."

~ * ~

The meeting went well with the two mercenaries. Hiidee was taller than me by several inches and larger framed than her wiry partner. She was of a dark brown complexion as that of walnut wood. Her light grey eyes matched the silver braids coiled atop her head. They made a striking pair. Neither showed any edginess at entering an edifice filled with witches. Wizards and witches, thanks in part to spell casters like the viper mages, instill a distrust and fear in most of the public.

The two left after we agreed to a meeting time the next morning – and that I would not be wearing the garb of a ringhop.

154

"What will you be doing the morrow?" I asked Lorenzo.

"Oh, a bit of this and a bit of that."

I studied him for a moment and said, "They say to keep friends close and enemies closer, but why is it that I feel the opposite with you?"

"Because my presence makes you feel safe?"

"No. Because then I know what you are up to."

~ * ~

A message had been received from Morgana's party saying they arrived and set up camp for the night. So far, they relayed, no sign of wizard or witch could be found.

"Why can they not transport themselves back for the night?" I asked the messenger. "You know – as they did to the viper mage stronghold."

"They carry weapons and apparatuses that will aid in their search, some with enchantments preventing a magical means of conveyance," she replied. "Leaving the equipment unattended, even for a night, be out of the question – some because they are too valuable and others because they are too dangerous to risk falling into other hands."

I returned to my room for the night. Lorenzo and I were informed that new quarters were waiting for us the next evening near the coven hall. Wards there, we were told, would be much more robust.

Morganna wanted a witch to accompany me for the day, seeing as Morgana was not available. I won the argument by pointing out that it was peculiar enough to be traveling with two female mercenaries, but accompanied by a witch as well was too outlandish. Such an odd accompanying trio would make too much of a distraction.

Morganna did place a spell that would alert her if I became injured. The witch shrugged her shoulders when I suggested that by then it might be too late for aid.

"Maybe, but I will be able to deal with your murderers," she noted.

"That be a comforting thought," was my reply.

~ * ~

Rahjar's crowd were more affable than yesterday, after a number of rounds on the house. A rather scruffy individual, said to occasionally provide muscle when collecting gambling debts, mentioned a tavern called the Sticker Inn. It was there, he said, those in need of illicit deeds could acquire such services. With the assassin guilds basically destroyed in what the Weekly Tattler headlined as the Case of the Annoying Assassins, only freelancers were now available for whack jobs. Most of them were out-of-work mercenaries.

The three of us now paused beneath the Sticker Inn's faded wooden sign swinging in a slight breeze.

"A rather unwelcoming signage," observed Hiidee, while gazing at the crude depiction of a knife being plunged into an unwary victim's back.

I was about to add a comment when the tavern door burst open and a scrawny figure landed face down at our feet. An apron-draped ruffian providing the fellow's means of flight dusted his hands, glared about and retreated into the inn's dark interior.

Hiilda prodded the sprawled figure with her boot. "Be you alive?" she asked in a voice suggesting little interest either way.

"If yah can call it livin'," he moaned, only then to roll over and scowl under the bright morning sky. Raising a grimy hand, he begged in a wavering voice, "Help a fella up, will yah?"

"That be not happening," Hiilda snapped. "Who knows what manner of plagues lurk beneath that dirt?"

"Oh, cruel lady, know that I was once a prince among men, a mover of cosmic events and renowned among the wisest of scholars," he spoke while struggling to his feet. "The loftier height one attains leads to but a harder fall."

I reached into a pocket and withdrew a fifty phenning piece. "A copper coin for you if you feel up to answering a few questions."

"What? A half mark? That be an insult. Crowned heads of state have flung gold and jewels at my feet for but snippets of my insights."

I stepped back to take account of the gaunt reprobate. He appeared

156

well into his years, though a strict diet of rum withers the hardiest of men. Straggly grey hair with traces of dirty yellow ringed his bald crown. I moved down wind. His stench was almost overwhelming now that he stood.

Still, his threadbare jacket and equally soiled tunic spoke of a once stylish and superior tailoring. Even his dog-eared boots in better days could have trodden the floor of any manor hall.

"A mark, then," I replied and tossed him a small silver coin. "What be your name?"

My two escorts snorted in unison. Their scowls signaled their thoughts regarding the beggar.

"It be Gymm Paughter, former Don of Alchemistic Studies at the Miskatonic Institute of Transmagic, recipient of the Royal Mastermind Medallion in Elemental Disciplines and past advisor to the Duke of Mahcokatah."

I eyed him in startlement. "You taught at MIT?"

He huffed up and chillingly replied, "Do you take me for a charlatan, dear sir?"

"Does the name Olmsted Aunderthorn sound a chime?" I asked.

My brother attended the Miskatonic Institute of Transmagic for several years until deciding to follow his own independent studies, though he spoke warmly of his time at MIT.

It was the derelict's turn to be surprised. "Aunderthorn, you say? Olmsted Aunderthorn from Duburoake? Why ask you?"

"He be my brother."

"Ah, then you be the private inquisitor. I hear occasionally of your exploits."

I retrieved a five-mark coin and tossed it to Gymm. "Here. There will be more if you meet us here at sun high, and you come bathed in clean garb."

I turned away and the two mercenaries followed close on my heels.

"That be a waste of silver," Hiidee opinioned. "It will only go to keep him in the cups for a week."

"Maybe, but he could prove a trove of information," I replied.

157

"Tongues wag more freely when paying slight heed to the ears of nearby beggars. Besides, there be no way I could question him when under assault by that reek."

"He also was a tutor to your brother," noted Hiilda.

"Yes, there be that," I admitted. "I am sure Olmsted would be upset to see one of his instructors in such a sad state.'

Our conversation ended as we entered the tavern. The mercenaries pushed me aside to pass first through the door and inspect the dark interior. Daylight was fighting a losing battle in passing through the grunge coated windows. The smoking oil lamps contributed little to furthering the room's illumination.

I gazed over the pair's shoulders to view as baleful a crew as I have seen in any inn. That impression did not improve as my eyes adjusted to the dim lighting. I faced a long bar upon entering the inn and the narrow room stretched to the right, furnished with eight or ten tables. The four patrons sitting at the bar turned at the sound of our entrance and scowled in greeting. A glance to the right revealed the dozen or more at the tables also casting suspicious and unwelcoming glares.

I squeezed past Hiidee and Hiilda to approach the bar. "I will have an ale and whatever my friends are drinking."

"The same," Hiilda spoke.

"Friends?" grunted the barmeister as he wiped mugs with a rag that would more likely dirty the cups than clean.

He could not have been more than five feet in height and had the thick ears and stocky build of a troll.

"Yes, friends," I replied. "They are just back from border skirmishes with the goblins and we celebrate their taking of more than one fifty thumbs."

Goblin raiding sorties out of the mountains are a perennial problem at Glavendale's southern border. Their attacks are impossible to predict. After their raids the goblins quickly disappear into the rock piles and crags of the foothills and wait to ambush pursuers. They are a cunning and murderous lot, almost impossible to kill with their nasty serrated pikes, tough hides and fangs filed to points.

Besides the guardsmen defending the border, royal payments are offered to bounty hunters for dispatching trespassing goblins. Since they are such fearsome creatures, even collecting half a dozen goblin thumbs would speak loudly of a bounty hunters prowess. My statement was followed by startled stares.

We picked up our mugs and set off for an empty table at the far end.

"Yah, sure. These two girlies killed…"

The scoff was abruptly silenced by Hiidee, who had stoutly cuffed the fool with her mug and kicked him in the ribs as he hit the floor. "Barmeister, another ale, and on this slobbering dullard who made me spill my own."

"Well, that be one way to make an entrance," I observed, after settling at a table.

"You disapprove?" Hiilda asked.

"No, no, certainly not. If anything, it might help. Local constables or CIA agents would not want to draw undue attention to themselves. Nondescript may work in many places, but take a look about. We have eye patches, scars, dungeon gang tattoos, more blades than a slaughterhouse and even mercenaries. Dull they are not."

Hiilda was brought her other ale and the inn quieted down to a usual midmorning raucousness. A few of the patrons even gave the intimidating Hiidee approving glances.

"What do you hope to accomplish here?" asked Hiidee.

I shook my head. "Maybe not much. I get the feeling the patrons of the Sticker Inn are a tight knit and lipped bunch. I would make a point of becoming a regular if I had the time. As it is, I doubt any here would care for idle banter with strangers. That only leaves me one approach – to act as one seeking the services of an assassin."

Hiilda glanced about the room. "I know places as this, though Hiidee and I are never as desperate to seek commissions in such environs. Sooner or later, someone will grow curious enough as to why we are here and all eyes will be upon us. There will be much chatter after we leave."

She was right. Halfway through our second ale one of the two in mercenary leathers limped across the barroom and without waiting for an offer to be seated, fell into the one empty chair. He and his comrade wore insignias showing they once served as lancers. The now free soldiers appeared to be in their mid-fifties. Unless one attained a high officer's rank, there was little demand for soldiers their age, which could account for their presence in the Sticker Inn.

"You are missing an invitation," growled Hiidee, "unless you be sitting but long enough to offer us an ale. That should take about five seconds."

Hiidee was obviously the cockier of the two.

"Ah, youth," smiled our visitor. "Such arrogance. That and youth will soon be gone, I can tell yah that."

It was probably no coincidence that a scar furrowing down his cheek and into his lip ended where two teeth were missing. He grinned even wider beneath the frigid glares of Hiidee and Hiilda.

"What do you want?" snapped Hiidee.

"Ah, but the question is what do you want?" he directed his reply to me. "You already have two mercenaries in tow and from their lovely baubles, they are highly proficient."

I looked about before leaning across the table and speaking in a conspiratorial voice, "There are some special services I require from which my overly scrupulous friends here baulk. I was referred to the Sticker Inn."

"Good, very good," he laughed. "Coming here as you are with two fancy fems and rapping poor Whuke on the head as she did. You make quite the stir. So much that none would suspect you of being anything but an over-moneyed popinjay wanting to whack a business or love rival, or maybe even a shrewish wife."

"I am sure I have no idea what you speak of."

"I be Wyrner. Me and my buddy Erroil, we been around." It was the mercenary's turn to speak in a hushed voice. "We was not always hanging in such dregs as these. Several years past, we had enough of foreign escapades and went into the hire of a caravan trader. We was to guard his shipment from Duburoake to here. There be quite the fracas along the way and even more in Stagsford with the changing of the kings."

I waited for him to continue. "Yes?" I finally asked.

"Hah. Let us end this dancing about. You and your buddy Spasm were on that caravan. You are Jak Barley, the ferret."

I shook my head in surrender. "That be private inquisitor."

He leaned back and smiled. "You would only be here for one reason, nosing about on some case."

I smiled slightly and took a slow draw from my mug.

He appeared amused by my silence. "Just what brings you here? Hmm, maybe the kidnapping of the viscount's niece? The ransacking of the sausage guild's quarters? Ah, maybe the suspicious death of the sergeant of arms for the city assemblage?"

Wyrner's snide grin and conceited manner did little to bolster a sense of trustworthiness.

"Oh, I know. Youse being dragged out of that witches' den and introduced to the now deceased Hvsun and his henchmen," he declared with an overly dramatic rise in his voice.

That brought a cuff to the mercenary's head. "Keep your voice down, you buffoon," snapped Hiilda. "If we craved our business flaunted about, we would hire a carnival barker."

Wyrner snarled in response and began reaching for a short sword at his side. The lout stopped short when he felt Hiidee's knife pressing against him beneath the table.

"What do you know of this?" I spoke as I eagerly leaned across the table.

"Tell your girly to get her sticker out of my side if you want to hear what I know," he growled through clenched teeth. "

I nodded to Hiidee. "Now, how do you know about the kidnapping and the torturers?"

"Hah. It be all about the street – some dupe from Duburoake hauled into Hvsun's workshop and all Hades breaking out with some freak dragon. It was not until yah stepped through that door that I figured just who that dupe was."

"What else be on the street?"

"Ah, that will cost yah. Me and Erroil been on a dry spell and it seems this information be of importance to yah."

161

"How much?

Wyrner leaned back and speculatively studied me in the same manner as a shady horse trader, musing how much coin he could squeeze from a bumpkin. "Four-hundred marks."

"How about four inches of blade?" Hiilda threatened in response to the outrageous demand.

I held my hand up for Hiilda to slacken and sarcastically answered, "I would be a fool to carry such coin on me, even if I were not visiting such a reputable tavern as this."

He shrugged. "Not my concern. That be my final offer."

"Will this do?" I reached into my pouch and then flung three green crystals upon the table. As well as the jewels of the mages, I had filled my pouch with the green crystal shards scattered about the desert floor.

All three mercenaries gasped. Though the torchlight was dim, an inner blaze caused them to gleam and sparkle.

"You. You cannot be serious," exclaimed Hiidee. "I have traveled Five Corners and never seen such gems. You throw them to this scum?"

I slammed my hand over the crystals as Wyrner hungrily moved to scoop them up. "Out with it."

The mercenary licked his lips and eyed the crystals intently. "Kairem. He be an out-of-work hired blade like meself. He was bragging how with the help of witches; he and a pal took a body from the backdoors of the academy to Hvsun's."

"Who be this Kairem?" I demanded.

"I heard of him." Hiilda answered for Wyrner. "A worthless troublemaker. I am surprised the knave has not yet been found in some back alley with a slashed throat. Besides a coward, he is of no honor and a thief."

Wyrner shrugged. "Ye, who be without flaw, fling the first scorpion," he quoted the Book of Trimp.

"Where can I find him?"

He leaned back again and crossed his arms. I glared at him for a moment and then slid one of the crystals across the table.

"Yah can find him at the Dragger Inn most evenings."

"What does he look like?" I drew back my hand holding the remaining crystals when he appeared hesitant to answer.

"Sandy hair. About your height. Missing part of an ear and favors his right leg. Gotta tattoo of a basilisk on his forehead and a gold front tooth."

"That could describe half the vagrants in this neighborhood. You know I will come looking for you if you speak falsehoods," I sternly warned, after tossing the remaining two gems across the table.

The crystals quickly disappeared into a pouch at his waist. I watched as he wordlessly pushed back his chair, stood and walked from our table.

"I cannot believe you gave him a small fortune in precious stones," Hiilda repeated her disbelief.

"Plenty more where they came from and they may soon not be that precious," I answered.

"Hear this." Wyrner's demanding shout stopped dead every conversation in the tavern. "We have a ferret here nosing about. He be after poor old Kairem. If we let this sneakabout leave here alive and word gets out, none of us be safe. We will have every gumboot in Stagsford thinkin' they can just stroll in here."

The scoundrel turned to me and snickered, "Yah did not think I would rat out a buddy?"

I was right behind Hiidee and Hiilda in leaping to my feet and drawing saber. Wyrner's call to arms jerked the early-morning drinkers from their sluggishness. At any other time with such warriors at my side, I would have felt more than safe. But we faced two dozen battle-scarred villains with broken-toothed leers and wolfish gleams to their eyes.

"I hope you be good with your blade, ferret," Hiilda muttered through clenched teeth.

"That be private inquisitor," I replied, "and not that good, but it does not matter."

Before the two could reply to my apparent fatalism, I hurled my ale mug though the closest grimy windowpane and stepped onto a chair to shout my own callout to the mob. "This be what Wyrner sold out his comrade for."

I scooped a fist-full of crystals from my pouch and held them above my head. To a rogue they froze with gaping mouths and wide eyes fixed upon the flashing green gems. A shared gasp erupted as I hurled the crystals through the shattered window.

Shocked silence was followed by curses and stampeding feet as the mercenaries fought to be first out the door. Wyrner was not among them. A slim dirk almost magically appeared in the villain's back and he collapsed to the filthy floor.

"I did not like the looks of him from the first," observed Hiilda as she stooped over the fallen mercenary to withdraw the blade from between his shoulder blades.

"Tell me, Barley, be this your usual mode of intelligence gathering?" Hiidee asked. "It seems a bit riotous."

"Not really. Wait until Lorenzo be involved."

~ * ~

We skirted the brawl outside the Sticker Inn and made our way to an eatery for a midmorning meal. The inn was on a little trafficked side lane and we sat in its garden. Several dwarf redwoods offered shade as well as nesting's for a flock of ruby-breasted fairies that buzzed about waiting for spilled crumbs.

It was a relief to sit in peaceful surroundings. I waited for our meal to end before laying out the puzzles before me. The faces of my otherwise hard-edged companions revealed their consternation as I detailed my captivity, escape and the magical extermination of the mages.

"The kidnapping by the necromancers be easily explained by their long-held grudges," I related. "It be the abduction leading to the torturers yet unsolved. I believe those behind the kidnapping and malspells to be one and the same."

"What about the pixie gold theft?" asked Hiidee. She was intrigued by that mystery.

"I believe I have that solved. It will take a return trip to Kaiserhelm and the results of what my brother Olmsted called invocation forensics.

The cask was sent to a witch who specializes in such."

"You say no wizard can aid in the crystal malspells?" asked Hiidee.

"Yes. That magic cannot be accessed by males – which means if wizards are behind the attacks, rogue witches are also involved."

Hiilda sighed. "I am used to intrigues among the courts that have hired Hiidee and me, so I should not be surprised it be the same among spellcasters."

"Hah," scoffed Hiidee. "Chronicles are full of such rivalries among wizards and witches. What think you caused the Wastelands?"

I looked at the large sundial set in the flagstones and commented, "Time to go. We are to meet Gymm Paughter outside the Sticker Inn."

"Best be quick," snorted Hiilda. "Needless to say, that be one tavern you can chalk off becoming a regular."

Chapter Ten

"I warned that be a waste of silver," Hiilda muttered as we waited across the street from the Sticker Inn.

"Patience," I counseled. "It be yet to reach high sun."

We were waiting in the recessed doorway of a hockshop. It took a couple fifty-pfennig coins to keep the proprietor from calling the constables on us as dawdlers. I stepped aside to allow a customer to enter the shop, but instead, the well-groomed fellow stopped and turned to face me. He appeared to be in his early sixties and was garbed in a tweed surcoat over a crisp white cotton tunic. His neatly trimmed grey hair matched his goatee.

Hiidee and Hiilda warily shifted their stance as the stranger failed to move on.

"Can I help you?" I asked.

"Can you?"

That voice. I stepped back to take in the stranger. "Very good."

I turned to my companions. Their looks were of puzzlement. "I would like to introduce Don Gymm Paughter."

"Not possible," Hiidee blurted.

"Possible," Paughter smugly answered.

"This reunion be poignant, but we need move on," Hiilda interrupted. "We are across from the Sticker Inn, whose denizen are likely still sotted and ireful."

I agreed. Two blocks away we turned into a narrow alley and stopped at the rear of an empty lot. Scattered piles of weed-covered bricks and fire-blackened timbers marked where a building once stood.

166

"It be amazing what a few silvers can accomplish," I dryly noted. "Why that guise?"

"Why else? To go about unnoticed. Things are whispered less softly when the only other ears are those of a broken-down old wastrel."

"What whispers are these?"

"Hmm," Paughter hummed to himself as he studied my face and glanced at Hiidee and Hiilda. "I am not sure you want to know."

When he did not continue, I asked, "Why be that?"

Looking warily up and down the alley, he spoke in a low voice, "There are ancient evils still about. They walk in the shape of man or drift through the night streets as foul, venomous fogs. This legion of darkness, this ancient obscenity – perhaps you and your friend Spasm might finally vanquish, especially with the help of the witch Morganna. This malignancy be injurious to all beings and must be confronted. Others have tried and died horribly for their struggles."

I gazed intently at his grim face. My two companions shifted nervously and glanced furtively about.

I took a deep breath and replied, "Yeah, that sounds pretty foreboding, all that evil and such. I am sure we can get around to it, but at the moment I have another case and your ruse in the local taverns might prove helpful."

"What?" I responded to the startled expressions of Hiidee and Hiilda. "You cannot spit without hitting a dire and foreboding threat. If it be as ancient as he says, it can wait a while longer."

Maybe I have been around Lorenzo too long.

Turning back to Paughter, I continued, "I will have my secretary schedule it. Right now, I need to know if you heard anything dealing with a kidnapping from the witch academy and a following delivery to local thumbscrews."

Paughter scowled at my response, but grudgingly revealed that he had overheard a vague conversation that could be related to my question. He paused for a second, then with a lift of his eyebrows asked, "Be that you?"

His reply echoed Wyrner's comments. There was chatter in the streets about a kidnapping from the witches' academy, but so far, the victim's identity was not common knowledge. If such an incident occurred in my home city of Duburoake, any mention of an unusual incident involving a private inquisitor and I would be the first suspect.

"Yes, I was the lucky lad. Actually, there were two kidnappings from the witches' academy. I doubt the second one gained notice as it did not involve your local torturers. I must find the names of the witches involved in my kidnapping. Just what have you heard?"

"Only that some of those involved met gruesome ends. That be your work?" he asked guardedly.

I sighed. "If you mean the torturers, it was not on purpose."

"How do you dismember someone not on purpose?"

"It be easier than it sounds. Now, what have you heard?"

"It be not just the torturers. One of the lads involved in the snatching was found floating in the river."

I grimaced. "Do not tell me, it be a scoundrel by the name of Kairem."

"No. He was a Lost Elf by the name of Burneyes. Now I did hear other gossip that a mercenary named Kairem has taken to ground. I do not know why, but he be avoiding his regular watering holes. Be he connected to your kidnapping?"

"According to a rogue by the name of Wyrner, yes."

"Hah, so you met Wyrner," Paughter scoffed. "He be a treacherous one."

"Was a treacherous one," Hiilda noted with a baleful laugh.

Olmsted's former professor studied the mercenary before replying, "I assume the past tense does not mean he has been rehabilitated."

"A Lost Elf, you say," I responded to Paughter's earlier statement.

Elves are known for being a decorous and gracious Little People. That cannot be said of those called the Lost Elves. They are of a tribe that disappeared generations ago across the Elgethian Sea. Some returned more than a dozen years back. What cruel land the elves found be not known, but those returning are of an insolent and twisted nature.

"Twice I have had the ill experience of crossing paths with a Lost

168

Elf called Ebert," I stated. "I hope there be not a third time."

A dead elf and a mercenary gone into hiding. It could only mean those hidden figures behind the crystal malspells and my kidnapping are cleaning up loose ends. I need find Kairem before those others do.

"We will not find Kairem at the Stagger Inn since he will be avoiding his usual haunts," I observed. "I need to return to see what Lorenzo has been up to. Hopefully, it has something to do with the case."

I gave my leave-taking to Paughter and promised not to forget the ancient evils that take the shape of man or drift through the night streets as foul, venomous fogs.

Chapter Eleven

I returned to the witches' academy to find my kit had already been moved to an inn next to the Stagsford Coven Hall. Magical wards about the coven compound had been expanded to include the inns circling the hall. After the creepy adornments at the academy, it would be interesting to see what the just-as-ancient environs of the coven hall would reveal.

A message left by Lorenzo related that quarters for the two mercenaries had also been reserved. Any worry they would shy from entering the almost-mythical realm of the powerful witches' sect was allayed by their keen response to the news.

"I wanted to be a witch when I was a youngling," admitted Hiilda as we rode a cab to the inn.

"What?" exclaimed her partner. "You never told me that."

"Yes," she sighed. "I did show early signs of power."

Hiidee was obviously surprised by the announcement. "You instead became a hired blade? Why not follow that path? Think of it, to be a witch. What be a strong sword arm compared to the flick of a witch's finger?"

"Hah. Do you think a halfling would be welcomed within such ranks?"

She had a point. Halflings of any mixed heritage often face scorn from both sides of their parentage.

"Early signs of power?" I asked. "Do you still have them?"

Hiilda turned to the window rather than answer.

I was as surprised by Hiilda's revelation as her partner. After a minute of silence, I prodded, "Come on, Hiilda. Do such traces remain?"

She shrugged. "What does it matter now? My life has taken me past such turns in the road."

I glanced at Hiidee. Her face remained a mixture of surprise and confusion.

"I will say this, Hiilda. Not all magic wielders come into their own as youngsters. My intended, Morgana, showed no signs of power 'til but a few years ago. Yet she will soon graduate as a novice witch. As far as being a halfling, I wager there are witches who would speak for you."

"Besides," I added with a laugh, "what snotty-nosed pupil would torment a classmate accustomed to hacking limbs and cleaving skulls?"

I dropped the subject for now, but planned on speaking of it later with Morgana.

Looming over the historic Stagsford neighborhood of Elvenwoods was the Glavendale Coven Hall. Lost in the fog of history were details on its construction. No doubt magic was used to evacuate the wide moat around the Stagsford Coven Hall and build up the prominence upon which the hall gloomily dominates.

Brother Olmsted says it still be unknown where the ebony blocks were quarried. The stonework voraciously sucks in all light so that it appears to be some portal to a world devoid of sun and stars. At night its lit windows seem to float in the dark sky. During the day, the hall is a shadow cast against a bright blue sky and its outlandish outline wavers as if viewed from across hot desert sands. Staring too long at the tortuous visage results in a dizzying nausea and pounding headache. Needless to say, the area directly surrounding the hall is not high-valued real estate. The sides of the inns facing the coven hall are windowless.

Though covens are scattered throughout Glavendale, Stagsford's hall be the oldest, and from the very beginning the site for the country's yearly assemblage.

Normally, these meetings are attended by a select handful of representatives from each coven. With the Grand Gathering called, all available witches will soon be descending upon the capital. I shuddered at the thought. Until meeting Morgana, I maintained a healthy regard for witches. Healthy in that knowing the less I had to do with the female magic wielders, the more likely I was not to suffer a plague of boils, puking up thumb-sized maggots or being reduced to a charred and oily smoking heap of rag and bone. I can credit Morgana's fearsome mother with one thing – at least partially inuring me to their daunting presence.

Our carriage came to a halt in front of an inn that attempted and failed to mimic the coven hall. Its black exterior was faded and peeling, though two dwarves were in the process of repainting the front. Several life-size effigies garbed as witches stood guard upon the porch roof. Above the entryway was red lettering that dripped as if bleeding from a wound. It read, "Any Witch Way Inn."

No doubt the hostel's regular guests were hayseed tourists from rural backwaters. They would have been cleared out in anticipation of the real witches soon descending upon the hall and other surrounding hostels.

"Classy place," sniffed Hiidee as we entered the lobby.

The witch motif continued inside. Crossed brooms on the walls, an iron cauldron near the stairway and a stuffed black cat on the front desk were some of the adornments. In one corner was a glass case offering souvenir fake wands and crystal balls, pointed black hats and cheap charms.

"I am not sure if the arriving witches will find this hokum amusing," I observed. "As with wizards, many seem to lack a sense of whimsey."

A nervous appearing desk clerk in an ill-fitting jacket obviously had the same apprehensions. He looked almost relieved to see that my female companions were only well-armed mercenaries.

"May I, ah, help you?" he asked in a trembling voice.

"New here?" I asked in response to his timidity.

"Yes, well, ah, no. I, ah, been working in the inn's livery yard for two years. Ah, the three working front ran off a couple days ago. The innkeeper, she, ah, cannot find anyone to replace them."

Hiidee sniggered and the clerk weakly smiled in response.

"We have retained rooms. My name be Jak Barley."

"Oh, yes. Two of your party are already here. A Witch Morgana and a Master Spasm. Oh, yes, here are your keys. One for you and one for the, ah, ladies. They be on the second floor. Ah, enjoy your stay."

I was looking forward to resting for the remainder of the afternoon. I would not admit it to my fierce companions, but the past several days had taken their toll. I purposely kept my back to Hiidee and Hiilda as I unlocked my door with a tremoring hand.

Morgana tells me male egos are as fragile as eggshells. I guess so. I would not harshly judge anyone showing wear after similar ill-treatments – chased by assassins and balaurs, in a sword fight for my life, kidnapped twice, in the clutches of professional torturers and held prisoner by the most malevolent necromancers imagined. All with little sleep. Still, I loathed showing signs of weakness in front of my companions.

"We will see what kind of fare the inn's kitchen offers come evening," I proclaimed in a forced hearty voice as the two continued down the hall to their own room.

I did not wait for an answer as I slipped through the door and closed it behind me.

~ * ~

I opened my eyes to see sunlight streaming across the foot of my bed. Judging by its angle, I surmised I had slept for at least four hours. The lie-down worked miracles – my body aches diminished and my head clear. It was now time to get a decent meal.

The narrow hallway was quiet. I debated knocking on the mercenaries' door, then decided to let them come down when ready. I did not have to wait. Morgana, Lorenzo, Hiidee and Hiilda were already stiffly seated at a long table.

"Morgana, back already? Great. Does that mean you have already discovered…?"

I stopped in mid-sentence and glanced from face to face. Except for Lorenzo, they all stared rigidly at a small troll I just now noticed. The diminutive figure stood away from a side entrance to the dining hall and appeared as immobile as my friends. He did not appear as a personage worthy of such enthrallment; garbed in a day laborer's rough wear of brown woolen vest, tunic and britches.

"What be the...?"

"Speak softly," Morgana interrupted, while slowly rising from her chair to make her way cautiously to the troll. She kneeled and carefully pulled aside his threadbare vest to reveal a small wooden box and four ivory tubes bound in leather straps to his chest.

"The troll, he says he was waylaid this morning," whispered Hiidee. "Remembers nothing but waking with the compulsion to visit here. Morgana says he comes with death by fire."

"This be the work of a witch or necromancer. These vessels are warded to imprison balefire," Morgana elaborated as she ran her fingers through the air in front of the troll's chest. "There are several containment-canceling spells running from this detonation box to the containers. Deactivated, any one of them will release the balefire that would turn this inn into a blazing charnel house."

"This blue thread deactivates if the leather bands are cut." Her hands moved along a flow of magic that was invisible to me.

"The green ribbon will deactivate the containment spell if any of us leave the room. This red annulling spell deactivates if there are magical attempts to defuse the hellfire. This yellow spell is a timer set to release the hellfire in, ah, about eight minutes."

"Is there nothing you can do?" I whispered.

"I did have lessons in incantations creating highly localized overpressure that rapidly distributes to equalize with ambient pressure – and ones also involving combustible magics like hellfire."

"And?" I asked when she paused.

"We did not get into these detonation spells before me. It be possible that simultaneously severing them all might not release the containment spell, but that be very difficult. I think I can cast a glamor mimicking the presence of you and the others, allowing for escape, but I must do it now," Morgana answered.

I detected a slight wavering in her voice.

"Not you?" I asked.

"I and the troll must remain to maintain the illusion."

I took a deep breath. "That be not happening, at least not where I

174

am concerned."

"No," I continued when she began to reply. "There be no argument. The others must leave, but I will stay."

She bit her lip and sighed. "I will first cast the glamor and briefly wait before attempting to neutralize the spells that would free the hellfire. Everyone, leave here as soon as I give the cue. You have but minutes to warn the others in the inn."

There was a tense silence as Morgana raised her hands to begin the incantation.

"If cutting all the threads at once does not work?"

Morgana smiled weakly. "I will not know of my mistake."

"*We* will not know," I answered and kneeled beside her.

The scraping of Lorenz's chair away from the table was as jarring as a banshee screech. He arose and crossed the floor to us.

"This is all very touching, but we have a busy day ahead of us." At that he tilted a brown glass bottle and drenched the wooden box on the troll's chest. "There. Who says beer is not just for breakfast anymore? Close your mouth, Jak, or the bar flies will get in."

I glanced from Lorenzo to the sopping troll and then to Morgana. "What the…?"

Morgana had fallen back off her heels and gasped. The troll sputtered as the mercenaries leapt to their feet.

"What, what did you do?" I managed to croak.

Morgana's laughter halted any further outbursts. "The threads are gone. Lorenzo, how did you do that?"

"Agh," I stammered. "It be that brew from his home world. Like Lorenzo, it be magic bane."

"Falstaff," he supplied. "The choicest product of the brewers' art – and the favorite of hipsters everywhere."

Morgana took a deep breath before asking, "Is not it a bit early to be drinking, Lorenzo? I worry you to become a hopeless sop."

"Too late for that," I said hoarsely as I helped Morgana to her feet.

"What just happened?" demanded the halfling mercenary.

Chapter Twelve

"Are you sure about this?" I asked Lorenzo for the fifth time as I clambered onto Adalbert's back. It was midday and I felt rushed to have packed and made ready for this crazy outing.

"Our probes revealed similar findings," Morgana answered for my friend. "That be why I could return so soon. Several signal outbursts we detected at camp came from beyond the crystal mountains in the heart of the Cythnian Desert. We believe that be where our adversaries be based. According to ancient lore, the area was once a fertile valley before the ancient Wizard Wars."

"Just how did you also come to this conclusion?" I asked skeptically of Lorenzo.

He smiled and shrugged. "While you were bar hopping, I was actually working. One cannot reside in a sterile wasteland without provisions. There must be outside suppliers and haulers. I just followed those leads."

"I still do not like it. I should be following up with the mercenary Kairem and a Lost Elf," I complained.

"You're just spooked because we're headed for Urbemmortis," he laughed.

I scowled but did not answer. How could I, since he was right? Urbemmortis – the city of many a bairn's nightmares – including my own. A staple of dark childhood fables of where the abandoned, gods-forsaken streets are still trod upon by grub-white ghouls and the ghosts of ancient residents, so evil they cannot pass onto where more mundane murderers, rapists, mutilators and genociders can. So said Marl the Adventurer in a trip recorded more than three centuries ago.

He described the city as, "Like the bones of a giant disease-ridden scavenger, it lies half buried in scorching sands that drift ceaselessly between its bleached ribs. The windows evilly glare forth as empty skull sockets. There remains the stench of death even as any once living creature now be but desiccated husks. A nauseous draft stirring the sands be such as a plague victim's lung-rotted breath. Half of my party now joins those brittle corpses interned a millennium ago. They died clawing at their bleeding eyes and screaming blasphemous curses."

"He died in a lunatic asylum soon after returning," I added after quoting the luckless adventurer.

"All right, it be torturous prose," I admitted beneath Lorenzo's mocking gaze. "Marl never claimed to be a poet and he was prone to mixed metaphors, but the fact remains that Urbemmortis be cursed and we travel there at our own peril."

"Yet there now appears to be some inhabiting the site," he noted.

"That also proves my point," I answered in turn while securing myself. "Whoever survives there be someone I care not to meet."

Already fastened in were the two mercenaries. I was now seated directly behind them and next to Morgana. Lorenzo was to the front. We waited only for Morgana's mother.

"What about you two?" I asked of Hiidee and Hiilda. "Does this not seem madness?"

"Maybe," answered Hiilda.

"Maybe?"

"Yes, maybe. Hiidee and I are getting no younger. We contemplate becoming conflict consultants. Such a venture as this will greatly enhance our marketing. Adding to that is working with the most feared witch in Glavendale. Not many can boast of that."

Though that was one brag I could usually do without, having Morganna along did slightly ease my disquiet.

Adalbert looked over his shoulder and in as a snide tone as possible for a dragon, said, "Do not be such a bedwetter."

"Hah. That be easy for you to say. You will be hightailing it to the clouds once we are dropped off."

"What whining be this?"

I jerked in my harness. Morganna relishes the startlement her abrupt appearances bring.

"I was just wondering if you keep a winter home in Urbemmortis. I hear the property values are quite affordable."

I may have been jesting, but for all I knew the fearsome witch did vacation in the city of death. I could see it. After all, her main abode is a former temple of Dorga, the Fish Headed God of Death. To my surprise, the witch ignored my jab and levitated to Lorenzo's side. A flick of her fingers had the leather belts rising like vipers to encircle her.

Minutes later, Stagsford was dwindling to that of a child's toy village. Except for the witches clad in some invisible warmth spell, the rest of us were garbed for the cold among the clouds. I wore a short, linen-lined leather surcoat since a cape would have beaten me merciless in the high winds.

Our small group, Morgana explained, was to only probe our enemy's defenses. The coven leaders decided reinforcing the protective wards about the Stagsford academy and hall was now the most critical mission. The always humble Morganna assured her fellow witches that she was more than capable of safeguarding our scouting party. I hoped so.

It was late afternoon when Urbemmortis came into sight. Adalbert circled several times before landing on a roof overlooking a wide plaza featuring a central debris-filled fountain. Long-dead skeletal trees guarded the entrances to streets radiating outward like spokes from a wheel hub.

I squinted in the glare from the sun-bleached structures. The white limestone buildings were two and three stories with small balconies facing the plaza. The centuries of blowing sands had worn away the sharp edges of windowsills and doorways. Wooden frames had long since disintegrated, though iron bars remained over many windows.

Stretching my legs, I gazed about and tried imagining the bleak landscape as it would have appeared a thousand years ago. It was no improvement. The parade of heinous figures carved into the mouldings would then have been in even sharper relief.

"They were a whimsical bunch," observed Lorenzo as he gazed at what appeared to be a hybrid weasel/lizard chewing at the throat of a young maiden.

Adalbert wasted little time in leaving after our camp supplies were unpacked and carted up to the third floor. I made sure a basket of cured meats, bread, dried fruits and cheeses had been packed, along with flagons of ale.

Morganna, with a wave of her hands, summoned a brief but fierce wind to blow the rooms free of debris.

"There will be no leaving this building without I or my daughter," ordered Morganna. In response to frowns from the mercenaries, she stressed, "Steel and muscle are no match for what is said to dwell in these accursed ruins. For me, Urbemmortis be an unknown. It has been shunned for so long there are no reliable accounts of what lies within these ruins. Even fables involving the original inhabitants are just that – fairy tales."

Hiilda nodded her head in agreement. "Fairies are always making up shit."

"What of Marl the Adventurer?" asked Hiidee.

Morganna sniffed. "That charlatan? It be said he traveled no further than the outlying taverns of Glavendale."

Lorenzo says there be no magic in his world, yet his silk-like shelters, barely heavier than smoke, sprang effortlessly into habitats large enough to hold three or four persons. He also had bladders that when blown into, were comfortable mattresses.

"Coleman's" he mysteriously replied, when I questioned him on the shelters.

~ * ~

I placed an arm about Morgana's shoulders as we gazed from a balcony to watch a swollen red sun begin to set. With a full stomach, an ale in one hand and my beloved at my side, I felt content. That was despite readying to spend the night in an ancient necropolis said to be swarming with armies of the dead.

"Did you hear that?" Morgana asked.

"Huh?"

"Listen."

I nuzzled her ear. "I hear nothing."

"There. Hear that?"

I sighed. Yes, I heard some faint, echoing clatter, but I did not want to admit it. It had been weeks since we had quiet time together.

I cocked my head. Were those voices?

"Come, we must investigate."

"Hold on. It be almost dark."

"All the more to act now," she replied, "before it becomes too dark."

She grabbed my arm and pulled me to the flight of stairs leading to street level.

"Wait. We must tell the others," I protested.

"We have no time. Besides, you heard my mother say we could leave if I be one of the parties. Do you not feel safe with me?"

The truth be that I would not feel safe in Urbemmortis with a dozen witches and mages. I made my feelings known with just a sigh and followed her down to the streets.

"There. It comes from that direction. Follow me," she declared excitedly.

We rushed down an avenue littered with the rubble of fallen, grotesque statues and the skeletons of the last wild beasts able to survive the advancing desert.

I grabbed Morgana's arm as we came to an intersection. I could hear clatter and voices. "Hold. Whatever hellish creatures we pursue, they be but around this corner."

Morgana licked her lips, took a deep breath and drew out her wand in preparation of a magical defense.

"Hold," I again ordered. "We cannot charge in blindly. I must first spy this out."

"Do it," Morgana tersely replied, almost too tense to speak.

I came to the last structure on the left side of the avenue and pressing myself closely against its wall, cautiously peered around the corner.

"What be it?" she whispered after a minute had passed.

I pulled myself back and answered, "Something beyond belief."

"What?" she impatiently asked.

I took one last peek and stepped back. "See for yourself."

After a brief hesitancy, Morgana placed a hand upon my shoulder and leaned forward. She gasped.

"So?' I asked.

"I, I do not believe it."

We stepped out into the street to gaze at a busy scene halfway down the block. Scaffolding covered the front of at least a dozen of the buildings. Several times that number of humans were apparently beginning work for the evening, climbing up the scaffolding or hauling buckets of rubble to a large pile of debris in the middle of the street. Witch globes were beginning to blaze to life, bathing the scene in a bluish light.

A large white sign with bright red lettering proclaimed, "The future site of Sunny Urbemmortis Haunt, a spooky oasis in the sands. Homes from fifteen hundred to four thousand square feet. Just minutes from a planned market and dragonport. Tell your friends."

Beneath it in smaller letters was, "Another project by Your Favorite Realtors."

We made our way to a woman examining parchments on a snapboard. She looked up to shout orders to several workers chiseling away at a bas-relief running beneath a roofline. "No, leave the fellow with the snake head and whatever that thing is with its mouth in its stomach. We need to leave a little ambience. Yes, go ahead and knock off that, ah, ugh. I cannot even look at it."

I cleared my throat and she turned to inspect us from head to feet. "You are early. The display units are not finished. The plumbing has been a nightmare."

"Sorry, but we are not whomever you are expecting," I said.

"Who then?" She stepped back and eyed us suspiciously. "What are you doing here? Spying for that masonry guild out of Macocahta? We told you, this be far out of your dominion. We will be filing papers for our homeowner's association next week."

Morgana stepped forward. "We are with a mission for the witch covens of Stagsford. What goes on here?"

The woman was startled. "You are what?" She looked both confused and slightly intimidated at the mention of witches.

"Witches? What concern be this to you?" she bristled while waving her hand at the bustling workers. "This be but a village revitalization."

"In Urbemmortis?" I asked. "Where the abandoned, gods forsaken streets are still trod upon by grub-white ghouls and the ghosts of ancient residents so evil they cannot pass on to where more mundane murderers, rapists, mutilators and genociders can?"

"You got it. Locale, locale, locale. Think of the bragging rights that come with living in the fabled city of death. At least that is what our marketing and investors are counting on. When one of our people came back and reported this place was as empty as a hobgoblin's date book, we knew we had to move fast. Think of it, a countless number of units just waiting to be flipped."

"Here in the middle of a blistering desert miles and miles from water? Who in their right mind would want or could live here?" I scoffed.

"It be not so hot in the winter and there be underground water we have tapped for the development. We plan on irrigating for croquet courses and putting in mineral baths. Many of our potential buyers will be older and only reside here during the cooler months. Our gross product margin will be unbelievable."

"We already have our realty office open for business," she continued, pointing across the street.

I could easily tell which of the buildings she referred to. It was the only one that had its window glass replaced. I shook my head in disbelief. What a crazy idea.

"For sure Urbemmortis be empty? No ghouls, demons, banshees, zombies…"

"Nada. Nothing," she cut me off. "We explored this city from end to end. Though we have noticed dragons occasionally coming and going from that tower."

She appointed to a tower in the center of the city, now a rosy hue from the setting sun. It was too distant to determine its height.

"We sent a worker to see who was there, but he never came back," she continued before cocking her head and examining us more closely. "Why again are you here?"

~ * ~

"So, Marl the Adventurer was a charlatan," said Hiidee, after Morgana and I related our visit. "All those thrilling bedtime tales are false? It was because of them that I took up the sword and sought adventure."

"At least the ones dealing with Urbemmortis," answered Morgana. "He might have traveled here, but the rest were fabrications to promote his speaking tours."

We sat around a witch's flame that cast dancing shadows across the roof. The stars brilliantly peppered the sky without street gaslights to dim them.

"Tomorrow, Lorenzo and I will investigate the tower," Morganna spoke. Until now she had remained silent. "It must be the site for those behind the malspells."

"I will accompany you, mother. This is my first case as a private inquisitor," Morgana firmly told her mother.

"I go where she goes," I added, just as determinedly.

"We go where the ferret goes," the two mercenaries spoke in unison.

"That be private inquisitor," I responded by rote. "It looks like we know what will be on tomorrow's schedule."

~ * ~

"What?" I exclaimed, then remembered we were to be discreet as we made our way into the city proper.

"You would buy one of these derelict buildings?" I continued in a

183

hushed tone. "That be lunacy. What would you do with it?"

"Look about you," Lorenzo replied with a sweep of his hand. "No matter how malevolent the original inhabitants were, they knew how to build. I wouldn't buy around here. As we circled Urbemmortis yesterday, I saw some choice real estate in the bordering hills. Rather palatial, in fact. It would be a good investment with the housing shortage now in Glavendale. Once the dragonport is finished, this will be a boom town."

Lorenzo be probably right, but for me it would be hard to erase memories from a lifetime of hearing foul tales of the city.

We walked single file, staying to the morning shadows of the buildings. Morganna and Hiidee led our party with Morgana and Hiilda to the back. We moved out of domestic neighborhoods into guild and market districts. The buildings were now four or five stories with many having display windows, minus any glass except for shards amongst the sand, and doors large enough for freight wagons. I guessed we had three miles to go before reaching the center and the tower.

"Nothing yet," spoke Morganna.

She gave such appraisals every ten minutes. The witch continually monitored for traces of magic. Morgana told me she and her mother would have walked even if not accompanied by the rest of us. The energy used with brooms would be detected if there were magic users in the tower.

I grew more nervous with every step. I was with two witches, but even they could be overwhelmed by superior numbers. What if our magical adversaries were backed by a garrison of hired blades? What chance would our four swords have against them?

"You seem a bit tense, little buddy."

"A bit tense?" I replied to Lorenzo. "We are only six, heading to who knows what awaits us at the heart of a primordial stronghold of mythical beings so malignant that even vague mentions of them were expunged from most ancient tomes. What if they have returned? A bit tense, you ask?"

"Here. You need a shot," Lorenzo replied in the vexing cheerful voice he uses in such situations. He pulled a flask from his pouch. I did not argue, but took a sip of the fiery drink he calls moonshine.

It slightly calmed me. Just what did the city builders look like? Were they the grubs with human-like heads in the murals? Maybe they were the upright cockroaches or the blue-eyed toads. It did not matter. They were all depicted as eager participants in truly vile pursuits.

With the rising of the sun came the oven heat of the desert. No wonder that renovation crew began its work in the evening. My eyes felt as if filled with grit and my sinuses ached deep into my head. I could imagine turning into human jerky, mummified by day's end.

A waterskin was passed around as we entered the heart of the city and gazed up at the tower looming fifteen stories above us. Morganna motioned for us to follow through a doorway. Once inside, I turned away from a faded mural depicting themes common to the other artworks we passed on our march – if one could ever link such nightmarish profanities to the word 'common.'

Lorenzo noticed my revulsions. "I think I will invest in a paint-making guild."

"There be not enough coatings to wipe such images from my mind. I would always know what horrors lie beneath," I replied, then turned to Morgana. "I am hoping, once established, our new private inquisitor agency will not specialize only in magical cases."

She knowingly smiled and touched my arm. "I should hope not. You are not alone in finding this case taxing."

I breathed a sigh of relief. "Thank the gods. I have had enough of irate mages. Give me a white-tunic embezzler or missing spouses. I am not eager to storm this tower, but if it means solving the case and returning to Duburoake, lead on."

Morganna stopped to study the surroundings. "I still detect no wards or magical activities. My daughter and I will head the climb to nullify possible curses or magical entrapments."

"I will also take lead," Hiilda spoke loudly. The halfling did not wilt beneath Morganna's glare. "There may well be traps that are not of a magical nature. I am well versed in pitfalls, arrow traps, snares, flooding rooms, whirling blades and falling blocks."

Morganna maintained her frostbite stare but for a moment, before coolly smiling and replying, "Yes, there is that. Please, lead the way."

Hiidee did not look happy at her smaller companion's volunteering, but remained silent.

I did not look forward to this venture for a reason beyond what magical perils we might face. There would be no elevators. The basement apparatus powered by draft animals would have been out of service for a millennium. It was exhausting just to think of fifteen flights of stairs.

Even battle-hardened Hiidee and Hiilda appeared tense as we entered the first-floor lobby. It was a vast open area, well-lit by the large front windows, but growing dimmer farther in. Sand drifts covered the flooring nearest the windows. Toward the back, nauseating floor mosaics were visible.

"There be the way," Hiilda observed and pointed to a door well.

We paused upon reaching it and looked through to see spiraling iron steps. The outer stairwell wall featured narrow windows. A thick layer of dust and sand was undisturbed. The top floors had not been gained this way.

Hiilda ventured first to closely inspect the steps at her feet as well as the undersides of those winding above us. She was satisfied enough to begin the climb and was followed by the two witches. Lorenzo and I were next with Hiidee guarding the rear.

The progression stopped as we were reaching the fourth floor. I leaned over the center railing and craned my neck upward. My companions' hushed tones softly echoed down the stairwell, though not loud enough for me to distinguish the words. Hiidee pushed past me and disappeared around the turn.

Lorenzo and I drew our swords. I did not want to impede any defenses the mercenaries or witches might be undertaking, but I chafed at the wait. Morgana's voice finally called down, "You can come up."

The four stood silently gazing at the scattered bones of what once were five or six halflings. Some of the larger bones were snapped as if broken for their marrow. Strewn amongst them were assorted pieces of dented armor and broken blades.

"The bones are brittle with age, but still long after the city was abandoned by its inhabitants," observed Morganna. "This scene played out less than two hundred years ago."

Hiilda kneeled to examine the broken skeletons more closely. "These are teeth marks. They died by beast and not magic."

I pushed a scrap of familiar cloth with the toe of my boot. "They were Blackwatch Goblins. They would not have gone down easily. I am not eager to discover what be capable of taking on a half-dozen goblins."

At the sixth landing we again halted. This time there was no way to tell what or how many met their end. There had to have been more than just a couple to leave such a large, now-dried mass of gore, specked with bits of hair, teeth and bone.

"This was magic," declared Morgana. "There be no doubt of it."

"There are no residual traces of magic remaining," her mother elaborated, "therefore this be not recent. It could also be several centuries old."

"There are also no signs of weapons," I observed, "which means they were probably witches or wizards."

Blackwatch goblins overcame by physical violence and others by magic. Were the perpetrators still around?

My legs were feeling the labor by the tenth floor. We climbed slowly enough that I was not out of breath. Sweat dried instantly in the arid air. As at the other landings, Morgana and one of the mercenaries did a brief exploration. So far, each level was found to be divided into two and three-room units connected by several hallways. There were no foot tracks, though bolts, nails, hinges and unidentifiable bits of iron littered the floors.

We paused at the thirteenth-floor landing.

"There is now an ambient presence of magic," the mother witch whispered. "It has been purposely muted so that only this close can it be detected."

"Fresh?" I whispered to Morgana.

"Yes," she whispered back.

On the fifteen floor we gathered about an imposing bronze door. No doubt everyone harbored questions similar to my own. What lay behind it? I took a deep, ragged breath that had nothing to do with climbing fifteen flights of stairs.

"There be a ward here," Morganna said as she brought forth her wand. "Move back. I will remove it."

I stepped forward and brushed my fingers across the metal. "This be new or recently burnished. There are no traces of green that comes with age."

The words were no sooner out of my mouth than the massive door explosively flew open.

"I warned you to stand back," I heard a taunting voice through the daze of being slammed backward and tumbling down several steps.

I painfully climbed to my feet as quickly as possible and drew my sword. The aches would inevitably make themselves known later, but for now that open door drew all my attention. As if frozen for a portrait, the witches stood with wands poised for either defense or attack, while the mercenaries warily stood with knees slightly bent and blades tightly clutched. Lorenzo was already out of sight.

Chapter Thirteen

"I am both frustrated and relieved," was my confession to Morgana as I sifted through the litter left behind. "I was not looking forward to some cataclysmic battle with maniacal wizards or madly grinning three-eyed goats, but that would have concluded this case. They must have seen us fly over yesterday."

"Still," I continued as she patted my arm, "no matter what, they left behind important clues in their rush to clear out. We now know there were several wizards and at least one witch."

The top floor was one large hall. Scattered about were toppled chairs and a small desk Morgana said was the type for crystal globes. There were also six bunks to the side.

"This belongs to an alumnus of the Stagsford Enchantress Preparatory Academy of the Occult Arts," Morgana exclaimed when I showed her an ink-stained quill. "It be from a Misty Mountain Griffin, rare enough that only the Stagsford academy uses them."

"Most likely that be Yansey, the graduate they said was unaccounted for. I am not sure she was here of her own accord." I held up a cord found near the quill. "This looks for shackling."

Morganna snatched the cord to briefly roll it between her fingers. "There remains a compulsory spell. No simple binding can hold a witch."

"According to the number of bunks, we are looking for five wizards and a hostage witch. Apparently not all Ghennison Viper Mages are dead," I added gloomily. Beneath one of the bunks was a forgotten purple peaked hat.

"While I was a captive of the mages, only their thirst for vengeance was mentioned," I related. "This group must be acting on its

189

own and was behind my first kidnapping and visit to the torturers – as well as the balauri. Working here saved them from the fate of their brethren."

Turning to Morgana and her mother, I affirmed, "It appears the mages are using a hostage witch for the malspells."

"She must be freed, and the vermin exterminated," Morganna spoke in a deceptively calm voice, but beneath, like an iceberg, was a coldness that spoke louder of death and vengeance than any shriek or curse.

I shivered, even in the desert heat. I could almost pity the surviving Ghennison Viper Mages – almost.

"Though that still leaves one or more witches at the Stagsford academy colluding with the mages. Someone on the inside aided in my kidnappings."

"I am sure the mages can be persuaded to name names," Morganna whispered.

I forced myself not to shudder.

"Where have they gone – back to their desert quarters?" I wondered.

"No. Death still stalks that warren," Morganna answered.

We continued our search of the top floor.

"These mages are certainly pigs," observed Hiidee from a far corner. "Look at this."

I had been sifting vainly through a small ash heap, most likely purposely destroyed parchments. I stood and walked to her side. There would have been the buzzing of flies and squirming maggots were this anywhere but the lifeless Cythnian Desert. We both contemplated their meal scraps of bone, gristle, fur and feathers.

"What be this?" I spied a blood-soaked foolscap.

It was a distasteful chore to retrieve the foul bit of wood-pulp paper from the rotting leftovers, but worth the effort. It had once been part of a meat wrapper. Written on it was, "If it moos, clucks, oinks or bleats – come to where the posh eat."

"Well, we now know where they have been," Lorenzo said from

over my shoulder. "I doubt Meats Be Us delivers out here."

"Meats Be Us?"

"A meat boutique."

"What? Make sense," I demanded.

"Haven't you been reading the Tattler? It's the latest rage. Meats Be Us is a craft butcher shop that specializes in hybrid meat cuts and sausages. You can buy steaks from a turtle crossed with an auroch, a chicken crossed with a mastodon, a unicorn crossed with a pig."

"That be so wrong," I sputtered, trying not to imagine such offspring.

"There are bills banning extreme crossbreeding before the Glavendale Assemblage," Lorenzo said, "but there is talk of dark coinage preventing passage."

"Dark coinage? Has the Tattler looked into this?"

"Their investigator died of an untimely 'accident' a month ago."

"Whatever." I was too mired in the current investigations to be distracted with the meat industry. "Where be Meats Be Us? It seems our only lead."

"In Iron Hill, a small village close to Stagsford."

"Iron Hill? Where have I heard that name?"

"It's a tourist town," Lorenzo patiently answered. "It was close to becoming as deserted as here after the mines petered out. Then a few of the remaining residents began marketing it as a quaint example of a more wholesome, bygone era. They have workshops on making flint kitchen knives and dishware from gourds, campfire cooking classes, gift shops, antique stores and Meats Be Us."

I was trying to fathom what Lorenzo was saying. "Meats Be Us is part of that? How is mixed-species sausage nostalgic?"

"The promoters point out we already have centaurs and sphinxes. Look at the chimera – part lion, part goat and part snake, or the cockatrice – part flying rooster and part snake."

"Yes, but we don't eat any of them," I feebly protested. "Anyway, Adalbert will be checking in early afternoon. I guess I need go to Iron Hill."

"First we check in with the covens gathering in Stagsford,"

Morganna firmly stated. "Head Mistress Kahlan will want an update on our progress."

"Or lack thereof," I responded.

"Not so," said the daughter. "We now know for certain the wizards behind the attacks are Ghennison Viper Mages and they are forcing a young spellwriter to create the malspells."

"There be that," I sighed. "At least a handful of Ghennison Viper Mages will stand out. Can you send a bulletin over the crystals asking to be alerted to their sightings?"

Our discussion was abruptly ended by a sharp echoing cry from Hiilda. "Jak! Come. You must see this."

All heads snapped to the mercenary standing to the far end of the chamber. As one, we swiftly made our way to her side. I involuntarily drew in a sharp breath at the sight of what had prompted her call.

Hiilda had found the owner of the discarded hat. Like a tossed-aside rag doll lay the crumpled body of a Ghennison Viper Mage. I dropped to my knees to examine the thoroughly dead necromancer. A powerful blade stroke had come close to decapitating the mage and left a black pool of nearly dried blood.

"Get not in the viper's fluid," Morganna warned me. "It will eat your flesh until you are naught but bone."

I climbed hastily to my feet. "It appears we might not have been the reason behind the mages' hasty flight. For whatever the cause, here lies one not quick enough."

"This be a puzzle," said Morganna as she turned to Lorenzo. "I would say this be your work if not for personally knowing of your whereabouts for the past two days."

"Why do you say that?" I asked.

Her daughter answered. "If this be the work of a wizard or witch, the death would be by spell or curse. You see it be not. Yet it be almost impossible for a non-magical being to physically attack a mage – except for Lorenzo with his off-world protection."

~ * ~

The anticlimactic march back to our encampment did allow me to go over the events of the past week. We now knew surviving Ghennison Viper Mages were behind the crystal malspells, with the aid of a young witch, either voluntarily or not. This case could only be concluded by routing the mages and ousting the one or more conspirators within the academy. Would the mysterious death of the viper mage complicate this?

I fell back to Lorenzo's side. "Come on, that dead mage. Spill it," I whispered.

"Whatever can you mean?" he answered.

"Now I am certain you know something," I hissed. "That false guileless tone be a dead giveaway. Be Michael involved?"

"What?"

"Do not 'what' me. Michael, your brother. As you, he is from a world devoid of magic. He could have killed the mage."

"Could have? Sure, but why? My brother doesn't get out much. I can't imagine him leaving Duburoake to travel halfway across the Cythnian Desert to battle Ghennison Viper Mages."

"Truly?" I asked.

"I have no reason to believe otherwise."

I believed him. I have never known Lorenzo to outright lie. That still did not mean his brother was not the culprit, only that Lorenzo did not believe so.

~ * ~

I was glad not to have continued straight to Iron Hill. The cellar-cooled ales at the Any Witch Way Inn had taken the edge off the bruises received at the Urbemmortis tower. A full night's sleep was also welcomed. Morgana reported to the senior witches of the covens, a task I gladly ducked. I could not imagine much worse than to be in the same room with a dozen easily-irritated masters of the magical arts.

But now I was at Iron Hill, only to find we arrived amidst an annual celebration. Families, as well as drunken celebrants, filled the narrow cobblestone streets. Market tents circled the village square and filled the side streets, offering an array of cheap tourist items and spicy foods.

"I shudder to think what kind of kind of crossbreed those drumsticks are from," I said.

They seemed to be a favorite meal and one alone had more meat on it than a whole turkey.

"Relax," replied Lorenzo. "They're from elephant birds. No, not because they are a cross between elephants and poultry."

Morganna remained in Stagsford to meet with the gathering witches. There was to be a central council meeting to discuss the attacks on the crystals as well as the Stagsford academy.

I felt safe from a magical assault among the thick press of beings. The panic created by the appearance of Ghennison Viper Mages would be warning enough. There was yet the danger of hired thugs and even though I was keeping a sharp eye out, an assassin would have no trouble suddenly emerging from the crowd. Hiidee and Hiilda were well aware of that danger and walked with hands on sword hilts, as did I.

"Here it be," Morgana announced.

Meats Be Us was an impressive establishment for such a rural village. It was three store-fronts wide and stood alone at the edge of the village, with a thick grove of trees to the back. The motto we had seen on the meat wrapper was emblazoned in bold red lettering beneath the roofline. A steady line of shoppers streamed in and out of the large double doors.

Once inside, we were met with a tumultuous array of spicy and smoky scents from the cases that lined the walls and aisles. Dried meats hung from cords over the main counter. Posters depicted a variety of bizarre creatures with names such as Porkapines, Bullphins and squirralope.

"I hope they observe the Human, Werefolk Accords that forbid the eating of flesh from intelligent creatures," I muttered. "That roast labeled as a lemurkey looks suspiciously like a skinned brownie."

"There be a chill spell on the fresh meats. Wizard's work," Morgana informed us.

"Can you tell which cabal? Viper mages?" I asked.

"No. It be too common a spell."

We arrived at the pay counter and I made my way to the front of a line.

"Excuse me. I need to speak with you a minute," I said to one of the clerks.

"What? You the crowned prince? Get to the back of the line and wait your turn," barked the human beanpole with pimples as red as his hair.

I flipped open my leather wallet and flashed my brass badge showing I was bonded and licensed by the Duburoake Royal Council of Public Safety as a private inquisitor. Yes, at a quick glance it could be mistaken for that of an inquisitor with the Glavendale Royal Constabulary. I am always happy to correct any such misconception – if asked.

"You would do well to cooperate with my investigation – or perhaps you would like to spend time somewhere dark and dank?" I snarled.

Notice there was no mention it would be a royal dungeon. As with the badge, I am happy to correct any misconception – if asked.

The dunce paled even more when he saw that I was accompanied by two fierce mercenaries and a witch. He frantically threw off his apron, waved us around the counter and called out, "Icky, fill in."

We followed him through swinging doors and into hellscape fit for an Urbemmortis fresco. Small creatures cried and screamed from stacked cages. Workers with bloody cleavers went back and forth from piles of assorted carcasses to butcher blocks. The smell was overwhelming. Even Lorenzo seemed rattled.

"Look, I just work in the front. Ask anyone. Do not know anything or want to. Yah have to talk to Dino. He be in the back office."

He was all too happy to scamper back to the front. It was a very unpleasant stroll back to Dino's office, so I will not go into greater detail.

"Whatdayahwant?" Dino fired off, when I knocked at the open door to his cramped office. His bloody apron spoke of him not being a hands-off boss. He came from behind his desk and again spoke a sentence

195

as one word, "Whoareyah?"

"Jak Barley," I snapped back and flashed my badge.

He grabbed my wrist before I could slip my wallet back into my pouch.

"A ferret, huh," he snarled. "Duburoake at that. Yah got no business nosing around here."

Dino's bluster quickly ended at the sound of Hiidee's and Hiilda's drawn swords. Morgana pushed her way to the front and in a voice doing her mother proud, curtly ordered, "Release him."

That, the portly proprietor did, and stepped back. In a forced halfhearted bravado he demanded, "What, ah, what do you want? You have no right to come barging in. I am a legitimate shop owner. And that was just malicious gossip about the gnomes."

I eyed the nervous butcher for a moment before turning and waving a hand at a pile of discarded offal, bones and fur. "I wager that be tasty fare for Ghennison Viper Mages."

Whatever Dino believed we were there for, it certainly was not that. "W-w-what? M-m-mages?" He pulled himself together and continued, "Ghennison Viper Mages have never visited my shop."

"He speaks truth," Morgana spoke softly. She obviously was relying on truth-telling magic. Yet the mention of the mages invoked a near panic response.

"Yet they are customers?"

His pursed lips and clenched jaw were answer enough.

"Recently? In the last couple of days? Have you delivered? To where?" I fired off my questions.

"We, ah, we do not deliver."

I grabbed his tunic and yanked him close, something I immediately regretted because of his rancid breath.

"I tire of this. My two friends here keep their swords as well-honed as any of your butcher knives, yet you should fear Morgana's impatience more."

M-M-Morganna," he blurted in fright at the name. "Ah, but she be too young. You canna fool me."

"Morganna be my mother and some say she seems but a kitten compared to me," my intended spoke in a chilling voice that even sent a shiver up my spine. I certainly hoped that was but theatrics and not a hint of things to come.

The dam broke. "The Boaster Lads, they buy chests of meat. Many at a time. I overheard one say they were but middlemen for mages. Yesterday they came, but wanted a fraction of their normal orders."

Boaster Lads – a gang known for a propensity for violence and insane hatred of halflings or any other non-human group. It would be just like them to align with the mages.

"To where?" Hiilda demanded after pressing her sword against Dino's throat. She as well was becoming impatient with the butcher.

"I-I, ah, I do not know. I swear."

The blade drew a trickle of blood. "Not good enough."

"I really do not know, but several will be here at noon for an extra box of smoked Liziger tongues."

I released the knave and warned, "We will be back. If there be any word that you have warned them…" I nodded to a glowering Morgana to complete the sentence.

"Yah, sure, yah have my word. But, ah, do not blame me if you come to wish you had never met them."

~ * ~

We killed time by strolling through the booths and tents, pausing to listen to the various troubadours and bards. Though the aromas drifting from the food tents were tempting, recalling the back room of Meats Are Us was enough to suppress my appetite.

I stopped to watch a fire breather and, at the end of his act, turned to make a remark to the others. They were not to be seen in the swirling mass of visitors. It was close to noon. My best course of action would be to meet them at Meats Are Us.

I waded into the crowd and was soon at the shop's rear pickup and delivery entrance. A foul-smelling creek flowed through the trees to the back of the shop. There was no doubt its defilement the result of killing-floor waste. I picked a concealed spot to watch for both my friends and the thugs – I hoped not for long, due to the stomach-churning stench.

"I regret there be not the time to make your suffering a week-long amusement."

There be no adequate description to relate the effect that death-rattle had upon me. I turned to view a visage as abhorrent as the voice.

I was barely able to reply without revealing my distress. "Ah, then we should choose a date that be more convenient for you. I believe I have an opening next…"

"Stop the prattle," the Ghennison Viper Mage hissed. This was a younger necromancer, in that his teeth and the whites of his eyes were only a light yellow and his wrinkles not yet deep enough to hide a nest of ants.

"What a coincidence to see you lurking in the shrubbery. Come here often?"

He ignored the quip. Even I could feel the energy buildup that had my hair beginning to rise. I was about to be toasted.

"Hah, Barley. You are the fool. Whatever pathetic weapon you think to surprise me with is useless."

I hoped the mage would not notice my hand sliding into my pouch. I did not answer. Lorenzo has always advised striking first and then having a chat – if there was anyone left to chat with.

With a flick of my thumb, I opened Lorenzo's gift and plunged it into the surprised necromancer's throat. Normal iron would have rebounded before reaching the mage, as well as turning white hot in the attacker's hand – but not with what Lorenzo called a Swiss army knife from his home world.

There was no time for gloating. I doubted the small blade could deliver a killing thrust. I spun around and sprinted to Meats Be Us. A loud gurgling was all the mage could muster.

Dino was standing outside his office when I burst through the door. His eyes widened and his mouth shaped an O as I flew past.

"You should be more careful who you invite," I shouted over my shoulder.

He must have somehow warned the mages.

I was halfway across the killing floor when the wizard stumbled in after me, still gurgling attempts at incantations. The wound did not leave him totally bereft of wizardry. Purple ropes of scalding light whipped wildly from his flaying hands. They sliced through butcher blocks, burned through the heaps of offal and slashed apart cages. Flames burst out about the room. The deafening screams of employees and freed animals added to the chaos created by the blinding oily smoke. A scream from Dino was abruptly cut short.

I continued blindly and blundered through the door to the salesroom. Buyers were already stampeding out the entrance. Nothing like screams of the damned to clear a room. I brushed a cuff sleeve across my weeping eyes and followed. Only upon reaching outside could I finally gasp in clean air.

Panic is contagious. Those milling in the street had no idea why the sudden onslaught of a terrified mob, but they enthusiastically joined the rout. I looked back to see the mage stumbling amidst a deluge of bizarre creatures as they exited the burning building.

No matter how I dodged left and right among the streets and alleys, the mage doggedly followed. The erratic attacks continued to send tents, wooden booths and permanent buildings ablaze. Two villagers attempting to tackle the crazed wizard were immediately cremated. I barely escaped a tumbling cupola that exploded into vicious shards when hitting the ground. I suddenly found myself running across the village green and, in the open, swerving to place a statue's pedestal between me and the crazed mage. A shadow warned me to dodge just in time, as a thirty-foot statue of General Lonbart came toppling down, its head rolling past me. The wizard was at least ending brawls at the village council over whether or not to remove the statue. Lonbart was a divisive figure in the Bayou Rebellion.

Rounding a corner and briefly looking back, I saw that the mage was not running, but gliding a foot off the ground. He now was using only one hand to spew his firestorms. The other was clasped tightly to his throat. His robe was wet with black blood. The mage's magic was obviously not up to healing wounds created by off-world iron. Would he ever weaken? The chase seemed to go on and on.

Damn! I barely missed being crisped. The streets were littered with rubble and smoke, but at least devoid of people and miraculously free of bodies. This would not go down as one of the more successful festivals, though it would be memorable. I now knew where much of the Ghennison Viper Mage's treasure would be spent – as a restitution fund.

I entered a bucolic street lined with elms. The quaint cottages were set behind picket fences amidst flowering bushes. Totally exhausted, I could run no longer. The only course was to hide in a bungalow before the mage appeared. That hope was quickly dashed. I threw myself to the side and a purple bolt passed but a foot away. That he no longer directed continuous streams of fire signaled he was weakening.

I turned to face the wizard with the plan to leap behind a nearby tree when the next charge was thrown. From there I would flee into a house and out the back door. He raised his free hand and I tensed in anticipation.

"Urg-g-g," the mage croaked and collapsed.

Bewildered, it took me a minute before cautiously approaching the fallen figure. Very little black blood puddled about him. Most bled out during the chase. A nudge from my boot drew no response. I wished for gloves when flipping him over. Eyes already clouding with death, stared back.

"There yah be."

What now? I straightened to face three loutish figures in aprons stained with blood and soot. The lead rogue gripped a cleaver. Though still shaken and tired, I would still gladly face Meat Be Us butchers anytime over necromancers.

"Yes, here I be. What do you want?"

"What dah yah think?" he snarled. "Yah burned down our shop and freed the meaties."

"Ah, excuse me. Your boss called in the mage who did the burning and freeing."

"But it was because of you," he replied.

The other two, clutching degutting knives, growled in agreement.

A swirling black cloud of smoke spread out eerily behind them.

"Fine. I see there be no arguing with knaves as you." I punctuated the comment with the rasp of a drawn sword. I was becoming irked.

My swagger was uncalled for. Each butcher outweighed me by forty or sixty pounds with biceps the size of smoked hams. They moved with the intention of encircling me. Where in hades were my friends?

I flinched as a blur sped over my head and into the midst of the ne'er-do-wells. A cyclone of feathers and fur tore into the lead butcher, followed by a wild spray of blood. You cannot scream with a torn throat. The remaining two stood stunned as their leader toppled backward. I was as frozen, gawking stupidly until one turned to run. He was overtaken, and his wildly flaying arms about his head did not save him. Nor the third and last rogue.

I took several steps back. It was too far to seek shelter in a cottage. I could only grip my sword and wait for the lightning attack to be repeated. Instead, the creature circled once and landed but not eight feet before me.

We stared eye-to-eye. It was one of Meat Be Us's escaped crossbreeds. With the head and body of a cottage cat, it came equipped with the beak and wings of an eagle and raking claws of a wolverine. An odd choice of mix for meat. It stood knee-high with a five-foot wingspan. I was at a loss of what action to take as it calmly approached. I remained frozen with sword held before me. That proved to be the correct response.

The creature closely circled several times before butting its head against my legs. Silent until now, it began loudly purring. It was, I decided, associating me with its liberation.

"Ah, nice kitty." I kneeled and began stroking between its wings. The fur was as soft as that of a regular cat.

"We've been worried sick about you, and here you are littering the place with corpses and playing with flying kitties," Lorenzo spoke as my accomplices approached.

"Careful," I warned Morgana as she rushed forward. "I do not know how the 'kittie' will react."

I needed not worry. It peacefully sat back and watched as Morgana slowly approached. Kneeling next to me, she scratched behind the creature's ears. It purred even louder.

"You seem to collect a strange menagerie of pets," Morgana observed. "How did this one come about?"

"It's his animal magnetism," offered Lorenzo.

"I am not sure. I think it associates me with its freedom and the destruction of the abattoir. It seems not to have a problem with anyone other than those of Meats Be Us."

She turned her head to take in the dead necromancer. "However, did you kill the mage?"

I looked to my friend. "It seems iron from Lorenzo's world is wizard bane. Too bad I lost it after the attack."

"I'll get you another one," he offered.

"That would be helpful, but how about in a larger size?"

Morgana moved to the mage's corpse. Reaching into her witch's shoulder satchel, she rummaged about until producing a thick chunk of chalk. I watched nervously as she drew a pentagram about the body.

"Ah, what are you doing? This be not of the dark arts, I hope."

"No," she answered while climbing to her feet. "I am not bringing the dead back to life; nor forcing a departed soul back into a rotting body. That creates a demonish shadow of a departed spirit, a perversion of what once lived. This be a spell; but allows us to question a newly-dead's soul before it departs."

"Somehow bringing forth even a current inhabitant of a Ghennison Viper Mage's corpse be not a calming thought."

I could see Hiidee and Hiilda agreed. They were taking several steps backward and nervously grasped the hilts of their swords.

"We are doing this because?" I asked.

"I hope this mage can tell us why they attack our crystal communications, who at the academy be a traitor and where the others have taken to ground with the kidnapped witch."

I was doubtful. "Even deceased, you think the mage will reveal all that?"

"We shall see."

It be dreadfully painful to hear the dead language of the even deader Xlantian race spoken by a human tongue. Why both witches and wizards rely on incantations spoken in such archaic and arcane languages has always puzzled me. Lorenzo was probably right when saying they be no different than barristers who use obtuse words and phrases to maintain their trade's exclusiveness. Whatever the reason, I and the others were forced to press the heels of our hands to our ears. The cat/eagle/wolverine was agitated as well and took to the air.

All eyes were glued to corpse which by now had taken on a greyish cast.

Drawing in a deep breath after finishing the spell, Morgana started off with a simple question, "Who are you?"

Even dead, the mage was still gurgling. Its answer was unintelligible. I cringed as the witch placed her fingers over the wound. "Who are you?"

"Mehdoohs."

I was seriously creeped. Hearing the voice of a living Ghennison Viper Mage be bad enough, but from a corpse… It seemed to emanate not only from the blue lips of the mage, but from the air about us.

"Are you behind the malspells attacks?"

"Yes-s-s-s," came a serpent's hissing.

"Do you hold a witch prisoner?"

"Yes-s-s."

"Where?" Morgana asked again after there was no answer. "Where, Mehdoohs, where?"

"Let me go. Now, I command you!" The mage's arrogance was surfacing.

"Where are they?"

"This be agonizing. Release me."

"First you must tell me where your compatriots are."

"Curse you, witch. I will not answer," the mage's shade howled.

I clenched my teeth at the hatred seething in the spirit's unnerving screech.

"Know that I will hold you until you speak."

A wail grew from a low hum to an ear-piercing shriek. It abruptly ended as Morgana rapped a ring against the mage's forehead. The ring's large jewel flashed a fiery red.

"Know that your histrionics serve you naught. Where are they?"

"Beneath the Stagsford Dorga temple ruins. In the catacombs."

"Why the malspells? What be the crystals to you?"

"Coin."

"What? You were paid?"

"Yes-s-s."

"Paid? To kidnap a witch? To disrupt crystal calling?"

"Yes-s-s."

"Who? Give me names. Who paid you?"

"Witches."

"What witches?"

The cadaver remained silent.

"What witches? Of what coven?"

Still no reply. Morgana sighed and stiffly climbed to her feet. "I could hold him no longer. He be gone."

"Whoa, witch. That was badass." All eyes turned to Lorenzo. "That's a compliment," he quickly responded to the wondering looks.

"Yes, that was badass," Morgana agreed with a laugh. "I wish my mother could have been here. Such binding be no easy task."

I was with Morgana when she belatedly discovered her budding powers and through her academy years developing those abilities. This clash with the mage's shade only reinforced what I was discovering. Morgana had come into her own as a witch – whether the idea frightened me or not. I could no longer think of her as a witchling.

One thing for sure that did frighten me – when the mage's shade said its accomplices were in the subterranean burial vaults for priests of the now deposed and deceased Dorga, the Fish-Headed God of Death.

Sergey journaled my near-death experiences with the foul deity in The Temple of Dorga, Fish-Headed God of Death, and the Case of the Seven Dwarves. It was in the last-mentioned chronicle that I first met Morgana.

Glavendale abounds with sects and cults that honest folks shun, but none were as loathsome as the devotees and diabolic priests of Dorga.

It was said all neophytes had to ride a goat naked and blindfolded while drinking the blood of an infant before entering the sect. I twice found myself a prisoner in the dank dungeons of the Dorga priests and their torturers. In the end, the Stagsford temple was reduced to rubble.

I could not help but think back to one of the incidents.

~ * ~

I was met at the chamber door by an apprentice torturer, a lanky lad with a swarm of pimples about his face like red ants pouring from a disturbed nest.

"Bring him in and chain him over there," the apprentice ordered the guards in a bored voice. "I be still heating the irons and yet to clean and polish the tools from the master's last task."

"I must say one thing for you torturers," I told the apprentice after the guards left and my hands were chained to the wall. "No cobwebs, rats or rotting skeletons lying about. Everything looks spotless. I am sure your mother must be very proud of you."

The apprentice was busy at a sink washing an assortment of knives, hooks, pliers and clamps.

"Shut your mouth, dead man," he snapped in ill humor. He turned to face me and pointed to one of the many strange contrivances that furnished the chamber. "See that? It be a spinning jenny. Just got 'er in. She slices, dices, chops and grates."

"Seems like a lot of machine just to make a salad."

He laughed, but it was not the kind of chuckling to bring joy to anyone's heart.

"That be right, dead man, and you be the carrot."

He went back to washing the tools of his trade. I prayed he would continue with his back to me. As quickly as possible for one with both hands chained, I propped up a foot against the wall and fumbled for my pouch of metal slivers. It took but another second to pick the simple lock.

Close by on the wall was a rack of oddly shaped knives. I carefully removed a blade and silently made my way to the apprentice.

"Do not move, my young torturer, or it will be your own blood that be scrubbed from the floor," I ordered, as I placed the blade against his throat. "Do what I say and you will live to burn and batter another night."

I led the lad to the rather whimsical device of gears and springs he called the spinning jenny. It came with manacles.

"You will never escape," he said, as I firmly secured him to the contrivance. "When you are returned, I shall ask the master if I may personally work on you. First, I will insert slivers under your nails and drive needles into your eyeballs. I will..."

"Put a cork in it," I ordered as I waved the knife under his nose, taken aback by the youngster's villainous outburst. He was glaring at me like a taxman who had just had his nose hairs plucked.

"I will have you begging for death, though it will be meaningless mumbles after I have cut the lips from your face," he began again.

I sighed and leaned forward. "One must not make such promises when tethered so."

Something clicked. Looking down where I had been resting my hand, I saw I had moved one of the several levers.

"No, you blockhead," screamed the apprentice.

"What did I tell you about such language?" I said and rapped him in the head with the knife handle.

"Pull it back, pull it back," the lad was now begging.

I looked down. Which one had I pushed? It seemed to me it was the third one to the right. I pulled it and suddenly there was a whirring noise. The entire contraption began a slow bending at odd angles.

"No, the other one, the other one," he was screaming again.

Now I was becoming nervous. I yanked on another lever and suddenly from the sides of the engine of torture emerged a whirling fan of blades. Pushing the lever in reverse failed to stop anything. I was now desperately shoving and pulling the levers. It was hard to think with him screaming so.

The apparatus was a clever device. Who would have guessed there were all those spinning screws and twirling blades tucked out of sight? I had to jump back when the blood began flying. It was a sight too horrible to contemplate. He was lucky in that I had activated so many of the machine's accessories at one time, so it was a quick death by slicing and dicing.

~ * ~

With the demise of Dorga and disbanding of his priesthood and devotees, the land was littered with abandoned temples. Morganna assumed residency in a deserted Duburoake temple. While many would find it unsettling living within walls claiming such dark histories, it seemed to suit my future mother-in-law. Big surprise.

I felt a calming moment when Morgana wrapped her arms about me. She leaned back to look into my eyes and whispered, "I was heart-wrenched when we could not find you. The village was ablaze, people screaming. I knew the mages be after you. Lorenzo said not to worry, you always escape harm."

"I told her it is better to be lucky than smart," Lorenzo spoke as he walked to our side. "Once again I am proved correct."

I flinched as a shadow passed across us. The abattoir escapee was back. It circled twice before landing and joining us.

Morgana scratched its head and spoke, "I believe I have found just the right house pet for my mother. Her black mamba died last year and I believe this one would fit right in. I shall name it Fluffy."

"If not, I believe Hiidee and I would have it join us," added Hiilda. "I would name it Throatshredder."

"Good," I sighed in relief. "I still must find a permanent home for a seven-headed dragon."

Another shadow passed over us. "Hah. You must be done here as there be nothing left to burn."

"Must I never leave your sides?" Adalbert huffed upon landing. "I briefly am absent and each time I return to find mayhem and ruin. Right here we have three skinbags that appear as through a meat grinder. And look, a wizard's corpse. This be by your hand, Barley? Am I right? Oh my, over there. Look. There be a building still standing. Do we need to wait for the ferret to make a clean sweep?"

"Very droll. That be private inquisitor, big lizard. For your information, the corpse at your feet be the culprit behind this chaos and ruin."

I paused. Fluffy, Throatshredder or whatever, gave an excited trill and launched itself onto the dragon's back. It happily continued its half mewing, half chirping. I held my breath as Adalbert craned his head about to examine the strange creature. One chomp from the cranky dragon and Fluffy would end as a meal.

"What be this?" he asked. After giving a quick account, Adalbert nudged it once with his snout and announced, "It will be called Scout. You skinbags have caused it enough distress. It stays with me. My hatchlings need a pet."

Chapter Fourteen

"Are you sure I need attend?" I whined for the third time. "After all, you are the spellcaster face of our partnership. I am just the ordinary, magicless private inquisitor."

"Nonsense," Morgana replied as she brushed lint off the outfit from my aunt's garden party. "You are the celebrated inquisitor who brought about the downfall of the death-god Dorga, destroyed the assassin's guild and prevented the return of the Dark Lords."

"Yes," I sighed, "but I would almost rather face all that again than a crowded room of witches – who are also the most powerful ones of the realm."

"Do not be the toddler."

The Stagsford annual gathering of witches included a banquet for the leadership of the Glavendale covens. It was an important social event in that it strengthened and created bonds among witches across the country. This year's assemblage was even more imperative with the attacks on the academy and crystal networks. The Grand Gathering was also an historic event for the covens.

"I should be preparing for tomorrow's visit to catacombs," I halfheartedly continued. "Chasing down the viper mages in those dank warrens be no simple task."

"You are right. It be a dangerous undertaking. With those witches arriving that you find so intimidating, I will ask Mother to lead a group to find the mages."

I admit part of me found the notion appealing. I was not looking forward to facing a group of necromancers in the bone-filled crypts of the Dorga priesthood. Who knows how many restless ghosts of the evil clerics still roam beneath the temple ruins? I must confess feeling a bit nervous at the prospect of meeting such spirits.

I have always felt uncomfortable with shades, even as a child when a playmate drowned in a pickle vat. His ghost displayed a nasty disposition and twisted sense of humor that he possessed in life – which must account for not continuing to wherever spirits are supposed to proceed. Too many times I was wakened in the dead of night by his cold clammy hands. That was the first time I called upon Olmsted's talents, well developed even when we were children. My hunchbacked half-brother trapped the malevolent phantasm in the body of a scum trout and we fed it to a particularly sullen neighbor lady who later puked up a bright green discharge. My stepfather would have beaten us both if he had not also loathed the old bat.

"No, that would be akin to releasing a pack of direpoodles in a pixie commune," I answered Morgana, my vanity getting the better of me. Once on a case, I pride myself for not being deterred by threats or peril. "They would fry the mages first and think about questioning them later. We need at least one alive to interrogate."

"Ah, I knew my brave private inquisitor would not shirk the challenge. If you are up to that, I know you can survive dining at the coven hall with my mother and her colleagues."

I wondered if her assurances were trustworthy when entering the high-ceiling banquet ballroom of the Stagsford Coven Hall. I found the yellowish light cast by the witch lights creepy. With usually just witches present for these gatherings, I decided it could not be to off balance guests. They must actually enjoy the baleful hue that made everyone' complexion that of a fading bruise.

"Ah, so what do you think of this lighting for our future quarters? I asked Morgana. "Go well with the carpeting? Maybe for the nursery?"

"Oh, no. It be too cheerful. We will need something more somber," Morgana matter-of-factly replied.

I gave her a side glance and she burst out laughing. "Do not worry, Jak. This hue is because of the hall's extreme protective wards. The spells affect the witch globe lighting."

"Good evening, Witch Morgana and Master Jak Barley," an apprentice witch greeted us. "Seats have been reserved for you. Please follow me."

A lengthy table ran along the far wall where seated were more than a dozen adepts from the various covens. Morganna sat between Head Mistress Kahlan of the Kuu Academy and Head Mistress Mirthia of the Stagsford Academy. We were led to a small table not far from the front – to be met with a frosty glare from its sole occupant. The ancient witch was as gnarled and wrinkled as a millennial troll tree.

Morgana ignored the look and greeted the ancient witch with a smile. I nodded while pulling out Morgana's chair.

"Hmpf. At least they be good for something."

"I beg your pardon?" Morgana replied.

"You should beg pardon, bringing a male into our coven hall. No respect for tradition. What next, elves? And do not sass me," she ordered when turning to me. "I may be old, but I can still hurl a curse. With a snap of my fingers, you could be covered with maggot-infested boils looking like tiny fish bowls."

"Grandmama, please behave yourself. He be a guest," pleaded a young witch as she seated herself. "I am Jasnora. You will have to excuse my great-grandmother, Heridine. She can be a bit tetchy."

I guessed Jasnora to be in her mid-twenties, as lean as the brooms witches ride and several inches above six-foot in height. Though her grandmama was pale in complexion with grey eyes, Jasnora was the color of mahogany. The young witch's frizzy black hair was that of a seeding dandelion.

"Excuse me, nothing. You can say what you want when you are one hundred and twenty in years," the elder witch snapped back. "I have attended far too many of these boring dinners. For camaraderie, hah. Just a chance to hear and spread the latest dirt on each other. Gossiping old cows, they are. And now we have a man here."

Glaring at me, she barked, "Well, what do you have to say for yourself?"

"I think you are an ill-mannered, grouchy old witch," I answered. "Could you please pass that pitcher of ale."

There followed a stunned silence. Jasnora paled and turned to her great-grandmother with an expression fearful of what would come next. Morgana tensed and I gently covered her closest hand to pause any defensive magics she might reflexively cast.

The elder witch's brows furled and she raised one hand. I squeezed Morgana's to reaffirm not to react. All eyes were on Heridine as her fingers slowly glided above the table to come to rest on the ale pitcher's handle, then to slide it to me.

"Hah, Morganna said you were an impertinent rogue," cackled the witch. "She be right. We cannot have one of our own marrying some milksop. Though speaking truth, I be not surprised. It would take some nerve to woo the daughter of Morganna."

I managed to pour myself an ale without spilling any. "May I?" I asked while nodding to Heridine's cup.

"Fill it up and keep 'em coming. It be the only way to survive the evening. If the speeches do not kill you, the dodo casserole will. You, Morgana. Have you nothing to say?"

"Only that I totally forgot something my mother once said of you."

"Ah, and what was it?"

"That you would burn down an orphanage if you could get a laugh," Morgana answered.

"And you, Jasnora. Were you in on this?" I asked.

"No, really. One never knows what Grandmama will do or say now that she borders on senility."

I finished filling the other cups and we continued our conversation until we were served. Heridine was right about the dodo casserole, as well about the following presentations given by the witches at the head table. Still, I would rather be bored around witches than the alternative.

Witch Kahlan gave an account of the investigation into the malspell attacks, derived from what was reported by Morgana and her mother. A hum of astonishment followed the telling of our trip to Urbemmortis, followed by an angry silence at the mention of the Ghennison Viper Mages and their misdeeds.

"So, you plan to seek the mages in the Dorga temple ruins. I must give you a warning," Heridine leaned over and said in a raspy voice.

"That be?" I asked, fearing to learn of some new threat in the catacombs.

"Leave early. Look at the faces around you. The attacks on witches and now the academy has incensed them. Hatred of the viper mages goes back centuries, but it was feared any retribution could lead to another wizard-witch war. Every sorceress here will be eagerly volunteering for the mission. They would turn your search for information into a mage massacre."

"She be right," Morgana agreed. "We need slip out that side door. First you, and then I will follow."

"One more thing," Heridine spoke in a lower tone, touching my arm as I rose. "No matter what they say, the Murky Forest Coven returns, and lies low waiting for its day."

Great, I thought as I made my way to the exit. The witches responsible for the depraved décor in the Stagsford Academy foyer are still about. Still, Stagsford Academy Mistress Mirthia said the Murky Forest Coven no longer exists and has not for more than a century. Even if the coven survives in secret, what could it have to do with the malspells attacks?

Morgana joined me in the hallway. "Why the face?"

"Did you hear what Heridine said? The Murky Forest Coven still exists."

"There have always been such rumors," replied Morgana. "Secret cults, dark conspiracies, clandestine world powers – they become obsessions. The Murky Forest Coven was like the bogeyman in children's bedtime stories."

"You were told frightening tales as a child before bed?" I asked.

"Of course. They were the only kind my mother knew."

~ * ~

"I am really not happy with this," I admitted to Lorenzo as we waited in the lobby for the rest to arrive. We were leaving while it was still dark to attract less attention. "I would ask that the mother witch join us, but I know Morgana would take it as having little faith in her abilities."

Truth be told, I would not feel safe if an entire coven joined us. That goes for Hiidee and Hiilda. Even a phalanx of mercenaries would offer little reassurance. I hate adventures.

I have had enough ventures into the bowels of the earth. I am developing an aversion to any place that could have grass growing above it. Adding salt to the wound be that this netherworld of mummies be beneath the ruins of a Dorga temple. Who knows how many vile ghosts of its priests roam the catacombs?"

"I am not done," I said as Lorenzo was about to speak. "Of the five mages at the tower in Urbemmortis, one was mysteriously killed there and another died at Iron Hill. That means three Ghennison Viper Mages are slithering through those burrows. Viper mages are the nastiest wizards known. They already hate me and, by now, probably know the part I played in their cabal's downfall. Think what would happen if I fell into their hands."

"Just think how they would look naked," Lorenzo advised.

"What are you babbling about?" I finally managed to reply after such a bizarre comment. "This be not like speaking before a scroll of the month club. We are talking necromancers."

"No. You don't have to actually think it, but you tell the mages you are imagining them naked. That'll weird them out enough to give you time to make a run for it."

"What be this about naked?" Hiidee asked as she joined us and dropped her pack at her feet.

"Jak imagining mages naked," offered Lorenzo.

"What? Yuck. That be so wrong."

"I was not imaging mages naked."

"Who said you were?" Hiilda wanted to know as she joined her partner.

"Lorenzo," replied Hiidee.

"Hmm," Hiilda murmured. "Does Morgana know about this? Not that I would criticize anyone for their sexual peccadilloes."

"Do I know what?" Morgana asked.

"That Jak imagines wizards naked," supplied Hiidee.

Morgana studied me for a moment before turning to my friend. "Lorenzo, have I not spoken to you about messing with poor Jak?"

In a repentant voice, just as fake as Morgana's chastisement, he answered, "Sorry, it was just a thought."

"Now that you have gotten this childish chatter out of the way, can we make plans for capturing the mages – or at least one of them?"

"Heridine!" I exclaimed in surprise. "What, ah…You are coming with us?"

"Let you children face Ghennison Viper Mages without an adult along? Not likely. Told Morganna I would watch over you."

"You volunteered or at my mother's urging?" asked Morgana.

Heridine chuckled. "Morganna did not, though she should have. There be a difference between self-confidence and over-confidence. When I warned of a horde of witches accompanying you, I did not mean you should go alone. Facing several viper mages is not something any witch should do alone. You, Morgana, should know better."

"That be why Jasnora and I will be joining you," Heridine finished, with a wave of the hand toward her great-granddaughter descending the stairway.

"Greetings. Are we ready to go?" the young witch asked in much too cheerful of voice for someone about to face evil necromancers in possible ghoul-infested crypts.

Morgana warmly greeted Jasnora. Though she did not show it, I believe my intended was relieved to have them along. As with me, her pride can overcome prudence. Morgana be eager to prove herself as a witch in her own right and not as the daughter of the most feared witch in Glavendale.

Adalbert waited for us on a knoll not far from our inn.

"What are we about today, Barley?" he asked in a sarcastic voice. "I am puzzled what kind of mayhem you be up to at a temple already in ruins."

I ignored his taunts and aided in battening down our kits. The mercenaries' gear included pairs of arrow-filled quivers, bows, barbed spears and hatchets. They each wore leather armor that included pauldrons over their shoulders and torso-covering cuirasses – signs they were taking today seriously. When mentioning this to the two, I didn't feel as fainthearted when Hiidee admitted they too hated underground hollows and anything to do with necromancers.

It was a short flight to the old center of Stagsford. Adalbert circling several times before landing allowed time to observe the ruins. Scattered sections of fire-blackened walls remained. Charred stubs of thick oak rafters poked up through the rubble. In my mind I could still see the forbidding temple as it stood before being destroyed in a battle both of torch and magic.

We clumsily clambered across the rubble in search of an entrance to the subterranean warrens. Large sections of the temple floor were collapsed to reveal the first of the lower levels beneath the temple. Scavengers had already combed through the debris for valuables. The temple priests were known for hoarding coin, gold and jewels bled from cowed followers. I would wager a keg of Duburoake Star Ale that none of the looters braved venturing into the warrens where deranged obscenities must lurk.

Yes, Urbemmortis proved not to be the toxic necropolis of legend, but a Dorga temple was different. I should know, having been a prisoner of the vile god's priesthood in their loathsome temples. I shudder when recalling the nauseating stench that drifted up from deeper levels. The jarring odor suggested slithering, abominable horrors dwelling in the sunless pits.

"I, Lorenzo and Hiidee will lead," Heridine announced, after we clambered down to a stairwell leading into the greater depths beneath the temple. "Morgana, Jasnora and Hiilda will bring up the rear."

That left me in the middle. I did not know whether to be insulted or relieved.

"That's because you are the most valuable of the group," Lorenzo commented, as if reading my mind. "Without our trepid private inquisitor, the case goes nowhere."

"That certainly be true," I replied, deciding not to question his earnestness. Now and then, even his most flippant remarks do mask sincerity.

As a child, an aunt once told me, "Paranoia is when you think everyone hates you and they do not. There might not be a name for believing everyone likes you when they do not, but you, my child suffer it."

Of the two mental aberrations, I thought when young, I would rather suffer the latter. It would make life more pleasant. Now, as a private inquisitor surrounded by rogues, thieves and madmen, it be safer to be paranoid.

The air immediately chilled as we picked our way down the steps. Lorenzo handed out the light sticks he calls flashlights. It was feared the mages might detect the use of magic if witchlights were invoked. The mercenaries seemed unimpressed with the metal tubes, probably believing it was just more magic.

"At the first hint of the mages," whispered Heridine, "muffle the lights."

What next? Past explorations in underground lairs, both natural and contrived, had brought me face-to-face with voracious wolf spiders; slimy, giant albino worms; ghouls; monstrous vipers; and massive, gelatinous blobs.

The narrow tunnels we now traversed lacked torturous carvings and murals. The Dorga priests saved that artwork for their above-ground chambers. The ceilings were low, forcing Lorenzo, Hiidee and Jasnora to crouch as they walked. I assumed behind the panels lining the walls were chambers containing dead Dorga priests.

"Now," whispered Heridine.

We immediately placed our hands over the lights without waiting to see what caused her warning. It became apparent as our eyes adjusted to the darkness. A faint radiance could be seen at the end of the long passage. It appeared to be originating from a side hallway. I could not tell if it was the glow of natural torches or that cast by wizard orbs.

Morgana and Jasnora made their way to the front and the three witches conferred in hushed tones.

"Let just enough light escape so as not to stumble. Hiilda, Lorenzo, come with me," ordered the senior witch. "We will see if the mages be nearby. The rest remain here."

Surprisingly, no one questioned Heridine's assuming leadership of the group. When it comes to angry necromancers, I am only too happy to have a seasoned magic caster leading the way. My job description includes a lot of duties, but despite many past interactions with monsters and magicians, none of my private inquisitor courses covered battling viper mages in stinking, corpse-lined vaults beneath a death god's temple ruins. There was no Angry Wizards 101 nor advanced classes in Crypt Spelunking. I wondered if the mercenaries were having similar thoughts.

The bit of light we let escape through our fingers cast small pools of light before our feet. It was an eerie sight to see our glowing, pink fingers hovering in the dark. Jasnora skirted around us to keep a better watch on her great-grandmother. I looked over my shoulder to see Hiidee scanning the darkness behind us. The mercenary was not going to let the drama to the front distract from possible dangers from the rear.

"I do not like this," I whispered. "Once around that corner, we have no way of knowing if they remain safe or in need of aid."

"I agree. I am not happy remaining in the dark," added Hiidee. "No pun intended."

I could feel Morgana fidgeting. "We will wait here as Heridine ordered," she whispered. "If we hear not in ten minutes, we will at least cautiously make our way to the side tunnel."

"Sounds good," I replied.

We waited only five minutes. That be when a blinding light flooded the tunnel, followed seconds later by a deafening roar and a scorching tsunami of dust and grit.

"Get down," I screamed and turned my back, waiting for the sting of stone shrapnel.

It did not come. Morgana or Jasnora had swiftly cast an invisible ward. As sea shrews in a glass bowl, we were within a protective bubble about fifteen feet in diameter. Outside, a maelstrom of churning dust and debris swirl swept about us.

"Lorenzo," I thought out loud. How could he have survived the inferno? With similar thoughts, Jasnora cried out the name of her great-grandmother and Hiidee chocked on that of her companion's.

"Heridine be a masterful witch," Morgana quickly responded. "She would as well have cast a protective ward."

"If she had time," Jasnora responded.

I looked about us. "Can you move this cover?"

Morgana looked at me questioningly.

"You know, can we keep this ward about us when walking?"

"Yes, if not too fast."

"We must find how they fared," I said. "How much protection does it offer? Be it only for fire and stone or also against other curses?"

"Morgana's spell wards only against earth and fire," Jasnora answered. "It be similar to the one I was about to cast."

"Jasnora, you must be ready to reply to mage attacks while Morgana maintains her ward."

She nodded her head in agreement.

We walked as quietly as possible with only the barest of light to guide us.

"What be this?" Hiidee asked. She had kicked something that made a dry rattling sound.

I opened my fingers to better light the tunnel floor. Jumbled in a pile were what looked like opaque shards of brittle parchment. Only when I looked closer did I see what was intermingled with other pieces – broken bits of insect legs. Before us were fragments of an exoskeleton.

"My gods," I gasped. "That be the remains of a cockroach – one that had to be as big as a small dog."

Hiidee kneeled for a closer look. "I have seen similar, but smaller such mounds as those shat out by owl lizards."

"Which means whatever ate it be much larger than an owl lizard," I added. I did not know what was worse, the thought of a potentially dangerous predator slinking about in the dark or the creepy thought of oversized cockroaches hiding in the shadows.

The dust storm and smoke were thinning as we reached the side passage. It was littered with stone shards, but no living or dead bodies.

"Now where did they go?" I asked in frustration. "Morgana, can you tell anything about that explosion? Was it mage-cast or a booby-trap?

And where is everybody?"

"I need to lower the shield," Morgana said.

I shrugged my shoulders. The air had pretty much cleared.

Both witches, with heads tilted back, closed their eyes and hummed. For either one alone, the sound would have not been out of the ordinary, but the combined harmonics created an eerie, wavering pitch and tone that set one's teeth abuzz. Hiilda looked at me as if asking, 'What kind of crazy sheise is this?'

"Nothing," Morgana said after opening her eyes and letting out a long breath.

"Same with me," the other witch echoed.

"We must search ahead," Hiidee firmly stated. "I am not leaving until finding Hiidee."

All agreed. No one was willing to abandon the three. Hiidee scratched an X on the wall to mark our trail. Ten minutes later we stopped at another side corridor. It too held no clue to the whereabouts of our companions, just the endless rows of bone vaults in the walls.

"Do we turn here or continue?" asked Jasnora.

That was a good question. One that I was at a loss to answer. I did not want us to split up, though if we did, it made sense to send Morgana and me in one direction and Jasnora and Hiidee the other. That way each party would have a sword and spell caster.

"What if Morgana and I continue on to the end of this passage and then immediately return," I offered. "You two explore this side passage until coming to its end or another side tunnel, and then return. We can decide where to go when we regroup."

The others nodded their agreement, though it was with little enthusiasm. I nervously watched as Jasnora and Hiidee disappeared into the dark.

"I think Lorenzo will be safe," Morgana whispered later, as the faint beams played back and forth before us.

"It be hard to imagine anything else, though I know he be not invincible," I replied in just as hushed a tone. "Yet how many times he has avoided what Sergey likes to describe in his stories as certain demise?"

We were treading as lightly as possible. The only sound was that of water dripping from the ceiling. Damp and chilly was the air, with a faint stink of corruption.

We stopped when coming upon an opening on our right. I pressed myself against the wall and was preparing to peek around the corner when Morgana whispered in my ear, "Here we are, the two of us."

I paused and answered, "Ah, yes, here we are."

"This proves we are an invincible couple. A force to be reckoned with. Yes?"

I was at loss to answer. "Well, I do not know if invincible be…"

"You know. I, a top-of-my-class witch, and you a renowned private inquisitor. If we are not up to such trials as this one, who would be?"

I could think of several. There was the mythical king and queen of Molina, both deaf and dumb, who led their army to sweep through the Northern High Plains and subjugated a dozen realms. What about the sorcerous Vzseul and her concubine Gledule, who despite being gluten intolerant, defeated legion after legion of demons? There were more, but I decided this was not the time.

"Why, ah, yes. We are the indomitable duo. They will sing ballads of us centuries from now."

Morgana squeezed my hand and in an unsteady voice that finally revealed her fear, said, "We can do this, right?"

"Sure, no problem. I stick 'em and you fry 'em."

"They are wrong, are not they, in saying it will never work out?"

"It? Work out?"

"Us."

I turned and whispered, "Whoever 'they' are, yes, they are wrong. Are you speaking of your mother, the students at the academy, who?"

"They call us a mixed couple, you know."

"What? Mixed?" That was a first to hear. "Do they believe I be part elf or munchkin? I know my mother is a little short, but…"

"No. You are non-magical and I be a witch." Her tone finally had a bit of mirth to it.

"Does that bother you?"

"Of course not. I could never love another as I love you."

We were holding the lights beneath our chins, which cast weird shadows up her face.

"I am glad you finally feel confident enough to speak of this. We need to discuss this further, but maybe after we have dispatched the mages and are safely home in Duburoake."

"Of course," she whispered back, and again squeezed my hand.

I took a deep breath and leaned forward with the flashlight to peer around the corner.

"Fick." I exclaimed and hastily hand-blocked my light. "No Way."

"What? Mages?"

"There be a damned piss dragon sleeping down the passage. Gods, I hate piss dragons."

I motioned for Morgana to retreat to where we could safely speak.

"How can that be?" she asked. "No piss dragon be small enough to fit within these narrow corridors."

"It be either a dwarf or juvenile. I think I know what has been dining on the cockroaches. Time to head back."

I had barely spoken when came a roar echoing out the side passage, "What? I smell skinbags? Where you? I hungry."

"Yup, that be a piss dragon," I groaned and gripped my sword hilt tighter.

Morgana brushed past me, planted herself at the entrance and drew forth her wand. I quickly moved to her side with sword raised.

"What are you...?" I was halted in midsentence when she raised her wand and spoke a quick sequence of unintelligible words.

"There," Morgana declared. "I cast a barrier. That will hold it."

The piss dragon arched its back against the ceiling and hissed, "Yum. Tired of bugs. Long time eat skinbags."

"Ah, Morgana. It appears to be wearing a brass anklet similar to the piss dragon's that breeched the wards at my aunt's garden party."

The dragon began easily ambling toward us.

"Umm. Good skinbags, tasty skinbags. Much better than bugs and…"

It will forever remain a mystery what else the dragon subsisted upon. It abruptly erupted into chunks of flying meat and bone. The inside of a piss dragon smells even worse than its outside.

Morgana lowered her hands and with a sigh, said, "That should do it."

I ran my light over the bloody mess. "I would think so. Remind me not to get into a domestic squabble with you."

"Jak, I would never do that."

"Good to hear."

"Not when I have so many other spells to fall back upon."

"Ah, well, yes. We should be getting back to the others."

We were back first, though I could faintly make out the approaching pink dots of two muffled flashlights.

"Anything?" Jasnora asked, when they reached us

"Just a piss dragon," I nonchalantly answered.

"Good. We also saw nothing," replied the witch.

"No, wait. I said PISS DRAGON." I could not help but raise my voice after her trifling comment. "You know, the vicious, insane dragons that relish disemboweling meals while they still live. The ones that will chew off their own tails and devour their young if hungry enough."

"Yes, but you had Morgana along."

That stopped me before I could stick my foot farther in my mouth.

"Ah, yes, thank the gods. Did it with a flick of her wand. The piss dragon had no chance. This time it will be the cockroaches feasting."

"What now?" asked Hiidee.

Another good question. We could pick one of the routes and begin a more extended search. On the plus side, we might find them. On the minus side, we could wander until dropping, they return here after we moved on, or we stumble upon the mages without the added clout of Heridine. It was out of the question to return to the surface without our companions.

I drew a coin from my pouch. "Heads it be continuing down this passage. After all, we do not know for sure if they were in the side passage when the explosion occurred or were past it. Tails, we take the side tunnel."

I was glad it was tails. Why else the blast if not for our friends trespassing? Our next question was what to do when we reach the first side passage. Turn or continue? Both witches voiced their frustration over not being able to detect Heridine. The ruins, they decided, were warded against such linking, either by the mages or residue magic from the temple.

Hiilda began marking walls at each intersection. My skin crawled every time I heard a scuttling from just beyond the circles of lights.

"Can it get any worse?" It was a rhetorical question. From past ventures I knew it could. The comment was motivated by my light falling upon the shed skin of a snake. And not the garden variety kind. Our lights skimmed along the skin as we walked past it. Five, ten, fifteen steps were counted off until coming to the skin's tail at twenty steps.

It could only belong to a Altoonian Sentry Viper; in my opinion, one of the worst examples of an invasive species.

According to Olmsted, they were first brought in by the Glavendale Royal Treasury three hundred years ago to discourage would-be vault robbers. With no native enemies to hold the serpents in check, they spread throughout the country either by connecting sewers and caverns or by intentional releases. If not for the valiant actions by the Old Town Rats in Duburoake and their counterparts in Stagsford and other Glavendale cities, municipal sewers would be swarming with the giant snakes.

We paused once to drink from our water skins, without the usual conversations that normally occur at breaks. I paused at each stairway before descending deeper into the bowels of the temple. I half hoped one in my party would say it was time to retreat. I was coming close to that decision when the sudden echoing of our footsteps spoke of us entering a large chamber. I removed my hand from the flashlight and played it about to reveal we had emerged onto a rough balcony at least twenty feet above the floor of a wide cavern. The walls showed no signs of pick or chisel. We were now in a natural cavern system beneath the ruins.

Soon, the others were shining their lights to the circular chamber below us. It revealed several entrances to the floor.

"I had no idea all this lay beneath the temple," Morgana said.

"How will we ever find the others?" Jasnora plaintively asked.

"We will," I replied.

"How?"

"By making them come to us. Morgana, you said using witchlights might alert the mages of our presence, right?"

"It be a possibility."

"Can you cast a globe to the floor beneath us?"

Morgana stared at the puddles of light below. "That would be no problem."

"What would you say," I aimed my query at both witches, "that if taken by surprise, you two could restrain a lone viper mage?"

"If taken unaware," Jasnora hesitantly answered, "but only if by surprise. It be easier to kill one."

"Yes, that might work," Morgana readily said, understanding where my questions were leading.

"Why not make them come to us?" I continued. "The three mages would seek out the use of magic in their lair, but most likely send but one to investigate. When that mage emerges below us, you two will ensnare him. From him we can learn the fate of the others."

"Your plan rests on the uncertain notion we will face but one wizard," Hiidee noted. "What happens if all three appear?"

"We slink back into the shadows," I replied.

Morgana and Jasnora began enthusiastically discussing the different spells that could be used. I winced at hearing of one and reminded them that the mage must be taken in good enough shape for questioning.

They finally agreed on a course of action, with Jasnora explaining, "We will place a witch light just within that entrance below us to the right. That way it be unlikely a mage would appear in the passage behind us."

"And hidden within that sphere will be a dozen highly compressed air orbs," Morgana continued. "When the mage inspects the witch light, the containment spell will vanish and there will be a heatless explosion."

"The mages always maintain a low-level shield," Jasnora concluded, "but the resulting concussion should stun the mage long enough for a binding."

"It beats wandering aimlessly until we run into a pack of wolf spiders or giant snakes," I said. "Do it."

Hiidee and I stepped back as the two witches mumbled incomprehensibly while waving their hands about. Ten minutes later, they guided a glowing ball of light down to the floor and about ten feet into the passage.

"When a mage approaches the globe, it will retreat to the center of the cave. The trap will be tripped when the mage again approaches. There be nothing now but to wait," Morgana informed us.

After retreating into the tunnel, one by one, members of our party disappeared into the darkness for several minutes. Epic poems never mention it, but even heroic figures need vent their bladders now and then.

We hunkered down and, under the light of just one flashlight, we broke out our fare and ate. I was ready for an indefinite wait, much like fishing in spots that proved poor. Yet it was but fifteen minutes before a howling, dust-filled wind sent our packs tumbling.

"Now," shouted Jasnora, and the two witches leaped to their feet.

Hiidee and I followed close on their heels. I rubbed my eyes upon emerging onto the balcony. Morgana called upon a breeze to clear the air.

"Well, that be unexpected," I observed. A good section of ceiling had collapsed. "I guess this means the mage is somewhere under that."

"Would he be dead?" asked Hiidee

Jasnora winced. "Probably not. He would have a ward preventing severe injury from blunt forces, even when stunned."

"Which means we have a pissed off wizard somewhere under that," I darkly mused. "Let me guess; when he becomes unstunned, he will be popping up?"

"I am afraid so," Jasnora agreed. Turning to Morgana, she said, "We best be ready. It still be possible to take him unaware."

Morgana floated another witchlight above the rubble. Several times, I imagined stirrings among the shards, which proved to be just that, my overworked imagination. It included picturing the mage angrily squirming about beneath the rubble like a giant larva.

"There," shouted Hiidee.

She pointed to a churning in the debris that grew as we watched. The purple peak of a viper mage's hat emerged first and the wizard soon followed.

"One, two, three," Morgana counted, and then both witches flung their invisible, combined spell.

The mage took but two steps before falling. Our witches came close to doing the same. I steadied Morgana and Hiidee stepped over to catch a collapsing Jasnora. The spell was obviously taxing.

"We will be alright," Morgana whispered. "Just give us a minute. We must still maintain this spell, though I doubt we can hold the mage for more than an hour. It be important we now get him back to the coven hall where others can help."

We planned all this earlier. Hiidee and I returned to a stairwell leading to the chamber floor. Then came the disgusting part – carrying the mage back to the surface. The witches were too taxed by the restraining spell to levitate the mage. I shuddered at the thought of just touching the revolting necromancer, let alone having to carry him all the way back.

"Ready?" I asked Hiidee as we crouched over the mage. Though paralyzed, his unnerving, raging red eyes said everything we needed to know about his state of mind. Gods help us if he managed to break free. We grimly lifted the mage, I by the feet and Hiidee at the shoulders.

At least this time we were not shrouded in darkness. A blazing witch orb led us, also sending catacomb inhabitants scurrying farther into the shadows. At worst, it was a tiring and tedious trip upward, for which I was very thankful.

Chapter Fifteen

"You know I have to," I repeated to Morgana. "Hiidee will not leave without Hiilda and I cannot have her go back down alone."

"Hah, what help would you be?" Hiidee broke in. "I can slip undetected through that rathole without being compromised by your plodding boots."

"I will have you know I was top of the class in Stealth and Stalking 101," I replied, before again addressing Morgana. "It takes both you and Jasnora to maintain the mage's restraint. There be no time to waste. You have to get this mage back to the coven hall before he breaks free."

Morgana was torn between fearing for my safety and knowing I could not abandon Hiilda and Hiidee. Adalbert was shifting impatiently, Jasnora was already seated, and the mage strapped to the netting.

"Do not worry. We will be careful," I promised, after giving her a quick hug and stepping away. "I know you will be back as soon as possible."

"I and half the Grand Gathering now that we have one mage safely captured," she replied.

I waited until the dragon dwindled to a small dot before motioning to Hiidee that I was ready to begin our descent. The mercenary downplayed the need for me to accompany her, and most likely wished I would leave for my own safety. Yet I knew Hiidee appreciated my decision.

"Try not to clomp along too noisily," she gruffly ordered as we began the climb downwards.

"I will be as a soft breeze."

"Hah, more likely hot air."

Hiidee took the lead. As a veteran mercenary, she was experienced in scouting hostile terrain. I turned off my flashlight and we proceeded with only her muffled light to lead us down through the dark mazes. We were returning to the cavern where we had captured the mage. The plan involved the notion that one or both mages would arrive to investigate their cohort's failure to return. We would follow the wizard back to his lair, where we hoped would be our three companions.

We paused at each turn or branching to look for one of the marks made earlier by Hiidee. I walked with sword in one hand and dirk in the other. My skin crawled at the rustlings in the deep shadows and when stepping upon the dry cockroach husks. I was really grossed out when a slimy trail crossed our path. I did not want to imagine what creatures fled before our dim light but was glad they were doing so.

We passed an open vault in the wall – its shattered seal scattered across the floor. My pace quickened after hearing a rustling from the dark cavity. I did not look in, having no desire to see what was making a nest among the bones.

We arrived at the chamber and again took watch in the balcony. Our wait might be in vain, but again, wandering the many passages and levels could prove just as hopeless.

I was surprised when Hiidee spoke after her insistence on silence.

"You need not have returned here," she whispered. "I know how you detest wizards and warrens such as these. Hiilda and I are but hired mercenaries, not like your cohorts, the witch and Spasm."

"What am I but a hired snoop? I would like to think that during these past several days we have grown a bond beyond just that of coin."

"As surprised as I am at such sentiments, I believe it be so," she quietly chuckled. "How else to explain Hiilda and I continuing to remain in your employment after realizing the dark foes involved. We are simple hired swords, used to, and only wanting to, face but steel and muscle."

Our conversation was cut short with a faint glow emanating from one of the passages below us. We hunched down and watched as the light grew brighter until emerged a wizard light followed by its viper mage. I held my breath and would have prayed not to be noticed, if not for having offended all the gods while still in childhood.

The light revealed the necromancer to be the age of a novice. The appearance of a Ghennison Viper Mage ages quickly, most likely due to the toxic black arts they trade in. This mage looked but ninety years of age, meaning he was in his twenties.

For several minutes, the wizard paced over the rubble, now and then kicking at loose shards of stone. Finally, a few non-magical curses were heard, and the mage retreated back into the tunnel. We were quick to make our way down and cautiously peer into the passage.

"Now," said Hiidee, after the wizard's globe had dwindled enough.

I left it up to Hiidee to decide when to pause and when to continue. Though I have performed many tailings, they were in the alleys and even rooftops of cities. She was experienced in more life and death situations, such as night infiltrations of armed enemy camps or settlements. Several times I worried we had lost our quarry, but each time a faint light appeared as we turned a corner or looked up and down a stairway.

How close to get? We retreated to take stock after turning a bend and seeing the passage emerged into a brightly lit chamber. Between us now and the wizard's lair were the shadowed entrances of three or four side corridors.

"We can dash forward from passage entry to entry," I said to Hiidee. "If we are lucky, there be a close hideaway to safely spy on the mages."

She shook her head in agreement and we made our first sprint to an opening not more than one-hundred feet from where we hid. After craning our necks around the corner, we repeated the sprint to the next side passage. We finally found ourselves crouched behind a large chunk of fallen rock.

"You hedge-born, crooked-nose cox comb. How a bedwetting churl as yourself was inducted into our cabal is beyond belief," screamed a much older viper mage. "You go back to where Xyzquin was sent and find him. He cannot have simply vanished."

The hedge-born, crooked nose, cox comb, bedwetting churl

mumbled something before heading back our way.

"I heard that, you fat-kidneyed knave," screamed the more senior wizard.

I wedged myself between the stone slab and the wall as Hiidee scrambled back to hide in a side passage. I watched as the mage unexpectedly stopped and squatted not far from where Hiidee hid. He was obviously defying the senior wizard. That was all good and dandy, but his insubordination was keeping Hiidee pinned down.

It was now or never. I creeped around the stone to survey the lair while the sulking mage stared down at his knees. I caught my breath. The necromancers were not kind to their captives. The kidnapped young witch lay unconscious on the floor. Heridine stood stiffly in an immobilizing spell. The biggest shock was seeing Lorenzo slumped forward in a chair with hands tied behind his back. Dried blood matted his hair.

In the time of knowing Lorenzo, I never saw him helpless or more than negligibly injured. I forced myself not to gasp loudly. The sight unnerved me. But was that a faint stirring?

The mage also noticed. "Are you awake, dullard," he snarled, and cuffed Lorenzo hard enough that his head snapped to the side. "We will have more fun, you and I, when you awake."

I gripped my sword helplessly. Regular steel would have no effect on the necromancer. The mage returned to a bench where a small burner heated a bubbling maroon liquid in a glass vial. The mage persistently turned to examine his captive, giving Lorenzo no time to begin freeing himself. I clenched my teeth as Lorenzo paused his handwringing just in time to avoid detection. The mage needed distracting long enough for Lorenzo to win free of the cords.

"Hey, you. Just what do you think you are up to?" I shouted as I stepped into the light. "I am the security guard for these premises, and you are not authorized to be here. I must ask you to pack your belongings and be gone."

I am not sure anything could have surprised the mage more as my absurd appearance. His mouth dropped open almost as wide as his popping eyes.

"What, ah, where...? Who are you?"

"Like I said, I am the security guard."

"Security guard? For the ruins of a Dorga temple? Do not be ridiculous."

"Ah, with the religion officially defunct, this property is now owned by Your Favorite Realtors.

"What?" he screamed. "The contractors behind the Sunny Urbemmortis Haunt?"

"Why, yes," I replied, while looking past the wizard to see Lorenzo squirming about. "We plan for luxury tower apartments as well as a development for first-time cottage buyers. It be prime real estate here in the heart of Stagsford. As someone getting on the ground floor, you could have your choice of…"

"Enough," the mage angrily hissed. "I am not interested… You, I know you. You are that ferret, Jak Barley."

"Barley, me? That be silly. By the way, that be private inquisitor."

"Augh," the mage choked out and raised his hands.

Just a few more seconds and Lorenzo would be free, but I doubted I had that little of time.

"Wait a minute. I do not think we have been properly introduced."

He ignored me and opened his mouth to begin one of those vile curses Ghennison Viper Mages are known for.

"I am thinking what you would look like naked."

The necromancer choked on the first word of the spell and looked at me in complete bafflement. "What?"

"I, ah, I am imagining what you would look like naked. Buck naked, yup."

For the second time I had him momentarily speechless.

"You pervert, I will…"

Lorenzo's flashlight was not deadly like the Swiss army knife, but it bouncing off the necromancer's head stalled his curse. He looked down at the flashlight in amazement, surprised at anything penetrating his ward. The pause was long enough.

Lorenzo stepped back from the falling body and said, "See. I told you that naked line would come in handy."

232

With the mage dead from a snapped neck, the spell holding Heridine and Hiilda vanished. Lorenzo caught the elderly witch before she could join the younger one on the floor. The seasoned mercenary was made of sterner stuff and remained upright.

"Quick, take her," he ordered and handed the witch off to me as the remaining mage entered the chamber.

That ended just as swiftly when Lorenzo stepped into the mage's hastily hurled spell.

~ * ~

I finished my inspection of the mages' haunt just as Heridine said she was recovered enough to begin the trek back to the surface. Hiilda made a makeshift stretcher to carry the still unconscious witch and we each took an end.

"You say there was another witch here," I again asked Heridine.

"As I said, the spells included a muffling ward as well as an enthrallment spell. I was only partially able to pierce the muting, though enough to detect the mages speaking with a witch. I could not tell what they were saying or the identity of the witch. It be she, I believe, behind employing the mages as a diversion, as well as assassins."

Hiilda had no recollection of anything after being spell bound. Lorenzo was unconscious from the tunnel explosion and had only awoken as I arrived.

"It does not matter. The surviving mage be now at the Stagsford coven hall. Morganna will make him talk," I replied.

It was Heridine's earlier mention of the mystery witch that prompted me doing a thorough search of the den. Discovered was an item causing some uneasiness, a matter I would need to discuss with Morgana.

Halfway back, a recovered Lorenzo demanded to take a turn with the stretcher. Hiilda's frown let it be known she did not need help from any male. I let Lorenzo finally take my end.

Having earlier related our capture of the third mage, I now went on to tell of the rest of our time in these catacombs.

"You look tense," Lorenzo observed.

"I will stay that way until I see blue sky. There remain horrific things slithering in the dark to worry about. I told you of the snakeskin. I would not be surprised if next a horde of ghouls falls upon us."

I was happy to be proved wrong. We emerged to be greeted by a late afternoon sun. A brief time later a dozen witches or more filled the sky like a flock of giant ravens. Morgana was the first to land and she rushed into my arms.

Several of the witches immediately kneeled by the unconscious witch and began restorative administrations. I waited until the witches stabilized the toxic spell; one they said was meant to kill. Further treatment could only be done back at the coven hall.

I asked for, and was given, her shoulder purse.

"So, you survived your foolhardy resolve to chase after wizards alone," Morganna spoke in her usual haughty tone.

Hiidee left the side of her companion to confront the witch. "Jak was not alone nor foolhardy. He was with me, and I could not ask for a braver being at my side."

Morganna retained her usual glacial countenance, but I suspect she was taken off guard by the mercenary's challenge. I knew Morganna well enough to know that if she took affront, she also respected bravery and honesty. Hiidee was not in danger as she stared down the witch, though she had no way of knowing that.

Adalbert appeared in the sky and lazily circled twice before landing.

"Ah, Hiidee, I think Hiilda may need help boarding Adalbert. She seems still weak from that spell," I said.

She nodded and left to join the others gathering about the dragon. Many of the witches had already climbed onto their brooms and were headed back to the coven hall.

"I never cease to be amazed by your good judgement in picking companions, but I cannot say the same for theirs," the witch said as we watched Hiidee walk away.

I was too tired for verbal jousting. "There be something I find perplexing regarding this case. It has to do with…"

234

"We can talk back at the coven hall," the witch interrupted. "I must leave with the others."

Slightly irritated, I nodded and turned to rejoin Morgana.

"I also have never doubted your courage," the mother witch said as I walked away, "no matter how foolhardy it be."

"Bonding, as Lorenzo calls it, with my mother?" asked Morgana.

"Yes. She says what a joy it will be when I join the family. Your mother cannot wait until we go vacation together to her favorite places, like the third level of Hades or Scorpion Death Wasteland Spa and Resort."

"Great. Those were always my favorite places as a child," Morgana replied while smiling sweetly. "If you ask nicely, I wager she would even go with us on the honeymoon."

"Oh joy."

~ * ~

We went to the Any Witch Way Inn first. I needed to wash and change to rid the stench of the ruins. Even after the bath, I could not bring myself to go immediately to the coven hall. I told Morgana I would catch up with her. I was not needed, anyway. The witches had the last surviving Ghennison Viper Mage. The truth would come out.

Morganna demanded she interrogate the necromancer in a private cell. When she came out, the sheise would hit the wind – which meant there was no need to tell her of my suspicions. There could also be an innocent explanation behind what I found. Still, I wish I had been more insistent.

Lorenzo was already at the inn's ale room and I joined him at the bar.

"You look a lot better than when I saw you last," I observed.

"Yes, that was one sucker punch. Didn't see that coming," he grudgingly admitted.

We sat in a comfortable silence, until I finished the ale and stood. "No getting around it, it be time to join Morgana at the coven hall. Coming?"

"No. I've had enough drama for the day. Going to bed with a good book."

I was but halfway to the coven hall when Morgana came rushing across the green.

"Over already?" I asked in surprise.

"No," she gasped and then struggled to catch her breath. "The mage be dead."

"Whoa. I did not think your mother would be that quick."

"The mage was dead when she went to the cell."

"How?" I asked.

"Several of the academy head witches viewed the body and said it was my and Jasnora's spell that caused the death."

"Sure, they would," I growled. "I must talk to your mother. I should have demanded so earlier."

I explained the comment as we returned to the coven hall, passing through several sets of witches guarding the parameters. Once inside, a novice witch led us to a sitting room where Morganna sat glowering in front of a fireplace.

"Morgana's and Jasnora's spell did not kill the mage," I blurted out as a greeting.

"Of course, it didn't," she snapped. "Damned fools."

"They are not fools." My reply drew the witch's full attention. "They are traitors."

"What?" she demanded in a voice that usually would turn my bones to jelly.

"The witch at the catacombs and also in Urbemmortis was Head Mistress Mirthia of the Stagsford Enchantress Preparatory Academy of the Occult Arts."

She looked at me in disbelief. "What proof do you have?"

I drew three quills from my pouch. "This one was found at the mages' Urbemmortis den and we naturally believed it belonged to Yansey, the young hostage witch who graduated from the Stagsford Academy. The quill be from a Misty Mountain Griffin, the mascot for the Stagsford academy.

"And this one was found at the mage's den in the catacombs. Again, from a Misty Mountain Griffin, and again believed to belong to the young witch.

"This third one I retrieved from Yansey's pouch. Notice the difference. I believe if we question Yansey when she regains consciousness, we will find the first two quills are not used by students or even most staff. They are from the tip of the wing, being much larger and more colorful than the rest of the wing feathers. They are used only for official documents and letters. Such quills as these sit next to the inkwell on Mirthia's desk.

"Now, observe how Yancey's quill is shorter and lacking in color, the sort used by students and even staff for daily classroom work.

"I believe the Murky Forest Coven still survives, but furtively, as Heridine believes," I concluded, "and that Mirthia and an unknown number of others at the academy are secret members. I have yet to discover why they would be so vehemently opposed to the crystal communications."

I was very glad I was not the target of the rage blazing in Morganna's eyes. "We cannot ask anything of the young witch," she growled through clenched teeth. "She reportedly died from the mage's spell, though I was first told she was expected to recover."

"She would have known of Mirthia's complicity," Morgana said, "so of course she could not be allowed to recover."

"I will go to meet with other coven leaders, ones I can trust, to plan what follows," said Morganna. "We must act as if nothing be amiss. They must not know their dark deeds are known."

"Too late," I observed seconds later, after picking myself off the floor. I had begun opening the door to the hall, only to be slammed back by a powerful blast that came close to tearing the door from its hinges.

The door shuddered from another powerful attack. I was not happy with how close the ambush came to pulverizing me. I only survived because whoever was out there had been too quick on the wand.

Morganna was staring intently at the door. "I would like to know how many are out there. Two or three are no problem, but more might present a nuisance."

"No matter," she continued after appearing lost in thought.

In one smooth motion, the mother witch spun about and drew her wand. This time I knew to quickly cover my ears and shut tight my eyes. I removed my hands after the thunderous roar quieted. It was getting so I would not think a room's décor complete unless littered with rubble. At least most of it had been blown out the gaping hole now centered in the far wall.

A curt "follow me" had Morgana and I quickly trailing Morganna. We found ourselves in a dark storage room. Its door led to another hallway. Stopping after taking the first turn, Morganna motioned to press ourselves against the wall. She softly counted to sixty and with wand readied, the witch stepped back into the hallway and sent forth a blinding burst of flame. It was followed by a scream cut short and a smug smile on Morganna.

"That should quell their haste in following," the witch said.

Many twists and turns later found us in a large chamber where witches were already gathering. Morganna obviously had sent out some kind of call. I was tempted to again cover my ears. The room was filled with shouting witches, all trying to be heard over each other. And they were irate. Morganna's call must have included the essentials dealing with Mirthia and the Misty Mountain Coven.

"SILENCE."

The hall abruptly quieted with Morganna's order. Even with my lack of magical talents, I could hear the witch's shout by both mind and ear. She quickly repeated what I reported. Morganna was finishing when two of the witches guarding the grounds burst in to report the frantic departure of a dozen witches. They had stampeded out the main door and took immediately to their brooms.

"They flee to the academy. We must follow," yelled a tall witch, almost scarecrow in appearance, and with blazing red hair.

That set off another witch stampede, this one by the would-be pursuers.

Morganna opened her mouth as if to speak, but instead shook her head and resignedly turned to her daughter. "The fools. That would be the last place to flee. Besides it being too obvious, there would be no warm welcome once the rest of the staff and students discover the vipers among them."

I had not seen Lorenzo arrive in the hall, but suddenly he was at my side.

"Did you hear all of this?" I asked.

"Quickly, daughter, we have our own search," Morganna spoke before Lorenzo could reply.

"What? Wait. Morgana cannot go without me," I objected.

"Oh? So, you have your own broom?" Morganna snapped as she took her daughter by the arm. "Come, we have no time to waste."

Morgana pulled free long enough to give me a quick hug and said, "There be no choice, I have to go with my mother."

They were out the door so quickly that I was left stupefied.

"Hey, buddy, this is what you signed up for. How many times were you off by yourself, leaving Morgana wondering where and what the hell you were up to?"

"But, but, that be..." I stopped midsentence. He was right, no matter how I hated to admit it. "Where do you think they are going?"

"Hard to say. For now, you should get some sleep and we can make plans in the morning," he replied.

"What? I am to sleep after this?"

"Sleep, pace the floor, go bowling, whatever. There's nothing you can do now. Here, smoke this. It might help."

~ * ~

I made my way to the Any Witch Way Inn's common room where Hiidee and Hiilda were already eating breakfast.

"What goes?" asked Hiilda. "This place be as empty as Urbemmortis."

"We had a bit of excitement last night," I answered, then went on to apprise them of last evening's happenings.

"You have not heard from Morgana since? That be bad," replied Hiidee, who was then shushed by her partner.

"I am sure she be safe," Hiilda quickly spoke, "being with her mother, Morganna."

You could tell the mercenary hated even speaking the notorious witch's name.

I looked around the empty room. "Have you seen Lorenzo?"

"He was here when we arrived," Hiidee said, "but left after eating."

I took a deep breath in annoyance. "Did he say where he was going or when he would return?"

"No, but he left this for you."

Hiilda held out the thin, pointed blade of a dirk – much shorter than a sword, but still longer than a standard hand knife.

"And," I asked before taking it, "did he say if it be from his home world?"

"No, but that you would be glad to have it."

Hefting the weapon, I detected no difference in the weapon to that of any locally forged blade. I thanked Hiilda and slid it under my belt.

"Spasm also said he spoke with a coven hall witch who said the posse had not yet returned from the chase. The others were not at the academy, so the posse followed a tip leading into the Megaoulas Mountains."

"Great. A wild chimera chase taking them far from here," I sighed.

"What now?" Hiidee asked, "and what be a posse?"

"There has been something bothering me from last night," I replied. "I need to go back to the coven hall."

Neither of the mercenaries protested. I remained surprised by their casual acceptance of such missions. Mercenaries are usually extremely wary of mixing with practitioners of magic. By trade, they put their trust in cold iron and warm flesh.

"Still, I cannot be in two places at once," I continued. "I need you to go to the academy and find who steered the witches to the Megaoulas Mountains. They could be furtive members of the Murky Forest Coven."

Hiidee looked at me inquisitively. "We were hired as babysitters, not as ferrets."

"That be private inquisitor, and I like to think of you as armed attendants. You are right, but I believe it be standard to pay bonuses when performing outside the agreed upon duties."

"Forget bonuses," Hiilda said. "Could this be to keep us from what you believe be harm's way?"

She was correct, though I would not admit it. As much as I find comfort in the presence of the two, their fighting skills and weapons would be useless in any confrontation with witches.

"No, I fear vipers remain among those at the academy. I would like to protect us from a surprise rearguard attack."

That was true, if not the real reason for sending them off. They grudgingly agreed.

~ * ~

I found fewer witches guarding the grounds on my way to the coven hall. Several times, I stopped witches in the hallways and gave a description of the person I sought. One finally directed me to the coven's enormous library. It was impressive. The three levels of floor to ceiling books are open to all witches, with one strongly warded vault closed to all but a select few. I did not even want to know the subjects of those tomes.

I found the witch Kylla with hands clasped behind her back She was staring out a large window overlooking the coven's extensive herb garden. She was the redheaded witch from the night before, who set off the false lead to the academy.

"My mistress said you would seek me out," the witch spoke with her back still to me. "You have proved to be an irritating thorn in our plans."

"I could say the same for your coven. But now your plans are revealed, and your members will be hunted down for punishment."

"Hah, you are the fool, ferret," the witch harshly laughed as she spun around, "but I can cure your stupidity once and for all, though even a dead dunce remains a dunce."

"That be private inquisitor," I replied, closing the space between

241

us. "Just where has Mirthia and your cronies gone?"

She laughed again. "Such curiosity for a walking corpse. They return to Urbemmortis, the last place one would suspect. They will be mounting unbreachable defenses. I can also tell you this; you will be sorely disappointed if you plan to use that off-world blade. I detect its void, a hollowness in the ether surrounding you."

She raised her hands and I leaped forward while drawing the dirk.

A blast of light and scorching heat flashed above me, seconds after I was painfully slammed to the floor. Shocked at still being alive, I rolled to the side and prepared for another lunge.

Kylla was no longer at the window, which now featured jagged pieces of glass surrounding a gaping hole like the buzzsaw teeth of a lamprey tiger.

"Well, do not be a layabout. We have things to do." Heridine stood in the library doorway, but after having mocked me for idleness, the elder witch reeled and barely managed to make her way to a nearby chair.

"Whoa, that spell was more draining than I thought," she huffed.

"I find this becoming far too much of a routine," I groaned, while stiffly climbing to my feet. "Still, rather battered than fried. Thank you for your fortuitous arrival."

"Lorenzo warned you would be showing up."

That stopped me in my tracks. "What, he did? Am I that predictable? Kylla said the same of Mirthia's warning."

"If so, it be more of a complex predictability than that of your misspent youth, which I am told consisted of whatever ale joint you would be next be patronizing."

I laughed at the old witch's humor. "Can you predict what I am to do next?"

"No effort in that. I heard Kylla's remarks. We head to the necropolis. There be a courier dragon not currently booked. I know she will take us to Urbemmortis."

"By 'we,' you mean the two of us and a swarm of other witches?"

"No time for that. There could still be dark art witches here and they would send warnings to their sisters."

242

"Why the hurry? Why not wait for Morgana and her mother, or even the other witches?"

"We can leave word. The longer our wait, the more time the outcasts have to dig in. Mirthia – she be the key. I do not believe the Murky Forest Coven secretly survived these many years. It be Mirthia, twisted by furtive studies in the black arts, who attempts to resurrect the vile coven as her own personal cult. She be the head of the serpent we must sever."

"Ah, Heridine, remember how you warned Morgana that there be a difference between self-confidence and over-confidence? I will add there be a difference between madness and living long enough to again have an ale at the King's Wart Inn. You cannot be serious in taking on a horde of witches – and ones who also just happen to be practitioners of the dark arts."

"As I said, we need only take Mirthia by surprise. The coven youngsters now treat me as a doddering old crone, but once I was as feared as your mother-in-law to be. There be more than brute force in spell casting. I still maintain the finesse, if not the raw strength of my youth."

"No, I have to put my foot down. It be suicide."

Chapter Sixteen

"Glad to meet you, Talonia," I exchanged introductions with the dragon. She was half the size of Adalbert, but still capable of carrying two passengers. "I hope Heridine explained there be danger involved with this trip."

"Oh, yes. I find it exciting. It be so boring flying back and forth among the same destinations."

I winced at the youthful eagerness in her voice. She reminded me of another young dragon whose bones now lay buried in far desert sands. Called a dispatch dragon because of her small size and duties, I recognized Talonia as of the Cinnabar breed with her dazzling red sheen.

"You are to drop us off and then quickly fly to the nearby mountains. Heridine will call you when we have completed our mission," I stressed, hoping we would still be alive to recall the dragon.

Talonia had not the speed or endurance of a large dragon like Adalbert, yet we still made Urbemmortis by late afternoon. Heridine instructed her to circle the tower previously used by the mages.

"There be no magic there," she yelled over the wind that comes with dragon riding. "I would detect the erection of barriers."

"Then they inhabit another deserted building," I yelled back." It will be like looking for lice in a snowstorm."

"What now?" asked the dragon.

I racked my brain. Where would I settle if I were a coven of malicious witches? Water. No matter what, they would want a water source. There was but one area I was aware of that was so supplied.

"Talonia," I ordered, "take us in that direction."

~ * ~

We paused outside the door and inspected the drawings in the window. They were of different buildings to be for sale upon completion of renovations.

"I have to admit they are pretty cheap," I observed. "Look at this one, 'Three stories, four bedrooms, three bathrooms, twenty-four hundred square feet, three fireplaces, covered stable in the back and a ten-minute walk to the market. All for two thousand marks.'"

Heridine pushed past me and I followed her into the sales office. The walls were covered with colorful conceptions as to how the area would eventually appear. There were beings grilling outdoors, playing croquet beneath deep blue skies and swatting perforated balls over a net.

"Pickleball," piped up a gnome after following my gaze to the poster. He was sitting on a highchair behind a desk. "Weird activity, but you bigguns are noted for that, no offense."

"Now what can I do you for," he asked, after sliding from the chair and walking out from the desk. "We have some choice properties, and they will be going fast."

"Will be going," I repeated the gnome's words. "What about now? Have you sold any recently?"

He eyed me with caution. "We have sold a couple."

"Any to a witch?"

"Ah, as I told the person before you, I am not allowed to disclose such information. You know, there are privacy concerns with our customers."

"What? Who?"

"He did not give me his name. I could not even make out his face. It was shadowed by his cowl."

I quickly flashed my badge. "I am not some person off the street."

"You are from Duburoake. We are not in your jurisdiction," he observed, despite the brief glance.

"What about my jurisdiction?" asked Heridine. She used an icy speech glamour that sounded as a voice discharging from the mummified lips of a long-dead corpse. I hate it when they do that.

It had the desired effect. "Why, ah, yes, we did. Sold it several weeks ago to a nice little witch. Said she was going to retire here. Wanted a large home so all the grandchildren could visit. I told her the property was in an area not yet scheduled for renovation, but she said she could take care of that."

"Where?" I asked.

He returned to his chair and thumbed through a stack of papers. "Ah, 108 Maggot Mirage Lane."

"We are here and the house be there," the gnome spoke while pointing to a wall map behind the desk. 'There' was located several miles away on a hillside.

~ * ~

We had Talonia drop us of several blocks from our destination. Heridine assured me she could walk the distance, but I kept to a slower pace as we passed deserted dwelling after dwelling. Their vacant windows jeered at us as if the hollow eye sockets of skulls.

"That be the one." I pointed to a dwelling perched on the hillside. "Quite the mansion, totally black and with all those pillars and ornate turrets. What now?"

"You call out Mirthia and I will burst the black heart that beats within her villainous chest."

"Hold on. Wait a minute," I protested. "That be your plan? We came all the way here to face these witches and this is all you can come up with?"

"It should work," she replied with but the barest hint of sheepishness in her voice.

"Should work? Should work? It should also get me fried. You sound like Lorenzo. Why not you call out the witch?"

"I could not catch her by surprise if I did so."

"No, we will do it my way," I firmly replied. "We do a stakeout. She is bound to come out sooner or later and then you can mess with her black heart."

"Every minute that goes by means their defenses increase. With even just a handful of skillful witches casting the wards, it would take months for all the covens in Glavendale to break through. I doubt they would be up for such a siege."

"You say you can smite Mirthia before she can turn me into a sizzling greasy puddle on the ground? For sure?"

"For sure."

"There be not the confident tone I would like to hear in your promise."

"Well, nothing be sure in this world," she replied. "You could be hit by a shooting star in an hour."

There was no use arguing. Ten minutes later I stood at the bottom of a long flight of black marble stairs leading up to the equally dark mansion. Against the pale desert dirt and sand, it was like a cancerous mole on a pale maiden's face.

I took one last deep breath and looked off to the side at Heridine, who crouched behind a wind-worn statue of a nude maiden with the head of a hyena.

"Mirthia, it be me, Jak…"

I was not able to finish. Like the buzzing of a thousand gnats, a cloud of radiant pinpoint lights swarmed about me.

"You, you trifling ferret," snarled Mirthia.

I shook my head, dazed by the abrupt change in scenery. I was in a large room, barren of furniture or wall hangings. A glassless sun window in the ceiling was the only source of light.

"That be private inquisitor. Nice to see you, too."

"So, you thought me foolish enough to make an appearance outside a dwelling I have been warding."

"As you said, it was just a thought," I replied. "I have come to take you in. Ready to surrender?"

She threw back her head and cackled insanely. I meant that literally. Mirthia was not the same person I last saw at the coven hall. She was totally disheveled, with wildly unkempt hair, red-rimmed eyes and the crazed expression of an escaped lunatic.

"You," she again screamed. "You will die grotesquely and with exquisite slowness. It was all planned, and you and your prying friends have ruined it."

"Ruined what? I do not understand why you are doing all this."

"The wizards," she shrieked. "They grow too powerful, and yet the covens ignore the danger. There must soon be a reckoning."

She observed my perplexed look and continued, "War. An all-out war. The filthy creatures must be wiped from the face of the globe."

"The covens would never agree to that," I protested.

"They would if they believed themselves to be under attack. If they believed the wizards were behind the malspells. It would have been the perfect irony to have those dullard viper mages unwittingly bring that about with their attacks on witches and the academy. That counterattack on the mages' desert warren should have had the other wizard cabals seeking revenge."

"And how did that work out for you?" I mockingly noted.

"Damn your impertinence. I did not reckon with the abhorrence the other cabals had for the viper mages, or their shock at the attacks on the academy. The assault at the Duburoake dragonport added to the bad visuals, even though that was by other viper mages hired to stifle your pixie gold investigation. Still, there were other avenues to take. They are now blocked by you and Morganna's bastard offspring."

I was not going to let her slurs on Morgana distract me, not when the answers to the case were now available. "Why the malspells? What did attacks on the crystal globes have to do with a wizard/witch war?

"It was another thing to blame upon wizards. Also, too free of communication might allow the covens to connect the dots of my machinations. In that I was wrong. We later realized the crystals be the perfect vehicle for spreading deceitful fabrications and lies."

"Just how many of you are there?"

That question had a startling effect. The witch's eyes rolled until only the whites showed, lips curled back and spittle flew from her mouth.

"You dare ask that? You dare ask that?" she shrieked.

Mirthia stepped back to reveal a crumpled form in the corner. It

248

was a dead witch.

"We had our wards up, but still, one by one, my acolytes died through the night," she shrieked with growing intensity. "But I will have my revenge."

She raised her hands and all I could think was, *Here we go again.*

And again, I was saved. The witch jerked upright as if stabbed in the back, which was just what happened. A slim blade protruded from between her shoulder blades.

"Well, that should take care of that," said the cowled figure that had crept up from behind.

"You sure took your time, Lorenzo. Waiting for it to be more dramatic?"

The figure did not answer, but pulled back his hood to reveal he was not my friend. I found myself staring into yellow eyes.

"You. You are the one who killed the mage at the abandoned brewery. You have been following us."

"More than you know," he replied in an eerily familiar voice.

"It was you who killed the mage in the tower."

"Right again. The others had already left by the time I arrived."

"I know who you are," I declared. "You are Michael, Lorenzo's brother."

His smile was enough of an answer.

"No wonder I first mistook you for Lorenzo at the brewery. You are of the same build and walk. But your eyes. They are the yellow of Felidians of the Kearal Islands."

"The yellow eyes are but...," he began, finger-poking an eye while his other hand was cupped beneath. Out popped a slight flake like that of a yellow fish scale.

"...a contact lens," he finished. "Great for disguises where they are unknown – and of course the green hair is just dye."

"Why? Lorenzo said he could not imagine you being involved."

"Normally not, but I was asked by a wizard friend to look into some suspicious activities by both the viper mages and a few unidentified witches. Someone found out and that was when I first received the death threats, followed by actual assaults. That really pissed me off.

"My tailing of your group gave me the needed information to get to the tower first. As I said, the party had left but for one slow viper mage. From him I learned the identity of the witches and that they were behind the threats.

"I watched you this morning and followed. When I realized your destination was Urbemmortis, I took to the clouds to pass overhead unseen. You didn't know how good a team we made. Too bad I always work alone."

"It was you at the sales office," I said, "but the gnome said he did not give out such information."

"He doesn't except when a few silver coins cross his desk."

I looked at the two dead witches sprawled on the floor and shuddered when remembering there were more bodies about. Maybe Lorenzo was the meek brother.

"Well, I have to go. It's been fun. Tell my brother 'hi' when you see him. I've a dragon impatiently waiting a few blocks from here. We're both eager to get back to Duburoake."

"Sure, ah, maybe I will be seeing you again when I return," I spoke to his retreating back.

"Not if I see you first," he laughed.

I took a deep breath and rubbed my eyes. It was over. The case was solved and I and my friends were still in one piece, not counting the aches and bruises I suffered.

"Jak, my lad, I hear you talking. Where are you?" Heridine came rushing into the room. "I finally found a way to slip through a ward's backdoor."

"Whoa, what have we here?" The witch came to an abrupt stop. She looked at me in confusion.

There were further voices coming from outside, followed by whole dwelling rattling.

"See," said Heridine, "they always want to use brute force."

Morgana rushed in with wand raised. She braked just as abruptly as had Heridine when seeing me and the two dead witches. Her mother followed in a more leisurely stride. Morganna sniffed when viewing the corpses. "That saves some bother."

I braced myself as Morgana flung herself into my arms. "We found the note you left and then we spotted a dragon here circling overhead. What happened? They let you get close enough with that dirk?"

"No, it was Michael," I answered.

"Lorenzo's brother?" snapped Morganna. "I am surprised. He does not get out much."

~ * ~

It was late, but I remained too wound up to sleep, and sat at the Witch Way Inn bar with Morgana, Lorenzo and the two mercenaries. I finished recounting my entire discussions with Mirthia and Michael.

"Your brother seems to have gotten both the looks and wit of the litter," I baited Lorenzo. "Your mother must be very proud."

"Actually, it be our sister, Matilda. She is the excitable one of the lot."

I shook my head and related that Morganna was to make a presentation on the matter the next day. I would send a full report to the King once I returned to Duburoake. It would be a bit convoluted with the separate groups of Viper Mages involved in the different cases, though they all had one thing in common – their wish for my early and painful demise. Sergey would get a less detailed recounting.

I had only one matter to finish – the stolen pixie gold. We would be flying to Kaiserhelm in two days where I would quickly bring that case to a successful conclusion.

~ * ~

"The baffling aspect of the theft was how could the pixie gold be stolen from a warded keg," I began my presentation.

With me were Baroness Vilhema Stee Hragen, Wizard Arkhjin and Morgana.

"Arkhjin was present when the pixies filled the cask," I continued, "as well as when the wagon master confirmed the gold contents before the keg was sealed and taken to Stagsford. It was reopened at the caravan gathering site, inspected and warded. Yet when opened in Kaiserhelm, river pebbles had replaced the pixie gold. Upon inspection, both Arkhjin and an independent wizard verified there had been no tampering with the protective ward between Stagsford and Kaiserhelm. It would seem the switch was an impossibility."

Both the baroness and the wizard listened intently. I paused for a purely dramatic flourish. "So, how did it happen? How could the gold have been switched with rock between leaving Stagsford and arriving in Kaiserhelm?"

"Yes?" my aunt asked impatiently when I paused again.

"It did not." I answered.

"What?" There was confusion in her voice.

"There was no switch after the cask left Stagsford."

"What are you saying?" the baroness demanded. "Of course, there was. When opened, there were only rocks."

"Correct. But, Arkhjin, did you not say the ward by the caravan wizard would have canceled any preexisting spell that could have worked a switch during shipment?"

The wizard licked his lips and replied, "Why, yes. That be a standard inclusion in such wards."

"The ward would have also canceled out other existing spells, correct?"

"Ah, it, ah, it depends upon the spell," he stammered.

"What about a glamour that would have a keg of rocks appear to be filled with gold?"

"What are you saying?" he suddenly shouted. "Are you accusing me of a wrongdoing? How dare you."

"Did I speak such? I only observed that if the stones are charmed to appear as gold, a sealing ward such as the wizards would dispel the glamour, and the contents would be revealed upon opening for what it be, rocks."

"I know what you are saying, and it be an accusation against me. The pixies were there as the gold was placed in the cask."

"Yes, and I believe the last pixie to see the gold before it left for Stagsford was with you and named Airahaka," I continued.

"Ah, yes. The poor pixie eaten by a giant centipede," he snapped.

"Hmmm. That was only conjecture, I believe. She did disappear, though," I said with a smile that made the wizard appear even more nervous. "Would it surprise you to learn she be living under an assumed name in the Amnesian Isles on Rum Island? It seems she came into enough coin to buy a kumquat plantation."

The wizard visibly paled, but remained silent.

"It helps me when a crime is committed against a sister to the king. It be so much easier to involve agents with the Royal Fraud Inquisition Agency."

I raised my voice to say, "You can bring her in now."

A bedraggled pixie came through the door, between a man and woman dressed entirely in black.

Morgana was ready for the moment. Caught off guard, before he could do no more than raise his hands, the witch brought out her wand and ensnared the wizard in an incapacitation spell.

"Arkhjin collaborated with the pixie to perform a slight of hand with the gold, most likely under the cover of an illusion spell hiding the switching of casks," I continued. "The keg with the stones masquerading as gold was transported to Stagsford, while he and Airahaka made off with the real pixie gold. The wizard at the caravan had no reason to suspect anything was amiss when the false cask with the masquerading rocks was opened, checked, resealed and warded."

"I can hardly believe it," gasped the baroness. "Arkhjin, how could you?"

"Agents are in the process of recovering your funds, most of which were hidden in offshore accounts," I concluded.

~ * ~

A week later, after a welcomed rest, I was back in my office. I was handsomely rewarded by the covens and allowed to keep the handful of precious gems I pocketed at the viper mage's desert lair. Those I gave as a bonus to Hiidee and Hiilda. I refused any remuneration from the Baroness Vilhema Stee Hragen. After all, she be family.

There was a knock on my door, much more robust than that of my secretary's. I cautiously crossed the room and looked through a recently installed peep glass. It was Lorenzo.

"Hey, buddy. Have I got a case for us."

I failed to hear the rest as I exited my window.

Also by Dan Ehl
at
Rogue Phoenix Press

*Jak Barley, Private Inquisitor
and the Case of the Cursed Golden Muskrat*

Chapter One

There was no time to consider why six masked thugs appeared bent upon my untimely demise. Varying in quality of weaving and cut, their garb had in common the color black. Sword waving hooligans erupting from the shadows behind the King's Wart Inn was enough to send me fleeing down the alley. Even if I had been wearing my sword in the ale joint, there was no way I could face such a motley crew and survive.

Ten minutes into the chase I had to admit these were no common ruffians. I should be able to outrun most of the gin-blighted cutpurses who skulk about Duburoake's more neglected quarters. That all six kept pace at my heels meant their profession entailed more than lounging in shadows to pounce upon hapless mugging victims.

I can maintain jogging for some time, but this relentless all-out pace was wearing me down and each breath was becoming a ragged gasp. As always, there is never a guardsman around when you need one. Taking to the brighter gas-lit streets in the hope of safety in numbers, I was sorely disappointed by the vacant avenues. The tavern patrons were by now safely behind their locked doors and even the ladies of the night were off the hourglass.

I turned a corner to be almost crushed by a heavy freight wagon drawn by a team of enormous draft horses. I was forced to dive and roll out of the way of the steel shod hooves and immediately continued my flight. A shriek from behind spoke of a not so agile pursuer. I took advantage of the momentary distraction to dodge into an alley and climb a rickety fire escape. I reached the rooftop as the remaining five arrived to spot me disappearing over the ledge.

The moonlight enabled me to see my footing, yet equally aided my pursuers. I dodged a chimney and a clothes rack of drying garments. The wooden ladder creaked under the weight of those following as I came to a three-foot gap and without slowing leaped the divide to land upon another roof.

I paused long enough to see that the hunters were again in fresh pursuit. Ahead was a pitched roof. I launched myself across the divide and fell to hands and knees to keep from sliding to the dark street below. My heart was hammering.

The chase continued from roof to roof. Startled eave rats scuttled out of my way with indignant squeals. I felt sharp stings at my ankles as several of the roof rodents reacted swiftly enough to use tiny swords no more than slivers of iron.

"Ack, you little rat bastards," I squawked after forced to hop several times before regaining my stride.

Another leap and another roof. From my rear came a volley of angry oaths as my pursuers ran the gauntlet of now thoroughly enraged rodents.

Two more roofs and again my pace was thrown off. This time it wasn't eave rats I disturbed.

"Oh, excuse me." I gasped after tripping over what appeared to be two young lovers watching the stars or whatever else young lovers do on a roof in early hours of a new day.

"Hey, yah arsehole," bellowed the man in the deep voice of a young bull. He leaped up and waved a sword. He was probably a warehouse guard taking a lengthy break. "Come back here and I will teach yah not to be disturbing me girl."

The lout would soon get plenty more chances to impress the maiden. I was almost to the end of the next roof when I heard the din of his introduction to my pursuers.

I braked just in time before a divide of about twelve feet. I forced myself not to panic and looked wildly about before spying a clothesline. I ferociously wrestled with a crossbeam until tearing it from the pole and then with my boot knife cut all the lines but one. I crossed to the other pole to free my remaining line. The makeshift grappling hook was whirled a half dozen times above my head until loosed across the divide at a pigeon coup standing on four stout legs. The first throw was too hasty and I missed by several feet.

I could hear the thugs drawing closer. I paused, took a deep breath and repeated the cast. This time the crossbeam reached the coop and wound twice about a leg. There was no time to test its steadfastness. I wrapped the line several times around my left hand and tightly griped it with my right. *Why me?* I just knew this was going to hurt. It did. I tried breaking the impact with my feet, but twisted sideways in my downward swing and slammed my shoulder painfully into the opposite wall.

"Where be the mucker?" one of the pursuers yelled in frustration.

I was far enough down in the shadows to be not easily discernible.

"He might have plunked over the side."

"He would make a pretty splat if he did," observed another voice, "but we were told to bring him in alive."

I squinted, not wanting even the whites of my eyes to draw their attention, to see four figures silhouetted against the starry night sky. They mumbled angrily amongst themselves while the cord cut agonizingly into my hand. Finally, after several minutes, they disappeared. I waited another minute before pulling myself upward. The thinness of the cord made the going difficult.

"Hah, here he be," cried one of thugs who had returned to the edge of the roof. "I knew the mucker be around here someplace."

I threw a leg over the edge and hoisted myself onto the roof. I hesitated between hurling a few insults about the stalker's parentage or making good my escape. Seeing the figure lift an arm above his head made me chose the latter. I dodged the knife and turned to continue my escape. Bruised and battered, but with the hot pursuit ended, I could now make my way with more care.

Who in Hades were these stalkers? Unknown survivors of the

demon-slaughtered Duburoake Assassin's Guild bent on revenge for my part in the massacre? Someone nervous about a current investigation or angry with a past one?

My brief thoughts were abruptly cut off by a lengthy bellowing from behind. I turned to see an oddly convulsing figure. Only after part of the shadowy figure split off did I realize one of the larger goons was using a smaller member of the group much as I had the crossbeam. The villain had spun around several times and hurled his comrade across the gap – no doubt trailing a clothesline.

I groaned and forced myself to run. Three roofs later they were again closing in. One of the chasers had pulled ahead of the others and I could hear him drawing closer. I imagined the painful plunge of a sword skewering me from behind at any moment. I heard the grunt of someone forcing that one more bit of exertion, such as for the wild thrust of a sword, but it was just as I leaped across another divided and luckily kept to my feet to continue running. By the clatter across the slightly pitch tiled roof, the oaf had stumbled.

Ahead was a parapet that prevented me from spying what lay beyond. The nasty blades at my back were enough for me to throw caution aside and leap blindly over the wall.

I was suddenly plummeting through utter blackness and it was only because I was so lacking in breath that I did not cry out in startled terror. A jarring halt and the sound of tearing canvas told me I had briefly landed upon and then plunged through a canopy. I braced myself for a brutal collision with the cobblestone street, but luckily landed feet first and was quick enough to soften the impact by letting my knees fold before tumbling once. I unsteadily stood and grabbed an empty fruit stand to steady myself. It took a dozen breaths for the dimly-lit scenery to stop its reeling.

The lead hound had enough wind left to howl as he found himself plunging into blackness. He shot unimpeded through the tear and landed with an unpleasant thud. The twist of his body said he would not be rejoining the chase. I turned and continued my flight.

There was no reserve of strength or wind remaining when I finally collapsed in an alley a half dozen blocks later. My lungs were on fire and I could not stop quaking. I knew I should continue my getaway, but I was barely managing to fight off a dizzying nausea.

It took several minutes before I could shakily regain my feet. I debated continuing my escape by taking to the sewers I had regularly plied as youthful delinquent. Then again, it was highly doubtful the remaining –

My contemplations were again rudely interrupted by the arrival of my mysterious assailants. Their silhouettes at the alley entrance now numbered only three.

"We have you now," panted one of the trio. "You are unexpectedly wily, I have to admit."

I drew the dirk from my boot.

"You have not seen anything yet." I attempted a bravado I did not feel. "Come meet my blade. It tells me it be thirsty."

"Ha-ha," chortled one of the thugs. "My blade tells me it be thirsty," he mimicked me in a falsetto voice. "That be so lame."

"Shut yah mouth, Clam," hissed another of the three. "Say that again."

"That be so..."

"Not you, yah arsehole. You, the one we have been chasing."

"Fick you." I was getting annoyed.

"Hah," said the one who appeared to be the leader of the gang. He turned to Clam and smacked him in the back of the head. "You pinhead. This be not Grouse the Limp Leg. You sicced us on the wrong knave."

"What?" I irefully squawked. "I nearly killed myself a half dozen times because you thought I was Grouse? I look nothing like that bald, potbellied churl."

"Hey, it was an honest mistake. Do not get your undies in a knot."

"What do we do now, Eel?" asked the third one who was probably named something like Lobster. They were obviously using false names.

"We kill him and go on looking for this Grouse."

"What!?" I yelped. "You just said this was all a mistake."

"It be a mistake, but we lost Crab, Sponge and Seaweed chasing you. You have to pay for that. We cannot let that go."

I was doing the math in my head. "Wait a minute. I know one of you got flattened by that freight wagon and other splattered from the fall, but what is this about a third one?"

"Sponge got whacked by some arsehole with a girl he bumped into on a roof."

"I do not suppose there is some way we can settle this without bloodshed?" I asked without much hope.

"No, I am afraid..."

My friend Lorenzo Spasm says one should not blabber before striking – just do it. Eel's reply was cut short by my underhanded tossed blade entering his trachea. As he began gurgling, I stepped forward to wrench free his sword and twirl completely around for the momentum needed to shatter the rib cage of Clam. My reluctance for needless violence provided the pause the remaining hooligan needed to decide it was time to flee.

My world had become a surreal stage and I would not have been surprised if curtains fell in preparation for the next act. One moment I was innocently stumbling out the backdoor of the King's Wart Inn after a comparatively peaceful evening of quaffing ale with my friends – and no more than twenty minutes later I was in a gloomy alley gripping a strange sword and standing over the corpses of two strangers.

"For someone who espouses a pacifistic attitude, you certainly leave a trail of mayhem and dead bodies."

"They started it," I snapped at the newest of shadowed figures materializing this night. "Now you show up. Great timing."

"It wasn't exactly a stroll in the park. Haven't you ever heard of sidewalks?" answered my friend, Lorenzo Spasm. "I would have been here sooner, but some crazy bastard on one of the roofs kept waving his sword in my face. And then there were these really pissed off rats. So, what's going on here? Jealous husband, gambling debt, trouble with the fashion police?"

"Mistaken identity."

There was a brief pause before he replied. "Okay, so don't tell me. It's probably some sordid tale of wretched indulgences that would spoil my pristine image of you."

I tossed the sword by one of the bodies and leaned against a moss-covered brick wall. "So, you are back in Duburoake. Do not tell me what you have been up to – probably some sordid tale of wretched indulgences that would only reaffirm my squalid image of yourself."

"Actually, I had to return home to collect on a lottery ticket and cast an absentee ballot," he answered in his typical gibberish.

Spasm claims to be an inhabitant of a parallel firmament – one similar to our world in many ways, but devoid of any magic. Partial proof of that claim is Spasm's immunity to spells. Any enchantment will rebound off my friend and back onto the mage or witch who cast the curse.

"Do you have one of your magic lights on you?"

"Not magic. I've told you before. It's what your brother calls metaphysics and alchemy. I call it a penlight," Lorenzo answered as he withdrew a slim metallic tube from a pouch on his belt.

I pulled the mask from the one called Eel and shined the circle of light onto the corpse's face. He was clean-shaven and looked about thirty-five to forty years old. I rolled a bit of his tunic between fingers and thumb. The fabric was heavy and felt like boiled wool; twenty to fifty percent denser, more durable and added proof against the wind when compared to regular wool.

After removing my dirk from the dead man, I moved the light to his shoes and sighed after I in turn checked the second corpse's footwear. The one called Clam was wearing a tunic of a similar dense fabric, though of a different weave and style. I patted both bodies down but came up with no purses or identity papers.

"By the dozen teats of the goddess Gendra," I exclaimed in resignation as I stood.

Lorenzo flashed on a second light and played it upon the corpses," Oh, I see what you mean."

"Yes," I wearily replied. "They are members of the King's Clandestine Information Authority. No identification means they could be of a number of organizations, but only the CIA makes a big deal out of wearing such trademark footwear as that made by Narmian Shoe Elves."

"So, this was really a case of mistaken identity?"

"Yes, they thought they were chasing Grouse the Limp Leg, a petty smuggler who mostly specializes in untaxed liquor and hashish. They realized their mistake after they cornered me and yet still plotted to kill me over the loss of their bumbling cohorts."

I handed my light back to Lorenzo and he extinguished both with a simple push of his thumb.

"I think it would be best if we put as much space between us and the bodies as quickly as possible." Lorenzo recommended. "I don't think anyone witnessed the chase except the couple on the roof and it was too dark for identification – especially after I whacked the snarling oaf's head."

I agreed and we kept to the thicker shadows back to my office and living quarters. Lorenzo had a small loft not far from my place, one of several scattered secretly about Duburoake. He called them safe houses.

"Why were you looking for me?" I asked when we were finally a half dozen blocks away from the corpses.

"I have a case for you."

"You are like a meddling mother trying to find her son a wife. I can get my own cases. As a matter of fact, I am swamped with would-be clients. Besides, your cases always come close to killing me."

I was not jesting. I have had enough adventurous encounters to last me a lifetime. I was ready to settle down and follow errant husbands or solve petty thefts. I dreamed of romantic exploits when beginning my career as a private inquisitor, but after the last couple cases being the target of lethal Reverian Assassins, vampires, zombies, demons and malevolent Ghennison Viper Mages, I was ready for boredom.

I was now known as the private inquisitor who brought down the malevolent temple of Dorga, the Fish Headed God of Death, while surviving the onslaught of some of the nastiest assassins and mages known to the Western Realms. This newly gained prominence appeared to be placing my services in high demand among the more prosperous merchants and guildmeisters of Duburoake – a change from past clients who were normally as empty-pocketed as myself.

I had just finished several outrageously perilous cases and was now able to charge what I considered exorbitant fees. I almost went into paroxysms when I first heard my secretary, Osyani, relate my new rates to a potential client.

"You've had a trying night," Lorenzo spoke in a soothing voice. "We'll talk about it tomorrow."

"Do not use that tone with me. It will not work. I can tell you now, I am not interested."

Other Books by Dan Ehl
at
Rogue Phoenix Press

*Jak Barley-Private Inquisitor
and the Temple of Dorga, Fish-Headed God of Death*

As a private inquisitor, Jak Barley's job is fairly mundane-finding errant debtors and missing property, or proving the unfaithfulness of roving spouses. It's not a vocation that makes many friends.

Though a frequent patron of dark, wretched bars seldom visited by the more fastidious citizens of Duburoake, he still can be squeamish about some things--such as ghosts and rabid magicians.

Barley's latest cases are just that more upsetting, dragging him into contact with sinister specters, malicious mages, irate harpies, creepy death deities and royal plots.

It will take all of his backstreets cunning to stay alive, as well as the help of alchemist Olmsted Aunderthorn, his half brother, who uses the latest metaphysical laboratory techniques in solving crimes.

*Jak Barley-Private Inquisitor
and the Case of the Seven Dwarves*

Private Inquisitor Jak Barley wonders if his drinking cohorts at the King's Wart Inn are playing an elaborate prank on him. What else is he to think when seven dwarves want his help against a wicked witch they blame for poisoning an innocent young maiden staying with them named Frost Ivory?

Jak Barley, Private Inquisitor
and the Case of the Dark Lords Conspiracy

Private inquisitor Jak Barley is ready for some down time after battling Ghennison Viper Mages, being attacked by piss dragons, and fighting off priests of Dorga the Fished Headed God of Death. That is why Jak was not a bit amused to have a scruffy mage insist that he is to be one of a group of questers decreed in an ancient prophecy that must cross the icy Alf Mountains to foil the return of the Old Gods. To do so meant using a map all too heavily dotted with "Here Be..." warnings that read like an "Idiot's Guide to Monsters."

And why are Westian Lizard Wizards targeting young red-headed maidens and who is behind the numerous and bizarre attacks upon Jak? Once gain Jak finds himself saying, "I hate adventures."

Jak Barley, Private Inquisitor
and the Case of one Damned Thing After Another

Jak Barley, private inquisitor, hates cases involving damned creatures like vampires and zombies, but that's just what he finds himself helplessly in the middle of. Jak has come to hate adventures. He would prefer the boring cases of his earlier years in the profession when dealing with errant husbands or minor pilferings. Still, somehow he finds himself eluding corrupt officials and creatures of the night that want to suck his blood and eat his brains. He does find help in his friend and publisher of the Weekly Tattler, as well as his mysterious friend Lorenzo Spasm from a parallel firmament – one similar to Jak's world in many ways, but devoid of any magic. He also finds support from his girlfriend, Morgana, an apprentice witch.

Jak Barley, Private Inquisitor
and the Case of the Annoying Assassins

Jak Barley, Private Inquisitor, is tired of adventures and is ready to take on only hum-drum cases offering no drama – those of missing husbands, unfaithful spouses, or fat merchants paying well for outing thieving employees – anything not involving traveling, swords, or the darker magics.

Yet once again his otherworldy friend, Lorenzo Spasm, drags him into cases involving corrupt CIA (Clandestine Information Authority) agents, murderous bank robbers, nasty goblins, furious dragon chases, demonic foes, and going uncover at an elders' RW (recreational wagon) park set atop a butte overlooking a harsh desert floor. To top it off, Jak finds himself the quarry of the Assassin's Guild after an anonymous adversary takes out a whack contract on him.

Myrlyn's Gate

Vladimir Dragol XIII had an immense task--convincing the world he was not following in his ancestors' bloody footprints.

When the chance to prove himself came in the form of an attractive princess on a quest to save world, how could he refuse? There was a slight problem – the princess loathed the Dragol line.

There was also the dilemma that others alluded to in the quest prophecy--a dragon trainee and wizard's apprentice--wanted nothing to do with the task.

Through Myrlyn's Gate was another foretold member of the quest who had no idea what was in store for him, including a midnight raid on the Dickeyville Grotto in the strange land of Wisconsin.

Nicotine Dreams

Trent Rowen believed giving up smoking was supposed to be a healthy life choice and that he needed all the help he could get, but he began wondering after the nicotine patches began giving him extremely colorful dreams. Having vivid dreams while on nicotine patches is not unusual, but waking up bruised and battered after battling the minions of Dorga, the Fish Headed God of Death, was not something included in the prescription drug's warnings.

Trent's friends begin worrying about their buddy's state of mind as he starts recounting visits to a dark and sinister world, where at the Crossroads Café he meets with a girlfriend long believed to be dead. Their skepticism is strained when Trent begins waking with items from his dream worlds. Worrying about Trent's sanity turns to worrying about his life as strange and menacing denizen begin entering their own waking lives.

www.ingramcontent.com/pod-product-compliance
Lightning Source LLC
Chambersburg PA
CBHW071455170626
46811CB00007B/2585